POCKETMONEY.COM

PAUL MICHAEL CURTIS

Paperback: 978-1-967820-46-7
Hardcover: 978-1-967820-75-7
eBook: 978-1-967820-47-4
Library of Congress Control Number: 2025909782

This is a work of fiction.

Ordering Information:

Prime Seven Media
518 Landmann St.
Tomah City, WI 54660

Printed in the United States of America

BOOK REVIEW

Sometimes we all need a story with outstanding narration. A type of story so captivating that we'll find ourselves unable to put it down. POCKETMONEY. COM is certainly that type of book.

Paul Michael Curtis wrote this fictional thriller novel, which centers on a young man named Mike Kinnerman, who was only 14 years old at the time. It was with the assistance of his father, Richard, and the brilliant Harry Schlecker that he established PocketMoney.com, which is an investment firm geared specifically for kids.

Mike then rose to prominence after making an appearance on the most popular TV show in the United States. The episode in question became an internet sensation, and kids from all over the world began lining up outside banks to purchase shares so that they could be part of it. After a period of six months, the business had amassed billions of dollars in its financial reserves.

Then, sometime in the month of October, Mike and his girlfriend Savannah lay on the riverbank, holding each other. At the time, everything seemed perfect, but they had no idea how drastically their lives were about to change at the hands of ruthless kidnappers.

You'll be on the edge of your seat as you follow Mike and Savannah's attempt at escape and the entire rescue operation in this story, and you will be furious with the media for their meddling in delivering news of the kidnapping. Something that we have seen before in movies but was still unique in its own way.

The author, Paul, also does a great job of describing the difficulties faced by a typical affluent New York City family in this novel. The troubled marriage of Mike's parents, Katie and Richard, is reminiscent of some of ours. Both were busy with their own jobs, but both of them made time to support Mike as he embarked on his own venture, and be there in his darkest hour.

You will find inspiration in Mike's unwavering dedication to achieving self-determination through the establishment of his own business. As some of the events in this story demonstrate, however, for a young person that age to launch a business in the real world, it likely to be an extremely challenging experience.

Lastly, with its gratifying conclusion and intriguing cliffhanger, this is one of the works you will find worthwhile. The characters are well written, and the scenarios will elicit the emotions you should be experiencing from reading the story. This is a story that you'll probably read again at some point in the future. A gripping, exciting and satisfying tale of family, action, and love. This book deserves a 9 out of 10 rating.

Table of Contents

ONE

Sipping iced bourbon in his old office chair Jake Carlson gazed at his wall of fame reliving every snapshot of a hard fought career. His reputation as a brutal litigator had long been the subject of Chicago barroom conjecture and his phones had never stopped ringing. Time however, had caught up with him and he no longer had fire in his belly. He was tired, burned out and ready to spend his autumn years in the house that he and his wife Grace, who passed away last spring, shared for fifty years. Bourbon helped. As he poured another shot over the rattling ice, Annie, his ageing secretary, spoke on the intercom. 'I have JB Walsome for you.'

Jake told her to put him through and grabbed the phone. 'Hi JB, wanna borrow some money?'

'Jake, you old dog, I thought you'd be fly-fishing by now.'

'Nope, too busy pal. To what do I owe this pleasure?'

'I have a proposition for you.'

'What is it?'

'You always were a grizzly old cuss.'

'Cut the bullshit let's hear it.'

'I'm proposing that we join forces on a class action. Believe me this one is a monster. Is your TV on?'

'No.'

'Tune in to CNN. I guarantee you'll call me back.'

Jake did so and reached for his bourbon as CNN reporter Bill Glaxon filled the widescreen with theatrical gusto.....

-They came from towns and cities all over the state. Some arrived in limousines; others could barely afford the bus fair. But they came, they had to, for they are the conscience of a nation. Compelled by a wave of emotion sweeping across the country they gathered around a leafy corner of Chicago's southern district cemetery. Never have I experienced such an eerie silence among so many. Leaders of different faiths stepped forward and led the desolate mourners in a final solemn prayer as pallbearers lowered fifty-eight tiny caskets into freshly dug graves. Some distraught mothers fainted, some could no longer bear to look; others fell to their knees in a desperate attempt to touch their child's flower-strewn casket for the last time.

The nation was in mourning.

Strangers hugged one another.

Among them was tough litigator Richard Kinnerman, one of many lawyers representing the grieving families. I caught up with him in the crowd and asked for his reaction to today's events; this is what he had to say –

'This is a "Tragedy of Innocence" and those responsible will face justice in a court of law, but there are no winners in cases such as these, it's about closure. When I saw broken-hearted families kneeling by their child's grave struggling to find a way of letting go, I found it hard to imagine how they'll overcome such a devastating loss. I intend to win this case for them.'

-That was Richard Kinnerman on a dark day for Americans. Bill Glaxon, CNN, Chicago's Southern District Cemetery.

Jake breathed out and leaned back in his leather chair. It was a huge class action all right and it was horrible. He asked Annie to reconnect him with JB Walsome in New York City.

'You were right, JB, it is a monster and as much as I'd like to get involved, I can't handle it, not anymore. My doctor will stop taking my calls if I do.'

'So that's a no.'

'I neither have the energy or the resources for a class action needing doctors, paralegals and a million-dollar campaign.'

'Okay, I feel a but coming…….'

'I'm seventy-three and long overdue for a heart attack, JB. I'll take a backseat on this one, but I'm willing to sign up plaintiffs on behalf of your firm for a percentage of the punitive damages. People in the state of Illinois trust me, and if we join forces I want the first trial to be in Chicago. Judge Harlan will certify our class action at Chicago's Federal Court. Do we have a deal?'

'Yes we do and you'll get all the support you need. That is why I came to you, Jake. Richard Kinnerman got involved in this tragedy the day it hit the news, and he's just told reporters that he wants to handle the trial, which I agree will be in Chicago.'

'Okay, but the vultures are circling, JB. So if were gonna be first to file suit we need do it real quick.'

'I'll have the brief ready in three days.'

Five weeks later, having witnessed another day of human misery, Richard Kinnerman arrived home after midnight and as usual the house was in darkness, even Piffin, the family retriever, was asleep in his basket. Katie and the kids had gone to bed long ago. He hadn't seen much of them lately and missed the morning scramble to get the kids to school, which Katie had down to fine art, and the bubbly report on their lives over dinner. But leaving before dawn and working 16 hours seven days a week had made him a stranger. Things were not great at home and with a huge trial looming in Chicago it could only get worse. He showered and crept into bed next to Katie, who was sound asleep. At five a.m., he was on the freeway heading back to new York.

Richard Kinnerman, age 42, was a partner at Walsome, Kent and associates, one of New York City's finest law firms. Thanks to Jake Carlson he was first to file suit in Chicago on behalf of 968 plaintiffs against Merryland Food Corporation; the company held responsible for the so called, "Tragedy of Innocence"

After months of evidence gathering and witness preparation Richard and his team were ready to argue the case at Chicago's Federal District Court against Merryland Food, Mercury Water and Alpec Science. Due to the high profile nature of the case many families had to stand at the back of the courtroom. Hard-nosed lawyers, representing plaintiffs from every U.S. state, had gathered to hear the outcome, which, if proven, would trigger the biggest class action in recent American history.

The plaintiffs, mostly young families, had unwittingly bought Merryland's contaminated baby food, which resulted in the tragic deaths of twenty-seven thousand four hundred and eighty-nine children, and left thousands on life support machines.

The cause: a drum of toxic waste awaiting collection at Alpec Science, a U.S. chemical research laboratory a few miles north of Merryland Foods, got swept away by a recent flood, and later crashed head-on into a ruptured water pipe owned by Mercury Water, allowing its contents to flow into the baby food process, according to experts investigating the case. The toxic baby food remained on sale for almost three weeks before scientists linked the product to the deaths of thousands of children.

On a bitterly cold Chicago Monday morning the selected jury took their seats and arguments began and continued for four long weeks before a packed courthouse. Hostilities finally ceased late on a Thursday morning, at which point Judge Harland adjourned for lunch and invited summations by the lawyers at two p.m.

Emery Wilcombe for the defence was first.

With righteous indignation Wilcombe rambled on for almost twenty-minutes about the no-stone-left-unturned evidence that, in his opinion, proved beyond doubt "the Tragedy" was an accident that occurred due to a series of unfortunate incidents over which no one had any control, and was therefore impossible to foresee or prevent. Raising his baritone voice he concluded that with those undisputable facts, the jury had no choice but to consider it "An act of God"

Wilcombe returned to his seat in a crowded silence.

Richard walked across the courtroom floor and stood before the jury. He had an honest handsome face and an easy way with words. He looked at every juror. He did not smile.

'This has not been a pleasant case for any of us, least of all the families, and I do not intend to trawl through the evidence yet again. I think you've all heard enough. Therefore, I have only one thing left to say; this was no accident, or an act of God, which the defence attorneys would have you believe. The facts have proven this terrible tragedy should never have happened. Yet here we are, and thousands of bereaved families are looking for you, the jury, to ensure this never happens again. Thank you.'

A murmur swept through the benches as Richard returned to his desk and joined his associates. Jake Carlson gave him a smug grin and nodded his approval.

Judge Harland adjourned proceedings until nine a.m. Friday, and said he would continue Saturday if necessary. Having served forty years on the bench he knew the outcome and wanted to get it over with; the families had suffered enough.

The defence attorneys headed for the nearest bar.

On Friday morning, as the jury continued their deliberations, Richard paced the courthouse corridor with a cell phone clamped to his ear talking to TV networks, reporters and senior partner JB Walsome, to whom he explained the jury was still out. Then he received a message from his wife urging him to call her, which she rarely did when he was in court. He pressed her number. 'Katie, what's up?'

'Sorry to bother you but I have a problem. My partner Geoff Batchett arranged a four-week tour of U.S. financial conventions to drum up business. Unfortunately, Geoff tripped and fell down a shopping mall escalator last night and broke his left arm and he's unable fly. It's too late to cancel the tour so I'll have to go, which means that we'll both be away, but I'm not sure what else I can do. Sally will look after Mike and Julieanne who, by the way, watch you on TV news every night and miss you terribly. I just hope that you're not going to make a big deal about this.' Katie said, and held her breath.

'No, I admire you for starting your own company and going back into the financial world after years of being a Mom, Katie, but have you asked Sally? We can't just assume she'll look after our kids whenever it suits us.'

'You know that is not the case. Sally has been an adopted aunt to Mike and Julieanne since her husband died of cancer nine years ago, they adore her and she loves them like a grandmother. What are you getting at, Richard, that I'm being irresponsible, that I shouldn't go?' Katie said, angrily, and bit her lip. The last thing she needed was another row with her husband. There was enough tension already at home, but she could not cancel the tour when meetings, flights and hotels had all been arranged.

Richard exhaled, 'No, do the tour, Katie. The jury has the case so I should be home in a day or so. Email me a copy of your itinerary and…have a safe trip.'

'Thanks, I will.' Katie said, a little surprised and hung up.

Katie had known for some time that her marriage was in crisis and that Mike and Julieanne were convinced they were heading for a breakup. She explained to her children why she had to do the tour, but they doubted she would have gone were it not for the ongoing rows. Riddled with guilt Katie started packing for her evening flight to Atlanta, watched by her long-faced children and Sally Brooks who felt that it was not her place to comment.

Richard returned to the courtroom and sensed the weight of expectation hanging in the air as the crowd waited for the verdict, which was rumoured to be forthcoming any time soon.

At 5-40 p.m. the bailiff informed Judge Harland the jury had reached a verdict and as they shuffled back to their seats, a buzz of speculation swept through the benches. A mob of reporters, barred from the courthouse by Judge Harlan, gathered at the court entrance waiting to report the verdict to the nation.

Merryland Food's lawyers sat staring into space. The CEO and board of directors huddled together to avoid eye contact with the plaintiffs. Standing arm-in-arm at the back of the courtroom the heartbroken parents had yet to overcome their grief and it was widely believed they never would.

The verdict was unanimous for the plaintiffs.

The jury found Merryland Food, Mercury Water and Alpec Science responsible for the tragedy. They awarded two hundred and fifty thousand dollars for "wrongful death" to the bereaved families of each child, and five hundred and seventy five million dollars in punitive damages. A gasp of relief filled the courtroom. The company directors leaned forward with their heads in their hands. Lawyers with thousands more plaintiffs were delighted with the verdict and looking forward to a huge payday.

The courtroom hummed with opinions. Families hugged one another. An undercover journalist, who managed to sit through the trial unnoticed, whispered on the phone to her editor.

Judge Harland thanked the jury and dismissed the court with a loud bang of his gavel, at which point the courtroom erupted into tearful uproar.

The bereaved families thanked Richard for bringing a sense of closure to their grief. He responded modestly to their gratitude, but their hollow-eyed faces, racked with pain for the loss of their child, would stay with him long after the headlines faded, and he thanked God his own children had not suffered the same fate.

After limp handshakes from the defence attorneys and a final debriefing with his associates at the Hilton, Richard took a taxi to O'Hare airport and caught the red eye to JFK, where his black SUV had gathered dust for six weeks. He longed to be home with his family in New Mayford, their redbrick oasis at the heart of a green valley seventy-nine miles north of New York City.

He slept throughout the flight.

TWO

Early the next morning, Julieanne knelt on her brother's bed and gave him a shake. Mike looked at her squint-eyed.

'What?'

'Dad got home around three-thirty this morning.'

'He's home, are you sure?'

'Yep, Sally found his shoes abandoned in the hallway

Mike rubbed his face. 'I need to talk to him. What's with the jeans boots and anorak, you going somewhere?'

'I've got a work experience day at the veterinary clinic, but Sally insisted I have breakfast first. God I want to hug her every time I see her.'

'Me too. Is she downstairs?

'No, she's doing her Saturday shop at the mall.' A car honked outside. 'That'll be Mr. Raker. Gimme a kiss I gotta go, and don't wake dad too early. Love you, bye.'

With his head entrenched in pillows Mike stared at the ceiling and went over the plan that he was about to present to his father. Then realising it was 9-30 he jumped out of bed, quickly showered and dressed. Grabbing his two precious folders, which contained two years of hard work studying the stock market and a detailed plan to start his own company, he went downstairs to the kitchen and made some coffee. It was almost 10 am; time to talk to his father. Buzzing with excitement he climbed up the stairs wondering if this would be a life-changing moment.

He was about to find out.

Gently opening the door clutching his folders, Mike entered the master bedroom and sat on the edge of his parent's king-size bed. His father was sound asleep with his head buried in several pillows and with some trepidation, he gave him a gentle nudge and whispered, 'Dad?'

Ignoring his exhaustion Richard smiled, his son's voice a reminder of why he had caught the red eye. He rolled over, his dark-circled eyes remaining closed.

'I know that voice,' he croaked, 'it belongs to a kid who lives around here; fourteen, five-nine, has dark hair, brown eyes and looks a lot like me.'

Mike grinned. 'Guilty as charged,' he shot back, brightly. He and his father enjoyed using legal jargon as playful banter.

'There had better be a fire or you're in deep water,' Richard mumbled into his pillow. 'Have you missed me?'

'Every day…..Dad, I need to talk.'

'Try the Samaritans.'

'I mean with you.'

'Cost you six hundred dollars an hour.'

'Objection council is being argumentative,' Mike rallied and folded his arms.

Richard smiled into his pillow. 'Objection overruled.'

'Not relevant councillor this is pro-bono. Charity begins at home, remember?'

'How could I forget, you already owe me two hundred and fifty thousand dollars for your education.'

Mike rolled his eyes. 'I'll pay you back when I'm famous, Dad. Can we talk? It's about my future.'

Richard sat up and yawned. 'Sounds like you need a fortune teller. I thought you wanted to be a lawyer.'

'That was six weeks ago I was younger then.'

'Wise guy, huh? Come 'ere.' Richard hugged his son and the six weeks they had spent apart became history. 'This had better be good or I'm calling the orphanage. What is it?'

'I've got an idea, Dad, and I need your help.'

'What's it gonna cost me?'

'Your approval and legal expertise.' #

'Mmm, that sounds horribly expensive. Have you done the groundwork, got a plan?'

'Yep, I've compiled it as part one and two. Here's part one,' Mike explained, handing his father one of the folders.

Richard fumbled around on the night stand for his glasses. 'Tell you what, draw back those curtains and go make us some coffee while I read this. By the way, is Julieanne okay? I called her a couple of times from the courthouse yesterday and left a message but she never came back to me.'

Mike opened the curtains. 'Yeah, Jules is fine. She's working at the vet clinic today,' he said, pausing at the doorway. 'So how'd it go in Chicago, did you win?'

Richard looked up. 'No son, there were no winners.'

Mike nodded wishing he'd never asked and went down to the kitchen, closely followed by Piffin who had a hungry look and was trying hard to make eye contact. When he returned with the coffee his father had just finished reading the first document, so he sat on the bed and waited for his reaction.

Richard peered over the top of his glasses. 'Did you write all this stuff?'

Mike gave him a questioning look. 'Don't you like it?'

'This is a real piece of work, son. I'm impressed,' he said, and sipped the strong coffee.

Mike exhaled and silently thanked Sally Brooks. Without her help it would have taken him years to understand the complexity of the financial markets. Ironically, his newfound knowledge had given rise to doubts as to whether the company idea was just a boyhood dream; it looked fine on paper, but could it work, was it legal? Would his father pat him on the head and tell him to get on with his studies, as Ms. Wilmot, his school principal had done.

He sat transfixed with expectation.

Richard closed the folder. 'Okay, you've got my attention. So why do you need all this stuff on the stock market?'

'This one will explain that, Dad.' Mike said, handing him the second folder. Richard flicked through the pages in silence.

Just stick to the facts was the advice his father had drummed into him since he was eight years old, and this was the defining moment. If Mike could not convince his father that his idea had real potential, then he would never convince anyone.

Richard took off his glasses. 'Helluva presentation, son, dyou want to talk me through it?' he said, and drank more coffee.

Mike took a deep breath. 'Okay. In America, pocket money is worth around 9 billion dollars a year and kids spend most of that on games, toys, and electronic gadgets. Take that to a global level and we're talking about 50 billion dollars a year, which is a huge market that no-one has taken seriously, except the games and gadget makers. Imagine what would happen if millions of kids used that money to buy shares in a company, which would invest it on the stock market. With an income of billions of dollars the company could become a Wall Street giant, owning investments in businesses and commodities all over the world. In short, if I can persuade a generation of kids to invest their pocket money in my company, instead of buying gadgets, games and other stuff, the sky's the limit. That's my plan.'

Richard closed the folder and looked at his son's eyes twinkling with dreams of changing the world. He was too young to know the glamour of Wall Street was a façade and that in reality it was the center of a ruthless world driven by greed. Richard had no desire to discourage Mike but he had no first hand experience in the business world, and before going headlong in at the deep end he had to learn that it's not just a walk in the park.

'Great in principle but it's idealistic. The stock market is not perfect, Mike, it crashes now and then. When that happens it's almost impossible to see it coming, and as a result, opportunistic investors can lose everything,' Richard explained.

'I know, but my research suggests that apart from war and natural disasters there are two reasons for that; political climate and greed. The meltdown due to the subprime mortgage crisis created by unscrupulous bankers is a classic example,' Mike said with some authority.

Richard smiled inwardly. 'Okay, am I correct in saying that you want to start a company?'

'Yes.'

'A company solely financed with pocket money?'

'Yep, by kids all over the world, is there a law against that?'

'No, but a company owned by youngsters means a whole new set of rules. The laws are very strict when it comes to kids and money, even trust funds, gifts, whatever, so before we go down that road I'll need a couple of days to check it out.'

Mike exhaled. 'But is it possible, Dad?'

'I'm not sure but it's a great idea, so don't get all down in the mouth. We'll talk again on Tuesday when I get home from the office. By then I'll know the legalities.'

Mike was relieved that his father even liked the idea, and although it was an anticlimax after all his hard work, he was sure the road to success would not be without disappointment.

On Tuesday afternoon, looking forward to his father's arrival, Mike jumped off the school bus and strolled home. Grabbing a pile of letters from the mailbox he went in the house and tossed them on the kitchen table. Then with Piffin at his heels he ran up to his bedroom and powered up his laptop. Ignoring a long list of emails, which he knew were nothing more than school gossip and spam, he called his best friend Mo Loose, nicknamed Moose; a long-haired 14-year old geek who attended the same high school as Julieanne, but unlike her brother she thought he was a weirdo. Moose was a self-proclaimed computer genius who had a thriving business on campus repairing laptops, tablets and cell phones for students, tutors and parents. Several corporations, which he had hacked and cracked, had offered him a lucrative career if he ever finished his education. Mike dialled his work number.

'Speak, I'm busy.' Moose said, curtly on speaker phone

'Hi, Moose.'

'Hey Mike, how's it goin?'

'Okay, things are starting to move. How's my website coming along?'

'I've been busy man, but don't worry it's gonna be fine. You wanted it for kids up to fifteen, right?'

'Yeah.'

'Okay, I'm on it. So when you gonna be ready?'

'I'm not sure. My dad's checking out the legal side. I should know tonight.'

'You're gonna take over the world man. Call me tomorrow.' Moose hung up.

Sally Brooks had a charity fundraiser to attend that evening and expecting to be home late she had left Mike and Julieanne instructions; casserole is simmering in the oven. Blueberry pie is in the fridge. Bed at ten. *Love Sally*

At seven-thirty, Richard parked his BMW in the driveway and climbed out briefcase in hand. Mike hurried out to meet him and together they strolled inside the house to his den; a spacious room with packed bookshelves, a cluttered desk, law certificates and family photographs covering the walls. A large bay window view of the countryside gave the room a comforting silence. Richard took off his jacket and hung it on the coat-stand. Then taking a thick folder out of his briefcase he sat in his leather chair and clicked on the onyx desk lamp.

Mike sat wide-eyed with anticipation as his father opened a thick document labelled "U.S. Company Law"

Richard began. 'Okay, I've looked at the legalities of setting up an investment company just for kids, and here's how it works. First, I'll have to be guarantor because you're under age. That means if you get a billion dollars into the company account and spend it on things you shouldn't, I go to jail.'

Mike chuckled, "Lawyers don't go to jail they're too smart."

'Yes they do, son. Okay, second, you'll need a bank account, which I can set up for you. Third, to trade at Wall Street you need a broker; a person authorized to buy and sell on the company's behalf and settle transactions through a security-clearing house. Now, according to U.S. law, the company must have at least five trustee-directors on the board, of which you'll be the chairman, but until you're eighteen I'll have to assume that responsibility. In the meantime, you will need a lawyer, an accountant and a company secretary, but I guess your Mom and I can take care of that for the time being. These are just some of the basics to get you started, Mike. The rest are regulatory procedures that I'll explain to you as we go along,' Richard concluded, leaning back in his leather chair. 'Any questions?'

'Yeah, but I'll get back to you. Right now I just wanna get the company started, Dad.'

Richard closed the folder and leaned on his desk.

'Owning a company is a serious business, Mike, and I want you to be absolutely sure before we go ahead with it.'

The front door slammed. 'I'm home!'

Mike yelled. 'We're in here, Jules!'

Julieanne gushed into the den and kissed her brother, and then her father whom she had decided to stay mad at until he stopped arguing with her mother. Sitting on the edge of Richard's desk swinging her long legs, she said, 'you look wasted, Dad.'

'Thanks. It was a tough case, Jules.'

'Hey, am I interrupting something here?' Julieanne asked, but before either could respond her cell phone rang. She looked at the screen and clicked it on. 'Hi, Mom…yeah I'm missing you too. Hang on a sec.' and jumping off the desk she hurried out of the room slamming the door behind her.

Richard huffed and shook his head. 'Your Mom told me that you were interested in the stock market, Mike, and how Sally Brooks spent a lot of time teaching you the basics, and even took you to the New York stock exchange. Now I understand why.'

'Yeah, without Sally I could never have done this.'

'So tell me, Mike, what prompted you to wanna learn about the stock market and start your own company?'

'Two years ago, I was sick for about three weeks and Mom had put daytime TV on for company. I think you were away on a case. Anyway, a program about U.S. pocket money came on and I was fascinated. When they announced that it was worth 9 billion dollars a year in the U.S., I sat up in bed and thought "What about the rest of the world?" That's what triggered the idea.'

Richard smiled. 'Well you obviously did your homework and I admire your determination. You certainly got my attention. It's a novel idea, Mike, but there's no guarantee that it'll work. The financial world can be very risky, even if you know what you're doing. There is one person who might be interested in getting involved, but I can't promise anything. First, I have to know that you're serious about doing this. So what's it gonna be?'

Mike looked across the desk at his father. 'I've worked real hard on this idea for two years, Dad, and I know that owning a company is a responsibility, but I can't create a market without it, so the answer is yes I want my own company.'

Richard leaned back in the leather chair and placed his hands behind his head.

'Okay, I'll set it up. What're you gonna call it?'

'PocketMoney.com.'

THREE

Three weeks later, at one thirty p.m. a black limousine pulled up outside the Kinnerman house. Chauffeur Charlie climbed out and stood by the open rear door. Mike checked himself in the hallway mirror and hurrying down the pathway he nodded to Charlie and sank into the rear seat. Charlie climbed in front and the limousine sped away heading for the freeway.

Mike was about to attend his first business meeting, which his father had arranged with Wall Street billionaire Harry Schlecker whose stock market genius had made him one of the wealthiest men in America. Mike's mission was to persuade Mr. Schlecker to be the broker of a company with nothing in the bank but an idea. The three p.m. meeting would take place at Mr. Schlecker's country mansion and he had sent his limousine to pick him up.

Ever since Mike was a small boy Harry Schlecker had been a regular visitor at the Kinnerman house, and although he hadn't seen him for two years Harry never forgot to send birthday and Christmas cards with gifts for both him and Julieanne, whom he affectionately thought of as a niece. Harry made no secret of his admiration for Richard Kinnerman. He also sent Katie a large bouquet of roses every Valentines Day, which always brought a giggle from Mike and Julieanne.

Richard had never mentioned it.

An hour later, the limousine pulled up at two wrought-iron gates attached to stone pillars, upon which sat a pair of bronze Bald Eagles. Charlie pressed a number on his handset and as the gates silently opened, the limousine entered Harry Schlecker's sprawling estate and rumbled along a narrow stony road for mile or so. Then beyond the distant trees a huge mansion suddenly dominated the landscape, which at first glance was not unlike the White House, in Mike's opinion.

They drove over a wooden bridge and veered right around a huge lake lined with bushes and willow oak trees. Rowing boats and a stylish launch bobbed about at a wooden jetty, from which a pathway led to a plantation style summerhouse protected from the elements by a cluster of conifers. Horses silently grazed in a nearby field. Mike noticed a black helicopter gleaming in the sunlight on a helipad outside the imposing mansion. At the grand entrance two white pillars, supporting an upper balcony, stood either side, from which a purple canopy gave shelter to a flight of carpeted steps down to the driveway.

Charlie drove around to the rear of the mansion and pulled up in a courtyard, where Greta stood waiting with her arms folded. Mike remembered meeting her two years ago when she and Harry Schlecker visited their house, but having no interest in girls then he had barely noticed her. Greta strode towards him as he stepped out of the limo's rear door. She was tall, slender and stunningly beautiful with blue eyes and blonde hair.

Greta's face lit up. 'Mike? My God, you're a young man now. It's been a while since we last met. For a moment, I thought you were from the agency. How old are you?'

'Fourteen,' Mike replied, trying not to stare at her. Greta wore flat shoes and she was four inches taller than he was.

'You're bound to be a heartbreaker, trust me. Come on, this way Harry is expecting you,' she said, taking his arm.

Greta led him through a sea of flowers and tapped in a code on a high security gate, which opened onto a pristine golf course. A yellow buggy sat parked nearby. They climbed in and as Greta drove along a tree-lined fairway towards a distant pond, Mike stared into space wondering if Mr. Schlecker would go for his idea. Minutes later, having parked the buggy a short distance from the 16th green, Greta jumped out and took his arm.

As they approached the green, Mike saw Harry Schlecker's imposing figure for the first time in two years and immediately sensed an aura of great wealth emanate from his larger than life persona. He looked to be in his late thirties and stood around five eleven with thick dark hair, a rugged handsome face and broad shoulders. His red polo shirt and green slacks flapped in the cross breeze as he putted the ball from twenty feet.

Greta whispered in Mike's ear. 'Harry's playing golf with four clients keen to invest in a new project, and so your meeting will take place between greens, is that okay?'

Mike nodded. *There goes plan A, he thought to himself.*

Greta caught Harry's attention and pointed at Mike. Throwing up his arms, he handed the caddy his iron and swaggered across the green. 'Hey, Mike, it's great to see you. How you doin kid?' he said, giving him a bear hug.

As a young boy Mike recalled feeling intimidated by Harry Schlecker. His New York City accent, resonating with confidence and attitude, left no doubt that he was once a streetwise kid. The priceless jewellery on his thick fingers, wrist and neck perfectly matched his garish personality. Dark bushy chest hair protruded from the open neck of his polo shirt, and beneath his suntanned forehead the large brown eyes of one of the wealthiest men in America were staring directly at Mike.

'I'm fine thanks Mr. Schlecker,' Mike said, trying to appear confident.

'Christ, look at you, all grown up. You were a beanpole last time we met. Now you got balls in your voice and some muscles. In a couple of years you'll be a chasing anything in a skirt, trust me. How's my little Julieanne, she okay?'

'Yeah, she's studying to be a vet,' Mike croaked. His voice was breaking and it sounded strange.

'Yeah I know, she's real smart, just like your mother. How's she coping with her asthma, Mike?'

'She has an inhaler but her attacks are pretty rare lately.'

'I'm glad to hear that. Julieanne is sixteen, so that makes you what, fourteen?'

'Yes.'

'Richard said that you wanna talk to me about an idea and I'm happy to listen, but as you can see I'm playing golf, so it's gonna have to be alfresco. Can you handle that?'

Mike forced a smile. 'Sure.'

'Okay, you got seven minutes, that's how long it'll take to get to next hole. Go!'

Mike took a breath and spoke with a passion he never thought himself capable of, which boosted his confidence. Harry listened but said nothing as he strolled along the fairway, hands behind his back nodding and grunting.

Mike paced alongside him like a used car salesman. 'With that size of investment Mr. Schlecker we could buy companies, commodities, real estate, and have a radio, TV and cell phone network just for kids. It would be a global corporation owned by young people in every country on the planet.'

Harry stopped and looked up at the heavens as though the answer lay out there somewhere while stroking his chin with the back of his fingers. It was a decisive moment because Mike knew that he'd be heading home by now if Harry had no interest in his idea. Encouraged by that thought he made one final pitch and by the time they reached the 17th hole Harry had his arm draped around Mike's shoulder.

'PocketMoney.com. You got me goin kid, I love it!' Harry said, pacing back and forth. 'And you got yourself a broker. But, and don't ever forget this, Mike.' He leaned forward, hands on his knees. 'Business is like war; you have to win or you're dead. As the broker, I'll be buying and selling on your behalf. Believe me that takes a lot of good faith, so you're gonna have to learn to trust me.'

'I do trust you, Mr. Schlecker.'

Harry stood up and shook his head. 'No you don't, but you will,' he said, with a smug grin. 'I usually don't do business with anyone without at least five million dollars in capital. That said, I know you, you're smart and I love your family, and if you pay attention you could retire by the time you're eighteen. So for once I'll make an exception,' he said, stroking his chin again.

Mike looked puzzled. 'What do you mean?'

'When you've got five hundred grand in the bank we'll start doing business, and for a genius like you that shouldn't be a problem when your website is up and running. In the meantime, I'll have a contract drawn up and get a copy of the company registration from Richard. Any questions?'

There was that smug grin again.

Mike rolled his eyes. 'About a million.'

'Yeah I know, but not today. You got what you came for go home and celebrate, it'll take me a couple of weeks to get the documentation together and set things up, and I've already got an idea how to get you started.'

Watching from the edge of the green Greta folded her arms and smiled. Whenever Harry was excited about a deal he always stroked his chin. Mike Kinnerman had nothing to worry about.

'Are you playin or what, Harry? It's your shot,' yelled one of the players, irritably.

Harry told Greta to take Mike home and walked off to join his playing partners. 'I'll be in touch, Mike,' he yelled, waving his right hand without looking back.

While Greta drove them back to the mansion Mike called his father and told him the good news. Richard, not at all surprised, said he would discuss it over dinner. Greta parked the buggy near the security gate and arm-in-arm they walked back through the gardens to the courtyard.

'Wait here, Mike, I'll bring my car around,' Greta said, and walked off towards the rear of the mansion.

Mike reflected on his meeting with Harry Schlecker until a blue Mercedes convertible sped around the corner and pulled up alongside him with the top down and music playing. He sank into the front leather seat and closed the door. As the Mercedes purred along the stony road towards the iron gates in the warm afternoon sunshine, Mike laid back his head and smiled. Days don't get much better than this, he thought to himself.

Greta was the most beautiful woman Mike had ever seen in real life, and although she was probably twice his age he was unable to take his eyes off her. Her flawless tanned skin, sinuous body and blonde hair was breathtaking. She could have stepped right out of Vogue magazine, in his opinion. His awkwardness in her presence persuaded him to keep quiet, but curiosity soon got the better of him and he began asking clumsy questions.

'Where are you from, Greta? How did you meet Harry? Are you a lawyer, where do you live, do you have a…

'Whoa, so many questions,' she said, laughing.

Mike turned to the window. 'Just curious,' he said, as though he were no longer interested.

They sat in silence for fifteen minutes. It seemed longer.

Greta knew that she had to break the ice. 'Okay, my name is Greta Hortchfelt and I'm from Norway. I am thirty-one and have a degree in architecture, asset liability management and business finance. I also speak five languages and have worked for Harry Schlecker for five years. I live in one of the mansion's west wing apartments. Will that do for now?' she said, hoping to placate his embarrassment.

Mike leaned back and closed his eyes; she was a goddess.

Knowing that she had captured his attention Greta spoke with genuine affection. 'You are a handsome young man, Mike, and very clever. You clearly have a bright future. So how does it feel to be Harry's new protégé?'

'Kinda weird it all happened so fast,' he said, as they entered New Mayford. 'Does Mr. Schlecker live up to his reputation? He sure acts pretty tough.'

'In business, he's ruthless. Underneath, he's a tabby,' Greta said, looking out the side window. 'This is your house, right?'

'Yep, thanks.'

Greta pulled up at the sidewalk and turned to her new young admirer. 'Listen, Mike, when Harry's excited about a new project he moves into the fast lane, and I'll guarantee he's on the phone right now changing your future. You have a winner, so go along with him. Believe me, Harry is always right.'

'Mr. Schlecker likes my idea but he said I have to raise five hundred thousand dollars before he'll get involved.'

'Harry always does that. It's just to remind clients that he's the one with the power. Don't worry about the money, Mike, it'll happen,' Greta said, and pecked him on the cheek.

Feeling his pulse race Mike climbed out of the car and stood on the sidewalk breathing in the remnants of Greta's intoxicating perfume. For the first time in his life he had a serious crush, and though nothing would come of it he couldn't help himself. Greta waved goodbye and he watched her drive away until she melted into the traffic on the distant freeway.

Then punching air, Mike yelled, 'Yes!' For him, it had been a life-changing day, a day that he would never forget.

He strolled up the garden pathway, his thoughts returning to the good fortune life had bestowed upon him. For two long years he had dreamt of owning a company as though it were a distant star. Now a brush with fate had made that dream come true, and with Harry Schlecker's undoubted genius to guide him his prospects seemed boundless. Although there were many problems yet to face Mike was convinced that PocketMoney.com would one day become legendary in the illustrious corridors of Wall Street.

He would not have long to wait.

FOUR

There had been no news from Harry Schlecker for almost three weeks, and Mike began to wonder if he'd changed his mind about getting involved with his venture. His concern however, turned to excitement when at six p.m. an email arrived on his laptop.

Dear Master M. Kinnerman, I have been instructed to inform you that PocketMoney.com is five hundred thousand one hundred and fifty dollars in credit. Kurt Leiner, The Manager. Chase Manhattan Bank, New York City.

Mike raced downstairs to the kitchen where his father had his head buried in a thick legal document. Dancing on his toes he explained that an important email had arrived from the bank and urged his father to look at it.

When Richard read the message, he knew the five hundred thousand dollars could only have come from one source; Harry Schlecker, and that he was using his own money to kick-start the company. He assured Mike that Harry had no rights or say in the company's business. It was purely a gamble, which he would not have taken were there any doubts about the venture.

Mike printed off a copy of the email and read it again before placing it in his desk drawer. With half a million dollars in the bank and the PocketMoney.com website ready to go online he had cause to celebrate, and said so. Richard chuckled and ruffled his son's hair as they strolled down the stairs with Piffin at their heels anxious for his dinner.

That evening, looking forward to her mother's homecoming, Julieanne went straight home from school, and having showered, washed her hair and wrapped herself in a thick towel her cell phone rang; it was David Raker, the local veterinary surgeon.

'Hi, Mr. Raker, I guess you forgot that I can't make the clinic tonight because my Mom's coming home.'

'No, I didn't forget, Julieanne, but a problem has cropped up and I wondered if you might help out.'

'What kind of problem?'

'A nasty virus has showed up at two of the local farms. Same one we had eight years ago. Foxes, birds and all sorts of wildlife can be carriers, and if it's not contained, hundreds of animals could get sick or die. I've quarantined the farms and notified the authorities. Local radio and TV are telling people to keep their pets indoors until further notice. I got all the latest vaccines for horses, cattle and pets, but first I have to inoculate the animals in the compound and I need your help.'

'I'll be there.'

'Good, I knew I could count on you. My wife Susan will pick you up and take you home when we're done.'

'I'll be ready in five minutes.' Julieanne said, and hanging up she pressed her mother's cell phone number.

One ring and Katie answered. 'Hi, sweetie, you okay?'

'Yes, but I've missed you.'

'I've missed you too darling. I'm about to collect my car at JFK and I can't wait to see you.'

'Me too, but there's a problem.' She quickly explained why Mr. Raker had called her. 'I have to go, Mom, is that okay?'

'Go, don't even think about it. You got transport?'

'Yes. Susan is picking me up and bringing me home. I might be late. Will you wait up for me?'

'You bet I will, and I'm proud of you. Now go help those poor animals. I'll see you later, love you, bye.'

By the time Julieanne had put on her work clothes, boots and a baseball cap a car horn honked outside. Richard and Mike had just walked down to the hallway when Julieanne raced down the stairs. She kissed her brother, ignored her father and bolted out the front door slamming it behind her.

Richard tightened his lips and shook his head. Then the house phone rang; he picked it up. 'Richard Kinnerman.'

'Hi, it's me, just got in from Washington,' Katie said, brightly. 'I'll be home in about an hour. Is Mike home?'

'Yes, and he's dying to see you, but Jules has gone out.'

'I know, she just called me. Keep Piffin indoors. Apparently, a virus has broken out at two local farms. Jules has gone to help Mr. Raker vaccinate the animals in the compound.'

'Oh, I wondered where she had gone in such a hurry. 'Okay, we'll see you when you get home.'

'I'm on my way,' Katie said, and hung up.

As the engine of her gold Lexus growled to life in the airport parking lot Katie looked through the droplets of rain running down the windscreen. Throughout her trip she had given a great deal of thought to her children and her floundering marriage with Richard. They were her whole life but Katie was no longer sure whether she could remain in a relationship that had descended to indifference. Hoping for a sign of reconciliation she drove out of the parking lot and headed for the freeway in the pouring rain.

Mike also wanted his mother's homecoming to be special and suggested to his father that it would be nice if they surprised her with dinner at Benitos Italian restaurant, Katie's favourite eatery. Richard agreed, and reserving a table for eight p.m. he went upstairs to freshen up.

An hour or so later, Katie parked in the driveway and hauling her suitcase to the front door she entered the hallway. Mike raced down the stairs and grinned with delight when he saw his mother open-armed wanting a hug. Katie's eyes misted over with joy as he wrapped his arms around her.

Richard strolled down the stairs and paused at the last step. Katie smiled, hoping for a friendly response. 'Hi, I'm home.'

How was your trip?' he asked, rather lamely.

Katie exhaled with disappointment. 'Fine,' she replied, with the same indifference.

Ignoring the gloom Mike led his parents into the kitchen; the family gathering space. Richard and Katie stood as far apart as possible and looked anywhere but at each other.

Piffin made it quite clear how much he had missed Katie and excitedly licked her face as she made a fuss of him.

'Would you like a drink?' Richard asked.

'Wine would be nice,' Katie replied, not looking up. Richard handed her a glass of Merlot. 'Thanks,' she said, and continued flicking through the pile of unopened mail on the kitchen table.

Mike's cell phone rang; it was Harry Schlecker.

'PocketMoney.com is keeping me up nights kid, it's brilliant, and in case you're worried about the 500 grand, don't be it's just a tiny investment to get you started. Right now, I'm negotiating a deal that's gonna put you in the TV spotlight, so make sure you're ready,' Harry said, and before Mike could ask for more details he hung up.

Piffin stretched out on the kitchen floor, head on his paws.

'Mr. Schlecker thinks PocketMoney.com is brilliant and he's negotiating a deal to put me on TV,' Mike said, excitedly.

Katie dropped a pile of letters on the floor. 'Schlecker!' Richard rolled his eyes. 'Katie, he's just helping Mike to get started that's all.'

Katie's eyes narrowed. 'You, let our son get involved with a man like Harry Schlecker?'

'Mr. Schlecker loaned me five hundred thousand dollars to start the company, Mom,' Mike added, innocently.

'What!' she yelled, with a look of horror. Piffin left the room. Richard poured himself a glass of Merlot. Katie gave him a cold stare. 'We need to talk about this,' she said, icily.

'Okay, I've reserved a table for us at Benitos. We can have a nice meal together and Mike can bring you up to date with his new venture,' Richard said, and drank some wine. Katie folded her arms and was clearly about to give Richard a lecture so he went on the offensive. 'And before we go to war we owe it to Mike to help him in any way that we can, is that okay with you?' he said, immediately regretting it.

Mike left the room and joined Piffin, who lay stretched out in the hallway with his ears up.

Katie slipped off her navy blue overcoat and carelessly threw it on the kitchen table. 'I'm done with war, Richard.'

'Fine, then let's try being responsible parents.'

'Allowing Harry Schlecker to give our son half a million dollars is hardly responsible!'

'Look…

'Don't use that "look" routine on me!'

Richard showed the flat of his hands. 'Okay, whatever.'

Katie felt that she was sinking in emotional quicksand. 'I was hoping that after four weeks away you might at least be pleasant.'

'We missed you, okay?'

Katie exhaled. 'I was looking forward to seeing my children, Richard, and perhaps catching up on our lives. That is clearly not going to happen is it?'

'You're tired and cranky, let's go eat.'

Benitos family restaurant seated around fifty people, its red-clothed tables nicely spaced on a split-level wooden floor with candlelit alcoves. Romantic Italian songs flavoured the room but it was the home made pasta, congenial buzz of conversation and numerous celebrities that made Benitos so popular.

The waiter led them to an alcove table. Richard ordered three specials and a bottle of red wine. A mountain of steaming pasta soon arrived, and as they dined Mike outlined his plans for PocketMoney.com and his ambition for a career at Wall Street. Mike had learned a great deal about the money markets but Katie had no intension of letting him loose on Wall Street just yet.

'Everything okay? The rotund waiter asked, showing all his teeth. Richard nodded. Katie forced a smile.

As the waiter danced away, Katie spoke with the affection of a concerned mother and the practicality of an accountant.

'PocketMoney.com is a wonderful idea, Mike, and with Harry Schlecker onboard I can't see how it can fail. And that's what bothers me.'

'But why, Mom? If PocketMoney.com is successful I'll have a career at Wall Street.'

'Yes but you're still at school, sweetie, and if you miss out on that you'll wind up serving hamburgers.'

Richard threw down his napkin. 'Little dramatic wouldn't you say? Mike's top in his class.'

'What does that mean? That he doesn't need to go school?'

'Goddam it, Katie, you're the most annoying woman I have ever met and….

'If you can't be civil then I'd rather you said nothing at all,' Katie snapped, and sipped her wine.

Mike lowered his head. 'Why do you hate each other,' he wanted to say, but wouldn't dare intervene.

Silence fell around the table. Richard thoughtfully sipped his wine and glanced at Katie's wedding ring as she began twisting strands of her auburn hair, the ones that always fell to the side of her face, which was now pale with anger.

Richard ordered coffees and a hot chocolate, and as the waiter left, he said, 'We need to talk about this, Katie.'

'This is hardly the place.'

'Rationally.'

'Fine, then try to remember that you are not in a courtroom you're having dinner with your family.'

Richard could withstand any amount of provocation in a courtroom, but Katie knew which buttons to press and could shake his composure at the bat of an eye.

He leaned over the table. 'Mike, do me a favour. Go to the rest room will you, son? Mike knew there was something they didn't want him to hear and dreaded to think what it was. Feeling a knot in his stomach he left the table. 'What is it, Katie? This is not like you. There's something else, something that you're not telling me,' Richard said, his tone softer, conciliatory.

Katie shook her head. 'I can't live like this anymore, Richard. I honestly believe that we need a break.'

Richard's face dropped. 'I see, so that's it. Have you thought this through? What it'll do to our -

'Don't you dare lecture me. I've gone through hell trying to make our marriage work but you won't let me.'

'Try harder.'

'I don't think I can, not anymore.'

'Fine, then do what the hell you want goddam it!'

Overhearing Richard's outburst nearby diners looked at him with disdain. Katie calmly sipped her wine.

'What made you come to this decision, Katie? Did something happen while you were away?'

'No, I've thought about us and our marriage for months, day after day… after every stupid argument, but I couldn't leave my children.'

'So what changed your mind?'

Returning to their table, Mike sat in his chair and stared at the tablecloth, wondering what they hadn't wanted him to hear.

'I met Andrew Stell, my old boss at Menton Corporation. He was at the San Francisco convention. We had lunch and, much to my surprise, he offered me a job.'

'I thought you didn't want to travel to New York anymore.' 'I don't. The job is in Tokyo. Three months starting October, with an option for a further three months in Milan and London.'

Richard slumped back in his chair. 'I see,' he said, clearly shocked and sat in thoughtful silence for a moment. 'So are you gonna take it?'

'I wasn't sure until tonight. Yes I am.'

'What about your company, and partner Geoff Batchett?'

'Geoff's comfortable with it. Menton have offered to buy my share and be a partner, which gives Geoff city status in the sticks and leaves me financially comfortable.'

Mike looked at his mother. 'Are you leaving us, Mom?'

Katie shook her head. 'No, Mike, I'm taking a job in Tokyo for a few months, that's all. I promise I will never leave you.'

An awkward silence fell as the waiter delivered their coffee and hot chocolate to the table. Sensing a discordant air the young man nodded and left.

Mike had experienced many of those angry silences and he hated them, their unspoken words a stark reminder that the love he had so cherished as a child had turned to icy hostility, which was now evident around the table. His father had spent six weeks in Chicago and his mother had just returned after a four-week tour of the States, and to end her welcome home evening with the news that they were breaking up was very distressing.

Mike stirred his hot chocolate amid the raging silence.

Katie sipped her coffee and glanced at the loves of her life. Richard, a handsome, highly intelligent man sat fiddling with a crumpled napkin unsure what to say or where to look, while her darling son sullenly stared at the tablecloth with his head bowed.

What had brought them to such a pitiful silence when they had everything? Katie wondered.

In a corner of the restaurant a family sang Happy Birthday to one of their two young kids as a waiter rushed to their table with a pink birthday cake glittering with ten sparklers.

Mike was very upset, and the fact that his mother had decided to work in Tokyo added enormous stress to what was already a family crisis and he was finding it difficult to deal with. Deeply disturbed by what he and his sister feared would happen his head was exploding and he could no longer stand it. He jumped up, pushed back his chair and headed for the door with tears running down his face and ran down the street in the pouring rain.

Katie threw down her napkin and ran after him.

Richard paid the bill and hurried outside. He ran up the hill and soaking wet climbed into his BMW. The engine growled to life and he turned on the headlights, but a line of traffic both ways prevented him from pulling out. As he tapped his fingers on the steering wheel waiting for someone to give way, he had to admit that he'd been sleepwalking through his marriage for some time, and tonight's episode was a wake-up call.

Katie felt the heel of her left shoe snap and hobbling along the drenched sidewalk, she found her son standing with his face against a tree. She stopped a few yards away, desperately wanting to reach out to him. 'Mike.'

Mike looked at his mother, his pain-ridden face bleached with emotion. 'It's not fair, Mom, it's just not fair,' he sobbed.

'I know it's not, Mike, I know.'

'Jules and me sat upstairs for months listening to the fights hoping you and dad wouldn't break up. She cries in her room every night, Mom, she can't take this anymore than I can.'

Katie held out her hands. 'Come here, Mike.'

Melting in the warmth of Katie's embrace Mike clung to her, and said, 'Jules and I know how unhappy you are, Mom, but if you go away we're afraid that we'll never see you again.'

The BMW screeched to halt beside them. Richard jumped out onto the waterlogged sidewalk and spoke with a warmth Katie had not heard in long time.

'I don't know what happened to us, Katie. We've been in an emotional fog for so long I didn't see it coming, and I don't think you did either. I know we have our problems, but there's nothing we can't fix if we've a mind to. Our kids have always come first and they need you, Katie,' Richard said, his eyes burdened and rain running down his face.

Katie raised a hand to her mouth in an attempt to conceal her emotion but to no avail. She buried her face in her hands and months of heartache and uncertainty ran through her fingers.

Mike begged her not to cry.

Richard could not bear to see his wife and son in so much despair. 'Let's go home, Katie, please,' he pleaded.

Tightening her arms around her son, Katie turned to Richard and looked wistfully into his eyes.

'We both need to go home, Richard, *we* haven't been there for quite some time.'

CHAPTER

FIVE

No one spoke throughout the journey home. Mike sat staring out of the backseat window. Katie, curled up in front, couldn't stop shivering. Richard kept his eyes on the waterlogged road until they were safely home in their driveway. It was still raining heavily. Katie hobbled along the pathway to the front door and entered the hallway. Mike followed her inside. Richard parked the BMW in the garage and hurried inside the house closing the door behind him. Katie and Mike had evidently gone upstairs to shower and put on dry clothes. Richard hung up his wet coat and did the same.

Katie moved her things into one of the spare rooms, hoping it would underline her concern for their troubled marriage. Richard made no comment but it had clearly shaken him. Mike, still upset about his mother leaving, lay face down on his bed.

Tapping on his door Katie entered. 'Sorry, Mike. I didn't mention this to you because I hadn't decided. Can we talk when Julieanne gets home?' Mike nodded, without looking up.

Richard and Katie went into the den and sat facing one another each side of his desk. Over a glass of brandy they talked candidly about their ongoing petty arguments, their once perfect marriage and their future together. There was no yelling or blaming one another for their acerbic confrontations, but Katie made it quite clear that she was no longer prepared to live in emotional turmoil. It was tearing the family apart.

'Marital indifference and petty squabbling is nothing short of parental irresponsibly, Richard. We snap at the slightest thing and say sorry the next morning, but sorry doesn't solve the underlying problem it merely keeps the peace,' Katie said, dispassionately.

'Katie, we're intelligent people. We solve our problems with reason, by talking them through and…

'We don't talk, Richard, we argue.'

He shook his head hopelessly. 'Your tone suggests that your feelings towards me are less than conciliatory.'

'My feelings are on hold right now.'

'Well mine aren't. And for the record, I've loved you since the night we first met, and I still do,' Richard snapped.

Katie sipped her brandy. 'I know you do, and it's for that very reason I'm prepared to fight for us, Richard. I want my goddam life back.'

Richard sank back in his chair. 'What're you planning to do?'

'I'm taking the job in Tokyo for three months, with further options in Europe. I believe a break will give us time to consider what is at stake here and let the wounds heal. A few months apart won't hurt either of us, but if that doesn't force us to focus on saving our marriage, then nothing will.'

Richard looked thoughtfully at the family photograph on his desk and turning to Katie, he said, with angry resignation, 'I'm disappointed to say the least, Katie, but you must do what you feel is right. I'm in court tomorrow so…. goodnight,' and kissing her on the cheek he left the room.

Julieanne arrived home at eleven and squealing with delight she ran into the kitchen and wrapped her arms around her mother, who revelled in the warmth of her daughter's affection. It was what she lived for. Bubbling with news Julieanne slipped off her muddy anorak and handed it to Katie, who hung on every word until she went upstairs to shower and climbed into bed. Mike was lying over his sister's feet when Katie entered her room. Handing them mugs of hot chocolate she sat on the bed.

'Mike has told me what happened at Benitos, Mom. Are you really going away?' Julieanne asked, her eyes wide and anxious.

'Only for a while, sweetie. Now listen, this is very important. The squabbles you heard between your father and I had nothing to do with you we were just lashing out at one another. There is nothing more important to us than our son and our daughter. I know it's hard for you to understand but I'm taking a break to give your father and I a little breathing space that's all. You are my family, my life, for always, and nothing will ever change that. Your father and I still love each other and when I return we'll make a fresh start, okay? Now I could really use a hug.'

Mike and Julieanne decided to make a fuss of Katie at every given opportunity, hoping to persuade her not to go away. They went shopping, to rock concerts, pizza-movie nights, ice-skating and ten-pin bowling. Richard worked late most nights.

One morning, when Richard had gone to work and the kids were at school, Katie confided in Sally Brooks of her planned trip to Tokyo over several cups of coffee.

'If you expect me to be surprised, Katie, I'm not,' Sally said, drawing on the wisdom of her years. 'I could see it coming, and now the bubble's burst. Normally I wouldn't agree to a mother leaving her kids, but knowing how much you love them and that initially it's only for three months, I think it's the right decision. I'll take care of them. Richard will pine I promise.'

Katie was angry with herself and Richard. They were both guilty of emotional dereliction to their children, and the distress that it had undoubtedly caused them was unforgivable. It was not something that she could put a plaster on and kiss better. They were psychological wounds that would need time and loving care to heal, which meant that her imminent departure to Tokyo would give rise to feelings of guilt and recrimination and be challenging for the whole family, especially for Katie herself.

Late on Monday morning, Katie met with Andrew Stell and Menton's directors at their Manhattan offices. After discussing the details of her assignment, Katie agreed to the Tokyo deal in which she would head a team assembled to baby-sit the merger of Menton's two largest clients - American and Japanese - and solve any transitional problems. She would depart on Friday, October 2nd, with a proviso that if she took the option for a further three months in Milan she would spend Christmas and New Year at home with her children. Katie signed the agreement and thanked Andrew for giving her the opportunity. Then after a celebratory lunch with the directors, she headed home in her Lexus looking forward to an evening with her son and daughter.

Saturday morning, Mike's cell phone kept on ringing until he picked it up. 'What?' he croaked. It was 6:30 a.m.

'Get up you got one hour to get ready,' Harry said, as though it was way past lunchtime. He'd been on the phone since 4 a.m.

Mike rubbed his face. 'Mr. Schlecker?'

'Time to hustle kid you're on NYTV Saturday Live coast-to-coast,' Harry explained, his voice charged with adrenaline.

'Now! Today?'

'Today. I'll pick you up in the chopper. Bring the family.'

Mike woke Julieanne and his parents as though the house was on fire. Saturday Live was the hottest show in America and a buzz of excitement swept through the house. Mike showered and dressed, but when Julieanne saw what he was wearing she rolled her eyes and dragged him back to his bedroom.

'You can't wear an egg-stained t-shirt and jeans on TV,' she said, tugging through his limited wardrobe. 'Here, put these on,' she ordered, handing him a blue shirt, beige chinos and the brown loafers he got for Christmas and loathed. Mike didn't argue.

After thirty minutes of mayhem, throughout which Piffin ran up and down the stairs barking and wagging his tail, the family assembled for breakfast in the kitchen. Sally Brooks popped in and asked what all the fuss was about. Katie handed her some coffee and nodded to Mike, who explained that he was appearing on NYTV that morning, to talk about PocketMoney.com.

Sally smiled. 'Oh my, well you'll have no problem answering their questions. And by the way, you look great.'

Giving her brother a smug grin Julieanne stood up and began pacing the kitchen floor with her hands in her armpits.

'Did Harry tell you what is happening, Mike? Like what you have to say or do on the show.'

'Talk about shares and stuff I guess,' he said, calmly.

'He didn't tell you? I'm nervous, are you nervous?' Julieanne said, still pacing. Katie grabbed her arm and sat her down.

The helicopter landed in the grassland behind the house, its drabbing rotors cracking the early morning silence. Sally kissed Mike for luck and promised to watch the show. Katie, Mike and Julieanne scrambled out the rear garden to the waiting helicopter, followed by Richard who noticed disgruntled neighbours peering through their curtains. Letters of complaint would surely follow, he thought. With everyone safely onboard, the pilot took off and headed for the NYTV building in New York City.

Janet, the director's assistant, waved to them from the rooftop helipad as they approached. Climbing out of the helicopter they followed her into the building and took the elevator down to the lavish TV studios. Ushering them into the control room, Janet introduced the director, Robert Colbert, who smiled and gave a firm handshake. Harry and Greta had gone to the boardroom for a breakfast meeting with the directors.

Robert Colbert led Mike and his family into a spacious TV studio with a shiny, black floor, a dazzling backdrop of the New York City skyline and a curved white table, upon which lay several yellow scripts and a silver laptop. The studio buzzed with technicians rehearsing camera shots and making final tweaks to the lighting. The PocketMoney.com website, now online thanks to Moose, shimmered on a large screen at the right of the studio. They followed Robert Colbert across the shiny black floor to a tall man in a pink shirt and blue slacks standing with his back to them. Robert tapped him on the shoulder and he spun around showing his extensive dental plan.

'This is Ritchie Nepp our Saturday Live presenter,' Robert said, patting his star on the back as a photographer clicked away.

Everyone knew TV superstar Ritchie Nepp. His face was a regular feature on magazine covers. He was thirty-something, six feet two with blonde hair and a handsome suntanned face; the all-American boy.

'Hi, I'm Richard Kinnerman, and this is my wife, Katie, our daughter, Julieanne, and our son, Mike, the reason we're here.'

'Good to meet ya'll. We've got one helluva show lined up,' Ritchie said. He shook hands with Mike and Richard and gave Katie and Julieanne a lingering kiss on the cheek, leaving them both a little flushed.

Ritchie explained the format of the show; 'I'm gonna ask you a series of questions, Mike, such as how it all began, can it really work, what about school et cetera. We'll get into more detail as the show progresses. For the finale', the cameras will take us into the PocketMoney.com website and reveal to the nation whether the kids of America are really interested in buying shares or just laughing at the idea. Whadaya think?'

The thought of failure was scary enough, but in front of fifty million viewers it was mortifying. 'Sounds great,' Mike said, forcing a smile. Richard told him not to worry about it.

Janet gave Richard, Katie and Julieanne a tour of the studio complex, of which there was three and one editing suite. Richard had once visited their local TV station, but this was in a different league and commented on how amazing they were.

'I know and they cost a fortune. We've got all the latest hi-tec equipment, cameras, lighting, the works,' Janet explained. 'Two years ago though NYTV was struggling against other networks. Then the press came out with a story that we'd rigged a phone-in competition. It was untrue of course, and they even printed an apology, but never revealed their source. There were rumours as to who the culprit was, but I won't get into that. Anyway, a few weeks later, after some bad press, advertising revenues dwindled and the company's shares fell off the cliff.'

'Enter Harry Schlecker, who bailed you out,' Katie said, with a hint of where-have-I-heard-that-before.

'That's right, Harry Schlecker bought thirty-five percent of the company, and one year later, NYTV was right back on top of the ratings. Can you believe that?'

'That sounds like Harry,' Katie said, feeling her daughter's arm around her waist. 'Maybe that's why he's a billionaire.'

Janet continued, 'Sure, Harry's a genius, but he's made a few enemies in the boardroom. My husband is one of the directors and tells me everything. Pillow talk, you know.'

'That won't bother Harry,' Richard said, glibly. 'What'd he do threaten somebody?'

'Yes, on Wednesday he summoned the board of directors and insisted that "Saturday Live", which is now top of America's TV ratings and earning huge advertising revenues, be solely devoted to Mike Kinnerman this Saturday. Of course, no one had heard of Mike and by all accounts the meeting turned ugly. Apparently, Harry threatened and bullied the directors until they gave into his demands. They're all in the boardroom right now getting ready to watch a show they're convinced will damage the network and their careers.'

Richard chuckled, 'It's not hard to figure. The Saturday Show will air PocketMoney.com to America's kids, and their response either way will send the ratings sky high.'

'I hope you're right,' Janet said, glancing at her watch. 'We'd better get back to the studio I have to take care of Mike. Follow me,' she said, already pacing along the corridor.

Janet led Mike to a dressing room where a young girl dabbed make-up on his face and brushed his hair. Then she escorted him into the studio and sat him in a chair next to Ritchie Nepp at the curved white table. As security ushered the invited audience to their seats, a buzz of intrigue gathered about the handsome boy's face on the monitor screens.

Minutes later, as the house lights began to fade, Janet yelled, 'Quiet please! Three thousand, two thousand…and…cue music!' The camera zoomed in for a close up of Ritchie Nepp.

'Welcome to Saturday Live. I'm Ritchie Nepp and we have an exciting show lined up, especially for you kids out there, so let's get right to it. My special guest today is Mike Kinnerman, founder of PocketMoney.com; a brand new company designed just for kids.' A camera zooms in on Mike. He smiles. Back to Ritchie, 'Okay, so tell us, Mike. How did it all begin? Did you wake up one night and go WOW!'

'Not quite, I got the idea from a TV show when I was twelve. Problem was I knew nothing about the stock market, so I spent a couple of years learning the basics from Sally Brooks, a Wall Street expert and family friend. Then with the help of my Mom and Dad I started my own company, PocketMoney.com.'

'Okay, let's imagine for a moment that this company of yours is successful. Success can be very time consuming and you're still at school, so won't that be a major problem?' Ritchie asked, turning another page of his script.

Mike shook his head. 'No, I'm committed to my education. Starting a company was just an early career move.'

The audience chuckled, as did Richard and Katie. Julieanne shook her head. *Why does he always have to make jokes?*

Ritchie went on. 'It sure was, but aren't you a little young to play the stock market, Mike?' he persisted.

'Yes, you have to be eighteen, but the company will have five trustees handling the stock market when we start trading.'

'PocketMoney.com is a company just for kids, is that legal?

'Yep, my Dad checked it out. He's a lawyer.'

'Okay, but do you honestly believe that you can persuade the kids of America to buy shares in your company instead of cell phones, games, bikes and gadgets?'

'When they realise that PocketMoney.com is owned by kids all over the world, yes I do,' Mike said, confidently.

Ritchie turned another page of his script and threw in a few tough questions, which for many company executives could have proved challenging, particularly about the stock market, but not for Mike. He'd done his homework, studied hard, and reeled off the answers without batting an eye, much to everyone's surprise, especially Ritchie Nepp.

Just before the commercial break Ritchie played America's number one pop video featuring top U.S. girl group "Femme X", after which he invited viewers to call the number on the screen if they had a question for Mike Kinnerman. Within seconds all the lines were jammed. Mike took twenty calls, mostly from kids who said that PocketMoney.com was a cool idea and many of their friends had bought shares that morning. One negative call came from a woman in Wyoming who had three kids.

'It's a goddam shame taking money off young folk,' she said, 'Let 'em grow up first.' The director bleeped out the expletive, cut her off and went to commercials.

As the ads dissolved to part two of the show Janet hushed the audience. Close up on Ritchie, who announced that it was time to visit the PocketMoney.com website. A Hollywood style fanfare magnified the moment. Mike felt his stomach tighten.

Using his laptop, which the technicians had linked to the huge screen, Ritchie entered the PocketMoney.com website and asked Mike which icon to choose.

'Shares and business,' he said, and held his breath.

The audience remained deathly silent.

'Oh my God!' Ritchie exclaimed. 'This can't be right. I must have pressed the wrong icon. It says you've had seven million six-hundred thousand five hundred and twenty-seven hits this morning from kids all over America.'

Robert Colbert ordered a close up on Mike Kinnerman.

Mike took a breath and leaned forward on the table, his heart pounding. 'No, that is the right icon.'

A murmur swept through the audience. Julieanne smiled with pride for her brother. Richard and Katie exchanged glances, both realising their son's Wall Street career had just begun. Janet rushed onto the set and handed Mike a bottle of mineral water. Close up on Ritchie. 'Does that mean the kids are actually buying shares, Mike?'

Mike could barely contain his excitement. 'Yes, every hit is a share sold,' he said, his hands shaking as he took a sip of water.

'And it's happening right across the country; New York, Los Angeles, San Francisco, Dallas, Washington, Chicago, Boston, Denver. My God, this is amazing. We're actually witnessing the birth of a new company owned by kids.' Ritchie put his hand to his earpiece. 'I've just been told that we're taking a short break folks we'll be right back.'

The audience hummed with opinions as the studio screens dissolved to ads. Robert Colbert summoned the production team for an urgent conference. Ritchie hurried to the control room and waited to speak to Robert, who was yelling into a phone at the network director. The crew repositioned the cameras while staff quickly polished the floor and sound teed up the logo music.

Alone in her office watching the "Saturday Show" with great interest Mike's school principal, Ms. Wilmont opened her desk drawer and withdrew Mike Kinnerman's file.

Katie, striking in a bright pink shirt, jeans, cowboy boots and a green suede jacket, sneaked up behind her son and whispered, 'Mike Kinnerman I believe you're about to become famous.'

Mike grinned. 'Proud of me?'

'Ridiculously, we all are. Enjoy the moment you're back to school on Monday,' Katie said, and returning to her daughter she noticed a commotion going on in the control room.

After a grovelling apology to Harry Schlecker for their lack of faith in his protégé` the directors shared a bottle of champagne. The show was, without doubt, a smash hit! One proclaimed.

Robert Colbert hurried into the studio. 'Quiet please! We're extending the program by thirty minutes. Mike, the viewers are asking for more details about buying shares, and so I'd like you to explain how it works. Ritchie will prompt you with some basic questions, is that okay?' Mike nodded. 'I gotta hand it to you kid you really got something, the ratings have gone through the roof.'

Mike smiled. 'Thanks Mr. Colbert. '

'Okay, quieten down everyone we're going live.'

'Five seconds!' Janet shouted. 'Three, two…and cue music.'

Ritchie Nepp welcomed the viewers back. 'Something very special is happening here today. We're witnessing the birth of an idea, an idea that is sweeping across America, an idea that has taken Mike Kinnerman two years to realise, which is a long time when you're only fourteen. So tell us, Mike, what's the deal here? Are the banks involved? How do kids buy these shares?'

'It's straight forward really. They go to a bank with a parent, relative or guardian, and after a short security process they can buy the shares, it's that simple. They're ten dollars each.'

'Okay, but tell us how it works, take us through the process.' 'When the kids buy their first share they'll get a biometric card; it's like a drivers licence. The card will contain their photo and personal details. Some banks may prefer a retina photo, the center of the eye, which takes a few seconds; others may use a fingerprint screen. As most kids can probably only afford to buy one share at a time the banks will register each one on their biometric card and their account. When they have twenty-five shares, certificates are issued.'

'So how do you keep track of all those purchases?' Ritchie asked, certain this kid could one day steal his job.

'All major banks are involved, but every purchase is linked to the Chase Manhattan bank, which will register each share sold on the PocketMoney. com website. Every account is code-linked to a facial photo, a retinal scan or a fingerprint scan.'

The audience hummed with opinions. In the control room, Robert Colbert shook his head. 'Christ, this kid is amazing,' he said, chuckling. Janet just smiled.

Ritchie continued, 'I gotta hand it to you, Mike, this is pretty substantial stuff. So what do the kids get out of it?'

'They will own a global organization, which means they'll have a say in what it does and receive an annual return on their investments. As the company grows, we plan to set up a global TV, radio and cell phone network just for kids, with offices in every city on the planet to get them involved locally. When that's established, we plan to merchandise our own collection of brands exclusively for our investors.'

'Wow, that's not a plan it's a campaign. So what happens when the kids reach sixteen, can they still buy shares?'

'Sure, if they're previous members. We call them A-shares, but we're still fine tuning those.'

'So what is the dream, Mike, what do you hope to achieve, apart from making money? Are you gonna be President one day? It sure sounds like it.'

'I'm not interested in politics yet, but if I can unite the kids around the world, anything is possible.'

More applause.

Richard and Katie glowed with pride as their son astounded the audience with an intellect far beyond his years, and it was quite clear to those present and beyond that PocketMoney.com and Mike's youthful charisma had swept the nation off its feet.

Ritchie Nepp thanked Mike for an extraordinary interview and while the credits rolled the camera zoomed in for a close up as he plugged the next show and thanked America for watching. When the studio lights went up the audience jumped to their feet and applauded Mike Kinnerman, who smiled and waved like a movie star as security guards ushered them out to the exits.

Harry Schlecker bounded into the studio with a grin needing no explanation. Greta followed on behind, her dazzling beauty lighting up the studio. Wrapping his arm around Julieanne's waist Harry could barely contain his excitement.

'Mike Kinnerman and PocketMoney.com is now the hottest story in America,' he proclaimed. 'Your peaceful family world in New Mayford is over. Mike is about to become world famous, and that success is gonna come at a price, which I'm sure he'll encounter at school Monday morning.'

Greta linked arms with Katie. 'This really is a life-changer for you all, especially Mike.'

Richard chuckled. 'I don't think it's quite sunk in yet.'

'Oh I think it has,' Katie said, nodding in Mike's direction.

Mike was staring at Ritchie's laptop shimmering with life on the white table. He watched as the number of young investors continued to rise on the PocketMoney.com website, and found it hard to believe that over seven million kids had gone to a bank that morning and bought shares in his company. If they had just bought one share each he would have seventy million dollars in the bank, and that was just the beginning.

SIX

When Mike's "Saturday Show" appearance found its way on to social media life changed dramatically for the Kinnerman family. Living in the sleepy picturesque town of New Mayford they had no idea that PocketMoney.com had captured the imagination of a generation of youngsters around the world.

They were about to find out.

Kids were reportedly queuing at banks and buying shares, just to be part of a company they could call their own. Poorer kids were cutting lawns, painting fences and running errands in an effort to raise the money to buy one share; others were selling discarded toys, clothes, old cell phones and video games. Some resorted to less honourable methods, one reporter said.

Mail carriers had begun delivering sacks of fan mail for Mike Kinnerman. Autograph hunters were knocking on the front door and several shady characters had rented rooms in New Mayford, on whom local police were keeping a close eye. Every morning outside their house the Kinnermans ran a gauntlet of reporters, some of whom attempted to board Mike's school bus, while others waited for him to arrive at the school gates. When police made three arrests on one such occasion Richard and Katie decided to drive their kids to school in future.

Their world had gone mad.

In the classroom, Mike Kinnerman was no different to any other student, and though his status in the wider world was fast becoming iconic there remained a sense of normality in life at school, which he was determined to preserve. There were those who were jealous for one reason or another but he refused to let it bother him. Most upsetting was the anonymous hate mail sent to his email address, which he neglected to change after his debut TV appearance. His father copied the emails to Sheriff Carver but was doubtful they would catch the offenders.

'Forget it, Mike, they're just losers with nothing better to do than attack successful people,' Richard said, with contempt. 'It's a fact of life unfortunately.'

Moose installed what he called "Fort Knox security system" in Mike's laptop, cell phone and the company website, which he said would eliminate malevolent bugs and unwelcome mail.

Determined not to lose any sleep over it Mike entered the school grounds each morning with a smile on his face. He looked forward to the familiar smell of the wooden desks, the polished corridor floors, creaky swinging doors, steamy changing rooms and the chattering voices of fellow students echoing in the arched hallways arranging dates, parties and rock concert nights. Most of all he embraced the challenges of his privileged education and the camaraderie of his school friends, knowing those precious years would soon be gone.

He would not allow hate mail to interfere with that.

By late July, youngsters scrambling to buy shares had spread around the world like a pandemic. As a result, billions of dollars poured into the company, which would gather dust in an escrow account until September 30th; a date agreed with the Securities and Exchange Commission, which required the company to have at least five trustee-directors on the board before trading could commence. Finding the right people however, would take time and Harry Schlecker wanted it done now. When Richard, Katie and Mike agreed, Harry approached a dozen highly respected financial experts as candidates for the post of director-trustees at PocketMoney.com. This gave the company a six-week breathing space to select the five most suitable and seat them on the board before stock market trading commenced.

One week later, always way ahead of the curve, Harry had another idea and called Richard to discuss it. 'We got the hottest company in the world pal, and we're not even trading yet. When the trustees are onboard in a month or so all hell's gonna break loose, so we need a war plan.'

Richard smiled. 'What've you got in mind, Harry?'

'Let's use this lull-before-the-storm to approach the world's big terrestrial companies with Mike's idea of a global TV, radio and cell network for kids. I guarantee we'll find a buyer, and it'll probably take a year to get it up and running. By then, we'll have cornered the whole goddam kid's market. Whadaya think?'

'Mmm, okay. Look around and see if there's any interest. I'll talk it over with Mike and Katie.'

Tuesday morning, Greta began researching communications companies capable of putting together a global network. A few hours later, she handed Harry a shortlist of five.

Harry sent memos to their company CEO's outlining a plan to franchise a PocketMoney.com global kids network. He invited them to respond with an "Expression of interest" to confirm their willingness to participate in a first stage auction. All five CEO's responded positively, some even enclosed exotic holidays, others offered expensive cars and sunshine condos. Grinning smugly, Harry called Richard to share the good news.

'I hope you're sitting down, pal. I just heard from five of the world's most powerful communications companies, and they're offering bribes to attend the first stage auction and bid for the global rights of PocketMoney.com's network for kids.'

Richard chuckled. 'I'm impressed. Where and when?'

'My place, six p.m. Saturday, black tie, and I want Mike there. Greta will pick him up and Charlie will take him home.'

'I'll talk to Mike and Katie and get back to you.'

Richard agreed to the meeting, which he would also attend. Katie and Julieanne, who had worked tirelessly to eradicate the farm virus infection, opted for a girl's night out at Benitos.

Late Saturday afternoon, wearing a new tuxedo Mike was on his way to Harry Schlecker's mansion in the front seat of Greta's blue Mercedes. Richard, only along to give advice, gazed out of the rear side window recalling how his son had spent two years developing PocketMoney.com, and as a result, five of the world's largest communications companies were now attending a meeting hoping to buy into his success. It was a great moment for Mike and Richard felt that it was a good opportunity for him to get a feel of the business. It was only a first-stage auction, which he could handle and learn from the experience.

Richard knew that Mike would make mistakes along the way, but under his watchful eye at least they would be minimal.

As they silently sped along the freeway in the early evening light Mike found it hard to take his eyes off Greta Hortchfelt, and although he hadn't seen much of her lately his adolescent crush had not diminished one iota. Wearing a black dress, a string of pearls, high heels and her blonde hair tied back in a black velvet ribbon she looked every inch a goddess. He was curious about this beautiful enigmatic woman. She had spent the last five years at Harry Schlecker's mansion, which surely meant that they had some sort of relationship, and though it was none of his business he was keen to find out.

'Greta, when I first came to see Mr. Schlecker you mentioned something about an agency. What did you mean?'

'Oh that, I thought "Company for Kids" had sent you. It's an agency we use to supply same-age kids as playmates.'

Mike looked at her. 'Playmates? Who for?'

'Harry's daughter, she's fourteen.'

'He has a daughter? Are you and Mr. Schlecker…

Richard leaned forward. 'Ease up, Mike, you're getting a little personal here.'

'Sorry, Greta, I didn't mean…arr….

'Forget it, and the answer to your question is no. I'm Harry's personal assistant, he's not married, and here we are.'

Leaving her car parked beneath the purple canopy Greta led Mike and Richard up the carpeted steps to the entrance of the great hallway: a marble-floored reception with glittering crystal chandeliers and a swirling staircase. A variety of paintings hung on the oak-panelled walls, of which one was a portrait of a black stallion named Sugar Bay. Mike was awestruck.

A tall African American in a tuxedo introduced himself as Henry. Handing Greta a note, he informed her that dinner was in the Blue Room in forty minutes. He nodded and left.

'Richard, why don't you have a drink with Harry, you'll find him in the Blue Room. I'll give Mike a tour of the ground floor.'

'Okay, see you later son,' Richard said, wandering off

Gripping Mike's arm Greta marched him along a corridor, its timbered flooring clacking under her high-heeled shoes, which made her a good seven inches taller than he was that evening and did little to enhance his confidence. Along the way Greta gave a commentary of the ground floor, which was everything Mike had imagined a billionaire's mansion would be. Glittering hallways, a lavish ballroom, a labyrinth of stately rooms with antique furniture and majestic fireplaces, above which hung portraits of former U.S. Presidents, lovingly cared for by the live-in staff, two pilots, maintenance workers and gardeners,' she explained.

Mike stopped to look at a large black and white photograph of a tall muscular black man. He was young and trim and wore white satin shorts and boxing gloves.

'Is that Henry, the guy I just saw in the Tux?'

'That's him,' Greta said, taking a leaflet out of a desk. 'Here, you can read this later. It's an article about Henry, but it's not something he likes to talk about, this way come on.'

They entered a spacious room with a library at one end and a fireplace, sofas and nests of tables at the other. In the far corner, a grand piano and a harp were resonating tunefully at the hands of two females in black evening dresses.

'Harry prefers live classical music, and so do I,' Greta said, as they approached the rear entrance. 'Now let's go outside.'

They stepped through the open French doors onto a red-tiled patio, which, according to Greta, was Italian. Then her cell phone rang; it was Harry Schlecker. She rolled her eyes, indicated five minutes with her fingers and hurried inside.

Mike strolled beneath the vined trellises and looked out at the lush green lawns, neatly cropped hedgerows, bubbling fountains and tennis courts. A swimming pool with a wood-deck surround and a selection of sunbeds shimmered silently at the center. A Hawaiian-style cocktail bar, aptly named *The Half Moon,* stood in a blaze of lights at the end of the patio. In the distance courtyard lanterns, dotted around a cluster of stables, glowed eerily in the balmy evening haze, beyond which acres of orchards and pine trees captured the fading horizon.

A slender young girl with long, black hair and wearing a red bathing suit suddenly ran bare-foot across the lawn, and plunging headlong into the pool she began swimming from end to end, seemingly oblivious to Mike's presence. Hurrying to the waters edge he knelt down and called out to her, but his affability gained him nothing more than a contemptuous glare. Shrugging his shoulders he suspected the young girl was Harry Schlecker's daughter and that another encounter was almost a certainty.

She was very pretty, beautiful in fact.

When Greta failed to return Mike went inside and found his way to the Blue Room: a long oval table the staff had prepared for the dinner guests stood in the center, from which a panoramic window gave a stunning view of a miniature Japanese garden with flickering red lanterns, tiny bridges and waterfalls. An open partition into the library enabled guests to hear the piano and harp playing over dinner.

The mansion was breathtaking, in Mike's opinion, and as he wandered around the room looking at nothing in particular, a collection of black and white photographs encased in glass caught his attention, so he decided to take a closer look.

The first was that of a young dark-haired woman sitting alone on dusty concrete steps in the doorway of a drab building. Her clothes were faded and worn and her forlorn gaze gave no hint of a smile to the camera. The others were of a group of young boys whose faces suggested life had not been kind to them. They looked shabby and hungry and their eyes burdened with the sadness of those with unreachable dreams. A small arrow pointed to one particular boy who bore a striking resemblance to Harry Schlecker, but the photograph was too grainy to be certain.

Harry strode into the Blue room and studied a laptop screen displaying business data on a wall table. Mike observed him with more than the usual interest, and wondered if that sad looking boy in the faded photograph was now one of the wealthiest men in America. If so, he was the epitome of the American Dream.

Harry yelled into his cell phone and marched out of the room snapping his fingers at Greta, who quickly entered and studied the data. Ignoring the business panic, which was no doubt making Harry even richer, Richard asked Mike to join him at the table.

'Remember, these big company hotshots are here to see you, Mike, so don't be intimidated by them, you can handle it. I'm just here riding shotgun. If you're unsure of anything, talk to me. I'll be in that chair by the window,' Richard said, I'm proud of you son, you'll do just fine.'

Mike nervously shuffled in his seat. 'Thanks Dad.'

SEVEN

A clattering helicopter landed outside. The side door opened and a group of shadowy figures stepped out onto the helipad. Greta hurried out to greet them, leaving her exotic perfume floating in the air like a mystic promise.

She returned with five powerful company bosses, to whom the waiters offered drinks and canopies. Smiling and seemingly relaxed the renowned group chattered away as though they were the best of friends in an effort to conceal their dislike for one another. Having dispensed with the artificial pleasantries, they were anxious to get down to business.

Harry Schlecker knew the five company bosses, but had only done business with one of them, so before arranging the meeting he had asked an FBI pal to check out their profiles. As a result, he knew exactly what they were worth, how much power they had, and that one was a member of a criminal organization.

'Glad you could make it,' Harry said, grinning. 'First, lemme introduce you to Richard Kinnerman, Mike's father, and one of New York's finest lawyers.'

Smiles and handshakes all round.

Mike studied the bosses' faces.

Harry continued, 'Just so as you know, Mike Kinnerman is gonna handle this meeting. If he's unsure or doesn't understand something, Richard will advise him or make it go away. Is that okay with everyone?'

'Let's get on with it,' someone growled, irritably.

Harry turned to Mike and told him to come meet the guests. Glancing at his father, he stepped forward.

The first was Sergei Gradovich from Moscow: a bald, thickset man whose croaky voice did little to enhance his English. 'Sergei is head of MosCom, a huge eastern company,' Harry explained. Gripping Mike's hand Gradovitch said something in Russian and laughed, displaying a mouthful of gold fillings and bad breath.

Next was Kurt Gunther, CEO of Eurogold: a giant European media company based in Berlin. Kurt had black staring eyes and a thin, pale face, which had clearly seen very little sunlight, and wearing a black dinner suit he resembled a character from Bram Stoker's novel, in Mike's opinion. They shook hands.

David Schwartz, CEO of U.S. Wymack Communications, the world's largest entertainment company, needed no introduction. It was common knowledge that when people use a phone, watch TV, buy magazines, music or movies he's making money. David was the most powerful man in the media business and Mike felt privileged to be in the same room with him.

Harry moved on to Linda Greenberg, CEO of Maximum; a U.S. media and communications company. Looking formidable in a black evening dress and purple tinted glasses Linda smiled generously and spoke with a west coast accent.

'Hi, Mike. I guess you know the whole world is talking about PocketMoney. com; it sure got my attention. And if you're as smart as I think you are, I reckon we can do business.'

Mr. Lo Yang, CEO of Kiatachi Electronics in Tokyo, bowed his head when introduced. As it was customary Mike also bowed when they shook hands, which prompted Mr. Yang to give the only hint of a smile he would give all evening.

Last was Jo Peterson, representing a wealthy South African client who wished to remain anonymous for the time being. Jo looked like a school team cheerleader, all teeth, legs and lipstick. Her dark hair was long and her black dress was short. She smiled, changed hips and shook Mike Kinnerman's hand.

Henry announced dinner was served.

* * * * *

An hour later, after five courses of self-indulgence peppered with false familiarity, the waiters quickly cleared the table, closed the doors and left. Jo

Peterson attached a webcam to her laptop and focused it on the table, giving her secret client a visual on the conversation. Then she dialled a number in South Africa.

Smoking a black cigarette Sergei Gradovich sat studying the evening's itinerary in Russian. Kurt Gunther, already on his forth beer, leaned over and whispered to Mr. Yang, who nodded with apparent interest. David Schwartz sat quietly weighing up the opposition. Jo Peterson whispered to her South African client on the phone whilst batting her eyelids at David Schwartz. Greta networked to ensure everyone was happy.

As Mike observed them from his seat at the end of the long table Richard spoke in his ear. 'One last piece of advice, son; this is business, not personal. No emotion, okay?'

'Okay, dad,' Mike replied. Richard returned to his seat.

Anxious to move on, Harry Schlecker asked if anyone had any questions or comments to make before business commenced.

Linda Greenberg said, 'Yeah, I was gonna mention it earlier but I got sidetracked; the way you handled that class action in Chicago was superb, Richard. It's a real pleasure to meet you.'

'Thanks, good to meet you too, Linda.'

'Mike, I want you to know that I never bullshit, so always be honest with me,' Linda advised. 'If something bothers you, don't go away wishing you'd said this or that, just ask, okay?'

'Don't worry he will. Right, Mike?' Harry said, chuckling.

Mike nodded. 'Yes, I will.'

Linda continued, 'Okay, you got five of the most powerful communications people on the planet around one table, and that should tell you all you need to know, so let me be frank. When the PocketMoney.com global TV network is up and running, I have no doubt that it'll corner the biggest market in the world: the kids. If we, the established companies, don't have a piece of that market we're all gonna have a long, cold winter, and I'm not afraid to say it to your face. Right now, you're the owner of the biggest youth organization in the world, and I need you to tell me what those kids want. Then I'll put my money on the table.'

The Russian banged his beer glass on the table. 'And I also!'

Everyone ignored him.

David Schwartz agreed with Linda, and went on to explain his thoughts in his usual soft business manner.

'You've captured the imagination of a generation of kids, Mike, and by default have become their spokesman, which means that you hold the high cards. I need to know exactly what those kids expect from us. It's a tough business, and I wanna be sure that we're all on the same page before the bidding starts.'

Harry stood up. 'Lemme answer that. We put a questionnaire on the website asking our young shareholders to tell us what they wanted. The priority answers are on page twenty-eight.'

The bosses opened the folders, which contained an analysis of the proposed network, and began to read. Greta placed coffee and an ageing cognac beside them. Having studied the answers, Harry invited them to pitch their business.

Gradovitch guaranteed a first class global network. Mr. Yang offered the same but with superior technology. Kurt Gunther said Eurogold would deliver a system years ahead of its competitors. David Schwartz listened. The South African made no comment.

Linda Greenberg promised nothing. 'My only reservation is our profit margin,' she stated. 'The kids want all those gadgets at a basic, almost nonsensical price, with cheap terrestrial costs and no premium rates, so how do we make money, Mike? I assume you expect us to make a profit.'

'The kids are demanding cheaper rates for their calls because their provider has ripped them off for years, and they refuse to accept that anymore, especially by a company in partnership with PocketMoney.com, which is now a global brand. Second.... Mike looked through his notes; a page was missing.

Richard hurried to his side. 'What is it, Mike?'

'I lost my notes, Dad,' he said, flicking through the papers.

Mr. Yang looked at his watch and exhaled.

Linda Greenberg leaned over the table. 'Are we keeping you from something Mr. Yang?' she asked, glowering at him.

Mr. Yang huffed, picked up his itinerary and returned his attention to Mike.

'Ah, here it is,' Mike exclaimed. Richard squeezed his son's shoulder and returned to his seat. 'Sorry, I lost a page.'

'Take all the time you need, Mike, no-one's goin anywhere.' Harry said, lighting a huge cigar.

Mike took a breath, 'Okay, second, to generate a profitable market, even with a captive audience, we need quality targeted programming linked to global and local sponsorship, with which we can offer airtime incentives.'

Richard and Harry gave a hint of a smile to one another. The company bosses murmured in agreement.

Greta winked at Mike and smiled.

Mike continued, 'I believe that all the major retail companies will choose to advertise on our network, to connect with the kids, and will pay a lot of money for the privilege. In addition, working in tandem with PocketMoney.com will raise the host company's credibility in their home market, giving them a higher profile. A higher profile attracts a wider audience, and a wider audience means higher advertising revenues; that's business. I'm happy to answer any other questions you may have.'

Sergei Gradovich and Kurt Gunther mumbled to one another. Jo Peterson consulted her South African client. Linda Greenberg smiled thoughtfully. She liked this young man. He was sharp and committed, and as long as the auction remained within the zone of financial reality she was ready to do business with him. David Schwartz, who had so far said very little, indicated that he was about to speak.

The room fell silent.

'You're a smart kid, Mike. I've listened to what you have to say and I'm impressed. There are still problems and unanswered questions we'll have to deal with, but that's the nature of our business. I believe the fundamentals for a deal are in place and that it's time to be pragmatic. I'm ready to back you.'

'That goes for me too, Mike.' Linda stated.

There were nods and murmurs around the table. Jo Peterson indicated that her client was also ready to bid. Harry asked the remaining two and the consensus was unanimous.

Mike glanced at his father and both smiled as the five bosses shuffled in their seats preparing for an unprecedented game of poker. Richard was pleased that Mike was committed and totally focussed on the game, and was certain that he would make a great lawyer if he ever got tired of Wall Street.

Greta pressed a handset and a wall panel slid open to reveal a huge plasma screen, which she had connected to her laptop to show a record of the bidding.

Gradovitch chuckled to himself. Greta glanced at him; he was the dark horse in the group.

Harry stood up. 'Okay, who's gonna start the ball rolling? I want dollars only,' he said, rubbing his hands together. This is like the old days, he mumbled to himself.

The first bid came from the unknown client in Cape Town; "three billion dollars" and no one batted an eye except Mike, who found it hard to believe that such a large some of money merited only a passing interest. Within half an hour, the bidding had reached a staggering five-point two billion dollars, plus incentives, and the room was thick with skulduggery.

Five of the world's largest communications companies were offering a fortune for the exclusive rights to PocketMoney.com's network for kids. For Mike, it was a life-changing moment, a moment that would transform his dream into reality. Yet despite his huge sense of achievement, he felt uncomfortable.

This was not like the NY stock exchange, where vast sums of money changed hands at the whim of faceless clients. This was close up and personal, a word his father had told him to disregard, but how could he? For him, it *was* personal. One of the bosses would inevitably become his business partner, and if he witnessed the conniving and backstabbing that afforded them that privilege, he would resent them for that very reason, which would seriously impair any future business relationship.

When the bosses arrived they were all pals, but that shallow veneer of kinship had long gone. Mike was convinced these powerful people would stop at nothing to get what they wanted, and it wasn't hard to imagine fistfights and revenge attacks from those who failed to win their bids. Ironically, Mike had already chosen his preferred partner, but his presence would in no way influence the outcome of the bidding; on the contrary, he was nothing more than a naive observer, an accessory to a war of power of which he wanted no part.

It was time to leave; get out of the room, away from the silent stares and false camaraderie, it was intimidating, unnerving.

Mike stood up to leave the table.

'Don't wander too far I'm about to spend a lot of money on you,' Linda said, steely eyed beneath her purple tinted glasses.

'Just stretching my legs,' Mike said, and crossed the room to his father. 'Is it okay if I don't watch the bidding, Dad?'

'Sure it is, and I don't blame you. The higher they go the uglier it'll get. Go get some air, son.'

Passing Harry Schlecker, who was tapping large numbers on a calculator screen, Mike headed for the door.

'Goin somewhere?' Harry asked, without looking up.

'Just going out for some fresh air. Money's kinda boring.

Harry looked at him as though he'd been insulted. 'Boring? Are you kidding me? Listen, Mike, air is not fresh it's free, and that's the only freebee you'll get in this world, so don't ever tell me money's boring again, okay? Go on, get outa here.'

Mike opened the door, and stepping out into the hallway he looked back at the long, oval table. All five bosses were staring at him menacingly.

He closed the door and breathed out

EIGHT

Standing by the pool in the warm September night air Mike gazed at the crystal blue water, wondering which of the bosses would be his partner; his favourite? He hoped so. Deciding not to dwell on it he ambled through the gardens in the falling darkness until a light in the distant stables caught his attention, and it occurred to him that it might be the young girl he saw in the pool who chose to ignore him. Throwing caution to the wind he headed in that direction, hoping he was right. If she remained hostile he would make his excuses and leave.

The stables were almost in darkness, except for the glow of a lamp in one of the stalls. Tiptoeing to the entrance, Mike gingerly put his head around the open door, and there was the young girl, wearing cowboy boots, jeans and a red sweatshirt, gently brushing a black stallion. He tapped on the stable door and the horse whinnied and stamped its foot nervously. The girl spun around and gave him a fierce look.

'What are you doing here?' she snapped.

Mike offered the flat of his hands. 'I came out for some air and saw a light, didn't mean to startle you,' he said, smiling, even though her manner suggested he was a horse thief.

She continued brushing as though he were invisible. In the glow of a lamp at the back of the stall he could see that even at fourteen she was tall, slender and beautiful with long, dark hair falling below her shoulders. Maybe she's nervous, he thought to himself trying to justify his reason for wanting to stay. He took off his bow tie, opened his shirt and stepped inside the stable.

'Wow, he sure is a beauty. What's his name?'

'Sugar Bay,' the girl replied with indifference.

'I saw his portrait. He's even more magnificent in the flesh,' he said, attempting to engage her in conversation.

The young girl continued brushing the gleaming black coat, seemingly unperturbed by the awkward silence. Then with covert curiosity she quickly glanced at Mike. 'Can you ride?' she asked, throwing a blanket over Sugar Bay's back.

'Sure, but it's been a while.'

The silence continued as she secured the saddle and bridle. Then ignoring Mike she led Sugar Bay out of the stable.

Mike sensed that she preferred horses to humans and that he was unwelcome. Feeling humiliated he decided to leave, but as he walked out of the stable she climbed onto Sugar Bay's back.

'Well, if you can ride, get on,' she teased, taking her left foot out of the stirrup.

The young girl was obviously toying with him but he refused to give up. 'Sure, why not,' he said, and grabbing her left hand he placed his foot in the empty stirrup and climbed on behind her.

He leaned against her back as she coaxed Sugar Bay out of stony courtyard. Then raising her whip, she said, 'Hold on tight!'

Mike tightened his grip around her slender waist as Sugar Bay thundered into the night, hooves pounding on the ground. As they raced blindly through the paddock, the girl's hair dancing in the wind behind her, a ghostly white fence suddenly appeared out of the misty darkness. She kicked the stirrups urging Sugar Bay to jump, but he stopped dead in his tracks and reared up in panic whinnying and snorting. Mike toppled backwards dragging the young girl with him and together they fell onto the dewy grass. Bruised and breathless they lay side by side in the silent darkness. Sugar Bay returned and rubbed his nose up against the young girl's face as she sat up.

'You okay?' Mike asked, brushing grass off his tuxedo.

'Yes, no thanks to you,' the girl retorted.

'Guess he didn't want to jump, huh?'

She stood up. 'I thought you could ride.'

'I could use a little more practice.'

'Obviously,' she sniped, climbing back onto Sugar Bay.

Mike scrambled to his feet. 'Look, I'm sorry, okay? What's your name, can I call you?' he pleaded, but she ignored him and cantered off towards the stables. 'Maybe another time!' he yelled, watching her ride away in the darkness.

Shoving both hands in his pockets Mike angrily strode back towards the house. He wanted to shout, jump in the pool or break something, but instead he chose a poolside sunbed and stretched out, wondering if he would ever understand females. He checked his watch; it was just after nine. They'd be calling him back in soon. He reached into his jacket pocket and pulled out the article Greta had given him earlier about Henry. The lighting was bright around the pool so he lay back and began to read it.

HENRY MAX

Henry Alvin was a quiet man who wanted a quiet life, but he was not always that way inclined. He was once a great boxer; a feared cruiserweight known as *Henry Max.*

Henry was born into poverty, and as black boy growing up in a tough neighbourhood in Atlanta his prospects were zero. So he took up boxing and dreamed that one day it would take him to a new life. By the age of nineteen Henry had fought all-comers on the county circuit and remained unbeaten. Tim Harvey, a leading promoter, decided that he was ready for the big time and signed him up. Two years later, Henry Max was earning top dollar purses and gaining a fearsome reputation. He trained harder and climbed through the ranks until he was just two fights away from the title. All the smart money was in Henry's corner. Then, and no one knows why, he took to fast living and his demons got the better of him. Henry lost his killer edge, the title and his fans. Predictably, his promoter Tim Harvey dropped him like brick in water, and when his trainer walked away, Henry disappeared.

The next time I saw Henry Max he was bare-knuckle fighting in underground car parks, winner takes all. For the rich socialites it was a thrill to watch a man get half beaten to death for a few hundred lousy bucks.

They even brought along their own champagne.

A sad epitaph for a giant of a man whom many believe could have been, and should have been, a world champion.

Raymond Stolly, Sports world

Mike folded the article and put it back in his pocket. Having only met Henry briefly, he had not taken much notice of him, but he certainly would now.

With his duties done for the evening, Henry stepped out onto the patio with a beer in his hand and the neck of his shirt open and strolled to the pool in the warm night air. Dragging a sunbed next to Mike he lay back, and said, 'If that was my money they're talkin bout I'd sure wanna be there.'

Mike said nothing. He was still annoyed at the young girl.

Henry sipped his beer and the longer the silence went on the more curious Mike became about the boxer. Henry stood around six feet two and had a rugged look about him. He spoke with a southern drawl and seemed to emit an air of contentment.

'Them there business folks seemed mighty impressed by you, so I guess you knows what you're doin,' Henry said, looking up at the starlit universe.

Mike sat up and leaned back on his hands. 'Henry, can I ask you a personal question?'

'Depends how personal.'

'How did you come to work for Mr. Schlecker?'

Swinging his feet off the sunbed Henry took another slug of beer, wiped his mouth, and said, 'Well now, that's a long story.'

'I read the article about your boxing career,' Mike admitted.

'Oh you did, huh?'

'Yeah, did you carry on fighting in the car parks?' he asked, hoping he hadn't touched a nerve.

'Yep, got a whole new reputation. The Friday night crowds got bigger. I was winning but didn't sleep so good no more cause I was gettin hurt. Guess I knew it was only a matter of time afore it was over. Then one night, I woke up on the floor bloody and broke. Money changed hands and the crowd went home. That is, all except one; Harry Schlecker.'

'Mr. Schlecker went to those fights?' Mike asked, swinging his feet off the sunbed.

'Harry loved boxing, but not those fights. They was a circus. Harry believed I was a man who'd lost his way.'

Henry took another gulp of beer and shook his head recalling his fall from grace, and the woman who broke his heart.

'Well I don't take no pity see. I told him. Whatever happened to me was my doin. But Harry can be God almighty persuasive when his minds made up. Anyways, he brung me here, gave me a nice apartment, and money in a bank account. Said I could leave whenever I was ready. That was twelve years ago. I got no plans to be anywhere's else. Found my quiet life.'

Greta opened the patio doors. 'You'd better come in, Mike, you're wanted.'

Mike stood up. 'I hope you don't mind me saying so, Henry, but I think Mr. Schlecker brought you here because you needed a friend. He obviously admires you. And so do I.'

Henry stood up and towered over him. Mike looked into his fiery eyes and could only imagine what a terrifying opponent he would make in the ring.

'Time to go, Mike,' Greta said, with growing impatience

'You gotta go,' Henry said, tightening his lips into a smile, his wrinkled face showing no outward signs of the beatings it had endured. Mike shook his hand and hurried off to join Greta.

Returning to the Blue Room Mike felt tension in the air as if a murder had been committed. Gradovitch sat alone, his only friend a glass of brandy. Kurt Gunther and Mr. Yang, seemingly now joined at the hip, sat whispering like rebels in a hung jury. Linda Greenberg and Jo Peterson were sitting at the table; neither was smiling. David Schwartz stood chatting to Richard and Harry, all of whom seemed relaxed. The musicians had gone and the room was strangely quiet. Waiters circled the guests, freshening drinks and changing ashtrays. Mike looked up at the plasma screen.

NINE POINT SEVEN BILLION DOLLARS

Harry Schlecker swaggered across the room, a smouldering Havana in his hand. 'Glad you could join us, Mike,' he said, with a measure of sarcasm. 'While you were on the missing list war was declared in here. I had to pull 'em apart at one point. The final bid came from Japan and Europe who teamed up to clinch the deal. They've guaranteed everything we asked for.'

Mike shook his head. 'They only did that to get the deal.'

Richard explained. 'It's a game, Mike, and it's not one for the feint-hearted. There are no rules, and when big bucks are at stake, it's every man for himself. No emotion, remember?'

'Forming a partnership is just a sneaky way of eliminating the opposition and lowering the risk, Dad,' Mike said, bitterly.

'But that's how big business operates. That amount of money makes company shareholders nervous,' Richard explained.

Mike made eye contact with Linda Greenberg, who opened her hands and shrugged with disappointment. David Schwartz raised his glass, his wry smile suggesting the war was not yet over. Gradovitch sat jabbering in Russian into his cell phone and, according to Harry Schlecker, Jo Peterson's South African client offered to form a partnership with David Schwartz, but he had flatly refused and she was almost in tears.

Any former sense of camaraderie between the bosses, false or otherwise, had long gone and the room now reeked of hate, greed and a longing to leave. Nevertheless, the evenings experience had done wonders for Mike's confidence.

Greta fluttered around the five bosses like a butterfly in a war zone pandering to bruised egos. As soon as the helicopter rotors clattered outside, the embattled group abandoned their drinks and prepared to leave. After the farewell smiles and limp handshakes, they hurried outside. Pausing at the door, Linda Greenberg turned to Mike, her purple tinted glasses disguising her disappointment. 'Whichever way the voting goes, Mike, I'm a fan. Be seein you.' Then she was gone.

An empty silence hung in the air and Mike wondered if those five people would ever be in the same room again, he doubted it. They played for high stakes, which meant a constant state of war, and having drawn blood at tonight's little skirmish, they couldn't wait to see the back of one another.

As the helicopter clattered away in the night, Greta returned to the Blue Room and summoned chauffeur Charlie to take Mike and Richard home. Pouring an ageing cognac she sank into an armchair, leaving her long legs dangling over the side and looked at Mike, reading his thoughts.

'Hey, don't look so worried this is only the first round,' Greta assured him. 'There's a long way to go yet.'

Mike frowned. 'What do you mean?'

'No decision can be made until the trustees are on the board. Tonight was just an "expression of interest" The five companies have all offered different types of deals, which I'll document for the first trustee meeting. That's when you, Richard and Katie also vote to select the winner, okay?'

'I didn't know that we could still vote. So the highest bidder doesn't automatically get the deal.'

Greta got to her feet. 'No, it's your company, Mike, you and the trustees make that decision,' she explained, and grabbed his arm. 'Come on, I'll walk you out to the car.'

Richard told Katie they were on their way home and strolled down the carpeted steps to the waiting limousine. After a goodnight kiss from Greta, which would keep him awake nights, Mike climbed into the limo's rear seat next to his father. He looked through the smoky glass window and noticed a shadowy figure leaning against the wall. Pushing his face against the glass he saw that it was Henry, who smiled and gave him a fingertip salute as the car sped away into the night.

PocketMoney.com was nine point seven billion dollars richer, albeit in principle, and Mike had been in the presence of true greatness; a status in life he hoped to aspire to. He had learned that big business is not for the feint-hearted, and that beneath the false smiles lay bitter rivalry driven by ruthless greed, which clarified many things, particularly as to why his father had been so overly protective.

Richard was concerned that Mike's success created a security risk and had warned him to be vigilant. Mike had scoffed at the idea, believing it was nothing more than the parental phobia of another era. Sure he was famous, and perhaps even wealthy, so what? Many young new age entrepreneurs had fame and money. Did they lose any sleep over it?

NINE

Richard Kinnerman spent the next nine days in Washington D.C. representing Brush - the number one ad agency - in a breach of contract dispute with a giant motor company, which had hired them to create and organize a national TV campaign to launch their new SUV. The protracted courtroom brawl concluded with a verdict for the plaintiff, Brush, which received six million dollars owed to them by the motor company, plus legal costs.

Brush CEO David Ratchem invited Richard to stay an extra night and celebrate over dinner, but he declined. He wanted go home and see his kids. David let it go and drove him to Dulles airport, where his Challenger 604 stood gleaming on the tarmac waiting to fly him back to New York.

Flight attendant Molly Stewart welcomed lawyer Kinnerman aboard the luxury jet, which he had all to himself. As the aircraft left the runway, he watched Washington D.C. fade to a distant glow from his window seat. Molly handed him a beer and some canapés. He thoughtfully returned to the window as the aircraft rose above a thick layer of clouds into orange sunlight. He was deeply concerned about his son, and his marriage.

PocketMoney.com had billions of dollars sitting in the Chase Manhattan bank, and Mike was fast becoming a global icon for a generation of kids; a combination that made him a prime target for those with criminal intentions, such as fraudsters, kidnappers, and weirdo's, in Richard's opinion.

He recalled one afternoon when reporters clashed with angry tutors at Mike's school-team football game. Local police made three arrests on that occasion. What if they hadn't been reporters and were organized criminals?

Richard shook his head. It didn't bear thinking about. He had bitterly complained to the publishing regulatory board, which responded with stern warnings to tabloid editors that Mike Kinnerman was still a minor and any further interviews would require his parents consent.

Richard closed his eyes and felt the aircraft slowing down as it began its long descent to JFK. He thought about Katie. Their relationship had become an emotional minefield and needed to be defused, but nothing he could say right now would deter her from going to Tokyo. He hated the thought of her being so far away, especially now, but had to admit that he had not been a perfect husband of late. Perhaps Katie was right, maybe a break would save their marriage. He hoped so. He did not want to lose her.

Assuming Richard had nodded off Molly gently tapped his wrist. 'Excuse me Mr. Kinnerman. We'll be landing shortly. Can I get you anything else?'

'No. Thanks.'

Sensing the frosty acrimony with her husband had thawed to emotional amnesty, Katie hoped their lives would soon return to normal. Moving into a spare room had clearly hurt Richard and she had been tempted to return to their bedroom, but despite her troubled conscience she remained resolute the space between them was the key to their marital salvation.

Katie spent the hot summer doting on Mike and Julieanne, which helped to restore the stability of family life. Once Katie had explained her reason for going away, their concern that she and Richard were breaking up grew less intense. Nevertheless, with only ten days left before leaving for Tokyo Katie was aware their safe sense of family unity remained a tinderbox of fragile emotions, and hoped her departure to Japan would not give rise to doubts about her unconditional love, or her return.

Tuesday morning, in a suite at New York's Plaza hotel, which Harry Schlecker had hired for the day, Richard and Katie interviewed candidates for the trustee-directorships required by law before the company could start trading. By late afternoon, they had selected five of the very best for the prestigious position, all of whom had outstanding careers in the financial world and were eager to get started. Once appointed, they would handle all the company's business and be guardians of its fortune. Their duties would commence on Monday, September 28th.

The following day, Harry Schlecker gave the trustees a tour of PocketMoney. com's new offices, situated on the top two floors of a towering New York City building, which he had renovated at a cost of 18 million dollars on behalf of the company. The next morning, in their new offices, the trustees interviewed candidates for their administration team, which Greta had arranged through various agencies. By close of business Friday, twenty-one young wannabees had signed a three-year contract beginning Monday, September 28th and the company was now ready for business.

Greta organized a dinner party at the mansion Friday evening, which promised to be a momentous occasion. The trustees would sign their five-year contracts and vote to select the winning bid for the global network, a decision that would include Richard, Katie and Mike. They would also authorize repayment of the 18 million dollars spent refurbishing their new offices, and Mike's five hundred thousand dollar start-up loan to Harry Schlecker's company Manhattan Investments Corp, which would thereafter be known as "The Broker"

Julieanne, a 16-year old twin of her beautiful mother, was born with a contagious smile and a warm personality and friends at high school flocked to her, but she was fiercely protective of her brother, and as they had grown older their relationship had deepened to that of spiritual soul mates. Julieanne was keen to share Mike's special evening, but Friday was animal clinic night and having missed several, she couldn't afford to lose the work experience, which the university required to attend her course. Mike assured his tearful sister that there would be other parties she could attend and promised to call her later from the mansion.

At five p.m. on Friday, Julieanne waved to her brother as she sped away to the veterinary clinic in Mrs. Raker's station wagon. An hour or so later, dressed in their best finery, Richard, Katie and Mike climbed into the waiting limousine and closed the door. With the prospect of a new era dawning for PocketMoney. com, a sense of expectation filled the air as they sped away in the hazy autumn evening light.

Arriving at the mansion forty minutes later, they climbed out of the limousine. Greta, dazzling in a navy blue evening dress, a diamond necklace and earrings, hurried down the carpeted steps to meet them. After her usual warm hug, she took Mike's arm led them up to the great hallway. Katie had often been to the mansion but its grandeur never failed to take her breath away, especially the picturesque gardens and trellised patio, upon which a female string quartet were currently playing a Mozart classic. Harry Schlecker, resplendent in a white dinner jacket, stood at the Half Moon bar entertaining the newly appointed trustees in his usual animated fashion, a scene perfectly illustrating his meteoric rise from poverty to decadence, in Katie's opinion.

Mike looked for the young girl but she was nowhere in sight. A female waiter offered Richard and Katie glasses of champagne. Mike settled for a coke.

Harry slowly cast his eyes over Katie, who wore a silky black evening dress with glittering accessories matching her emerald eyes. 'Welcome to our little soiree, Katie, you look wonderful,' he said, pecking her on the cheek.

'Why thank you, Harry,' she beamed, pleasantly surprised.

'Julieanne called me. She was upset that she couldn't make the party tonight. You gotta admire her dedication.'

'It was a tough decision, but she's fine,' Katie explained.

'She's my little sweetheart,' Harry said, and turned to Mike. 'It's about time you met the trustees, kid. Follow me.'

'You do look lovely,' Richard whispered. Katie smiled.

Harry made the introductions. 'Mike, this is Penny Bowman; a fearless lawyer and terrifying business woman.'

Penny chuckled. 'He's just kidding. Ugly divorce, I fought to keep my daughter. Nice to meet you, Mike,' she said, offering a soft white hand, her eyes steely blue beneath her red glasses.

Harry went on. 'Jenny Grant, our lovely commodities expert.'

'You've caused quite a stir,' Jenny said, with a wicked smile.

'Sorry about that,' Mike said, grinning.

Harry moved on. 'Mike Coswell, our Canadian stock market analyst and karate black belt.'

He grabbed Mike's hand. 'Great to meet you, son.'

Mike nodded, 'You too Mr. Coswell.'

Harry continued, 'Winston Bliss, financial markets expert.'

'Pleasure to meet you, son,' Winston said, wrapping his hands around Mike's. He was tall, black and ageless with greying hair and the warmth of a favourite uncle. Mike liked him right away.

'And finally, Malcolm Connors, director of the International Banking and Commodities Alliance,' Harry explained.

'Hi, Mike, good to meet you. I thought I'd seen it all until you came up with PocketMoney.com. Congratulations.'

Mike shook his hand. 'Thanks Mr. Connors.'

Harry cursed as his cell phone rang. 'I'll be back in a minute, Mike.' he growled, and walked off clamping it to his ear.

Richard and Katie joined Mike. 'So what do you think of the trustees son, dyou like em?' Richard asked.

'What can I say, their profiles are amazing.'

'We chose the very best and they can't wait to get started, so take it as a compliment,' Katie said, linking arms with her son.

'Sure, with people like that how can we fail?'

Greta took a call and hurried inside the house. Richard and Katie mingled with the trustees. Mike listened as they discussed acquisitions and derivatives, and soon realised that everything he had worked for was now in capable hands.

A loud splash in the pool brought a smile to his face. He spun around and saw the young girl crashing through the crystal clear water. He watched her, thoughtfully. She obviously wanted to be alone; no surprise there, but their paths would cross one way or another that evening, he would make certain of it.

Katie Kinnerman, whose business acumen equalled her peers, broke away from the lofty conversation. Her imminent departure to Tokyo had persuaded her to clear the air with Harry Schlecker, who was still pacing the patio, yelling into his cell phone.

Whilst waiting for Harry's call to end Katie recalled how they met at a fundraiser for Republican Gary Chambers at the Marriott Hotel. Katie had left university with an honours degree and began working for the Menton Corporation. Harry, a rising star at Wall Street, made a b-line for her and they were soon exchanging life stories. Katie agreed to have dinner with him the following week, after which Harry filled her apartment with roses; he was smitten.

Two months later, after nights at the opera, a string of society events and candle-lit suppers at New York's finest restaurants, Harry proposed to her. Katie was both surprised and flattered but she was not ready for a serious commitment and flatly refused. Harry pursued her for months, sending flowers and gifts but she ignored him. Two years later, Katie married Richard Kinnerman.

Pocketing his cell phone Harry approached her.

'I'd almost forgotten how beautiful your house is, Harry.'

'If you hadn't turned me down all those years ago it would be yours now,' Harry said, never missing a chance to remind her.

Katie never failed to smile when Harry's roses arrived for her every Valentines Day. However, the roses were also a reminder that their little romance was over long ago, and right now Katie was in need of Harry's assurance.

'I'm going to Tokyo next week, Harry, and my son's future is partly in your hands, so it would be nice if we could move on.'

'If that's an apology for breaking my heart, I'll think about it. And talking of your son, where is he? I don't want him doin his disappearing act again tonight.'

'He's over there, talking to a young girl by the pool.'

Harry grinned. 'That's my daughter, you met her yet?'

'No, she's very beautiful.'

'She's quite the little princess. I adopted her five years ago. You haven't been here for what, six years?'

'I know, but you did tell us about her. Why have you never brought her over to meet Julieanne?'

'She's really screwed up, Katie, doesn't wanna meet anyone, but that'll pass. She's the best thing that ever happened to me.'

'Funny, I never thought of you as the fatherly type.'

'You'd be surprised, there's a lot you don't know about me.'

'I don't doubt that, Harry, but I'd rather remember you as the ruthless, irrepressible young man from Wall Street who tried to steal my heart,' Katie said, and kissed him on the cheek.

'Think yourself lucky, Katie, not many people know me that well,' Harry quipped, and walked off.

Henry announced dinner was served in fifteen minutes.

Crouching at the poolside, Mike asked the young girl if she was joining them for dinner.

'No,' she said curtly.

'Why not?'

She climbed out of the water and wrapped herself in a thick pink towel. 'I prefer to eat in the stables. You can bring me a tray in one hour, if you like,' she said, and walked off.

Mike had never met anyone so irritating, and wondered how she could possibly swim with a chip that size on her shoulder.

Throughout dinner, the trustees focussed their attentions on Mike Kinnerman, who quickly became a fan, a feeling that was mutual. Then having discussed details of the five global network bids, three players remained in the game: David Schwartz of Wymack, the Japanese-European Alliance, and Maximum, Linda Greenberg's company.

As the trustees had no personal assistants until the 28th Greta took down the minutes of the meeting. After another lengthy debate, Jenny Grant asked Mike what *he* wanted. Forget the money, which company had *his* attention?

'I think Linda Greenberg knows what the kids want. If it was up to me, I'd sign a deal with her tomorrow,' Mike said, honestly.

Harry threw in a wild card. 'When David Schwartz makes a genuine offer, it can't be ignored,' he said, emphatically.

Penny Bowman disagreed. 'I don't like the way that guy does business; it's sleazy. I think he'll screw us further on down the line, and then force us to renegotiate the contract.'

Katie stood up and when she spoke everyone listened. 'This network deal is a world changer, and it scares me. The pit-falls are enormous and there is no margin for error, and so it's time to make a decision. Let's take a final vote.'

Harry stood up, waving his arms. 'Whoa, think about who you're voting for. This decision will affect the company for fifteen years, so for Christ's sake make the right one.'

Harry asked for a show of hands and the vote was unanimous for Maximum. The trustees would inform Linda Greenberg that she had won the network deal. A press release would follow. Lawyers would then fine tooth comb every clause of the contract.

Having made their first company decision, the trustees were clearly satisfied with the outcome. PocketMoney.com was now in business with Maximum; a U.S. company they could trust. Linda Greenberg, an exceptional woman, had guaranteed delivery of a global phone, TV and radio network for kids, with offices in every country on the planet in six months.

Mike Kinnermans' grin reflected the general sentiment.

Henry brought in a model of a silver skyscraper; complete with miniature trees and cars, and placing it on the table he gave Mike a friendly nod and left. The trustees gathered round.

Harry explained. 'When I agreed to be the company broker I asked Greta to find us a building, and believe me she's an expert. Due to an insurance fraud this property had been empty for three years and it was in the hands of administrators. Greta offered to take over the building for one dollar, plus the running costs. They agreed, and gave us a ninety-year lease. It was a dump, so I put up 18 million dollars for the interior redesigning. Here's a copy of the contract, signed by Richard and Katie Kinnerman and the administrators Partman Bachs.'

'Now it's a brand new building, and it looks fabulous.' Greta said, having redesigned the entire interior herself.

The trustees agreed. 'Superb offices, wonderful space,'

'But do we need a building that big?' Mike asked.

Richard explained, 'No we don't, and so we kept the two top floors and leased the rest to Atlantic Oil…

'Which more than pays for our costs,' Katie interjected.

Mike looked at his mother. 'Are you serious?'

'Pretty smart, huh?' Katie said, raising her eyebrows.

Mike smiled. For one dollar, he owned a towering building?

Harry asked the waiter to pour the champagne. It was time for the trustees to sign their contracts. Greta told the photographer to set up his camera in front of the table.

Richard and Katie signed the five-year contracts on behalf of Mike, giving the trustees autonomy to govern the company as they see fit. The trustees signed against their names, followed by Harry and Greta, who witnessed the event. Then they gathered around Mike for a group photograph, an enlargement of which would hang on the wall at the company's New York offices.

For all those present it was a momentous occasion, especially Mike whose dream had become a reality. On Monday morning, with a board of trustee-directors in place and Linda Greenberg as a partner, PocketMoney.com would begin trading on the stock market; a day that would signify the beginning of a new era, an era offering unlimited promise, not only for those in the room but for millions of young investors around the world.

The waiters handed out flutes of pink champagne, of which Katie allowed Mike one glass. Harry and Greta linked arms and as the happy group gathered in a circle, Richard raised his glass and proposed a toast to the fledgling company. Their optimistic voices responded in unison.

'To PocketMoney.com!'

Mike felt a warm tingle run down his spine.

Katie walked to the panoramic window and looked out at the flickering lanterns dotted around the miniature Japanese garden, her mind six thousand miles away.

TEN

High on a cloud of success Mike decided to take a tray of food to the young girl, who having so far rejected him had become a challenge. Henry agreed to organize her dinner tray, and while he did so Mike called Julieanne and told her the exciting news.

The stable door was open when Mike arrived, and much to his relief Sugar Bay was in the next stall. A lamp glowed within.

'Room service,' he said, tilting his head inside the doorway.

Sitting cross-legged on the floor the young girl fought back a smile. 'Very funny. Bring the tray over here,' she said, her voice less welcoming than he would have liked.

Mike handed her the tray and sat facing her as she removed the silver cover and sliced into a salmon salad. He studied her in the flickering light. Her dark hair fell wildly below her shoulders, leaving loose strands to fall over her olive-skinned face, which nature had defined with fine, dark eyebrows, high cheekbones and a mysterious smile. Her soft, young voice, enhanced by an endearing accent, added mystique to her charm, but her coral blue eyes seemed to betray a hidden sadness.

'Are you mad at me?' he asked.

The girl glanced at him nonchalantly and continued to eat in silence, at which point he took an interest in a strand of straw and began fiddling with it. Finishing off her salad with a glass of mango juice, she placed the tray on the floor and leaned back against the wall, wrapping her arms around her knees.

'Why is it that when a girl does not respond to a boy's interest he thinks she is mad at him? Is that a dysfunctional hormonal disorder linked to rejection, or just a male ego problem?'

'Whoa, I think we got off on the wrong foot here. Could we start over?' Mike asked, nicely. 'What's your name?'

'Miss.'

'Okay, Miss, I get the feeling you'd like me to leave?'

'Your feelings are of no concern to me.'

Silence.

Sugar Bay broke wind loudly in the next stall. Miss covered her mouth in an attempt to hide her grin. Mike howled.

More silence.

'Look, I'd like us to be friends, is that possible?' he asked.

'Why?'

'You're very attractive, obviously intelligent and…

'That is an observation not a reason to be friends.'

Mike refused to give up. 'It's a start. I promise not to bite and hey, you might even like me. I'm happy to call you Miss, but it would be nice to know your name.'

Silence. Miss sat like a statue. She was stonewalling him. Mike fiddled with a strand of straw and considered leaving. Sugar Bay snorted and stamped his foot. He softened his tone.

'Are you okay? You seem pretty down.'

Miss stared at her red Nike's. 'I am not very good with people at the moment. I prefer my own company.'

'Why are you so unhappy?'

Miss jumped up, her eyes watering, and ran out of the stable. Mike raced after her, wondering what he had said to upset her. In the shadows of a full moon he saw her running away towards the distance lake, and eventually caught up with her at a wooden jetty by the lakeside.

Mike leaned on his knees catching his breath. 'Look, I'm sorry, I didn't mean to upset you.'

Miss glanced at him and without responding knelt down and flicked a switch beneath the jetty boards, giving life to hundreds of coloured lanterns in the trees around the lake. A fluttering of wings followed as unseen nocturnal creatures hurriedly searched for a dark space. Miss climbed down the steps and jumped into a yellow rowing boat, and taking a seat she grabbed the oars and looked up at Mike. 'We can talk on the lake if you like.'

With their knees almost touching Mike observed her as she rowed in silence. Noticing his enquiring look she gave a hint of a smile. A tiny beauty spot sat on her left cheek. She wore a gold crucifix around her neck and a cheap pink plastic watch on her left wrist. A gold bangle of a snake curled around the top of her right arm, above which was a small tattoo; **RIO**

Reaching the center of the lake she let go of the oars and sat in silence gazing at the stars. Then leaning back on her hands, she said, softly. 'My name is Savannah, Savannah Cordeiro.'

Mike's pulse went up a notch as their eyes met and remained focussed in curiosity. 'Mike Kinnerman,' he replied, his heart beating at the sound of her name.

Captivating in a red sleeveless t-shirt and tight blue jeans Savannah clasped her hands around her knees. 'I know who you are I saw you on the Saturday Show. Do you like being famous?'

'It's okay, my friends are cool about it, but I get a rash from reporters they're a pain in the ass.'

Savannah gazed at the coloured lanterns around the lake and said, almost whispering, 'It is quite magical here at night.'

'Yeah, it's beautiful,' Mike agreed, finding it hard to take his eyes off her, and wondered why such a beautiful girl would hide from the world. He chose his words carefully. 'I take it you're not from the U.S. Can I ask where you're from?'

'Rio de Janeiro,' Savannah replied, trailing her fingers in the cool, black water, her eyes suddenly distant.

'Brazil.' That explained her accent and beautiful olive skin. 'Do you have family there?'

Savannah fiddled absently with her gold crucifix. 'My mother and father are dead,' she said, her voice laced with bitterness.

Mike exhaled. 'Oh God, I'm…I'm sorry.'

'They were murdered,' she added, gazing into the water as though all her dreams lay at the bottom of the lake.

A morbid silence filled he air. An owl hooted and creatures scurried about in the lakeside foliage. A dark cloud slowly sailed across the moon like a ghostly face. The lake was still. He could hear her heart beating. 'Murdered?' he said, wide-eyed.

'A firebomb was planted in our house when I was nine years old,' Savannah explained, pausing to keep her emotions in check. 'It was the day before Christmas Eve. My mother and father were decorating our Christmas tree when…'

'Whoa, are you sure you want talk about this right now?'

'Yes, that is why I brought you here. There is no one else I can talk to, and I thought….' She turned away and wiped her eyes. She had promised herself not to cry. 'Obviously I was wrong. I am sorry.' she grabbed the oars. 'We will go back.'

'No don't, please. Tell me what happened. I want to know.'

Savannah glanced at him and fidgeted with her hands.

'I…was in the bath when the fire erupted. There was a loud bang, and then I heard my mother and father screaming in agony downstairs in the living room, a sound that will haunt me for the rest of my life. The bathroom door was on fire and tiles were falling off the walls. My eyes were stinging and black smoke was tearing at my lungs. Even now, I sometimes wake up in the night choking on that smell. I thought I was going to die. I lay in the water too terrified to move. Then miraculously two fire fighters smashed the bathroom window and dragged me to safety. I was too afraid to be embarrassed. They saved my life.'

'God, you must have been terrified.'

Savannah stared somewhere far away and shook her head. 'I watched our beautiful house collapse in flames with my mother and father inside. It was horrible…horrible…. she wailed and broke down sobbing in her hands.

Mike wanted to reach out to her, to comfort her, but she was lost in her horrific memories, and so he waited until she ran out of tears. 'I am so sorry,' he whispered. 'Are you okay?'

Savannah sniffled and nodded. 'I was lying in the ambulance when I heard the police say the fire was started deliberately, that someone had murdered my mother and father. I wanted to die too,' she said, wiping her eyes.

Hearing Savannah describe her parent's murder, perhaps for the first time, Mike could not even begin to imagine her sense of loss. She was emotionally unloading and who could blame her. Unable to find any words of comfort he listened in silence.

Savannah continued, 'I had no other family, except Christina Sanchez, a distant relative I had never met. The police traced her address and forced her to take me in. Then a few days later, Harry Schlecker came to Rio and my life changed forever.'

'Why did Mr. Schlecker go to Rio?'

'Harry owned a freight company called Palinda Shipping, and my father was the general manager. He made it successful. Harry stayed at our house several times a year and became part of our family. He brought me presents, patted my head and called me princess, which I hated, and still do. When the Brazilian police informed him what had happened, he was devastated and blamed himself for the death of my parents. I had become an orphan and it must have tormented Harry because he flew to straight Rio and refused to leave without me. He was an orphan too.

* * * * *

Harry Schlecker hired a private investigator in Rio, and by the time he arrived at Rio's Galeao Airport, he had found out all he needed to know about Christina Sanchez. When Harry called at Christina's filthy house and found nine-year old Savannah tearful and disorientated he almost broke down. He was aware that Christina used drugs and was heavily in debt. She looked every day of her forty years, and her swollen, red eyes confirmed her liking for alcohol and tobacco. She was a good time party girl with a succession of loser boyfriends, and the last thing she wanted was a kid around the house. Harry knew that and after several large tequila's Christina was willing, for fifty-thousand dollars, to let him adopt Savannah. Harry paid her; he would have paid anything. He called Fabio Roberto, a trusted friend in the Brazilian government, and asked him to help with the adoption papers. Forty-eight hours later, after the short journey to Galeao airport, Savannah, still terribly distraught, was on her way to the United States aboard Harry Schlecker's Gulfstream jet.

'Did they find out who torched your house?' Mike asked her.

'Yes, it was Carlo Jose' Almeida, a so-called friend of my father. They used to work together at the docks. Carlo and several other men came to our house

Friday nights, to play cards and get drunk while my mother cooked dinner for them.'

Mike felt their knees touch. 'How did they get him?'

Carlo was involved with a known drug syndicate. These men secretly persuaded the six captains of Palinda Shipping to deliver cocaine shipments at various ports in the Caribbean. They left weighted packages with homing devices close to the shore, which local fishermen collected at night. When my father found out what they were doing, he threatened to call the police if they did not stop. The syndicate bosses became suspicious of Carlo's loyalty to my father, so they ordered him to plant a firebomb in our house and threatened to kill his family if he refused.'

Mike shook head and exhaled. 'So that's why Mr. Schlecker blamed himself. How did they link the firebomb to Carlo?'

'Two men in the syndicate were arrested on another murder charge, and for a lesser sentence one of them told the police how Carlo murdered my parents, and why.'

'God, this is unbelievable. So what happened?'

'Carlo broke down in the courtroom and confessed. I was there as a witness. The judges gave him two life sentences: one for each of my parents. A week later, according to news reports, he was found murdered in his cell, and good riddance.' Savannah exhaled and clenched her hands to stop them shaking. 'It feels strangely uplifting to have told someone. I have lived with those memories every hour of every day for five years.'

Savannah was clearly a victim of her past and very lonely. She had desperately wanted to share her pain in a bid to find some measure of closure. But why had she never spoken about it? Didn't she have some sort of counselling, Mike wondered.

'I can't begin to imagine what you've been through because it didn't happen to me. But you've gotta move on, Savannah, you can't let that guy screw your life up too.'

'I know, but memories cannot be erased just because they are horrible. Telling someone what happened is different, it is like closing a door a little further on the past.'

'I understand that, but fate opened another door. A billionaire adopted you and brought you to the States to live in a fabulous mansion. That must have blown you away.'

Savannah glanced at him. 'Yes, but I became a prisoner of my new life. I have never been to school here, my tutors come to me. Sugar Bay and Greta are my only real friends, and Henry is like a big brother. He has been teaching me to box.'

Mike raised his fists. 'Boxing?'

Her voice was intoxicating.

'Yes, Harry built a gymnasium for Henry behind the stables. It has a boxing ring, punch bags, weights and exercise machines. Did you know that Henry was a famous boxer?'

'Yeah, I met him one night by the pool and we talked. He's an awesome guy. Did Mr. Schlecker mind you boxing?'

'No, not until I was thirteen. Then he ordered me to stop and hired Tina May, an ex military instructor, to teach me self-defence. We train three times a week.'

'Well that stuff is obviously working; you look great, better than that. But why won't Mr. Schlecker let you go to school?'

Savannah gazed across the silent lake remembering the dark green uniform and beret she wore every morning walking to school with her father, who would always remove his straw hat to kiss her goodbye at the gates.

'I am forbidden to mix with other kids until I go to university. I am to be a young lady, dine at the finest restaurants and attend the society balls,' Savannah said, feigning a wretch.

'Trust me, you'll fit in nicely. Trouble is, you're living in a bubble. No friends, no clubs, no movies, no hot dogs.'

'I know, but Harry will not let me to do anything like that.'

Savannah clearly needed to make new friends, but Mike was reluctant to introduce her to the boys at school they would be all over her. He had a better idea. 'Tell you what; come to my house for dinner on Sunday and meet my family.'

Savannah leaned on the side of the boat; her mind returning to hot summer days and happier times when she would laugh and dance on Copacabana beach with her family and friends, when after school the boys played volleyball on the white sand while the girls swam in the warm, clear ocean. It was a magical time, a time when the innocence of youth had promised to last forever.

It seemed so long ago now, another life in a different kind of bubble, a life of family security and affection. But a cold-blooded murderer had destroyed that sense of belonging, and Savannah doubted she would ever feel the warmth of family love again. She thought of Mike and how unkind she had been to him, yet he had persisted in gaining her attention. She glanced at his reflection in the still water, and a sudden impulse forced her to grab his hand.

'I *will* come for dinner, but not this Sunday. I have passed all my exams and Harry is sending me on vacation to St Lucia. He has a beautiful house there. I will be back next Friday.'

'Sounds wonderful.'

'St Lucia is paradise. I am like a dolphin there.'

'Yeah I've seen you swim. You'll like my sister, Julieanne, and my Dad, a lawyer with a wicked sense of humour.'

Savannah chuckled. 'I like him already.'

Mike rowed back to the shore while Savannah, smiling at her own thoughts, trailed her fingers in the cool water. Having shared her terrifying memories with someone her own age, she seemed more relaxed, unburdened somehow, a different girl entirely from when they first met. Mike likened her to a swan with a broken wing, and he wondered if her anger was simply to disguise her fragile emotions and protect her safe little world. Whatever the reason, she now appeared to be reaching out for friendship.

He silently promised to always be kind to her.

With the boat secured, they climbed up the steps to the jetty, and as Savannah knelt down to turn off the tree lights she caught Mike staring at her. She coyly took his arm and as they strolled to house in a comfortable silence, Mike asked her if she would like to meet his parents who were there that evening. Savannah tensed up. After months alone in the stables, which had done little to enhance her self-confidence, meeting her first boyfriend's family could prove disastrous. Her heart however, disagreed and for the first time in her life she wanted to look beautiful.

'Yes, all right, but first I must change,' Savannah said, and racing up the curved marble staircase, she yelled, 'Wait for me outside the Blue Room. I will be down in ten minutes!'

Mike stood at the foot of the stairs until Savannah had gone. Then floating along the corridor in a wonderful daze he returned to the Blue Room, which was now thick with cigar smoke and stale perfume. The trustees, clearly enjoying their own company and the cognac, were noisily discussing strategies to take over the financial world. Richard, Katie and Greta sat quietly chatting at the dining table. Harry was on the phone. Tired waiters circled with coffee and brandy. The string quartet had left.

Mike anxiously stood waiting by the door. Katie wondered why her son was pacing back and forth looking so agitated. Then the clatter of heels suddenly echoed along the corridor, and when Mike saw Savannah hurrying towards him, wearing a blue fitted dress, sparking earrings and positively glowing, he knew Greta was no longer the most beautiful girl he had ever seen.

Savannah smiled, and taking Mike's arm they entered the Blue Room. Every head turned, including Harry Schlecker who grinned with obvious pride. Introducing a girlfriend to his mother and father was something Mike had yet to experience, and as they approached them he took a deep breath.

'Mom, Dad, please meet Savannah Cordeiro, Mr. Schlecker's daughter. Savannah is fourteen and comes from Rio de Janeiro.'

'Savannah, it's nice to meet you, I'm Richard,' he said, gently squeezing her shaking hand. She smiled angelically.

'I'm Katie, and you are beautiful,' she said, realizing why her son was anxiously waiting with a sparkle in his eyes. 'If you are not considering a modelling career I shall speak to Harry.'

Savannah hated compliments but managed a nervous chuckle. 'No, I am studying to be an architect, like Greta.'

'Now that's a great career if you have an eye for it,' Richard said. 'A lot of hard work though I imagine.'

'Yes, but if something is a passion it is never tedious, in my opinion,' Savannah rallied.

Savannah was clearly nervous. Greta handed her a small glass of red wine. When Katie asked about her family life in Brazil Mike felt compelled to rescue her, but there was no need. Savannah soon captivated Richard and Katie with stories of her sun-kissed childhood in the beautiful city of Rio de Janeiro, but never mentioned her mother and father's murder.

Harry broke away from the business chatter and put his arm around his beautiful daughter. 'So, you've met our young genius, Mike Kinnerman. I'm sure you'll find him a lot more interesting than talking to horses.'

'Depends on your point of view,' Savannah retorted.

Harry deflected the sarcasm. 'Did you show Mike the lake?'

'Yes, we rowed to the center. Mike has invited me to dinner when I return from St Lucia. Is that all right?'

Katie wondered why Savannah was so cold towards Harry.

Harry kissed her forehead. 'Course it is.'

'I'll drive you over, sweetie,' Greta said, knowing that it was an emotional leap for Savannah.

Harry checked his watch. 'I hate to break up the party but its late princess, and you got a piano lesson at eight, remember?'

Tightening her lips Savannah handed Greta her empty glass.

'We'll breakfast on the patio at nine,' Harry added, then his cell phone rang and he marched off clamping it to his ear.

Savannah politely said goodnight and as she walked out into the corridor, her head held high and heels clacking on the wooden floor, a wave of adulation swept through the Blue Room, mainly from Mike who couldn't take his eyes off her.

Greta summoned Charlie to take the Kinnermans home. The red-faced trustees, who were staying overnight, yelled goodbye as Harry and Greta escorted them out to the waiting limousine. After the hugs and promises to call tomorrow, they sank into the limo's rear seat and closed the door.

Charlie drove out through the gardens and followed the road around the dark, silent lake. Mike looked back through the rear window at the glowing mansion, and wondered if Savannah was standing at her apartment window watching him leave. Something happened out there on the lake when they were alone, knees touching and their eyes focussed on one another, something special. An unspoken connection, a moment when two people forge a bond of emotional unity, and for Mike, the feeling was almost overwhelming. It was a moment that had proved to be the very pinnacle of a monumental evening and, still reeling from the unforgettable encounter, he was already counting the hours to their Sunday rendezvous.

Savannah, what a beautiful name…

ELEVEN

Bormont Correctional Facility was designed to prepare those who had served their time for re-entry into the outside world. The regime was relaxed and inmates could make their own decisions, as long as they stayed out of trouble. With freedom only months away everyone kept their heads down, waiting for the day they would walk out through the gates.

Rick Netty, aged 31, stood six feet two with blonde hair, ice blue eyes and had a muscular body. He was currently serving six years for the manslaughter of a drunk in a barroom brawl who happened to be in the wrong place at the wrong time. He pleaded self-defence. The incident had left him with a long scar across his face and was a constant reminder he was not invincible. He had spent the first five and a half years in Latchmore penitentiary; a dangerous overcrowded facility, with a collection of rapists, drug addicts and violent criminals, but managed to stay out of trouble. He was now an inmate at Bormont and shared a cell with Rylan Mitchell, who, like Netty, was due for release any day.

Rylan Mitchell had city hands. He was six feet tall and very overweight, with light brown hair, shifty hazel eyes and a boyish face that belied his 44 years. Prior to receiving a four-year sentence for fraud, with no parole for lying under oath, Mitchell was a successful entrepreneur and liked to rub shoulders with the rich and famous at New York's social gatherings. His success however, became the subject of barroom conjecture by those who suspected his business methods were less than ethical, including the FBI, who believed that he was involved in criminal activities and had money hidden somewhere sunny.

Mitchell still had connections in the financial world, some of whom were indebted to his generosity, and upon his release he intended to pay them a call. In the good years, Harry Schlecker was his trusted broker and he often visited the mansion. But when the FBI arrested him for fraud Mitchell swore he was innocent, claiming his broker had set him up. Furious, Harry gave evidence that put him in jail. Since then, Mitchell had threatened Harry with all manner of torture if he didn't return his lockbox key.

Prior to his arrest Mitchell knew the FBI was investigating his assets, but they didn't know that he had ten million dollars hidden in a lockbox at Grand Cayman National Bank. It was money he'd made from shady land deals with the Pentagon, and if the IRS found out he'd go back to jail for a long time. So when Harry Schlecker offered him an investment opportunity, the building of a shopping mall in Dallas, Texas, he gave him the lockbox key, the password, his social security number and his mother's maiden name in a sealed envelope as collateral. Harry accepted that and agreed to have the contract ready the following week. Two days later, the FBI arrested Mitchell for serious fraud. The following month the shopping mall deal fell through, due to a land dispute. As security against retribution, Harry kept the lockbox key.

Rylan Mitchell now held a deep hatred for Harry Schlecker, and with his release due any day, he was aching for revenge.

Mitchell was a reasonable chess player and having to share a cell with Rick Netty, he tried to teach him the art of the game. Netty was a crew-cut roughneck and not the type Mitchell would normally associate himself with, but in jail he had no choice, so differences were ignored. As the weeks passed by, they talked at length about their uncertain futures.

With no chance of parole to look forward to Netty read the newspapers and watched TV, to keep up to date with the outside world. Nothing was of much interest to him, except cartoons and grisly war stories, but when he read an article detailing the sums of money that bankers and football players earned, and a 14-year old kid owning a company with billions of dollars in the bank he was sick with envy. It didn't seem right, not when he was sitting at the bottom of the pile, with no money and no future.

It burned him up inside.

Every stinking day. Every sweaty night.

Netty, like his father, found his calling in the marines, but his penchant for violence led to three years in a military prison and a dishonourable discharge. Netty thrived on military life, he was born for it, and after being kicked out of the marines, no one was surprised when he joined a band of redneck mercenaries who fought any war, as long as the price was right.

His last job, ensuring the safe delivery of a cocaine shipment for a Colombian cartel, had opened doors to serious connections in the South American drug trade, which Netty hoped would be his salvation when he got out of jail.

That night, a guard banged on the cell bars and informed Netty that he was being released a day early, and told him to be ready at eight a.m. Netty, too wound up to sleep, talked to Rylan Mitchell in the darkness of their cell about a plan to make a great deal of money. Mitchell initially scoffed at the idea, and dismissed it as pure fantasy, but after staring at the cell wall most of the night listening to Netty's idea, he began to show some interest.

'It'll take money and contacts to set this up,' Mitchell said, liking the idea more by the minute. 'I get out in a couple of days and I'm going to New York. A few old pals there owe me serious money. I can make this happen, and it could work, but it's gotta be a military type operation. Tell no-one about this, Netty, and I mean no-one. With a good plan and the right people, we'll be out of the country before anyone can blink. Then you can go work on your suntan. What are you're immediate plans?'

'I'm goin to Houston,' Netty said, pacing back and forth. 'Got friends down there with plenty of cash and a place for me to stay. Then I'm goin to Mexico. There's a team of bad-assed guys down there we can use to make this happen, as long as you get things organized in New York. Being an ex con, I'm sure to get a hard time when I leave the country, so I'll ask my army pal to tag along. That way I'll get across the border without killing anyone.

'If you get in any trouble the deal's off,' Mitchell growled.

'Stop whining, that ain't gonna happen. It'll take me a week, maybe ten days to tie things up down there, and when I get back I'll expect a green light from you, understood?'

Mitchell nodded. 'Okay, call this number when you're back in Houston,' he said, handing Netty a slip of paper.

'Make sure you got the money. I don't wanna set this up and find you've come up short. People down there get mad if you don't pay,' Netty said, with a voice that made Mitchell shiver.

Dawn was breaking. The overcrowded cellblock echoed with prisoner's voices. A guard strolled passed the cells.

Mitchell was aware that Netty was a dangerous psychopath, who thought nothing of killing anyone. He had no conscience whatsoever. It was a way of life to him. Even so, Netty's low life talents would come in handy for what they had planned. After that, he would get as far away from him as possible.

'You leave the money to me, Netty. What do you think I am some kinda back street hustler? I've earned more money than you'll see in a lifetime,' Mitchell said, almost spitting blood.

'Maybe so, but you're still in jail,' Netty shot back, meeting Mitchell's gaze.

'So what? I got plenty hidden away and I'm not relying on some asshole to get me over a goddam border because I got a bad temper. We do this my way or not at all, so listen carefully. When it's all set up, go to New York and call me on that cell number. Then we'll meet up at my hotel and check every last detail of the plan, deal?' Mitchell said, offering his hand.

Netty's muscular arm rippled as he gripped Mitchell's soft white hand. 'Deal.'

The guard unlocked the cell door. 'Time to go, Netty.'

New York City, Saturday, September 26th

Relieved to be back in New York, Rylan Mitchell checked into a suite at the Ritz-Carlton Hotel, Central Park. After sharing a stinking jail cell with Rick Netty, he took a deep breath and embraced the spacious luxury. He had missed it and vowed never to go through that again. Never. He ordered lunch, unpacked and took a hot shower. Then savouring the comfort of a blue silk shirt and beige slacks, he started working the phone. Many well-known high flyers owed him favours and it was payback time. One was Ramon Salero, whom he had bailed out after getting into debt to the tune of twenty-five grand, with some nasty characters due to his gambling addiction. The number rang.

Ramon picked up 'Yeah?'

'Your telephone voice needs a little tweak, Ramon, you never know who's gonna call,' Mitchell said, drolly.

Rylan, my God, where are you?'

'I'm at the Ritz-Carlton. Maybe we can meet up for a drink. I just wanted to make sure that you're still in town.'

'Yeah, got married to a nice lady. Got a job with a future too. The bad ole' days are over, Rylan.'

'Glad to hear it, you owe me twenty-five grand, but maybe we can work something out. We'll meet up next week, okay?'

'Sure, I ain't goin anywhere.' Ramon disconnected.

Mitchell called a list of people who owed him large sums of money, and to his surprise most agreed to repay their debts. Two slammed the phone down. Netty would pay them a call.

Mitchell was a member of "The Domingo Club" a private drinking and dining establishment two blocks from Wall Street. Around five p.m. on weekdays the club was full of movers and shakers from the financial world, and for those who liked to be in the eye of the storm, or watch the high rollers spend their bonuses, it was the place to be. Mitchell had arrived in New York on a Saturday, which meant that only a dozen or so people were in the club, but that didn't bother him he just wanted to get a feel of the place before doing a big hello-I'm-back. Black and white photos of celebrities patronizing the club hung on the wall behind the bar, and red leather-seated booths lined one side of the oblong room. Mitchell bought a chilled bottle of Bordeaux and sat in one of the leather sofas around the huge empty fireplace, which in winter blazed like a furnace. Some twenty minutes later, an unshaven man in a crumpled grey suit strode across the room with a beer in his hand and sat on a nearby sofa. Spreading the Financial Times out on the low wooden table in front of him, Mitchell sipped his wine and began reading an article about a troubled company called Stella Electronics.

The house music played softly. A couple entered and stood chatting at the bar. The man in the crumpled grey suit suddenly spoke, 'Huge company Stella, shame they got into so much debt.'

Mitchell turned to the man. 'Yeah, they overstretched their investments by the look of it,' he commented.

The man offered his hand. 'Jonathan Shelleck.'

'Rylan Mitchell,' he said, shaking his hand.

The waiter approached. 'Will you be eating with us, sir?'

Mitchell nodded. 'About fifteen minutes.'

Handing Mitchell the menu the waiter left.

Shelleck went on. 'Rumour has it the bank pulled the plug on Stella cause they're about to lose the government contracts. Their research team moved to Panama over a year ago.'

Mitchell eyed Shelleck with suspicion. 'How do you know that? There's nothing in the press about it.'

'I worked for Stella in Panama until a few days ago.'

'Oh really, why dyou leave?'

'I didn't, they fired me. Got an expensive social habit, and in Panama it's like buying candy. One day they found cocaine in my locker and that was it. Bye bye Stella.'

'Sorry to hear it. I've never touched drugs. So what are you doing now?' Mitchell asked, but had no interest in losers.

'Oh I'm just biding my time. Got a little plan,' Shelleck said, vaguely. 'They're gonna regret firing me that's for sure.'

'Is that right, well according to the Times Stella's talking to a potential buyer but they don't say who,' Mitchell reported.

Shelleck huffed. 'Course not, they're not allowed to, but I know who they're talking to.'

Suddenly keen to hear what Shelleck had to say Mitchell sat up. 'I'd be interested in knowing that. What's it gonna cost me?'

'Depends what its worth to you. I'll give you a little freebee; they're in talks with a broker named Harry Schlecker. That's all I'm prepared to say right now.'

Mitchell's blood began to boil. 'I need more that that.'

'You'll just have to trust me.'

'I don't know you.'

'Let's just say that I didn't leave Stella empty-handed.'

'What do you mean?'

'Can't say anymore unless you wanna do business.'

Mitchell rolled his tongue around his mouth. It was what Shelleck hadn't told him that he found intriguing. He was shady and untrustworthy, but appeared to know who Stella's potential buyer was, and if Harry Schlecker was involved Mitchell wanted to know too, price no object. 'Tell you what, Jonathan; come to suite 107 at the Ritz-Carlton tomorrow morning at eleven. If you don't show up we never met.'

Shelleck stood up and straightened his jacket. 'You got a deal,' he said, and walked off without looking back.

As Mitchell watched him head for the exit the waiter strolled over. 'So what will it be, sir?' he asked.

'I'll have the beef, make sure it's rare.'

'Very good, sir.' The waiter took the menu and left.

Mitchell's cell phone rang; it was Rick Netty. He clicked it on. 'Netty, where are you?'

'I just got in to New York. It's all set up, but we need to talk.'

'Take a cab to the Domingo Club, the driver will know where it is. I'll be waiting.' Mitchell said, and disconnecting he smiled, raised his glass and whispered, 'Here's to you Harry. I'm about to ruin you're life you son-of-a-bitch.'

TWELVE

On Saturday afternoon, Harry Schlecker's Gulfstream jet landed at George Charles Airport, St Lucia and taxied to a halt in a similar line of toys. Co-pilot Alan Cobb opened the door and carried their only passenger's baggage out to the waiting driver. Bursting with excitement, Savannah jumped out of her seat and hurried down the aisle to the exit, where Captain Marsh, Angelina Rosa, and Alan Cobb were waiting to say goodbye. Thanking the crew for a nice flight, Savannah gave them a hug and said that she would see them next Friday

'Have fun, Savannah,' came the collective response.

'I will. Bye!' she yelled, scrambling down the small flight of steps to the sun-baked tarmac.

Jeremy Ben, a tall, African American and owner of a local security firm, stood leaning against a black Cherokee SUV with his arms folded in his usual white shirt, blue tie, beige slacks and sunglasses. Grinning broadly, he said, 'Hi, Miss Savannah, nice to have you back. We're gonna have fun, right?'

'You can count on it,' she replied, climbing onto the rear seat, her blue eyes dancing at the thought of a week in paradise, and lowering the window she breathed in the warm clean air.

Jeremy curled his six-foot two frame into the front seat and turned around. 'I put a nice chilled bottle of mango juice in the cooler. I hope it's still your favourite. And you better put on your seat belt Miss Savannah, you know the rules.'

Savannah grabbed the mango juice and secured her seat belt. Since her adoption, she had been to St Lucia many times with Harry and Greta and was well aware of the rules imposed upon her. Surprisingly, Harry had allowed her to travel alone for the first time, and she was wide-eyed with excitement.

Harry Schlecker had hired Jeremy Ben, ex Special Forces, to protect Savannah whenever she was in St Lucia. He became her shadow, but she barely noticed him whilst swimming in the warm Caribbean and sunning herself on the silky white beaches. But Jeremy was always there, somewhere in the crowd, as she strolled around Castries bustling streets, shopping in boutiques with her titanium American Express card, or sitting outside a café in khaki shorts, a skimpy red top, a floppy straw hat and sunglasses eating pastries and sipping coffee.

Jeremy Ben had once guarded the U.S. President, and as far as he was concerned Savannah was no different. He left nothing to chance.

Savannah loved visiting the island of St Lucia. For her, it was a sunshine paradise, with a unique vibrancy not unlike that of Rio. Harry's beautiful house was the home that she had dreamed of as a little girl; an imposing eleven-bedroom palace, with a mosaic patio facing a swimming pool with wood-decking and hammock-style sun beds surrounded by a tropical garden, beyond which lay an endless white sandy beach. The house was home to five live-in staff; Nanny Coombes, her husband Jonathan, who was deaf, a male chef, and two housemaids, Cindy and Dorleen.

In her late twenties, Nanny Coombes was a teacher at the New York Children's Institution, in which Harry Schlecker spent most of his orphaned youth. Her real name was Mary, but everyone affectionately called her Nanny; they still do. Nanny had been an inspiration to young Harry, so much so that when the institution closed down years later, he invited Nanny and Jonathan to take care of his house in St Lucia and make it their home.

When Savannah arrived at the house, Nanny squealed with delight and wrapped her arms around her, like her mother Gabriel used to do, and she wallowed in the warmth of her affection.

After the horrific murder of her parents, which Savannah had yet to overcome - Harry vowed that he would never let anything bad happen to her again. Ironically, when she arrived that day Nanny noticed a sparkle in her eyes, and wondered if Harry had told her the house in St Lucia would be her 21st birthday present. When Harry said no, she knew there was only one explanation; Savannah had a boyfriend.

* * * * *

With five days left before Katie's departure to Tokyo, an uneasy air of anticipation descended on the household. Piffin followed Katie around as though he could sense she was leaving. Mike and Julieanne insisted on staying up late. Richard made a point of coming home early from work, and Harry Schlecker sent Katie a bouquet of orchids. Late afternoons, the whole family and Piffin walked to the river in the autumnal sunshine; a simple pleasure they had not shared for some time.

Outside the house, reporters and tourists remained a constant challenge, but they were learning to live with it. A mail van now delivered Mike's fan mail to a small warehouse in New Mayford, which PocketMoney.com had leased for a year. Monday through Friday a dozen senior citizens sat around a table answering fan letters, with a standard reply from Mike Kinnerman.

The days sailed by, and then it was Thursday their last day together, which Katie spent packing and making farewell calls to her friends. That evening, they walked to the river for the last time for the next few months. Later, Sally Brooks joined them for dinner, throughout which Piffin lay under Katie's chair, head on his paws as their chatter danced around everything but Katie's departure, until Sally burst the bubble.

'I got you a nice little going away present, Katie,' Sally said, handing her a yellow gift-wrapped box.

Inside she found a Japanese language course; a book and CD. 'Perfect. Thanks, Sally, I shall need this.'

Julieanne pushed back her chair and ran up the stairs. Richard called out to her. Katie stood up and showed the flat of her hands as if to say I'll deal with it. Julieanne was lying face down on her bed when Katie entered her room and sat beside her. 'Hey, this is not like you. What's the matter, sweetie?'

'What do you care, you're leaving us,' she said, tearfully.

Katie exhaled. 'Come here.'

'Leave me alone. Isn't that something I have to get used to?'

'Jules, we talked about this. I'm not leaving you.'

'No? Tomorrow you'll be six thousand miles away, and you don't think that's leaving us?

'We'll talk every day, and I'll be home before you know it.'

'Is that supposed to make me feel better?'

'I'm not having this conversation. Get a good night's sleep. Tomorrow, you will come to JFK and kiss me goodbye. I'll ask Sally to bring you up some hot chocolate. Now get into bed,' Katie said, and left the room regretting her harsh tone.

When Mike was in bed and Sally Brooks had returned home, Richard and Katie talked about their relationship over a couple of brandies in the den. Katie sensed Richard's eyes telling her not to go, to change her mind, to work things out, but that wasn't the answer, of that she was certain. Staring into her brandy glass she said, 'Believe it or not, going to Tokyo is a daunting prospect for me, Richard.'

'Then don't go.'

'Then what? Go back to where we were; accept this feeling of reconciliation between us, when I know it's just a reaction to my leaving? No. That doesn't solve the problem, it just confirms my belief that spending time apart will save our marriage.'

'I don't accept that, and you know what? I'm finding it kinda hard getting used to the idea that my wife will be living in some goddam apartment in Tokyo.'

'I'm sure you'll manage.'

'Your confidence in me is overwhelming.'

'You're a great father.'

'I used to be a great husband.'

'No comment.'

Silence. A sip of brandy.

'I'm not going to argue the point. The kids know why you're going, and I think they'll be okay. And Sally's here. I'm gonna miss you, Katie, and I want you to call, email, whatever, every day or so. I don't want us to lose our pulse.'

'That's a promise,' she said, getting out of her chair.

Richard walked around the desk and held her in his arms. 'Don't let go of us, Katie,' he whispered.

Katie kissed him. 'Us is all I have, Richard,' she replied, and pausing at the door, she smiled and went up to her room.

Minutes later, Julieanne crawled into her mother's bed

* * * * *

As the blistering sunny days passed by, Savannah continued her passion for collecting shells from the seabed, and basking on the beach eating melons with the sea lapping at her feet. Being Brazilian she had soon tanned to a stunning bronze on the silky white sands of Rodney Bay, with her guardian nearby in the shade. It was already Thursday and having breakfast with her feet in the pool, Savannah made her morning call to Harry, and asked if she could come home on Saturday instead of Friday. Harry agreed, and told her to be at the airport at three p.m.

Delighted, she said, 'Now I can go to the market on Saturday morning, then have a swim before I go home.'

'I've never heard you sound so happy princess.'

Savannah smiled. Harry was right, she *was* happy for the first time since her parent's death. Mike Kinnerman had reopened the door to her life, of that she was certain. 'Yes, I am very happy.'

Choking back the emotion, Harry took a breath. 'Buy yourself some clothes princess, I know you love doin that. Greta sends her love. Call me tonight, okay. Bye sweetheart.'

After a short shopping spree, Savannah sat outside a café and asked Jeremy to join her, and with some reluctance he sat down.

'You sure are growin up fast Miss Savannah.'

A young waiter arrived. 'A mango juice, coffee and two club sandwiches please,' Savannah said, coolly. He nodded and left. 'I am surprised you even noticed, Jeremy.'

'Can't help it, on the beach an all, you're mighty pretty. I'm happily married and shouldn't even be lookin at you, but I got to that's my job. Harry pays me to protect you, cause you're not yet aware of the ways of the world. But I won't always be there, and I don't want nothin bad to happen to you Miss Savannah.'

'I know that, Jeremy, but there is something you should know about me that I don't like to talk about. Harry adopted me after my mother and father were murdered in Rio. My father worked for Harry, and he felt responsible for me.'

Jeremy had often wondered why Harry was so paranoid about Savannah's security; now he understood. 'Oh I'm sorry, I didn't know. You've seen bad things. I was gonna warn you about fast friends and to stay alert, but you're already there, right?'

Savannah nodded. 'Yes.'

The waiter placed their order on the table. Savannah thanked him and took a sandwich.

Jeremy leaned on the table. 'My advice is to enjoy what you have right now. You're probably still hurting after what happened to your folks, but try to hang on to the good times, not the bad stuff, it's in the past. You got a hell of a lot goin for you.'

'I know how lucky I am. Without Harry I would be living on the streets of Rio now,' Savannah admitted. 'But I would rather not talk about that. I am on vacation, and nothing bad will happen to me in St Lucia. I have you to look after me.'

'It's always a pleasure having you here Miss Savannah, but don't get hung up about being beautiful, that's God given.'

'I know it is, but I have always hated compliments about my looks, except from my mother.'

'You'd better get used to it cause in a couple of years you're gonna be stopping traffic, trust me.'

Savannah chuckled. 'Let's find another beach this afternoon, one with fishing boats, a coral reef and a cafe nearby?'

'I know just the place ma-am.'

'Excellent.'

THIRTEEN

New York City, Friday October 2ⁿᵈ

Harry Schlecker informed the media that Friday was the official opening day of PocketMoney.com's headquarters in New York, and at two p.m. its founder Mike Kinnerman would be there. The reporters knew that it was just a PR stunt to put the building on the map, but it was, nevertheless, a major story and certain to attract a large crowd.

Early that morning, Julieanne came down for breakfast and apologised for last night's outburst.

'Forget it, sweetie, sit down and have some juice and cereal,' Katie said, grabbing her hand. 'Your father's making pancakes.'

Julieanne grinned. 'I'll have two, Dad, please.'

'A wise choice, you won't regret it,' Richard replied, busily.

Julieanne kissed her brother. 'You look nice for a change. Is your girlfriend joining you today?'

'No. She'll be here on Sunday....I hope.'

Katie nudged her arm. 'Don't go there it's a touchy subject.' Julieanne continued teasing, but Mike was no longer listening. He was visualising Savannah's beautiful face, long legs and coral blue eyes, but his daydream ended abruptly when Sally Brooks, who had called in to say goodbye to Katie and drive Julieanne to school, planted a kiss on his cheek. Katie handed her a mug of coffee and they sat chatting at the breakfast bar.

The pancakes were perfect.

Harry's limousine pulled up outside the house at seven-forty a.m., and marching up to the front door Charlie carried Katie's baggage to the car. Sally and Julieanne came out on the porch and waved goodbye as Richard, Katie and Mike, ignoring a bunch of yelling reporters, climbed into the limo's rear seat and sped away. Mike's school Principal, Ms. Wilmont, had reluctantly given him the day off, and it would prove to be both frantic and emotional, beginning with an appearance on breakfast TV, and then a string of interviews with New York's hottest talk shows and magazines throughout the morning.

When the limo parked outside PocketMoney.com's towering building at two p.m., the crowd could hardly contain themselves. Grim-faced police officers were directing irate drivers away from the chaos, and people were hanging out of high-rise windows to see what was happening below. As Mike climbed out of the car, a wave of reporters and dignitaries lunged forward, all wanting to shake his hand. Amid the frenzy, he signed a bunch of autograph books excited fans were shoving at him. Then after a photo call at the red-carpeted entrance, Harry Schlecker ushered him through the glass doors to reception, followed by Richard, Katie, Greta, a camera crew and several hand picked reporters.

Mike looked at the reception area in amazement.

A revolving glass fountain, with seven statuettes of kneeling children holding out their hands begging, stood glittering under a galaxy of spotlights at the center of a blue marble floor. Staring at a bank of CCTV monitors behind a wooden desk, the uniformed security guard glanced up and nodded as the group stepped into the shiny new elevator.

Harry pressed a button marked PMC, and a breath later, the doors opened at PocketMoney.com level one, a spacious office reminiscent of a busy newspaper. Beneath rows of spot lighting, young executives sat hunched over desks strewn with paperwork, phones and laptops. They all stood up as Mike approached and shook their hands, while reporters and a camera crew captured the moment.

'Okay, that's enough for now,' Harry said. 'Now let's go see the executive suite.'

The top floor had a thick blue carpet and a hive of tinted glass offices surrounding the area, at the center of which secretaries sat behind a circular desk, typing and answering phones beneath the spot lighting. Harry led the group to the boardroom and entered. Gathered around an oval table cluttered with paperwork, phones and computers the trustees were studying market prices on a huge plasma screen. Behind them a tinted window gave a panoramic view of New York City. They stood up and gave the incoming group a warm welcome.

Richard, Katie and Mike joined the trustees for an update on current events, but as the company had only traded for one week there was little to report, bar a few investments needing no safety net. Company accountant Winston Bliss handed out the weekly financial status report, and announced that PocketMoney.com's assets currently stood at thirty-one billion dollars, and rising.

Mike sat wide-eyed in disbelief.

'And when I give you my first cheque, you'll be even richer,' Linda Greenberg said, gushing into the boardroom, unmistakable in her purple tinted glasses, camel coat and crimson ankle boots. Wrapping her arms around Mike, she said. 'We're partners now and I guess that's why David Schwartz is sulking off campus.'

Mike grinned. 'Hi, Linda, it's great to see you.'

'I know it is,' Linda quipped, removing her coat. Then having touched cheeks with Harry, Richard and Katie, she summarised a progress report; 'I want you to know that Maximum is working 24/7 on setting up the TV, radio and cell network for kids, and it looks like we'll be ready in the spring.'

'Way to go, Linda, you're a goddam dynamo,' Harry bawled.

The trustees murmured and nodded. Greta handed her some coffee. Linda chuckled, took a sip and continued her report.

'We have people in every country on the planet setting up offices for support teams and local interest programmes. Global industries are falling over themselves to advertise with us, and hundreds of production companies are offering programmes for consideration. This is a huge undertaking, but thanks to many dedicated people its working. I guess that about sums it up for now. If you got any questions, shoot,' Linda said, and sat down.

Richard stood up. 'On behalf of us all, Linda, thank you. You truly are an amazing woman, and we're lucky to have you.'

'Thanks, Richard, but that goes both ways. Mike, come sit here and watch me sign this agreement.'

Penny Bowman handed out copies of the agreement, which their lawyers had tweaked to everyone's satisfaction. Each copy was then signed and initialled by all concerned, and two witnesses. Maximum had agreed to pay PocketMoney.com eight point two billion dollars in six tranches over three years and, according to their number crunchers, they would break even on the fourth year and look forward to profits thereafter.

Linda had to leave to attend a meeting with the broadcasting authorities. There were complicated licensing issues to deal with and she wanted it done now. Pulling on her coat, she embraced her new partners and suggested a weekly progress report and a by-weekly meeting. Then after hugging Katie and promising to call her in Tokyo, Linda strode away, and there was not a soul in the room without a smiling face as she hurried to the elevator dictating orders into her cell phone.

Jenny Grant joined Mike at the table and placed an envelope and a document in front of him. Katie sat beside them.

'Inside the envelope is a pin number, Mike. Learn it and burn it. This is a black titanium American Express card, endorsed by your parents and the trustees. The card has no limit, so if you decide to buy an airline call me first. Sign here and on the back of the card,' Jenny said, with a wicked smile.

Katie raised an eyebrow. 'You will be sensible, right?'

'Yes, Mom,' Mike replied, and placing the card in his pocket he noticed a picture of a beach on the cover of magazine, which prompted him to ask if Savannah had return from St Lucia. He crossed the room to Harry Schlecker, who was chatting to Greta, and said, 'Mr. Schlecker.'

'Yeah, what is it, Mike?'

'Is Savannah back from St Lucia yet?'

'No, she extended her trip,' he stated, and before Mike could ask him when she was due back Harry took a call.

Mike sighed with disappointment. Savannah was not coming on Sunday and he was devastated, but as he turned to walk away, Greta whispered in his ear, 'She'll be home tomorrow.'

* * * * *

Savannah spent Friday afternoon exploring a deep coral reef at a secluded beach, and at five p.m., she reluctantly asked Jeremy to drive her back to the house. It was her last night in St Lucia and she was determined to enjoy it. Having showered and put on a red t-shirt and shorts, she grabbed her new digital camera, a birthday present from Greta, and photographed the entire house. Then she asked Jeremy to take several photos of her hugging Nanny and Jonathan, and one of her alone by the pool in the crimson evening light.

Nanny had arranged a dinner party for Savannah's last night, and when her friends Tom and Erica arrived Jonathan motioned for everyone to sit down at the patio dining table. The two young housemaids, Cindy and Dorleen, who liked Savannah because she had been kind to them, began serving a farewell feast. It was a starlit night and sitting at a candle-lit table, Savannah once again found herself captivated by the resplendent beauty of St Lucia.

After calling Harry the next morning, Savannah grabbed her beach bag and climbed into Jeremy's black SUV. Saturday was market day in Castries and the streets were bustling with tourists. Jeremy sat outside a café while Savannah went into a photo store and spoke to a female behind the counter.

'I would like two sets of prints and a disk please?'

The store assistant nodded. 'I'll need to download them first. They'll be ready in one hour.'

'Fine, and could you print one of my pictures on a seashell?' Savannah asked, producing a blue shell from her bag.

The assistant smiled. 'Yes we can, but that'll take a few days I'm afraid, Miss. I'm alone here this weekend, so it'll be Tuesday at the earliest.'

'If I give you my address would you post it to me? I will pay for it now with dollars,' Savannah said, disappointed.

'Sure, write down the address while I download your photos, then you can show me which one you want printed.'

Savannah handed her the camera and the pale blue seashell. A notepad lay on the counter, on which she wrote down the mansion address, C/o Harry Schlecker. The assistant returned and handing Savannah her camera, she spun the desk screen around to reveal a miniature set of her photographs.

'The one of you alone is beautiful. Is that the one you'd like me to print on the shell?'

'Yes. I will collect the prints when I have finished shopping.'

'Fine, that will be fifty-seven dollars, including postage.'

Savannah paid the bill and headed for the market, with Jeremy in tow. An hour later, having bought a few trinkets and collected her prints from the photo store, Jeremy drove to the beach and watched her plunge into the crystal-clear water.

At twelve-thirty, Jeremy stood up and pointed to his watch. Savannah reluctantly dried herself off and dressed. Arriving at the house, she went up to her room and packed her suitcase. Jeremy hauled it out to the car, along with her shopping bags, and placed them in the trunk. Nanny had made Savannah a light lunch and sitting with her feet in the pool she looked at the distant beach, the tropical garden and tranquil beauty of the house for the last time. Then she went to the kitchen and gave Cindy and Dorleen fifty dollars each and hugged them goodbye.

It was time to leave. She wrapped her arms around Nanny and said, 'Thank you for looking after me. I will be back in January. I miss you already,' and using sign language repeated the words to Jonathan, who hugged her tightly.

'We'll miss you too darling, Savannah. Call us when you're safely home,' Nanny said, sniffling.

Savannah sat in the SUV's rear seat and sulkily snapped on her seatbelt. Jeremy grinned, and as they sped away heading for George Charles airport, she frantically waved goodbye to Nanny and Jonathan and looked with longing at the beautiful house until it was no longer visible.

Having smiled her way through immigration and customs, Savannah dragged her suitcase out to the airfield, with Jeremy in tow laden with shopping bags. When she saw Harry's Gulfstream jet and Rosa waving to her at the exit she knew that her vacation had ended. Then as the flight crew hauled her bags and baggage onboard, she handed Jeremy a small gift and told him to open it.

Jeremy raised his eyebrows. 'You're gonna get me in trouble with my wife buying me things,' he said, discovering a red tie. 'Hey, that's real nice. You tryin to tell me something?'

'You wore a blue tie every day. Red will suit you, trust me.'

Jeremy grinned. 'Thanks Miss Savannah. I gotta tell you I've never seen you lookin so happy. So…is there a lucky guy?'

Smiling coyly she gave him a hug. 'Thank you for looking after me, Jeremy. I shall answer that question in January.'

'I'll get in training for that. Take care of yourself ma-am.'

Savannah chuckled as she boarded to a welcome by the crew. As the Gulfstream roared into the air, Savannah watched St Lucia fade to a dot in the sea, and whispered, 'Bye, little Rio.'

* * * * *

With business of the day concluded, Katie strolled to the window and gazed at the city traffic below. In a few hours, she would be on her way to London, a decision she now secretly regretted. Harry watched her look thoughtfully through the tinted glass.

Greta squeezed her hand, and whispered, 'I'm here if you ever want to talk, Katie. You have all my numbers.'

Richard said nothing, believing comforting words were meaningless, and that Katie's pent-up emotion would manifest itself somewhere over the Atlantic Ocean.

Harry's pilot picked Julieanne up at school and flew her to PocketMoney.com's rooftop helipad. He informed Harry that she had arrived but was in no mood to face a gathering, and had gone down to reception to wait for her mother.

Harry disconnected. 'Julieanne's at reception, Katie. I guess it's time for you to go. Charlie's waiting outside with the limo.'

Keen to avoid lingering goodbyes Katie hugged Harry, Greta and the trustees, who promised to send her a weekly report. Then quietly slipping away, Katie, Richard and Mike took the elevator down to reception in silence. Julieanne watched the elevator light pass through the floors, and as the doors opened, she grabbed her mother's arm and they walked to the waiting limousine. Charlie drove through the city traffic to JFK Airport and pulled up at the terminal. Julieanne became overly bubbly and Katie knew that tears would follow. Keeping her laptop and shoulder bag she checked her baggage at the airline desk, who told her that calls for boarding would commence in two hours. With little time left to share they had coffee at a table outside a café and sat staring at Katie, who kept making excuses to go to the ladies room.

When they announced boarding for Katie's flight to London, where the company had arranged for six members of her team to join her on a jumbo jet to Tokyo, Mike and Julieanne glanced at one another. Masking her emotions Katie walked with her family to the departure gate, where crowds of loved ones were saying goodbye, and last minute calls for late passengers rang out on the PA system. The area was chaotic, the emotion palpable.

Taking a deep breath Katie turned to face her family. 'Well, this is it. I guess it's time for me to go.'

Julieanne tearfully threw her arms around her. 'You will call and let us know you're okay?'

Katie held back her emotion. 'Of course I will, sweetie. We'll talk all the time, I promise.'

Julieanne sniffled. 'The house won't be the same without you, Mom. Nothing will.'

'I'll be back before you know it, my darling. Mike, aren't you gonna give me a hug too?'

Mike wrapped his arms around her. 'This is gonna be hard for us, Mom. I'm really gonna miss you, we all are.'

'I'll miss you too. You are my life, and don't ever forget that. I'll call you when I get there, okay?'

On the verge of tears Mike and Julieanne held Katie tighter. Richard turned away.

A female voice on the PA system announced the final call for passengers boarding the flight to London.

The noise level rose as people said their last goodbyes before letting go. One hysterical woman had lost her boarding pass. Cleaners arrived to mop the marble floor where someone had just vomited. More people arrived to board a flight to Paris.

Then a mass exodus ensued.

Katie locked eyes with Richard, who was clearly struggling to keep his composure. He kissed her long and hard on the lips, and then gently pulled Mike and Julieanne away. Katie held their gaze for a moment, then whispering *goodbye* she hurried through the departure gate with her hand to her mouth forcing herself not to look back. Their eyes followed her swaying raincoat and red beret until she melted into a sea of fellow travellers.

Then she was gone.

Richard led Mike and Julieanne away and exited through the terminal's automatic doors. Sullen-faced they sank into the limo's rear seat. Charlie closed the rear door and sped away into a heavy stream of traffic leaving the busy terminal. Twenty minutes later, they pulled up outside the PocketMoney.com building. Richard thanked Charlie as they climbed out, and entering reception they took to the elevator up to the heliport.

Buckled up on the rear seat of Harry's helicopter, they sat in their own silence as the pilot flew them back to their empty house in Beechwood Avenue, where Katie's perfume lingered in every room, and Piffin lay gloomily in his basket.

Alone with her thoughts somewhere over the Atlantic Ocean, Katie leaned back in her seat and looked out the window into the endless darkness. Her mother and father would not have approved of her decision to leave, and there would have been an awful row. Sadly, they were no longer of this world, but every now and then Katie could still hear their voices advising her, sometimes telling her what she should do. Now, at thirty-five thousand feet and a little closer to heaven, their voices were loud and clear and their message unmistakable; she had just made the biggest mistake of her life.

FOURTEEN

Sunday, October 4th

Mike had been up since six a.m., expectantly pacing the kitchen floor. By seven-forty, he was starting to panic. At eight-thirty, his cell phone rang, caller unknown. His heart sank; it was probably a reporter. 'Mike Kinnerman,' he said, irritably.

'Mike, it's me, Savannah. You invited me to your house. Do we...still have a date?'

Mike looked up and mouthed the words *thank you*. Melting to the sound of her voice, he said, 'Are you kidding? I can't wait to see you. Please tell me you're leaving now.'

Savannah giggled, disguising her relief. 'I will be there in one hour. Bye,' she said, and hung up.

He ran up the stairs and showered, then rummaging through his wardrobe he put on a blue shirt, khakis and Nike's.

Forty-nine long minutes later, Greta's blue Mercedes pulled up outside the house; top down, music playing. Mike stood in the driveway, his pulse racing as Savannah stepped onto the sidewalk looking radiantly beautiful in a short blue skirt, a spaghetti strap pink top, blue shoes, chic sunglasses, her pink plastic watch and matching purse. Strands of pink and blue ribbon in her long, dark hair fell on her suntanned shoulders in the warm autumn sunlight. She smiled and did a little twirl.

Unable to take his eyes off her Mike kissed her on the cheek, and said, 'You look absolutely amazing,'

Savannah smiled, coyly. 'Thank you.'

A black tinted windowed van slowly drove past the house.

Jumping out of her car in shorts and a t-shirt, Greta strode over to Mike. 'Happy now?' she whispered, giving him a hug.

'Delirious,' he quipped.

Greta chuckled and, deciding that she had already stayed too long, wrapped her arms around Savannah. 'Call me when you're ready to go home, sweetie.'

'I will. And thanks, Greta.'

'Have fun you two,' Greta yelled, closing the door as she slid behind the wheel, and waving goodbye she sped away towards the distant freeway.

Huddled over the bamboo veranda table Mike and Savannah talked as though they were on a desert island. Richard observed them through the kitchen bay window; they seemed completely engrossed in one another. He had rarely seen his son happier.

Richard brought out coffee and quassants and left them alone to talk. Yawning sleepy-eyed, Julieanne joined them at the table.

'Hi, you must be Savannah. Mike said that you were coming today. I'm Julieanne, and we're gonna be friends, okay?'

'Yes, all right,' Savannah said, liking her instantly.

At eleven-thirty, a jeep parked and beeped outside the house. Jumping to her feet Julieanne explained that her boyfriend Jake was taking her to the county fair. She kissed Mike and hugged Savannah, and then sped away in a cloud of raunchy rock music, much to the annoyance of the late Sunday sleepers.

On Sundays, lawyer Kinnerman shuffled about in jeans and a sweatshirt doting on his kids, which today included Savannah, who seemed quite content to sit on the veranda in the autumn sunshine and talk about nothing in particular. For Mike, it was hard to imagine a better way of spending a Sunday morning.

'Can you ride a bike?' Mike asked.

Savannah drained her coffee. 'Yes, where are we going?'

'To the river, but first my dad wants to take some photos of you and me, so smile.'

Richard clicked away with his digital camera, while Mike and Savannah sat smiling and glowing with happiness in each other's arms. Then reminding Mike of the possible dangers out there, he warned him to be vigilant.

Savannah frowned, wondering why he would say that.

Mike rolled his eyes. 'We'll be fine, dad.'

Richard strolled with them to the rear gate and watched as they rode off together, laughing without a care in the world. He chuckled, shook his head and returned to the house.

Due to the autumn county fair there was not a soul about as they cycled along the walker's path. It was exceptionally warm for early October, and the golden leaves, crisp from the long hot summer, fluttered silently to the ground in the autumnal sunshine. A gentle southerly breeze sailed across the browning landscape where drays of red squirrels were already busy gathering winter food. Mike chased a rabbit, but it was too smart for him and he fell off his bike, landing face down in the grass.

Savannah knelt down beside him. Are you alright?' she asked, concerned that he may be hurt.

Mike turned his head and grinned. Just wanted to know if you cared about me, that's all.'

'Not at all,' she said, playfully slapping his head, and rode off towards the river giggling like a schoolgirl.

Lying on the grassy riverbank beside an ancient willow, they gazed affectionately at one another in the breezy silence. It was a perfect day; warm and captivating, which seemed to mirror the deepening bond between them.

'What were your parents like, would they have liked me?'

Savannah smiled. 'I am certain of it. Pedre, my father, was a kind man and lived for his family. My mother, Gabriel was a true angel, a beautiful woman in every way, and I worshipped her. At weekends we would go to Copacabana beach and party with our friends until sunset. We had a perfect life. I was very happy.'

'Your eyes seem to light up when you talk about Rio. Maybe we could go there one day,' Mike said, dreamily.

'Rio is a magical place. I never wanted to leave until…

The birds suddenly left the trees en-masse and headed south. A helicopter clattered somewhere in the distance. Mike sat up and scanned the horizon. There was a military base in the area and its personnel often flew by during training exercises. The helicopter disappeared into the distant woodlands, and Mike silently cursed himself for overreacting.

Savannah folded her arms. 'Hey, remember me?'

'Sorry I was…doesn't matter,' he said, glancing north again.

Savannah snuggled up to him. 'I like it here.'

'This is my special place. I tend to see things more clearly when I'm here on the riverbank. Clean air, trickle of fresh water and the rustle of trees; that's a powerful silence. We used to have family picnics here in the summer when I…..Holy shit!'

A helicopter suddenly appeared out of the dense trees on the other side of the river and hovered in front of them. It was a green Bell Huey, once a military favourite. Mike had a model just like it in his bedroom. The side door was open. A man was looking at them through binoculars. It glided over the river.

'Oh my God!' Savannah gasped, gripping Mike's arm.

Their bikes lay half way. Mike's mouth went dry and he felt sick. The voice in his head screamed, *do something!*

Richard was in his den when he heard the distant helicopter. *Why do they always have to exercise at weekends?* He mumbled, instinctively peering through the window, but the river was not visible from the house. Then the phone rang; it was Jim Barker, an old law school pal who was going through a nasty divorce and needed a sympathetic ear. 'Jim, how's it going pal?'

Scrambling to his feet Mike pulled Savannah up, unaware his cell phone had fallen into the long grass. The Huey uhovered menacingly thirty yards away, its nose pointing directly at them. Mike stared at the tinted cockpit window, his heart racing and his face taut with fear.

They knew we were here. Someone has been watching us.

Gripping Savannah's hand he yelled over the clattering noise of the rotors, 'We need get out of here, now!'

Hearts thumping and knees buckling they frantically ran in the direction of Mike's distant house. Glancing back, Savannah saw the Huey swoop around and follow them. 'Who are they, what do they want with us?' she yelled, breathlessly.

'Me I guess!' Mike answered, sucking in air.

'You mean kidnap?'

'Don't let go of my hand.'

As they scrambled through the long grass, their feet crunching on fallen leaves, Savannah tripped and fell into a hidden gully. The Huey circled overhead, its rotors whipping up a whirlpool of dust and leaves. Mike dragged

Savannah to her feet and they raced towards a distant cluster of tall chestnut trees. They could hear men yelling overhead amid the clattering noise of the rotors and sickening stench of aviation fuel.

Escape seemed unlikely

Like gazelles fleeing a hungry lion they zigzagged through the rugged landscape, the Huey hovering above them waiting to pounce. Having made it to the chestnut trees, they crouched down and looked at the distant red brick houses, both knowing their chances of outrunning the Huey were slim. Mike cursed himself for not heeding his father's warning.

The Huey circled overhead and time was running out. Mike reached for his cell phone; it was not there.

'Damn, where's your phone?'

Savannah looked for her purse. 'I must have dropped it when we ran away. What are we going to do?'

Mike exhaled. 'If we go back for the phones, they'll grab us.'

'Then we have to run to the house.' Savannah said, shaking.

The Huey suddenly sank to the ground. Two men jumped out. 'Run! And don't stop for anything!' Mike yelled.

Surely, someone would see them.

The men jumped back onboard, and soaring into the air the Huey hovered over them like a dragonfly shadowing their every step. Someone yelled, Go! The Huey swooped down and a thick heavy net dropped over Mike and Savannah, dragging them to the ground. They pulled, kicked and yelled in a desperate attempt to break free, but their efforts were in vain. Terrified and unable to move they lay trapped in a whirlpool of dust and leaves as the clawing net tightened around them like a giant spider.

'I can't breathe!' Savannah shrieked.

The engine roared and with a surge of power the Huey rose high into the air and sped away heading due south, with Mike and Savannah curled up inside the net gasping for air. Mike's hands were bleeding. Savannah's pink watchstrap snapped and slipped through the net, which now swung wildly at the end of two cables high above ground.

Someone shouted, *winch 'em up.* The net sailed up to the side door. Two muscular men, wearing black balaclavas, pulled the net inside, released it and let it drop to the floor. Mike and Savannah yelped with pain. Forcing open the net the men stood over them menacingly. One slapped Mike's face and kicked him in the ribs, then dragged him to a corner face down. The other, covered in tattoos and reeking of stale cigarettes, grabbed Savannah's hair and dragging her screaming across the metal floor, he shoved her face down next to Mike and spat at her.

That was the last thing they would see for seventeen hours.

Wearing black hoods and their hands bound with duct tape they lay face down on the metal floor. One man pulled back their hooded heads and coldly threatened to kill them if they became a problem. When neither responded, he let go and joined the pilot. Slamming the side door shut, the tattooed thug lit a cigarette and sat cross-legged on the metal floor admiring Savannah's legs, which were shaking uncontrollably.

Their kidnapping, which had taken less than eight minutes to execute, had left no evidential trace. Furthermore, their absence would go unnoticed for several hours, by which time they could be anywhere. Their only comforting thought was that Richard had been aware of the possible dangers and would no doubt be the first to realise something had happened to them.

At some point later, they heard the pilot yell, 'We're just east of Harrisburg, Pennsylvania approaching Mallard airfield. This place is perfect, been deserted for years.'

The Huey landed and an eerie silence fell as the rotors slowly wound to a halt. The respite however, proved to be short lived when a few minutes later, a jet thundered by overhead and landed with a screech of tires on a nearby runway.

Covering Mike and Savannah's heads with a blanket, the men led them across the runway and dragged them up the steps into the waiting aircraft. Placing them in seats at the rear of the cabin, they cut the tape off their wrists and warned them not to remove their hoods or make a sound.

They listened to sounds around them; a car pulled up outside. A door slammed. The car sped off. Someone entered the aircraft. The cabin door shut. Men greeted one another. A croaky-voiced man congratulated the kidnappers on their success. Cans popped and cigarette smoke filled the cabin. Then the men moved further down the cabin, much to Mike and Savannah's relief.

Barely audible under his hood, Mike leaned close to Savannah and whispered, 'Are they talking Spanish?'

'No, Portuguese,' she replied, softly. It was her native tongue in Brazil. 'The croaky voiced man is Javier.'

The engines roared as the jet gathered speed along the runway and took to the air. Levelling off at thirty-five thousand feet, the pilot set a new course heading due Southwest.

Frightened and disorientated in their hooded darkness Mike and Savannah had lost all sense of time and location. They were at the mercy of ruthless kidnappers who would no doubt demand a ransom, and may even murder them. Mike wondered how they would prove their captive's identity. There had been many high profile reported incidents of kidnappers cutting off fingers and ears as proof of life, but the very thought of such an extremity was sickening. In any case, the FBI was powerless to negotiate a ransom until their kidnappers chose to make contact, which could take months, maybe even years. Meanwhile, they would rot in a stinking hole in some God forsaken country where no one gave a damn whether they lived or died.

Mike closed his eyes; *surely, this can't be happening.*

Savannah feared for their lives, but having borne witness to the dreadful murder of her parents, the brutality of human beings no longer surprised her. She had flown in many jets with her father and Harry Schlecker, and as far as she was concerned they were all the same. One such jet had taken her to America to begin a new life, a life that had so far given her everything but the affection she craved. Her solitude and growing cynicism had led to contempt for the mansion, the limos, the Gulfstream jet and the prestige' and baggage that went with it. Now she was on another jet, this time with her hands bound and a black hood covering her head. She almost smiled at the irony. Having no idea what these men might do, she was preparing for the worst. But they would not see her fear, only her contempt for their cowardice.

Hours of fearful uncertainty passed as their terrifying journey into the unknown continued. Someone attended to the small cuts on Mike's hands, but after that, other than an escort to the rest room and an occasional cold drink, there was no further contact with their kidnappers. With no means of escape, they sat alone at the rear of the cabin lost in the drone of the engines, wondering what fate had in store.

Their lives had stopped. Time was meaningless.

Hours later, the aircraft landed with a screech of tyres on the tarmac and taxied to a halt. The door opened.

'This won't take long,' Croaky voice Javier said.

The cabin remained locked in silence until Javier returned with a group of men and closed the door. Joining the kidnappers they began laughing and boasting of their criminal activities.

Savannah whispered, 'Eight men posing as airport workers have boarded. They hid four crates of cocaine in the hold while corrupt ground crew refuelled the jet. We are in Mexico City.'

As the jet roared along the runway and took to the air, more cans popped and the men began celebrating. Predictably, the mood began to change. A brawl broke out and several of their drunken tormentors paraded up and down the aisle, bringing a frightening sense of unpredictability to the cabin. One man spoke crudely in Portuguese to Savannah. Someone dragged him away.

Aware of her vulnerability, Savannah escaped into her forced darkness and pictured the riverbank, where she and Mike had lain in one another's arms on a perfect Sunday morning.

No one could see her tears beneath the hood.

Mike reached for her hand; it was warm and comforting and he thanked God for her presence. Whatever dangers that surely lay ahead, at least they would face them together. He leaned back in the seat, his eyes flickering with fear and exhaustion. Then his mind slowly slipped away as the constant whine of the engines and the acceptance of their uncertain fate made sleep involuntary.

He found only darkness.

FIFTEEN

By five p.m. Richard was concerned that Mike had not returned or called to say he'd be late. He tried Mike's cell phone but it went to voicemail, so he left a message urging him to call. When there was no response Richard instinctively knew something was wrong. He shared his concern with Harry Schlecker and asked him to try Savannah's phone. That also went to voicemail and with a heightening sense of urgency, they agreed to give it thirty minutes before deciding what action to take.

Richard anxiously paced the kitchen floor. Mike would never wander off without telling him, of that he was certain. He looked through the kitchen bay window. The sun was going down and it would soon be dark. Grabbing his jacket he opened the door and headed for the river. If there were any clues to their whereabouts surely he would find them there.

He found their bikes abandoned on the riverbank. Beginning to fear the worst he searched the area and found a cell phone in the long grass; it was Mike's and his heart sank as the probability of their abduction became a reality. Then beneath a willow tree he found Savannah's pink purse containing a few personal items and her cell phone. He scanned the distant landscape, hoping to see something, hear something, anything, but there was nothing, just the October wind rustling through the trees in the looming darkness. They had vanished. Something had happened to them, something terrible. It was time to call the authorities.

Richard informed Harry what he had found at the riverbank, and said, 'They've gone, Harry. They've been taken.'

Harry froze. 'Taken? But Savannah was….Christ, what are we dealing with here, maniacs, pro's, terrorists, what?'

'I don't know but we'd better find out. We'll talk later.'

Harry called FBI Director Vernon Bentram, with whom he had a long friendship and explained what had happened. Director Bentram agreed to assign a few agents to look into it. Harry was keen to hire a private investigator and post a huge reward on his website for information leading to their whereabouts, but Director Bentram cautioned him against knee jerk reactions.

'Forget it, Harry. Crank sightings worldwide on the internet is the last thing you need. If they've been kidnapped someone'll make contact. Let's wait until we know what we're dealing with.' Harry reluctantly agreed and hung up.

Richard alerted Sheriff Carver and within minutes his patrol car pulled up outside the Kinnerman house, blue lights flashing. Inquisitive neighbours peered through their windows.

Sheriff Tom Carver was like family to Richard. They grew up in Bridgeport and went to the same schools, until he went on to study law at Yale University. When Richard's parents died in a Canadian boating accident he almost fell apart and sank into a crater of grief. Tom dropped everything and stood by him until he found his way out. When Mike was born Richard and Katie asked Tom to be his Godfather. He was honoured and had loved him like a son ever since, so for Tom this was personal.

'Who's the girl, Richard?' Sheriff Carver asked.

'Harry Schlecker's 14-year old daughter, Savannah. She and Mike are pretty-much smitten and he invited her over for the day. I took a photo of them this morning. I'll print it out for you.'

Richard's throat tightened when he saw their happy smiling faces on his computer screen. He pressed print and waited for the picture to drop in the tray.

The Sheriff rubbed his face. 'How's Julieanne taking this?'

Richard shook his head. 'She doesn't know yet, Tom. What the hell am I gonna say to her?'

As they walked to the patrol car, Tom explained that in cases of missing people the authorities have unilateral procedures.

'The state police wait 24 hours before putting out a nation-wide alert. Once they cross a state line the FBI get involved, and they'll find 'em, believe me.' he said, reassuringly.

Sheriff Carver drove away, leaving Richard with an empty feeling in his stomach. In 24 hours, Mike and Savannah could be anywhere, perhaps even dead. He went into his den, poured a brandy and anxiously paced the floor, glancing at the phone on his desk. He could only imagine what Katie's reaction would be to the terrible news. His dilemma was whether to break her heart that evening, or wait until morning and hope for good news, perhaps a sighting, or even a phone call from the kidnappers informing him that Mike and Savannah were alive. Either way, it was not a call he was looking forward to, and after considering the options he reluctantly decided to wait.

* * * * *

Mike woke up with a dry mouth and his head spinning. When he felt the hood he almost panicked, then it all came flooding back, along with the fear and nausea; it was not just a bad dream. He rubbed his numb legs in an attempt to get the blood flowing, and suddenly realized the cabin was silent; the aircraft had landed. Having no idea if it was day or night, where they were, or if they were alone, he thought about removing his hood, but caution persuaded him to wait. He reached for Savannah's hand and felt her soft skin on his fingertips. 'Are you awake?' he whispered.

'Yes, my body aches, I am hungry and scared, and I wish I was in St Lucia,' Savannah said, coughing with fatigue.

'I can't tell you how good it feels to hear your voice.'

'Me too, I cannot believe this is really happening.'

'I know, but we'll come through this, I promise.'

Savannah gripped his hand. 'I want to believe that.'

The door opened. The sound of boots crunched down the aisle and stopped beside them. Croaky voice Javier asked if they were awake. Mike nodded his hood. Savannah gave him a mouthful of abuse in Portuguese. Javier ignored her and nodded at one of the men to place a tray on the backseat table in front of them.

'As long as you behave no harm will come to you,' Javier said, with a hint of menace. 'There is coffee and rolls in front of you. We are going outside. You can remove your hoods to eat, but make sure you put them on before we return. Oh, and I advise you to use the bathroom you have a road trip ahead of you.'

'What time is it and where are we?' Mike asked.

'It is five a.m. Monday. I cannot tell you where you are but you slept for ten hours. This is our second stop,' Javier explained.

Mike coughed. 'I feel like shit, were we drugged?'

'We gave you a mild sedative, nothing harmful.'

'Are we in Venezuela?' Savannah asked.

'Enjoy your breakfast,' Javier croaked. The boots marched off down the aisle and exited down the steps.

They removed their hoods and looked squinted-eyed around the empty seated cabin. Savannah took a cheese roll and sipped the strong, sweet coffee. Mike did the same and looked out the right window, but all he could see were a few airport perimeter lights and twinkling dots on a distant hillside. To his left further down the runway, there was a building with one light on.

The place looked desolate.

Savouring her coffee, Savannah said, 'I have a feeling that we are in South America, but I have no idea where.'

'And they don't want us to know. We're at a small airfield in the middle of nowhere and it looks deserted. They're obviously planning to hide us somewhere off the beaten track,' Mike said, glancing again out the window. 'It'll be light soon.' Draining the last of his coffee he jumped out of his seat.

'Mike, what are you doing?'

'I'm gonna look outside. Stay here.' He crouched down and crept along the cabin to the exit. Lying on the floor, he peered around the bottom of the doorway. The flight crew were standing on the misty runway smoking and chatting. Parked alongside the jet was a van with its rear doors open, into which eight men were hauling packages from four large crates. One of them glanced up, and for a split second he and Mike were eye to eye. Mike quickly pulled back, hoping the man wouldn't give him away. Strangely he did not. He cautiously looked again as one of the men closed the van's rear doors and led the others to a nearby dusty bus in which they all sat down.

A tall man in some sort of official uniform was standing at the foot of the aircraft's steps, talking to a well-dressed man with a small grey beard, whom he referred to as Javier. Beside him were two men in army fatigues; one was tall and muscular with a blonde crew-cut, the other was bald, stocky and heavily tattooed on his arms and neck; their kidnappers, Mike was certain of it. Javier handed an envelope to the uniformed official who nodded and marched away. Then entering the well-lit bus Javier strode down the aisle to the fifth row. Turning to the man on his left, he pulled out a revolver and shot him in the head. Mike gasped in horror as the man recoiled against the blood-spattered window. The others on the bus sat motionless, one of whom was the man he had been eye to eye with moments ago.

Javier ordered two of the men seated nearby to carry out the dead man and place him in the back of the van. As the van sped away, he stepped off the bus and joined the kidnappers at the foot of the aircraft's steps.

Blonde crew-cut said, 'What was that all about?

'He was an undercover agent for Mexico's anti drug agency.' Javier explained. 'He infiltrated the cartel months ago, but we had a tip-off and waited for the right opportunity to kill him.'

Mike looked at the man who had chosen not give him away. He was dressed like a peasant and sat alone at the back of the bus, but something about him suggested they had killed the wrong man, and that perhaps their tip-off had come from the anti drugs agency. Mike hurried back to his seat in an agitated state.

'They just shot a guy on a bus,' he said, his hands shaking.

Curled up on two seats Savannah sat up wide-eyed. 'What!'

'That guy Javier said the man was an undercover agent. This whole thing is a set-up for some drug cartel. I'll explain later. Go use the bathroom before they come back, hurry,' Mike urged.

Javier returned and found them seated with their hoods on. He ordered one of the men to bind their wrists.

'It is time to go my young friends. I wish I could promise you a nice trip, but unfortunately that is not the case,' Javier croaked, with underlying sarcasm. 'Alright, get them out of here.'

Blonde crew-cut slapped Mike's head. 'Time to go, sonny.'

Gripping the back of Mike's neck he marched him down the aisle. Savannah gave tattoos a tirade of abuse as he dragged her kicking to the exit. Placing a blanket over their heads, to avoid satellite surveillance, they dragged the youngsters down the steps and shoved them onto a stinking mattress inside the back of a van. Sliding the side door shut the men climbed in the front and the van sped away.

Dawn had broken and dewy morning air flowed through the open side windows. Mike and Savannah welcomed its coolness beneath their hoods, but as the sun began to rise, the heat in the back of van became unbearable.

As the hours and miles rolled by, they lay together in their hooded darkness, afraid and soaked with sweat in the unforgiving heat. They slept, but had no idea for how long. When they awoke, their throats were dry and the van was barely moving. The smell of coffee and cigars permeated the air. Nearby, they could hear people chatting, laughing, car horns beeping, phones ringing and a cacophony of music. For Savannah it all sounded familiar; they were stuck in city traffic, but where? After a stuttering mile or so, the van turned onto a smooth highway and continued at speed for some distance before veering off to the right. Then after several stops and sharp turns, the van came to a screeching halt.

They smell of the ocean and squealing seagulls filled the air. Cranes thundered somewhere in the distance, their chains banging on metal containers. A welding torch fizzled nearby. Carts and barrows rumbled over cobblestones, and boats chugged by with diesel engines gurgling in the water.

The side door slid open. Two men pulled Mike and Savannah out, and covering their heads with a blanket, they marched them up a steep gangplank onto the deck of a boat. Then lowering them down a flight of steps, they dragged them along a passageway through swinging doors until a voice grunted, 'In here.' A key turned noisily in a lock. A door creaked open.

The men shoved them onto a bunk inside a stale-aired cabin. 'Rule one; never take off the hoods until the door's shut, okay?' A man warned, ripping the duct tape off their wrists.

Both nodded their hoods in silence.

Then someone entered the cabin and spoke with an articulate American accent bordering on arrogance.

'Well well, Mike Kinnerman, the famous young billionaire. I can't help but admire your astonishing achievements. And if you behave yourself, you may even live to enjoy it,' he said, his veiled threat striking fear into Mike's imagination.

Crew-cut and tattoos chuckled at the intimidation.

'And you must be Savannah, an exceptionally beautiful young lady, I hear. Good morning.'

Savannah took a breath. There was something familiar about him. 'Who are you?' she asked, curtly.

'If I tell you that I'll have to kill you. Still want to know?'

Savannah did not respond. She had remembered the face that matched his voice, and ironically she was glad to be wearing the hood, knowing her eyes would have betrayed her. His name was Rylan Mitchell, once a regular visitor at the mansion, until Harry Schlecker's evidence put him in jail for fraud. She had disliked him on sight. He always had a token blonde clinging to his white dinner jacket, and his ostentatious jewellery perfectly matched his roguish personality. He appeared suave and worldly and, though not particularly handsome, there was something dangerous about him, which was no doubt a magnet for some women.

Savannah knew that it would be foolish to mention his name, but she was unable to curb her curiosity. 'Why did you kidnap us? We have done nothing to you,' she pleaded, innocently.

'It was the boy we wanted. You just happen to be there my dear. However, Harry Schlecker has something belonging to me, and your presence will ensure that he returns it,' Mitchell said. 'I know you're afraid, but this is strictly business. Be reasonable, and you'll go home in one piece, fair enough?'

Savannah nodded her hood. She despised this man.

'What if they refuse to pay a ransom?' Mike asked.

'Then you will die,' Mitchell replied, with indifference. Mike wondered if he was smiling. 'There are tracksuits beside you. Put them on and the crew will launder your clothes. You will have new jeans and sweatshirts tomorrow. Meanwhile, I'll have some food brought down, and I don't want to hear another peep out of you. Okay, lock it,' Mitchell ordered, and left the room.

They sat in silence until the sound of boots faded along the passageway. Then removing their hoods, they both flinched under the glaring overhead lighting in their small cabin, which had two bunk beds, a maroon carpet, a porthole and a pink-tiled bathroom, into which Savannah quickly dragged Mike and closed the door. Barely whispering, she explained that she had recognised

Rylan Mitchell's voice. Mike praised her coolness for not mentioning his name, but both admitted to finding a strange sense of comfort in knowing who their kidnapper was, even though he would kill them if he knew they were aware of his identity.

Savannah drew back the porthole curtain and found it blacked out with some sort of plastic. Mike took off his belt, and using the buckle he scratched off the black coating. Then with their heads touching they looked out the porthole and saw the quayside of a bustling marina, beyond which lay a golden sandy bay curving around a sprawling city, with a backdrop of thick forests, dramatic mountains and a cloudless blue sky.

Savannah stepped back, her eyes wide with disbelief. 'Those sounds and the smells, I knew they were familiar. Mike, we are in Rio,' she said, wrapping her arms around herself.

Mike looked at her. 'Rio de Janeiro, Brazil?'

'Yes, it means River of January in Portuguese.'

'I know, and we're five thousand miles from home.'

'Four thousand eight hundred and sixteen,' Savannah stated, and wiping her eyes she returned to the porthole and looked out at the beautiful city in which she had spent her childhood. She remembered visiting the marina many times with her father, and sitting down there on that quayside bench, waving to the sailors as the boats sailed out the harbour.

'We are in Marina da Gloria, and that is the city of Rio at the foot of Corcovado Mountain, which has the statue of Christ the Redeemer at the top,' Savannah explained, her eyes clouding with memories. 'Beyond the marina are Flamengo, Copacabana and Ipanema Beach. Many hotels are along that strip. At the mouth of the bay is Sugarloaf Mountain. Behind us is a cruise terminal and Santos Dumont Airport. Up there on the hills are the "Favelas" Shanty towns where poor people live.' Savannah paused and took a breath. 'This will not be easy for me, Mike,' she whimpered.

Mike placed his arm around her. 'I understand that, and I'm sorry I should have seen it coming, but there's nothing we can do about that now. At least we're together, and no matter what, I promise we'll make it out of here.'

'I really needed to hear you say that,' Savannah said, sniffling. 'By the way, you need a shower.'

'I know.'

Locked in their tiny cabin, they looked through the porthole at the outside world continuing as usual. Drivers in open top cars were cruising along the beach highway, tapping their fingers and chatting on cell phones. Brightly coloured scooters, driven by seemingly fearless teenagers, weaved their way through the coast road traffic, narrowly avoiding passengers clambering on and off crowded busses. A band of rollerbladers sailed across the marina, passing a circle of children holding hands as they danced in the sunshine. On the nearby quayside, with lines of glamorous yachts swaying in the tide behind them, groups of tourists were smiling at cameras for their friends back home.

It was just another day in Rio

CHAPTER

SIXTEEN

K atie sighed with relief as she entered arrivals at Narita airport and saw a Japanese girl holding up a board with her name on it. Introducing herself as Chia, she led Katie out to a black Toyota SUV and placed her baggage in the back. Promising her a tour of Tokyo on Monday she drove out the terminal.

As Tokyo is 13 hours ahead of New York, when Katie called home at eleven a.m. on Sunday to say that she had arrived safely it was ten p.m. Saturday in New Mayford. Still reeling from the heart-wrenching goodbye at JFK, Katie's long-distance call to Richard, Mike and Julieanne only reinforced her determination to save her marriage. She promised to call again on Tuesday at eight a.m. New Mayford time and tearfully said goodbye.

Alone in her new apartment, Katie looked out at the dazzling city of Tokyo and New Mayford suddenly seemed far away.

* * * * *

As the western stock markets close at weekends Harry Schlecker spent Mondays at New York's Stock Exchange, feeling the pulse of business, which fluctuated at the slightest whiff of rising gas, oil and mineral prices, and sneaky political statements leaked at the weekend to prevent panic buying and selling. He'd have lunch with a few financial heavies and promise to play golf soon. He'd stop and chat to the young whiz kids who were keen to whisper the latest hot shots. He'd send flowers to several of the CEO's personal secretaries, who'd call to thank him and pass on snippets of their hottest new investments. Networking was part of the game and Harry was an expert. He threw money around at fund-raisers and charity functions, but never enough to be vulgar. Harry was seriously wealthy and had nothing more to prove. His illustrious career had earned him the financial world's respect, and an undisputed reputation as King of Wall Street.

While Harry was out of the office on Mondays, Greta caught up with chores too time consuming to deal with on other days. Monday, October 5th however, the day after Mike and Savannah's disappearance, proved to be different. She and Harry spent the morning cancelling meetings and talking to the FBI, CIA, state police, hospitals, farmers, walkers clubs, helicopter rentals and aviation authorities, hoping for a sighting or a lead to Mike and Savannahs' whereabouts, but to no avail. At midday, Harry flew to New York City and met with someone whose name he did not disclose. Greta manned the phones and trawled through Harry's weekend emails, until she came across one that literally took her breath away. She read it again, and began pacing the office floor, wrestling with her conscience and conflict of loyalty. The email had arrived at two a.m. on Sunday, October 4th from Brimson International, a respected Wall Street investment company.

> Harry, $75,000 is in the account. Thanks. As agreed, the fax alert will arrive at 2:20 p.m. next Thursday, and will recommend PocketMoney.com buy Stella Electronics on Friday prior to the last bell. I will also attach a copy of the sensitive details you provided. Matchmaker.

Greta was aware that Harry had a dark side, which manifested itself whenever he wanted something. In that event, he would use every dirty trick in the book to possess it, even if that meant first destroying it. The Brimson email had all the hallmarks of a Harry Schlecker dirty tricks campaign, but the implication of conspiracy against PocketMoney.com was beyond the pale, even for Harry, and Greta was unsure what to do about it. She could be wrong it may be quite innocent. In any case she did not intend to confront Harry with it yet, not while Mike and Savannah were missing. Instead, she saved a copy and concealed it in her apartment. Greta had never doubted Harry's integrity, but she would review that opinion in the coming days. Meanwhile, as difficult as it was she would attend to business as usual, knowing circumstance may force her to take a course of action that would undoubtedly end their relationship, and possibly her career in the United States.

* * * * *

Devastated by Mike's disappearance Sally Brooks wept as though he were her own son. Knowing things may get worse she offered to look after Julieanne, who was inconsolable since Richard had told her that Mike was missing, feared kidnapped.

Heartbreaking words Richard hoped he'd never have to say.

As Sally prepared breakfast in the Monday morning gloom, Sheriff Carver arrived. Richard led him to the kitchen and poured some coffee. Tom was pleased to see Sally, and knew that it was just like her to help out at a time of crisis. He gave Julieanne a warm hug and said the police were doing everything possible to find her brother, but deeply disturbed, she ran up to her room in a flood of tears. Sally followed her up the stairs.

The sheriff placed a document on the breakfast bar. 'I got this from Bormont Penitentiary. It confirms Rylan Mitchell's release five weeks ago. I thought you should know,' he said, and waited.

Richard had only rubbed shoulders with Mitchell at a couple of functions, but his business reputation was not exactly a secret.

Then he made the connection.

'Christ, Harry's testimony put Mitchell away. Are you saying this is revenge? That he kidnapped Mike and Savannah?'

'I didn't say that. I'm just makin you aware it's a possibility. I've dug up some background on Mitchell. It ain't much, but it tells you what kinda guy we're dealin with if he's involved.'

'I can hardly wait.'

'His real name is Edward Laycock. He's forty-four and born in Philadelphia. He has no record of violence, but there's long list of felonies for which he served time when he was in his twenties. Then he changed his name to Rylan Mitchell and moved to New York. A few years later, he rose to celebrity status in the business world and went to all the right parties. Even got his picture on the front cover of Time magazine. This is a guy with Latin American drug trade connections who managed to smell of roses for years. Then his luck ran out and he went to jail for fraud. His lawyer asked for leniency; said he was a victim of society.'

Richard shook his head, and said, 'Yeah, well he's paid to say that, even though his client's obviously a career criminal.'

'It gets worse,' the sheriff continued. 'While he was in prison he hooked up with an ex marine, a real bad ass, who had a pal waiting for him in Houston when he was released. They're both mercenary's into war, drug running and kidnapping for a price.

Sally bustled into the kitchen. 'Carry on don't worry about me I'm making breakfast for little Julieanne.'

Richard leaned over the breakfast bar. 'Are you saying these guys are working for Mitchell, and that they kidnapped my son?'

'Hold it right there, Richard, I didn't say that, so don't start jumpin to conclusions.'

The thought of Mike and Savannah kidnapped by anyone, let alone ex cons, was a nightmare scenario, and Richard was finding it hard to be objective. 'So what are we dealing with here.'

'One is Rick Netty, six two, crew-cut blonde and got a nice scar across his face. Report says he's a psychopath. The other is Colin Wilson, five ten, bald and heavily tattooed on his arms and neck. He murdered his father when he was twelve. They're scum, and if they're involved we have reason to worry.'

Richard shook his head. It was getting worse by the minute. Mike and Savannah maybe in the hands of psycho/mercenaries, Julieanne was inconsolable, and he had yet to inform Katie, who would no doubt blame him. 'What else, Tom?'

'According to the FBI Mitchell first met Harry Schlecker at a benefit for Congressman James White. They became fast friends and he appointed Schlecker as his broker. It was then, the FBI believes, that someone introduced Mitchell to a Pentagon official, who agreed to authorise land requisitions. Whether it was Harry Schlecker or not, no one knows. Mitchell got involved in serious real estate deals and apparently made a fortune. But that all ended when Schlecker's evidence sent him away and he had to share a cell with a low life like Netty. It was a long fall into the gutter, and he must be aching for revenge. Mitchell's now a free man and seems to have kept his head down, but my gut feeling tells me he's got something to do with Mike's and Savannah's disappearance.'

'So what are you gonna do, Tom?'

'Good question. I told the FBI what I told you, but they're not convinced there even was a kidnapping.'

'What! Are you kidding?'

'No, but look at it from their point of view. There's been no ransom call and there's no evidence, other than two missing kids. Hundreds of youngsters go missing every year and most of them turn up safe and sound. If it makes you feel any better, I believe Mike was the kidnap target, not Savannah, she just happened to be there, and that this is about greed not revenge. But what I think don't mean diddlysquat. Rylan Mitchell's not even a suspect, and without any evidence we're just pointing fingers in the wind.' The Sheriff finished his coffee and headed for the door. 'Keep your spirits up, Richard, we'll find 'em. I'll see myself out.'

Richard called the FBI and spoke to agent Rachel Froy. He requested a news blackout on Mike and Savannah, to prevent hoax calls and armchair speculation, which might just antagonise the kidnappers and place them in even more danger.

Agent Froy flatly refused and went on to explain why.

'A nationwide alert will be posted later today to get a public response, which is usually positive to kidnapping, if that's what really happened. But a news blackout on a high profile citizen is virtually impossible Mr. Kinnerman. Someone always leaks the story for a few lousy bucks, and when it hits the headlines, all hell breaks loose, screwing up the investigation. I'm sorry to be so negative, sir. I'll keep you posted.' Agent Froy hung up.

At a five p.m. media briefing the FBI confirmed Mike and Savannah's sudden disappearance. Agent Froy read a statement acknowledging the FBI had listed the youngsters as missing, but added there was no evidence yet to suggest a kidnapping. The investigation was still ongoing, she explained. The story hit the U.S. six o'clock news, and minutes later it was global. Reporters camped outside the Kinnerman house and Mike's school, hoping to get a reaction from tutors or students. Julieanne was now lying in bed distraught and mildly sedated.

* * * * *

It was seven-thirty a.m. on Tuesday in Tokyo. Katie was standing alone at the panoramic window of her 40th floor office staring vacantly at the glowing city, her face pale and her eyes red and tearful. Mike and Savannah's disappearance had hit the breakfast news, and having seen their smiling faces on CNN and Japanese TV news, she was in a state of numb disbelief. Concerned about Katie's emotional state, her PA, Julia Whiteman informed Simon Wyler, one of the directors.

Simon swept into Katie's office and pulled up a chair. He had not yet seen the morning news. When Katie told him that her son was missing, believed kidnapped he was visibly shocked.

'Kidnapped! Oh my God, I'll call Andrew Stell, Katie. Take compassionate leave. You have my full support.

Katie nodded. 'I'll speak to my husband first.'

Katie called Richard's cell phone but it went to voicemail, so she left a message. Then she phoned home and spoke to Sally Brooks, who was clearly upset as she explained that Julieanne was in bed after suffering a severe asthma attack. Doctor Morton had given her a mild sedative. Richard had gone to an FBI press briefing in New York and was due home at any time.

As Simon marched out of her office, Katie called Richard's cell phone again and left another message urging him to call her. Then she checked available flights to New York.

* * * * *

Mike's best friend Moose had been lying in bed for three days suffering from some sort of bug. His computer flickered with life on his desk, but he lacked the energy to get up and play. Instead, he lay on a bunch of pillows watching cartoons while his emails piled up, of which there were currently 226 unopened.

Shocked kids around the world were calling and emailing the PocketMoney. com offices, asking for news of Mike Kinnerman. In response, a young executive posted a bulletin on the website confirming Mike and Savannah's mysterious disappearance on Sunday, October 4th, their whereabouts still unknown.

That evening, Nanny Coombes called Harry Schlecker from St Lucia. 'I've just seen the news about Savannah. I can't believe anyone would do this. It's just terrible,' she said, tearfully.

'Yeah, it is, Nanny, I was gonna call you later. It's a black day for all of us,' Harry said. 'I can't tell you what I'm feeling right now, except that I wanna kill the people who took her.'

'Jonathan's crying in Savannah's room, and our little maids, Cindy and Dorleen are heart-broken. Jeremy came to see us a few minutes ago, and I have never seen him so angry.'

'We all are, Nanny. When I get any news I'll call you.'

'We're praying for her safe return, Harry.' Nanny hung up.

Richard had hoped for good news before calling Katie, but her emotional voicemail left no doubt that she had seen the breaking story on Japanese TV. He dialled her Tokyo office and held the phone away from his ear. Katie was predictably distraught, torn between anger and heartbreak. She had warned of impending disaster if they allowed their son to go into business at such an early age, particularly with a man like Harry Schlecker.

'Mike is fourteen years old goddam it! Now he's at the mercy of lowlife murdering scumbags. How could you let that happen? Why the hell didn't you call me? My God, he could be dead by now! Dead!' she yelled, almost screaming.

Richard let Katie get it out of her system. She was furious and had every right to be. Their son had been missing for two days and she had only found out by watching CNN.

'Do we know who did this, Richard? Are the FBI involved?'

'The FBI is on the case, Katie, but there is only speculation as to who did this, and why, so let's not go there until we know.'

'It's what you're not telling me that is worrying.'

'I should have called you sooner, Katie. I am sorry. Guess I was hoping for a miracle.'

'We'll need one. Call me later,' Katie fumed, and hung up.

Richard had worked hard for a partnership at Walsome, Kent and Associates, the law firm in which he had been a litigator for eleven years. Throughout that time he had earned the respect of his peers, including judges who were quick to offer their support at a time of crisis. JB Walsome, deeply concerned about Richard, decided to have chat with him and maybe offer some advice.

At eleven the following morning, Richard took the elevator to the top floor of his firm's building. JB Walsome's PA, Annette offered a welcoming smile and escorted him to JB's office, which had a million dollar view of New York City. The two men shook hands as Annette stepped out to make coffee.

'Good to see you, Richard, though I must say you've looked better.' JB said, his face gaunt with concern.

'I've felt better,' Richard said, taking a seat facing the desk.

Richard had known JB and his wife Emily May since he left university. They adored Katie, Mike and Julieanne, and over the years JB had become a fatherly figure to Richard and they were close as can be. Both treasured that relationship.

'So how're you holding up, Richard? This terrible business must be taking you to the wire.'

'Oh I'm way past the wire,' he replied, hopelessly.

'I take it there's been no news of Mike and Savannah.'

'No. The FBI has no idea where they are. They're not even convinced there was a kidnap. Julieanne's sedated after a severe asthma attack, and Katie is out of her mind with worry in Tokyo. Things are just great, JB,' Richard said, cynically.

JB sank a little further into his leather chair and clasped his hands. 'What can I do to help, Richard?'

Annette brought in some coffee, and left, closing the door.

JB poured two strong cups and handed one to Richard.

'You're concerned about my workload with this crisis, but it's not a problem, JB, it's almost therapeutic. However, if I get a call from someone who knows where Mike and Savannah are being held captive, I'm gonna jump on a plane and go find them.'

'I've already anticipated that, Richard. I spoke to Beth about it and she's keeping me up to speed with your clients, in case I have to hand them over to one of the partners in your absence.

'Thanks, Beth knows everything I know.

'We've been close for a long time, Richard, and there's not much we can't say to one another, so let me say this. I pray to God that call comes soon. When it does, you may wind up in a foreign country chasing shadows without a friend. So allow me to remind you that you have a friend here, and if you need anything, anything at all, call me day or night and I'll arrange it.'

Richard's eyes sparkled with gratitude. JB promised to call Julieanne and Katie to reassure them that he was just a phone call away if they needed anything. The two men shook hands and parted, both knowing their friendship had deepened.

Julieanne had become withdrawn staying at home, which was unlike her, so the next morning Richard drove her to school and her eyes lit up. Pulling up at the entrance, he told her to call if she had another asthma attack, and promising to do so she ran inside waving excitedly. When he arrived to pick her up at four-thirty, she had a large group of friends around her. She climbed into the SUV and waved to them as her father drove out the campus.

Richard understood why Julieanne needed to be around her friends; they were a huge part of her life, her world. A world in which she was studying hard to be a veterinary surgeon, but since her brother's disappearance she had put her dreams on hold.

The kidnappers had gotten to her too.

Leaving the BMW in the driveway Richard and his daughter walked around back to the kitchen, where Sally Brooks was busy preparing dinner. Wrapping her arms around Julieanne she gave her a hug and helped her off with her overcoat. Richard tightened his lips; Sally truly was a Godsend. He shuffled off to his den and checked the messages, but there was nothing from Mike, Harry Schlecker, Sheriff Carver, or the FBI. Disappointed, he sat behind his desk and stared out the bay window. He had a horrible feeling that distant helicopter he heard on Sunday morning belonged to the kidnappers. He shook his head despondently.

Determined to stay positive he googled kidnappings. Current *reported* kidnaps worldwide had reached a staggering 20,000, and many never returned. Which meant that Mike and Savannah's chances of survival were slim at best, but Richard vowed never to give up. He had to believe they were alive and that good news would come from someone, somewhere, anywhere, it didn't matter. He would go to work each day and pray for that call.

Julieanne's asthma attacks had become less frequent since her return to school, and outwardly she appeared to be coping with Mike's disappearance. That evening, she opened her heart to her father for the first time in months, and realizing his little girl had grown in to a beautiful young woman, he regretted not giving her the attention she needed.

Richard held her in his arms for a long time.

Then the phone rang; it was Katie.

As soon as Katie spoke, Richard knew that she was on the edge of despair. Her voice sounded small and plaintive, and he visualised her sitting alone on the floor of a dark room.

'This is hard for me, Richard. I really don't know what to do. I just want my son back,' Katie said, tearfully.

'We have to stay strong, Katie. Kidnapping is about money, life is just a commodity. All we can do is wait for the kidnappers to call. I've arranged for our cell phones to accept collect calls. I don't know what other options we have right now.'

That was not what Katie wanted to hear. She was emotionally distraught on the other side of the world, watching reports of her son's kidnapping on CNN as if it were a bizarre soap opera.

'What if nobody calls, Richard? I have a problem sitting here in Tokyo, knowing my son is in the hands of a bunch of goddam kidnappers. I can't think, I can't eat and I can't sleep,' she said, as though she wanted to break something, anything.

Richard had no answer to give her.

Katie went on, 'I don't know the answer to this one, Richard, but I refuse to wait for a goddam phone call that may never come. We have to go find our son. I'm coming home. My flight to JFK will arrive at four-thirty p.m. on Friday, and I really need you to be there.'

It was not a request.

Richard could have told her there was nothing they could do until Mike and Savannah's whereabouts were known, or that perhaps it would be better to wait before flying around the globe on an emotionally charged sense of parental guilt. Instead, he kept those thoughts to himself, because deep down he was glad Katie was coming home, for many reasons, though he wished it were under happier circumstances. Julieanne was clearly yearning for her mother's affection, and her presence would bring a much-needed sense of unity to their fractured family.

'I'll be waiting for you at JFK, Katie.'

CHAPTER

SEVENTEEN

Rio de Janeiro, Thursday, October 8th

There had been no further contact with the kidnappers, and it looked as though life in their isolated cabin would continue until a ransom was paid, or they were killed, or both. Moored at a wharf on the port-side the boat faced seaward, which meant from their tiny cabin on the starboard quarter they could see the ocean, the marina quayside and the winding beach road to downtown Rio. Inevitably, the solitude and silent tedium gave way to listless resignation, and as the minutes turned to hours and the hours to days, they stood at the porthole watching the outside world go by, wondering if any sort of rescue was underway.

It seemed doubtful.

When footsteps approached in the passageway, they replaced their hoods and sat on the bed. One of the crew brought them a tray of food, coffee and water three times a day, which, as it was their only contact with the outside world, was an event they found themselves looking forward to. Savannah had the bottom bunk. Mike had the top. The air was stale and the beds were hard.

Frequent showers became essential.

Days were long. Nights were longer.

On Thursday morning, their fifth day of incarceration, they began to wonder if the boat would set sail or remain in Rio. When a crewmember entered the cabin with their breakfasts, Savannah spoke to him beneath her hood.

'We have been in this cabin for four days and we need some fresh air,' she complained. 'Can we go on deck?'

'No no, you stay here, maybe one more week,' the man said. 'Then you go to farmhouse till ransom is paid.'

'The guy with the crew-cut, is he still onboard?' Mike asked.

'You mean Netty.' His eyes narrowed. 'Stay away from him,' he warned, tapping Mike's hood.

The name "Netty" would now haunt him and he wished he'd never asked. 'So is the boat staying moored?'

'No, had engine problem. Had to fly part from far away. Men fitted good this morning. I think captain sails in one hour. At sea, maybe you go on deck, huh?' the man said, and locking the door he walked off down the passageway.

Mike took off his hood and paced the cabin. 'We gotta get off this boat before it sails,' he said, his voice sharp, edgy.

Savannah huffed. 'How, smile sweetly at Rylan Mitchell and plead with him to let us go?' she shot back, cynically.

'I know it sounds crazy, but we gotta figure out something.'

'What, run up to the deck and jump off the boat?'

'Why not? All we need is a diversion to keep the crew busy.'

Savannah glanced at him and shook her head. 'These men are evil and dangerous, Mike. Are you not afraid?'

'Afraid, no I'm terrified, but if we give up we're dead, and that's not gonna happen. What about starting a fire?'

Savannah stiffened; she hated fires. 'Here, in the cabin?'

'No, the bridge, if we can find a way out of here.'

'Overpower the man who brings the food. Can you do that?'

Mike's eyes narrowed. 'Yeah, if I can surprise him.'

'I will help, I can fight too.'

'Don't even think about it.'

'Why not? They are going to kill us anyway.'

'I don't think so, not until they have the ransom money.'

Savannah gazed out the porthole. 'I suppose anything is better than sitting here, but first we have to get the boat away from the wharf or the crew will chase us.'

'We'll worry about that when we're out of here.'

Using a splinter of wood Mike pierced two tiny holes in his hood, which would allow him to see where the man was standing. Their escape would take courage, an element of surprise and a portion of luck. None of which had been forthcoming lately.

Lunch came with the usual sound of boots in the passageway, but it was a different man today; he was singing. They sat on the bottom bunk, and with nervous anticipation replaced their hoods. Turning the key in the lock the man kicked open the door and let it slam against the wall. A fat, bald Chinaman with a cigarette in his mouth and wearing a filthy vest, shorts and boots walked in carrying a tray of food and closed the door with his foot.

'Lunch my young friends,' he said, cheerfully.

As a seasoned "Back Receiver" for his school junior football team Mike was fit, fast and strong. He was not a violent person by nature, but like most creatures when cornered, he could be, and this was one of those times. A matter of life or death.

As the Chinaman placed the tray on the floor with his back to them, Mike ripped off his hood, jumped up and kicked him in the crotch. Groaning, he fell forward, banging his head on the wall. Savannah took off her hood, ran to the door and opened it; the key was in the lock. The passage was clear. Staggering to his feet, the Chinaman charged at Mike, his eyes bulging like a mad man. Savannah fell to the floor and tripped him up. Mike side-kicked him and he fell, banging his head on the wooden bunk frame and passed out. Mike locked the door and threw away the key.

Turning right, they ran along the passageway and stopped at a slatted swinging door. Easing it open, Mike saw two men walking towards them, both were yelling. He quickly pushed Savannah into a nearby cabin and closed the door. The men stopped right outside and continued arguing in Portuguese.

Savannah whispered a translation.

'He is a courier for a Colombian drug cartel that owns this boat. He delivered a shipment of cocaine to the boat last night, which came via several routes, including our jet, and he wants his money,' Savannah reported. 'They are taking us to Cuba. At sea they will rendezvous with ships at night and deliver the cocaine, but the courier says he has done his job and wants no part of it. He has a family and refuses to get involved with kidnapping.'

The argument escalated and they fought fiercely, until the man agreed to pay the courier's money. Neither said anything further, and as their footsteps slowly faded down the passageway Mike and Savannah sighed with relief.

Mike whispered, 'That's why we're in Rio. This boat must be a registered tourist charter, when really it's a front to deliver cocaine for the drug cartels. It's clever, damn clever.'

Savannah looked puzzled. 'I don't understand.'

'They deliver the cocaine at sea, then sail to Cuba and hide us at a farmhouse. Weeks later, someone calls PocketMoney.com, probably from another country, and demands a ransom, but the two are not remotely connected.'

Savannah's eyes narrowed. 'What are you saying, Mike?'

'If someone does trace us to Rio, we'll be in Cuba and our chances of being found are zero. Bottom line is, no one's coming to rescue us, so we need to get off this boat, now!'

Mike opened the cabin door and gingerly put his head out; the passage was clear. They ran to the next slatted door and eased it open. There was not a soul about. The next passage, grubby and dimly lit, led them to the hold entrance in which they could hear banging and men shouting. To their right, a flight of steps led up to the deck. Savannah tugged Mike's arm and nodded for him to follow her. Reaching the top, she cautiously raised her head and looked around in the sunlight. The deck looked deserted.

She pointed to a tinted windowed hub. 'That's the bridge.'

Crouching down they crept along the varnished deck to the bridge, which, since the vessel had docked, was empty. Savannah crawled to the port-side and peeked over the trimmed rail. Mike knelt beside her. On the wharf below, wearing a peaked white hat the ship's captain stood talking to Rylan Mitchell; both seemed engrossed in the conversation. None of the kidnappers or crew appeared to be on deck, which meant they were probably below in the hold; they hoped so.

They crawled inside the bridge and peering over the window frame, Savannah took a breath. The boat was identical to one owned by Georgiou Angelis; a three-masted schooner, seventy-five metres long, with two 480 horsepower engines, seven cabins and quarters for twelve crew, which he taught her to sail when she and Harry went island hopping around the Caribbean.

She stared at the maze of electronics, trying to remember the correct procedure; it was two years ago. Then it came to her. She checked the security system; it was off. Breathing a sigh of relief, she turned the key, clicked several switches, pressed a red button and the engines sprang to life with a throaty roar.

The captain looked up at the bridge through his sunglasses, his weather beaten face lined with a questioning frown. Savannah shoved the powerful engines into forward gear, and then jammed the throttle wide open with a crowbar. The schooner suddenly jolted forward and the sound of hurried boots rumbled below. She turned to Mike, her eyes glazed with fear and exhilaration.

'Time to jump in the water,' she said, visibly shaking.

Mike found a lighter, a can of fuel and a pile of money, which he pocketed. Ordering Savannah outside, he quickly sprayed the lighter fuel over the control panel, walls and carpet and set it ablaze. The bridge exploded into fireball, and as the electronics and woodwork began to melt, they made a run for it.

As plumes of smoke poured out of the bridge, the captain and Mitchell ran for the gangplank, but as they did so, the mooring ropes snapped under the engines forward thrust, wrenching the schooner away from the wharf, and leaving the two men standing at the quayside as the gangplank fell into the sea.

Mike and Savannah raced along the deck to the rear of the boat, hoping the fire would distract the crew long enough for them to jump overboard. As the huge schooner gathered speed, taking a piece of the quayside with it, the crew arrived on deck and stared in disbelief at the mayhem; the bridge, now a blazing inferno, had smothered the boat in a thick fog of smoke.

Fearlessly jumping into the sea Savannah swam along the quayside wall. Mike tried to keep up with her, but she was like a dolphin. The crew appeared at the aft rail, yelling and shaking their fists, some considered jumping in after them, but the raging fire forced them to run back and turn on the hoses. The flames rapidly spread along the varnished deck and wooden framework, and with thousands of gallons of fuel below; the schooner was a time bomb waiting to explode. Netty and tattooed Wilson jumped onto the quayside, as the boat snapped away from its moorings and headed seaward with no one at the helm.

The schooner was worth ninety-six million dollars.

They swam through the oily seawater around the far side of the wharf and scrambled up the harbour wall's rusty ladder. High on adrenaline, they crouched down behind a metal container; their survival now depending on luck and pure instinct.

The crew prepared to abandon ship as the doomed schooner sailed on crashing into anything in its path, its throttle jammed open in the burning bridge. Unaware their captives had escaped Mitchell and the captain looked on helplessly as the blazing boat, containing a seven hundred and fifty million dollar shipment of cocaine and two American hostages, headed towards the sea in a cloud of swirling, black smoke.

Crawling behind abandoned wooden crates and barrels Mike and Savannah slipped passed Mitchell, who was too preoccupied with the burning schooner to notice them. The captain called one of the crew and told him to bring the kids ashore.

'I can't they've escaped,' the crewman yelled. 'It was those damn kids who started the fire!'

When the captain told Mitchell the kids had escaped after starting the fire, he began foaming at the mouth and smashed his cell phone on the ground. He yelled at Netty and Wilson. 'For Christ sake find those damn kids or we're dead!'

Inquisitive onlookers had gathered at the quayside, many of whom were posing for cameras, with the blazing schooner in the back round. Burying themselves among the burgeoning crowd Mike and Savannah jostled their way through, and with freedom in sight they frantically ran towards the city, hoping to disappear among its tourist crowded streets. Then their luck ran out. A huge truck suddenly pulled away from the quayside, giving Netty and Wilson a clear view of them racing away to freedom.

Heads down they charged after them.

EIGHTEEN

At the far end of the marina a young man parked his red scooter outside a café` and strolled inside, leaving the engine running. A moment later, he charged out yelling, *"Stop!"* as his scooter sped away in the traffic. Arriving at the café` Netty and Wilson leaned on their knees breathing heavily. The young man, clearly a U.S. tourist, was pacing back and forth yelling and cursing.

'What's up, kid?' Netty asked.

'Two kids, they stole my scooter,' he said, flaying his arms.

They ran back to a lock-up at the marina buildings, in which a Kawasaki silver Ninja 500 Roadster, owned by one of Netty's mercenary pals currently in Afghanistan, stood gleaming under a white sheet. Ripping off the cloth, Wilson jumped on and started the engine, which sprang to life with a high-pitched scream. Netty climbed on behind him and they sped away, tires burning along the beach road.

A loud explosion suddenly rocked the marina.

With Savannah clinging to his waist giving directions, Mike weaved the red scooter through Rio's crawling traffic. Once they had safely distanced themselves from the marina, she told him to take a right at the next turning.

'Where are we going?' he yelled, over the engine's noise.

The U.S. Consulate, Avenida Presidente Wilson. It is only a short ride from here,' Savannah explained. 'Turn right at those traffic lights. The building is further down on the right.'

They caught a red light. Mike pulled up and searched for a hostile face among the crowd crossing over. The lights went to green. He took a right and followed the road for half a mile or so.

'There, on the right.' Savannah yelled, pointing to a U.S. flag outside a white building with a black metal-rail fence.

'Okay, we'll dump the scooter and run for the door.'

Mike slowed as they neared the consulate, oblivious to the silver Kawasaki racing towards them. In that split second, a small boy ran onto the road. His mother screamed and ran after him. Savannah yelled, 'Cuidado! (*Look out!*)

Wilson turned to avoid hitting the boy and his mother and the Kawasaki skidded off the road onto the sidewalk and crashed into the consulate's iron railing fence, throwing Wilson and Netty to the ground. Dragging her son off the road, the distraught mother hurried away, clutching his hand and nervously glancing back as the two men struggled to get up.

Savannah stiffened with dread. 'Mike, they are getting up we have to go! They will not let us reach the consulate!'

'Okay, hold tight!' he yelled, revving up to pull away. Then a marine stepped out of the consulate door and surveyed the scene. Mike waved to him. 'Hey, over here, we need help!'

The marine walked forward and stopped; his eyes hard and staring. 'What's goin on out here?' he asked, with attitude.

Wilson stood up and showed the flat of his hands. 'A kid ran into the road and we're a little banged up, that's all.'

Savannah yelled, 'No, he is lying. Help us, please!'

Netty stood up and with blood dripping from his face he ran to the scooter and lunged at Savannah, who screamed in terror as Mike slammed it into gear and raced away. Picking up the dented Kawasaki, Wilson climbed on and started the engine.

The marine yelled, 'Hey you! Wait a minute!' He marched forward. 'I said, wait a minute!'

Ignoring him Netty jumped on and they screeched away.

The marine tried to get the licence plate but it was moving too fast. Shaking his head, he marched back inside the consulate.

After a nerve-racking journey through Rio's crowded streets, which for part of the way they joined a group of kids weaving their scooters through the traffic, Savannah told Mike to turn left. He did so and pulled over at a payphone in a tree-lined street packed with cars parked bumper to bumper. Savannah ran to the payphone. Mike joined her, leaving the engine running.

Savannah told the operator that she had escaped after being kidnapped, and pleaded with her to make a reverse charge call. The recent kidnapping of her daughter's school friend prompted the operator to help her, and after illegally connecting her to a U.S. operator friend Richard Kinnerman's cell phone rang. She handed Mike the phone and went outside to keep a lookout.

A whining motorcycle suddenly entered the street. Savannah froze and held her breath as the Kawasaki raced up behind her and screamed passed stopping a hundred yards away.

Then it spun a round.

For a split second, she stared at it unable to move.

Richard took the call. 'Mike! Mike! Is that you?' he yelled, glancing at his son's photo, hardly daring to breath.

The Kawasaki mounted the sidewalk at the end of the street and raced towards the payphone. Netty clenched his teeth as streams of blood ran down his face from a gash on his forehead.

'Yeah, Dad, it's me! We've been kidnapped!'

Richard sprang to his feet. 'Oh, Christ, where the hell are you, Mike!' he yelled, but his voice was lost when Savannah entered the booth screaming, 'Mike! They found us! Quick, we have to go!' Richard yelled into his phone. 'Mike! Talk to me, please! What's happening, where are you?'

Mike's body went rigid when he saw the Kawasaki hurtling towards him along the sidewalk w,ith bloody-faced Netty and a tattooed man onboard. 'Dad we're.....oh shit!' he dropped the phone, leaving it swinging and ran out to the scooter.

The Kawasaki screeched to a halt beside the payphone. Netty jumped off and hurled himself at Savannah, but Mike was already racing away, engine burning. Blocked in by parked cars tattooed Wilson raced along the sidewalk, looking for a space to re-enter the road, by which time the scooter had vanished.

Richard gripped the phone, his mind in overdrive. He'd heard Savannah screaming, men yelling obscenities, terror in Mike's voice and a screaming motorcycle. He kept calling Mike's name into the swinging payphone, hoping that he might return and tell him where they are, then someone entered the phone booth and replaced the receiver. Richard tried tracing the call but it was hopeless. Slamming down the phone he began pacing back and forth, his head spinning with both relief and anxiety. Mike had confirmed their kidnapping, but having managed to escape they were on the run and in grave danger, but who was chasing them, and where were they?

It was one a.m. in Tokyo when Richard informed Katie of Mike's horrifying call. Sobbing with relief, she demanded to know every detail. The call lasted an hour.

* * * * *

Following Savannah instructions Mike drove through a maze of Rio's backstreets, cluttered with washing lines, car wrecks and overfilled trashcans, before pulling up in an alley behind a shabby apartment block. Savannah jumped off, leaned on her knees and vomited. Then she looked at Mike, her eyes glazed with terror.

'We have to leave Rio, Mike. If they find us, they will kill us,' Savannah said, unable to stop her hands shaking. 'I mean it.'

'I know, I know, I'm scared too, but we did it, Savannah, we got away from those creeps. If I can let my dad know where we are he'll come looking for us.'

'No! Listen to me, Mike; this may be our only chance to get away. We have to leave now!' Savannah yelled.

'Hold on. Why don't we *call* the U.S. Consulate?'

'How, from another payphone? We did that and it almost got us killed,' Savannah snapped. She'd clearly had enough.

'Then let's go to one of the big hotels. We'll explain that we were kidnapped and need the consulate to pick us up.'

'A hotel? You mean sit in the lobby and wait for the marines to arrive? If Mitchell is no longer on the boat, then he is in one of the hotels. Netty will be watching for us at the U.S. Consulate, while the crew and God knows how many others are out there searching for us. Mitchell will not stop until he finds us, Mike. He will go to jail for life if we get away. Comprende?'

There was that anger again. 'Okay, we'll go to the cops?'

Savannah shook her head derisively. 'You do not understand. South America has a serious kidnapping problem with powerful drug cartels and corruption at every level of society, and you want to go to the police? If we stay in Rio, **WE DIE!**'

Mike breathed out heavily. 'What dyou wanna do?'

'Head for Brasilia. There is a U.S. Embassy there. When we are far away from Rio and feel safe, we will call for help.'

Mike nodded. 'Okay, but I've gotta contact my dad.'

Savannah relented. Mike had just spoken to his father and he was clearly emotional. 'Alright, what do you have in mind?'

'A computer store to send an email.'

'Why not steal a cell phone.'

'No, we're amateurs. We'll get beat up, or wind up in a police cell, or worse. We could buy one. Where's the nearest store?'

'No idea, but I do know a computer store. Then we leave.'

Savannah directed Mike through more of Rio's backstreets, acutely aware that Mitchell, Netty and others were combing the city determined to hunt them down. One more mistake and they would never leave Rio alive, of that she was certain.

Wilson pulled over and parked the Kawasaki at the roadside. Netty jumped off and called Mitchell. 'We lost 'em,' he said, pacing the sidewalk.

A police car sped by, its siren wailing down the street.

'You lost 'em? You lost 'em? Netty, if they get away we're dead. Go find them. They gotta be somewhere in Rio.'

'I don't think so,' Netty said, coolly. 'They got hold of a kid's red scooter and I reckon they're heading north.'

'Damn it! Okay, I'll call Lucan, he'll find them. Meet me at the heliport.' Mitchell hung up and dialled a number.

'The third ring a husky voice answered. 'Mitchell?'

'Yeah, I need you to find someone in Rio, it's urgent.'

'Who is it?' Lucan growled. He was a corrupt undercover cop for Rio's serious crime squad and the pay was lousy.

'Two American kids; boy and a girl, both fourteen. They ran away and I want you to find them. Five thousand dollars cash.'

'Mmm, five thousand dollars,' Lucan said, pondering over the price. He liked Mitchell to think that he was doing him a favour. 'I'll find them, but if it's the two American kids I saw on TV, the price just doubled, and I won't need a photo.'

'You're a real piece of work, you know that? Okay, it's a deal, but I want them back in one piece, you got that?'

Lucan chuckled. 'How long they been gone?'

'A half hour, they stole a red scooter. They're heading north. Call me when you find 'em. I'll pick them up in the chopper.'

'Bring the money.'

Savannah pointed to a multi-story car park and told Mike to drive up the ramp to level five, knowing few cars used that level due to the burning sun. Ducking beneath the barrier, they sped through each level to the top and pulled up between two large trashcans. Savannah jumped off the scooter and paced back and forth, her face pale with anxiety.

Mike joined her. 'Hey, we'll be okay, I promise. Here, take this,' he said, handing her the money he found on the boat.

'200 Reais is about 114 dollars. At least we can eat tonight,' she said, folding the money into her jeans pocket.

'Wait, it gets better,' Mike said, removing one of his Nike's. He lifted the insole and pulled out his American Express card wrapped in polythene and elastic bands.

Savannah's face lit up. She had one just like it in her lost purse. 'With this we can stop at a hotel on the way to Brasilia; there are many. There we can eat, call for help from the safety of our room and rest overnight. Then hopefully, someone will come and rescue us. I still think we should leave now.'

'No, let's send the email. Then we'll get outa here.'

A Fiat saloon drove up the ramp and they held their breath as it parked nearby. An ageing couple climbed out and glanced at Savannah, whose sullen look no doubt gave the impression that she and Mike were having a lovers tiff. The woman smiled as she and the elderly man shuffled to the elevators.

'I will send the email, Mike. You will get lost in the shopping mall. Tell me Moose's email address,' Savannah demanded.

Mike knew that sending an email to his father, who rarely used his laptop and had no interest in social networks, would not be the best option. Moose on the other hand, a computer fanatic, would see the email right away and pass it on, and with only a few seconds in which to send it, he was a much safer bet.

He shook his head. 'No, it's too dangerous.'

'Give me one of those rubber bands,' Savannah ordered.

Tying her long, dark hair back into a ponytail she stared at a nearby empty parking space. 'My father used to park our green Volkswagen there and read the newspaper, while mother and I went shopping in the mall,' she said, her eyes misty with fond memories. 'I am sorry, Mike, I told you this would be difficult for me,' she whimpered.

Mike held her in his arms. 'I know, its okay, its okay.'

Sniffling, she wiped her eyes. 'How do I look?'

'Is that a trick question? I've wanted to say this ever since we first met; I love the sound of your voice, your sunshine smile, those big blue eyes, the way you get mad sometimes and…

Savannah kissed him on the lips for the very first time. It was a moment that he would never forget. 'Me too,' she whispered. 'Now wait here. I will be back in ten minutes.'

Feeling as though he could fly but also racked with guilt for allowing Savannah to endanger her life, Mike watched her walk to the elevator and press the call button. When the doors pinged and slid open, she looked at Mike and smiled.

Then she was gone.

CHAPTER

NINETEEN

Harry Schlecker had requested an urgent meeting with Richard and the trustees at nine a.m. on Thursday, and when he and Greta entered the boardroom at eight-fifty, they were sitting around the table with their arms folded. Quickly dispensing with the morning pleasantries Harry sat down and opened a thick folder.

Greta felt a knot in the pit of her stomach. If the Brimson email was true, then Harry was about to implement a conspiracy.

Penny Bowman spoke 'This is a sad day. We're all praying for Mike and Savannah's safe return. If we can help, just ask.'

'Thanks,' Harry said, busying himself with paperwork to hide his emotion. Greta handed him strong coffee. 'At least we know their alive, thank God. Right now, all we can do is hope the FBI get a lead on their whereabouts. In the meantime, as tough as it is, it's gotta be business as usual.' Harry sipped his coffee.

Richard added, 'I have to admit this has taken me to the wire. Mike means more to me than I can put into words. That phone call from him tore me apart, and I lie awake at night, wondering how they're surviving, or if I'll ever see him again.'

The trustees nodded sombrely. A short silence followed.

Harry stood up. 'As you know, since Mike and Savannah's kidnapping share sales have rocketed. Add to that several major hits on the stock market, this company now has thirty-six billion dollars in fluid assets. I'm proposing that you invest in a company called Stella Electronics. Hand out the papers, Greta.'

The trustees glanced at one another. Richard ran his fingers through his hair unsure if he could handle this today.

Harry continued, 'This document will tell you that Stella's shares have gone south and they're in trouble. They've managed to stay afloat by selling a few foreign assets, but if they continue on that road they'll be dead in six months. Their government aviation and naval electronics contracts are about to end due to an incoming president, and rumours at Wall Street suggest an undisclosed company will get the new contracts, meaning Stella's out in the cold. But that's bullshit, someone's lighting fires.'

'So what's the bottom line, Harry? Sounds like it'll take more than money to solve their problems?' Richard commented.

Harry went on, 'Stella employs around one hundred thousand people worldwide, so they need a lot of cash for monthly pay checks. They have contracts in many countries, plus assets in oil, gas and pharmaceuticals, but when the bank found out Stella was losing its U.S. contracts they walked away, leaving them with no cash, which smells of dirty politics. Stella's been a favourite with the government for years, but someone obviously wants that to change. If they can find a buyer that understands their market they're back in business. The usual cronies are predicting a landslide election, and the favourites are already throwing their weight around, so it's time for a little strategic manoeuvring. I can lobby my sources at the Pentagon for the new contracts, so we won't have to deal with this new bunch of crooks.'

Penny studied her nails; others cleaned their glasses.

Harry drained his coffee and went on. 'Most of what I've just told you about Stella is common knowledge, which means that other companies are gonna bid. So I looked at their books, and after meeting with the directors, they agreed to go with us, albeit in principle. However, if we don't make an offer in writing today, they'll have no choice but to go to auction, which is virtually a hostile takeover. Their lawyers are waiting for our offer. If they accept, buy Stella tomorrow. Our lawyers are prepared to handle phase one of the purchase over the weekend. I know it's short notice, but you're gonna have to trust me on this one.'

Silence.

Fingernails tapped, some glanced at their watches. Greta sat still, wrestling with her conscience. A helicopter clattered past the windows. At the central desk, secretaries were busy taking calls and messages. Harry sat back and folded his arms.

Trustee Jenny Grant, all business in a white blouse and black skirt, got to her feet. 'Harry, you're a very smart guy and highly respected at Wall Street, but this just doesn't add up.' she said, leaning over the table. 'You're asking us to buy a company that is all but dead in the water for how much?'

'Six point eight billion dollars,' Harry confirmed, as though it were loose change.

The trustees breathed out and shuffled uncomfortably. Jenny shook her head disparagingly. 'Well I can give you my answer right now, and that's a firm negative,' she stated, without any hint of compromise and sat down.

The others unanimously agreed. Stella Electronics was in free-fall on the stock market, and to gamble on its recovery would be sheer madness. Greta saw the storm in Harry's eyes, he was clearly preparing for verbal combat.

The scent of perfume and coffee hovered around the table like a dark chocolate. The trustees scribbled useless notes on company notepads. Harry pulled off his tie and began pacing the room. He was famous for using his hands to express himself, and the louder he spoke the more animated he became.

'Lemme ask you this; dyou trust me?' A resounding yes was the response. 'Okay, then ignore the figures and listen to what I'm sayin!' he yelled, taking a stance at the head of the table. 'I helped build this company and I thought you, the trustees, had the balls to make it a giant, but when I put the best deal in town on the table, along with my credibility you….'

Fearless lawyer, Penny Bowman refused to be lectured by anyone. 'That's enough, Harry! You've had your little tantrum. We'll conduct business as we see fit, that's why we're here. You're the broker, remember?' she said, her eyes steely cold.

'You're damn right. I'm also the guy who recommended you as a trustee, so don't talk to me as if I just got off the boat. If your head wasn't so far up your ass you'd see it was a good deal.'

Penny jumped up and ripped off her red glasses. 'You know what Harry? You can always tell when someone comes from the gutter; the stench never leaves them,' she snapped, gathering up her papers. Jenny Grant attempted to calm her down

'Sit down, Penny, this is not a courtroom,' Harry barked.

'I will not sit down, nor will I be spoken to like that by you or anyone else! Just who the hell do you think you are?'

'I'm the broker, remember?'

Stock market analyst Mike Coswell, a karate black belt, spoke up. 'Your art of persuasion is not exactly subtle, Harry. We all have a point of view here, so let's respect that.'

'Fine, let's cut to the chase. I'm offering you an investment opportunity worth zillions, and you're looking at me as though I'm a contagious disease.'

Richard had heard enough. 'Harry, the trustees may disagree with you, but that doesn't undermine your credibility.'

'Oh, but it does, Richard. This is not a game where two-bit lawyers argue over petty legalities; this is the real world. Dyou think the market gives a shit about points of law, or being fair. No! They eat up little guys and spit em out for profit, and if that ain't why we're here, then we're all wasting our time.'

Company accountant Winston Bliss stood up and banged his black fist on the table. 'Thanks for the lecture, Harry, but you're wrong damn it! This company was built on integrity, and I will not allow that to be tampered with.'

A few murmured in agreement. Penny seethed steamily.

'I'm rarely wrong, Winston, and you know that,' Harry said, intimating at his legendary Wall Street status.

'Then what are you sayin; that we got no opinion here?' Winston said, using his baritone voice like a weapon.

'No, I'm telling you to look at the facts, the bigger picture.'

Penny lit a cigarette. She was trying to quit, but not today. Greta offered her some coffee and a neutral smile.

Richard decided to intervene; someone had to be the devil's advocate. 'I think the deal's risky at best, Harry.'

'You're wrong, Richard. Stella's a goddam platinum deal, but this board is weak, it has no guts, no killer instinct.'

'Take a deep breath, Harry, you're crossing a line here,' Mike Coswell cautioned, and standing up he walked to the window.

'Harry crossed that line the day he opened his mouth,' Penny Bowman sniped, venomously.

Jenny Grant spoke from her chair. 'It must be nice living way up there in the o-zone layer, Harry. Why don't you tell us lesser mortals how to win the goddam lottery, because that's exactly what you're asking us to do.'

Malcolm Connors, elder of the trustees, stood up and offered the flat of his hands. 'Look, this is getting us nowhere. We're all supposed to be on the same team, that's why we're here, so let's try and be reasonable shall we.'

A debate of sorts continued, but an underlying contempt for Harry's heavy-handedness remained, so he lowered the bar.

'Penny's right. I *am* the broker, and in six months we've done pretty well, some would say remarkable. But when you stop taking my advice I may as well not be here. So I'll say it again, you'll just have to trust me on this one,' Harry said, calmly.

More silence

The heated bickering had stopped but tempers remained short, and so to defuse the anger Richard suggested a short break. Harry was clearly not about to give way, and his arrogant stance backed up by his legendary track record had sown enough seeds of doubt to suggest that he might even be right about Stella.

Harry said that he had something to attend to and would be back in fifteen minutes. Reaching the door, he turned to face the trustees. 'I know you'll do the right thing,' he said, and calmly walked out, closing the door behind him.

Richard told the trustees to disregard the heated sentiment and resume their discussion. Greta circled the table with coffee in an attempt to defrost the room, and wondered where Harry had gone as there was nothing in his diary. She no longer trusted him.

Harry returned exactly fifteen minutes later, and closing the door he leaned against it, hands in his jacket pockets. 'So, what's it gonna be?' he said, flexing his eyebrows.

Mike Connors clarified the board's decision. 'We've agreed to go with you on this, Harry, but only with a view to peeling off the deadwood, turning the company around and selling it as soon as we can make a profit.'

Harry nodded. 'You might wanna rethink that later. Make an offer today. If they accept, buy it tomorrow just before close of business. That'll delay any counter offers until Monday, by which time we'll have a protocol established, and phase one of the contract signed. On Monday, we'll announce that we bought the company. The Wall Street boys will huff and puff, but so what.'

'What if they don't like our offer?' Penny Bowman asked.

Harry smiled. 'Trust me, they will.'

Greta's back stiffened. Harry's telling smile confirmed her belief that he was involved in a conspiracy, but she would need more than gut feelings and a tenuous email to prove it.

Richard had a few queries about the Stella deal but he knew that would lead to another war, which seemed pointless when the trustees had decided to go along with it. Besides, his mind was elsewhere: a payphone in a foreign country.

Executive maid Trina Cano served their lunch, after which discussions on the Stella Electronics deal began in earnest. If the morning had been challenging, the afternoon would take them to the wire. Penny Bowman dictated the company's offer to her PA, Wendy Berryman, who typed the first draft and handed a copy to Richard, the trustees and Harry for their approval. At four-thirty, after several amendments, Penny Bowman faxed the agreement to Stella's board of directors, and their lawyers.

Stella would notify the trustees later that evening if they were happy with the offer, which seemed likely.

With business of the day concluded, a sense of relief filled the boardroom. The air had cleared, but only until the next brawl, of which there would no doubt be many. The Stella fiasco had left the trustees with a bitter taste of resentment for Harry's arrogant stance. Nevertheless, beneath the theatrical indignation a growing sense of belief that it might even prove to be a good deal secretly smouldered. If so, bruised egos would soon heal.

Greta and Wendy gathered up the reference paperwork and filed it away. Harry informed his pilot they were about to leave. The trustees put on their coats, and agreeing to call one another that evening they strolled out to the elevator. Harry and Greta took the stairs up to the heliport.

Richard called his office and spoke to Beth, who was on red alert for any contact from Mike, and together they went through next week's diary. Then he checked the messages at home, but there was nothing new. He was hoping that Mike would find a way to call again, but he had obviously not been able to, which was even more cause for concern.

The elevator took him down to the basement parking facility, where his BMW stood in line among an assortment of SUV's. Having spent his entire working life in New York City Richard had yet to get used to the traffic, and doubted he ever would. He drove through the barrier and crawled through Manhattan, taking several calls from clients before joining the home crowd on the freeway, which as usual was gridlocked. With no choice but to sit behind a long line of tail lights barely visible in the autumnal mist and fog of gasoline fumes, Richard replayed that chilling collect phone call in his mind; Savannah's terrified screams, the high-pitched whine of a powerful motorcycle, violent men yelling obscenities and the terror in Mike's voice.

Then worst of all, the silence.

CHAPTER

TWENTY

Rio de Janeiro, Thursday, October 8th

Rio de Janeiro's once grand municipal building was now a 21st century shopping mall, but somewhere within its walls the musty smell of old courtrooms and offices still lingered in the air. There was a sale on that day and the mall was heaving with shoppers all looking for a bargain.

Savannah stared at the elevator wall as shoppers entered and departed at each floor. When the doors opened at ground level, a wave of those desperate to part with their money swept her out into the bustling mall. Burying herself in the crowd she strolled along the marble floor avoiding eye any contact.

Extron Computers had a promotion going on that day with an open invitation to come in and browse. Outside, amid bunches of coloured balloons, two young girls in short skirts were handing out leaflets. Savannah took one and strolled inside.

The store was full of youngsters and techie-types huddling over the latest gadgetry. Wandering down the aisles she noticed a laptop with google on its screen and made a b-line for it. A sales assistant wearing a white name-tag *Ricardo* strode over showing some teeth and offered to help. Pretending to know very little about computers Savannah chose a top-of-the-range and asked for detailed information; price no object. Ricardo explained the basic features and left her to think about it while he pounced on another potential customer. Seizing her chance, Savannah returned to the laptop, and opening email she entered Moose's address and began typing the message: *Moose, its Mike. We've been kidnapped. Call my Dad. Tell him we've escaped and we're…* A hand grabbed her arm; it was Ricardo, and this time he wasn't smiling.

'This store is not an internet café young lady,' he growled, and dragging her to the door he shoved her outside. 'Come back when you want to buy something,' he said, and hurried inside.

Cupping her hands around her eyes Savannah looked through the window. Ricardo was pushing his way through the crowd to the laptop. She could just see her unsent message flickering on the screen. A group of kids were laughing and pointing to it. *Press send please*, she whispered. Ricardo had almost reached the laptop when one of boys moved the cursor to the send button. *Don't touch it!* He yelled. The boy froze, but a young girl in the group cocked her nose defiantly and clicked send.

The message was now at Moose's house in New Mayford.

Waving the youngsters away, Ricardo turned off the laptop. Savannah took the elevator to level five, and as she stepped out of the opening doors, Mike ran over to meet her. 'What happened, are you okay?' he asked, concerned about her.

'I was thrown out before I could finish the message, but I said that we were kidnapped and have escaped. I saw the email go. If Moose really *is* a genius, then he will know it came from Brazil.'

Mike nodded. 'Trust me, he'll know. Are you okay?'

'Yes. Now we must go. I will drive,' she said, climbing onto the scooter. 'I have one thing to do before we leave Rio.'

Using a maze of backstreets Savannah drove to a picturesque suburb on the outskirts of Rio, and weaving her way through its tree-lined avenues she stopped at an arched gateway, and looked up at the sign before parking under a tree inside the gates.

It was a vast cemetery; a place of tranquillity where dreams had ended and only memories remained. They passed old women dressed in black sobbing on their knees at the graveside of lost ones. Bouquets of colourful flowers lay in abundance all around and candles silently flickered below photographs of the deceased attached to their headstones. Statues of cherubs and angels kept watch over the endless lines of neatly tended plots, which were forever silent but for the sound of birds singing.

Clutching Mike's arm Savannah led him through a labyrinth of neatly manicured pathways. He glanced at her in the unspoken silence; her face was pale with solemnity. Then she froze, placing her hands to her mouth and stared at a black marble grave. Fresh flowers lay at the headstone, and she frowned as though puzzled by who might have placed them there. Hesitantly, she stepped forward and knelt beside the beautiful grave. Then lowering her head, she whispered a prayer and began to sob.

There were two gold lettered names on the headstone: Pedre and Gabriel Cordeiro. Realizing Savannah's murdered parents lay there Mike inhaled deeply, suddenly overcome by the enormity of her loss. Savannah was only nine years old when she last saw their grave on the day of the funeral, and had never grieved. Mike moved away to allow her some privacy, but he could still hear the heart-wrenching sound of her sobbing. He glanced back and saw her lying across the grave hugging the stone, with tears running down her face. He could find no words to describe the moving scene, except perhaps that she was a child again, grieving at last for her beloved mother and father.

After barely moving for some time, Savannah gently kissed the headstone and rose to her feet. She looked at Mike, her eyes glistening with pain, and threw her arms around his neck. Neither said a word as they walked arm in arm to the gateway in the eerie silence. Savannah climbed on the scooter and revving the engine as though it were her soul speaking, she drove out through the gates savouring the comfort of Mike's arms around her.

It was time to let go. She would never forget them.

At the next junction, Savannah turned left onto highway BR 040, the main artery to Brasilia, which an overhead sign indicated was 753 kilometres; 430 miles. Knowing that driving a scooter on a busy highway was extremely dangerous she hugged the grass verge. Huge trucks, buses and cars thundered by inches away on the cracked tarmac, which the blazing sun had partially melted, leaving a haze of carbon monoxide hovering over it in the humid air. Nevertheless, convinced their long journey home had begun they embraced the warm breeze in their faces, and with the sprawling countryside passing by on either side their newfound freedom was almost overwhelming.

Brasilia 753 kilometres

* * * * *

Lucan took highway BR 101 out of Rio, which followed the coast northward to the port of Vitoria. Wearing a checked shirt, jeans, boots, a baseball cap and sunglasses he could be mistaken for a farmer. His rusty red Toyota pick-up truck looked as though it should have been scrapped years ago, but under the hood was a four hundred brake horse-powered engine and when he put his foot down nobody passed him. He pulled over and stared at the road. Mitchell said the kids were heading north, but intuition told him they would not risk leaving on a boat they would head for a U.S. Embassy. Crossing the central barrier he drove back to the junction and turned right onto highway BR 040 to Brasilia.

Twenty miles out of Rio Savannah noticed a red Toyota in the rear-view mirror. A few miles further on it was still there.

'I think someone is following us, Mike.' she yelled.

Mike glanced back and saw the Toyota some distance behind them. 'Get off the road as soon as you can,' he ordered.

A sign indicated a parking area ahead. Savannah drove in and pulled up outside a café, which had closed. An arrow for "Devil's Leap" pointed to a narrow pathway across the fields.

'This is a parking lot for walkers. If we go under the barrier and follow the track, we can hide until our stalker has gone.'

'Okay, go for it,' Mike said, over the engine noise.

Keeping an eye on the mirror Savannah sped along the dusty walker's path through the arid field. Then her heart sank when she saw the Toyota crash through the hedgerow and race towards them, leaving a cloud of dust in its wake. She opened the throttle until the scooter's engine screamed at the edge of its capacity. Mike looked back at the Toyota and wondered who was chasing them, Mitchell's men or someone even more sinister?

Savannah didn't see the river until they were almost upon it, and only at the last second did she manage to avoid disaster and follow its snaking bank. Now, with the river on their left and the Toyota closing behind them it looked as though their luck was finally about to run out. A narrow wooden bridge for cattle and walkers appeared up ahead. Mike yelled at her to cross over, but as she slowed to take a left turn onto the bridge, the Toyota raced up behind them and rammed the scooter's rear wheel. Savannah lost control and screamed as the rear fender crashed against the bridge's corner post. Mike fell to the ground, but fortunately was unhurt. Jumping to his feet he dragged the scooter away from the post and climbed back on.

'Go!' he yelled, looking behind him for the Toyota.

Savannah opened the throttle but the engine spluttered and died. The Toyota pulled up at the bridge. She pressed the starter. Nothing. The driver's door opened. She crossed herself, pressed it again and the engine sprang to life. Slamming it into gear she sped across the bridge, turned right and followed the track along the riverbank. Unable to cross the bridge the Toyota maintained a parallel pursuit on the opposite side of the river. Mike captured a mental snapshot of a dark-haired man with a down-turned mouth staring at them beneath his sunglasses. The man grinned and gave him a fingertip salute.

The path suddenly veered left up a rocky mountainside, and as the scooter strained against the upward slope, the Toyota spun around and headed back towards the highway.

'He's gone, keep going!' Mike yelled, but moments later, the scooter puttered to a halt. He jumped off and looked at the fuel gage; it was empty. 'Damn it! I should have checked. How stupid is that? Well we can't go back we'll just have to keep going.'

Savannah nodded. 'This path will take us over the mountain and back to the highway. There we can find a hotel and hide.'

Abandoning the scooter they trekked up the mountain path until it was nothing more than a narrow track with a sheer drop on the right. It looked bleak ahead and on a path that seemed to be going nowhere, they had almost reached the point of turning back when a yawning tunnel loomed ahead. They crept through the dripping cavern to a gravelled area, where a tiny path snaked left around a cliff face, and a waterfall thundered from above into swirling river far below. Having no choice but to follow the tiny pathway, they gripped one another's hand and nervously inched their way around the winding cliff face, and then to their horror they found themselves standing at a dead end with their backs pressed against a towering wall of rock on a tiny ledge named "Devil's Leap"

Lucan called Mitchell. 'I found the kids.'

'Where are they?'

'On a cliff called Devil's Leap. I'm at the top and can see them, but I can't get to them by car, so get the chopper out here.'

'Okay, the pilot knows where it is. We're ten minutes away,' Mitchell said, and hung up.

Having slowly inched their way back around the cliff face to safe ground, Mike and Savannah sighed with relief.

'Can you believe it? After all that we hit a dead end. I should have checked the fuel,' Mike grumbled, venting his anger.

'It is not your fault I was driving,' Savannah said, scanning the distant landscape. 'I have a feeling that the man following us is working for Rylan Mitchell, and he is close by.'

'You're probably right, and if we're gonna get out of this we have a decision to make.' Mike said, staring at the nearby cliff.

Savannah walked to the edge and looked down at the murky swirling river far below. 'You decide.'

They paced back and forth glancing at one another until a distant clattering helicopter forced them to make a decision. Mike looked up the rugged mountainside; surely there must be another way out, steps, a pathway, something. Then he caught a glimpse of Lucan watching them through binoculars.

'Holy shit, you were right. I just saw the guy who was tailing us. He's up there, at the top of the waterfall.'

'And that will be Rylan Mitchell,' Savannah said, pointing to the distant helicopter heading towards them.

They had only one choice left.

Mike looked pale. 'Are you okay, with heights I mean?'

'No, not really, hold my hand,' Savannah lied.

'Okay, don't look down.' he said, swallowing his fear.

Nervously gripping one another's hand they walked to the cliff edge, and with a huge rush of adrenaline jumped into mid air. For a split second it felt as though they were in slow motion, but as they fell faster and faster, their clothes pinned to their bodies and Savannah's hair blowing wildly behind her, the murky river came hurtling towards them. Then everything went black as they crashed beneath the deep swirling water.

Lost in the murky darkness they let go of one another's hands. Mike burst to the surface gasping for air as the current swept him away. Then Savannah surfaced, and realizing Mike was in trouble she frantically swam after him. Lying backwards she held up his head as the raging torrent tossed them about like dolls amid the floating debris. Coughing and spluttering they helplessly drifted downstream holding on to one another.

In what seemed like an eternity the river eventually narrowed and the ferocious current, now tamed by a barrier of rocks, gently washed them onto a pebbly shore a mile or so downriver. They crawled out of the water and collapsed on the riverbank in the blazing afternoon sun. A dense forest bordered the shoreline and the air was thick with mosquitoes. Somewhere in the distance the relentless waterfall thundered like a giant turbine as they lay exhausted on the desolate riverbank, wondering if this was where their lives would end.

The clatter of a helicopter echoed along the river, and Mike knew that it could only be Rylan Mitchell. Struggling to his feet he looked left along the shoreline. A concrete bridge stood some distance away, which he guessed was the highway, and parked by the railing was the red Toyota; the driver had obviously followed them downriver. He pulled Savannah to her feet and they quickly scrambled into the forest. Hidden in thick, low-hanging trees they watched the helicopter hover over the river, with Rylan Mitchell standing at the open side door scanning the riverbank through his binoculars. Netty and tattooed Wilson were kneeling beside him waiting to pounce. They would show no mercy.

Both knew their only hope of escape was to go deeper into the thick forest, and so they set off in search of a pathway through its giant weeds and dense vegetation. They were making headway when caution forced them to stop at a large, brown swamp, which stank of decay and may be home to *Jacare* (alligators) Savannah warned. They stood very still before carefully stepping around it, but after years of natural decay the rotting bank suddenly gave way and Mike slipped into the thick slime up to his neck.

'Mike! Stay very still!' Savannah screamed, lying face down at the swamp's edge. She frantically reached for his hand, but he kept sinking until only his face was visible. She grabbed a fallen branch and held it out to him, but he just looked at her with helpless resignation and sank beneath the bubbling slime.

A pair of yellow eyes rippled in the swamp some distance away and disappeared beneath the surface.

Frantically plunging her arm into the thick sludge Savannah desperately fished around for Mike's hand but it wasn't there. He had gone. Panicking, she tearfully began screaming his name.

'Mike! Come back. Please come back!'

'Swamp quicksand, mind out!' The man said, crashing to the ground beside her and stretching out his arm.

Too stunned to respond Savannah moved aside and held her breath as the man plunged his muscular arm into the slime and fished around for a hand. Long moments passed. Then he pulled Mike to the surface covered in brown sludge and sucking in air. Savannah almost wept with relief. Dragging Mike onto the bank he turned him on his side. Disorientated and stinking of rotting vegetables he lay in the long grass hawking for breath.

Something suddenly moved in the tree above Savannah. The man had also seen it. 'I want you to slowly back away,' he said, pulling Mike out of harms way.

Savannah looked up and froze with fear as a huge black and yellow snake slithered down a thick branch towards her. Terrified, she slowly stood up and backed away towards the man, who now held a revolver in his hand. The long snake hung motionless from the branch and stared at her, its eyes black and lifeless and its fanged mouth wide open ready to strike.

'That's right, keep walking this way,' the man said, calmly, leaning against a tree in a khaki uniform with his arms folded and the pistol back in its shoulder holster. He looked about thirty, six-feet two with blonde hair and spoke with an English accent.

Unable to stop her hands from shaking Savannah knelt beside Mike, who was still clearing his lungs, and said, 'Who are you?'

'No need to be afraid,' he said, offering the flat of his hands. Savannah sensed there was something dangerous about him; an air of calmness, a confidence in his voice, a demeanour borne of those with military experience.

Mike coughed. 'Thanks for fishing me out. I'm real glad you were here. But why are you here, and what do you want with us?'

'There are some nasty people chasing you, one not far from here. If you go any deeper into this dense forest you will almost certainly die, so I am afraid you will just have to trust me. Come on, this way,' he said, matter-of-factly and walked off.

They looked at one another wondering what to do. Their first instinct was to run away, but where to? The man had saved Mike's life and seemed to know his way around, but what was he doing there, in the forest? Believing his timely presence was no coincidence they decided to follow him at a distance.

A violent explosion suddenly shook the ground. The man put his hand to an earpiece and spoke in whispers. 'Don't worry, that had nothing to do with you,' he said, and continued walking as though he were out for a stroll.

Mike couldn't figure him out. 'You never said who you are or what you're doing here?' he said, not expecting a response.

'You can call me Colin,' he replied, without looking back. 'I am here on business.'

'Are you alone?' Mike persisted.

'There were others, but they've gone now.'

'How did you know where we were?' Savannah asked, the distance between them now only a few yards.

'I'm afraid I can't answer that, sorry,' he said. 'This way, it's not far now.'

He seemed friendly enough so they continued to follow him and silence prevailed amid the screeching of hidden wildlife and crunching of rotting bracken underfoot. The damp septic air, a breeding ground for mosquitoes, had spawned squadrons of the vile creatures, which relentlessly attacked Mike's stinking skin as they trekked along an almost invisible pathway.

At a small clearing, Colin raised his hand signalling for them to stop. He stepped under the low-hanging branches and removed a pile of green foliage camouflaging an army jeep.

'Hop in,' he said, folding himself into the driving seat.

Believing good fortune may have finally smiled upon them they climbed onto the rear seat and huddled together. Colin drove down a steep, grassy bank into a fast flowing river and told Mike to wash off the slime; he did so, but the pungent stench remained. With water bubbling halfway up the doors Colin eased the jeep out of the river and drove up the opposite bank. Quickly scanning the area he turned left and headed for Rio.

A mile or so down the road they approached the bridge that Mike saw earlier from the riverbank. Colin changed to a lower gear and slowly drove by observing the charred remains of a red Toyota pick-up truck smouldering at the railings.

TWENTY-ONE

Larry Harbourne had spent a lifetime building his company, The Madison Corporation, which supplied commercial airlines and the military with fittings and gadgets for top-of-the-range jets. Now aged fifty-eight he enjoyed the trappings of success.

But the road had been long and painful.

Already wealthy by the time he was twenty-four Larry fell in love and married Patti Anderson, a British girl. Four years later, they had a son, Jamie. They had a perfect life: a beautiful home in Rowayton, Connecticut, a Grand Cayman Condo, a beach house in Florida and a loving circle of friends. Patti was adamant that Jamie have dual nationality and finish his education in England. After several heated discussions, Larry relented and applied for Jamie to attend Cambridge University.

Five years later, Jamie was on his way home with a degree in Spanish, Portuguese and biochemistry, and had already decided on a military career. It was six p.m. Christmas Eve and bubbling with excitement Patti stood waiting to greet him at JFK's terminal eight arrivals. Larry, snowbound in Washington D.C., was trying his best to find a way home but it looked doubtful.

After an emotional homecoming reunion, Patti led Jamie out to her black Range Rover and as they drove out the terminal she could hardly get a word in edgeways. With the glow of the airport fading behind them Patti took the slip road onto highway 95 and headed for Norwalk, Connecticut. It was well below freezing and the highway, bumper-to-bumper with those going home for the Christmas holiday, shimmered with black ice. Jamie was all news and insisted on telling his mother about his British conquests. She laughed and asked him to spare her the sordid details.

Neither saw the bus in front spin out of control, hit the central barrier and bounce across the highway until it was too late.

Patti slammed her foot on the brakes, but the wheels locked and skidded over the ice. They hit the corner of the bus side on and Patti's head smashed through the side window, severing her carotid artery. Patti never regained consciousness. Jamie suffered cuts and bruises but he recovered, though his broken heart never would. Twenty-four vehicles were involved in the accident; nine people were dead and many were badly injured.

After Patti's funeral Larry had lost the will to live and started drinking and gambling. Deeply concerned about his father Jamie put his career on hold and stayed at home to help him fight his demons. After weeks of torment, clouded with alcohol and grief, Larry could no longer bear the thought of holding back his son and ordered him to get on with his life; he would deal with his problems. Reluctantly, Jamie gave in to his father's wishes, and with his blessing enlisted in the United States Marines.

Jamie endured eighteen months of intense training as though he was born for it. He was a natural, and having unique language skills his unit commander recommended him for Special Forces, which had always been his goal. Four years later, after tours in Iraq and Afghanistan, Jamie received orders to lead a covert CIA unit based in Brazil, as part of a reactionary force against terrorist groups and organized drug cartels in South America.

Meanwhile, his father Larry was slowly drinking himself to death and owed a small fortune in gambling debts. His company, the Madison Corporation, was about to go to the wall.

Harry Schlecker had known Larry and Patti Harbourne for many years. They were good friends and often met at business conventions, played regular golf and dined together. When Harry attended Patti's funeral he offered to help, but Larry was a proud man and refused to accept a handout from anyone. Harry watched Larry's company fall of the cliff, and after confirming reports that he was drinking himself into the ground, he confronted him with a few home truths. Larry though, did not want to hear it and told him to leave, but knowing he was a lost soul Harry persisted in persuading him to seek help at a rehab clinic in California - a caring facility in which he could rid himself of his demons and come to terms with Patti's tragic death. In his absence, Harry offered to babysit the Madison Corporation, and when Larry gave him authorization to do so he set about saving it.

At Harry's expense, Larry spent five months at the clinic, throughout which sobriety gave him a chance to grieve for Patti for the first time. He took long walks remembering her laughter, her soft skin, long auburn hair, and how she took his breath away whenever she entered a room. He missed her terribly, but he still had Jamie, who was a constant reminder of the love he was so lucky to have shared with Patti.

After months of soul-searching Larry arrived home tanned, fit and well, and most of all grateful. He no longer had any debts and his company was once again thriving.

Harry Schlecker had given him back his life.

When Mike and Savannah's disappearance hit the headlines Larry called Ben Brakker, a CIA operative and lifetime friend. Over lunch at a Georgetown riverside restaurant Larry asked Ben what he knew about their disappearance, if anything.

'Not much,' Ben said, vaguely. 'Two suspect charters flew to Brazil via Mexico the same day the kids went missing, but they came up clean. Our satellite picked up a burning boat in Rio's marina, but that could have been anything: an accident, a drunken party, who knows. We also have nice photos of Somalia pirates, missile sites, Mexican gunfights and illegal border crossings; you won't believe the stuff we see on satellite surveillance.'

Larry stroked his chin. 'Brazil, huh? Jamie's unit's there.'

'Yeah I know. he's working with us. Look, there's something you should know. One of our people down there saw a memo on this and inadvertently mentioned it to the wrong person. Since then the Brazilians have been kinda twitchy, and if it turns out to be true, they want it to go away quietly. If a story of a famous American kid, kidnapped and taken to Brazil, hits the headlines it would be political dynamite. They already have a kidnapping problem, and the last thing they need is a global icon winding up dead in their country. Tourism accounts for about eight percent of Brazil's GDP and they wanna keep it that way.'

Larry ordered more drinks. 'I suspect you know a lot more than you're telling me, Ben, but I gotta know, are they in Brazil?'

Ben's back stiffened. 'Don't go there, Larry, it's political, it's classified, and I don't know.'

Larry sat back in his chair. 'I wanna get them out, Ben.

Ben glanced at a young couple as they sat down at a nearby table. Field habits die-hard. 'Why the interest?'

'The FBI's not convinced it was a kidnap. I am, and I wanna find them. I owe someone, but he must never know about this.

Ben nodded. 'Gotcha, Harry Schlecker, about six years ago. He stopped you falling off the cliff, right?'

'You're the only one who knows about that.'

'It's a graveyard secret. So what's the connection?'

The waiter hurried over and delivered their beers to the table. 'Anything else?' he asked

'No. Thanks,' Ben said, waving him away.

'The girl is Harry Schlecker's adopted daughter, Savannah. She's a real nice kid,' Larry explained.

'Ah, now I get it. Look, we don't know if they're in Brazil. Even if they were and we could get them out we'd deny it ever happened. The CIA is reluctant to share information with the FBI, or the NSA, even though the so-called "Wall" is down.'

'Make it happen, Ben, I'll cover whatever it costs, help me out here.

Ben tightened his lips and stared into his beer. 'Mmm, lemme think about it.'

That evening, Larry got a call from Ben. 'Forget the rumours. There's no hard evidence to prove the kids were on a boat in Rio that caught fire and managed to escape, okay?'

Ben was obviously being ambiguous for security reasons, but he was also telling him what they really believed happened.

Ben continued, 'If you really want to help by anonymously repaying your debt to Harry Schlecker, then you can do so by transferring seven hundred and fifty thousand dollars into a numbered account linked to an unspecified Special Forces Unit. The money will go towards financing a covert operation, which is currently underway in Brazil. Jamie is team leader.'

Rio de Janeiro, Thursday, October 8ᵗʰ

As summer is almost a permanent fixture in Rio de Janeiro most of the hotels are fully booked, beaches are crowded and the roads are in a permanent state of gridlock.

That day was no different.

Colin weaved the open-top jeep through a line of cars, buses and trucks tailing back along the highway. It was still warm and a thin layer of carbon monoxide hovered just above the scorched tarmac. He pulled up at a red light, alongside open-top cars, with drivers tapping their fingers to music and talking on cell phones. A bunch of skateboarding kids sailed over the crossing in front of the jeep and waved to Savannah. One boy, who looked no more than twelve, gave her a loud wolf-whistle, and she smiled a little embarrassed as they raced away laughing.

A mile or so down the road Colin pulled into an out of town shopping center, and leaving the jeep in a corner bay he led Mike and Savannah through the parking lot to an unlocked dusty green Fiat. After fumbling around on the floor for the keys he sank into the front seat and told them to jump in the back. Then as he drove to the exit Mike looked for the jeep but it was gone, which left him in no doubt that Colin was not alone and that he was the real deal, perhaps CIA, or had he seen too many movies. Either way, he was not about to ask him. Crunching the ageing gearbox into first Colin turned left and headed for Rio, which according to the road sign was twelve kilometres.

It was Thursday evening, five days since their brutal kidnap in New Mayford. It seemed longer. Much longer

As they entered Rio and headed downhill to Ipanema beach, Mike and Savannah looked for the silver Kawasaki at every turn, on every street, but to their relief it was nowhere in sight. Turning left at the golden sandy seafront Colin followed the beach road around the marina. There was no trace of the schooner, which sank in the bay, much to their delight, but the marina was just how they remembered it: large groups of tourists, lines of swaying yachts, children playing and endless traffic cruising by.

A different boat had moored there now; another millionaire's toy with sleek lines, tall masts and a shimmering pool on deck. Savannah shuddered, recalling the sense of hopelessness, fear and solitude they had endured for four terrifying days while staring out the porthole at unreachable freedom.

Savannah sat back and closed her eyes. They were safe now. Colin took the slip road to Rio's Galeǎo International Airport, and grabbing a ticket at the barrier he drove in and parked at the first empty bay. Wide-eyed with anticipation Mike and Savannah jumped out and followed him inside the busy terminal building. Every face turned away from the stench of swamp still on their clothes as they marched to the departure gates. There an armed guard stood watching each passing traveller. Colin produced his I.D. and whispered to him.

The guard nodded. "Through there, sir," he said, pointing to a door marked *Airport Personnel.* Pushing it open Colin led them along a corridor to a security door, which opened onto the airfield where several empty jets awaited their next journey. They walked towards a large hanger with its doors ajar and entered. Inside, a silver Hawker 800 jet stood gleaming at the center, which Colin confirmed was Mike and Savannah's transport out of Brazil. Gathered around a circular wooden table a group of men were talking to two pilots and an attractive flight attendant wearing a light-blue uniform.

Mike noticed the missing jeep parked in a corner.

The men stood up and saluted as Colin approached. 'At ease men. This is the package,' he said, sweeping his hand towards Mike and Savannah, who were filthy and reeked of swamp.

'The package?' Savannah protested. She trusted him now.

Colin smiled. 'For want of a better phrase, yes. I will explain later, now take a seat,' he ordered.

The seven young men, all wearing combat fatigues, nodded and made room at the table. No names were given. One stood up and walked to a nearby door marked *kitchen.* Moments later, he returned with a tray of coffee and sandwiches, which Mike and Savannah devoured like starving orphans.

Susan, the flight attendant, got up from the table. 'There is clean clothes and a hot shower upstairs, and don't forget to wash your sneakers. Savannah, if you need anything let me know. This way,' she said, heading towards a metal flight of steps.

Showered and wearing new jeans and sweatshirts Mike and Savannah, no longer smelling like a toilet, sat back down at the table. The pilots boarded the aircraft and began a pre-flight check while Susan prepared refreshments in the galley.

Colin walked away and spoke in whispers to his phone. Mike and Savannah studied the group around the table, who looked to be in their mid to late twenties. They seemed decent, polite young men, who out of uniform could be doctors, architects, dentists or taxi drivers, but they were not they were Special Forces; an elite group of highly trained men whose current mission, according to Colin, was to protect them until they were safely out of Brazil.

Surely, they could be in no safer hands.

Savannah feared for their future.

Colin sat down and poured some coffee. He was slightly older than the other men were but clearly had their respect. 'Operation Blackbird is on,' he announced. 'We leave at 22:00 hours.' The men nodded and began gathering up their equipment.

'Where are we going, Colin?' Mike asked.

He drained his coffee. 'We'll talk on the plane, come on.'

Following Colin up a short flight of steps they entered the aircraft: a luxurious jet with fourteen leather seats, two tables and a pale blue carpet. Choosing two seats at the rear of the cabin they curled up together. Colin knelt on the seat in front and faced them. The other men gathered around a table further down.

For Mike and Savannah it all seemed vaguely familiar.

'We are going to Caracas, Venezuela,' Colin said, glancing at his black Wenger Swiss watch.

Mike frowned. 'Why Venezuela?'

'The U.S. Embassy in Caracas will get you home.'

'But why not go to the embassy in Brasilia?' Savannah said, finding the implications unsettling. 'It is only two hours away.'

Colin thoughtfully rubbed his chin. 'I can't tell you that, but there *are* reasons.'

'Can we call home and let our parents know?' Mike asked.

'Yes, as soon as we get to Caracas.'

Savannah huffed. 'So we are to quietly leave the country. A famous young American kidnapped and taken to Brazil would be bad for the tourist trade, right?'

'Something like that,' Colin replied, evasively. 'Look, I know you are Brazilian, Savannah, but don't take it personally there is a lot involved here.'

'Last year there were 307 kidnappings in Sao Paulo alone. What about them?' Savannah persisted.

Mike squeezed her hand. 'Hey, ease up, Savannah, he's on our side, remember?'

'I am sorry, Colin. I am tired and still very frightened by what has happened to us. But it seems so unfair.'

'I know, but that is a government problem not yours. Right now you have enough problems of your own. Your fears are understandable, but they will pass. You have shown extraordinary courage and we are all proud of you.' he said, without sounding the least bit condescending. 'I am trying to get you home, but it's complicated and I have to play by the rules, so keep the faith. Now buckle up we'll be taking off shortly.'

Colin joined his men further down the aisle. Savannah nestled up to Mike and looked out at the shimmering perimeter lights and mini luggage trucks racing back and forth to tourists jets arriving from all over the world.

The pilot parked the Hawker at the end of the runway and waited for clearance to take off. A few minutes later, the interior lights dimmed and with a surge of roaring power the Hawker thundered along the runway, passing the brightly lit terminal, and soared into the air.

Wrapped in one another's arms Mike and Savannah looked out the window as the resplendent city of Rio de Janeiro slowly faded to a distant glow in the Brazilian night sky.

Their terrifying nightmare was over.

TWENTY-TWO

Lucan had to admire the youngster's tenacity as he watched them float downriver and crawl onto the riverbank, but when a jeep and a Fiat carrying men in combat fatigues parked under the nearby thick trees, he knew he was in trouble. Abandoning his Toyota, he climbed over the bridge railing, scrambled down the bank and ran west along the shore, glancing back as he called Mitchell to warn him that a covert military unit was in the area. Netty and Wilson said they could handle it, but Mitchell said no, and ordered the helicopter pilot to pick up Lucan and return to Rio.

When they touched down at Rio's heliport tattooed Wilson said he wanted to cash out, that he was going to Mexico to join a band of mercenaries. Mitchell was glad to get rid of him, but he was also ready to give up the chase. The kids had escaped and no doubt called the FBI, if so, he would be on their wanted list in a matter of hours. The plan had failed. It was time to disappear; get a new name, a new passport, a new life.

Following Mitchell out of the heliport Lucan disagreed, and said for ten thousand dollars he would track the kids down and hold them at a safe house. Mitchell considered this and decided he had nothing to lose. If Lucan failed, that would be the end if it, but if he managed to recapture Kinnerman and the girl….he ran his fingers over his face, a smile forming at the corner of his mouth; maybe this time we'll get lucky he mused.

Mitchell agreed the deal.

Returning by bus to the police compound Lucan tapped and entered his chief's untidy office. 'Sir, I need a break. I've been undercover for six months, and I'm beat,' he said, and waited.

Without looking up from his paperwork the chief took a long draw on a cigarette. 'Okay, go party for a couple of weeks, and stay out of trouble,' he barked, grabbing his ringing phone.

The kid's dramatic escape bothered Lucan as he drove an ageing police Honda to his downtown apartment. A military unit had appeared when they ran into the forest, which he believed was no coincidence. If so, they now had help to get out of Brazil, and it would not be by car, or boat; they would fly. He packed an overnight bag and drove to the airport, siren wailing.

Parking illegally at terminal two he ran inside to departures and waved his police badge at the security guard. 'I'm looking for a boy and a girl, both 14, white American. Have you seen them?' he asked, as though they were terrorists.

'No, but I only came on duty at nine,' the guard said.

Lucan went to the airline desks and checked outgoing flights but there were no such passengers, so he barged his way into the control tower and demanded flight information, but was met with a wall of contempt and ordered to leave. It was 9:58 p.m.

Cursing under his breath Lucan rode the escalator down to the crowded terminal, and shoving his way through to departures he demanded to go airside. The guard opened a door and pointed down the corridor. Lucan brushed passed him and ran to a door at the far end. He stepped out onto the tarmac and studied a line of jets, which were all in darkness. Further away to the right was a large hanger with its doors wide open. Lucan smiled, but as he ran towards it the roar of jet engines shook the night air. He spun around and watched a Hawker jet thunder along the runway and take to the air.

As the Hawker faded into the night sky Lucan had no doubt the kids were onboard, and that Colombia or Venezuela was their destination. If so, it would be a long flight, which meant they would need to refuel before leaving Brazil, and he believed they would do so at Manaus International airport, which stood at the edge of the Amazon rainforest

Finding no available direct flights Lucan settled for the 23:30 to Brasilia, and then a connecting flight to Manaus at 07:20. With an hour or so to kill, he bought a cold beer and sat outside the bar watching the chaos. A family had missed their flight and they were yelling at the uniformed girl behind the desk. Armed police dragged two drunks away for brawling. Angry passengers were queuing at the lost luggage desk, while their kids screamed and a tinny PA system announced arrivals and departures.

Lucan chuckled, he'd seen it all before. Then he noticed a familiar face at the Varig Airline desk. Her name was Silvie and she was married to one of his colleagues. Their eyes met and he strolled over to say hello. As they chatted, he asked if she knew anything about the Hawker flight, which took off at 22:00 hours.

'No, my shift just started, but I'll check the flight list for you.' Silvie said, pressing a key on her computer.

Lucan drummed his fingers on the desk while Silvie searched for the flight details. She was very attractive.

'Ah, here we are, one four zero. It's a diplomatic flight going direct to Caracas,' Silvie explained. Did she have a number for the Caracas airport manager? 'Yes, of course.' She wrote it down. Lucan thanked her and wandered off tapping his cell phone.

The number rang a few times before a husky, brusque woman answered. 'Yes, who is this, what do you want?'

Lucan gave her his police credentials and went on to explain. 'I am calling to inform you that two fugitives involved in a recent Rio murder are on their way to Caracas on flight one four zero, which I believe is a diplomatic flight. I am sure you understand that we would be disappointed if they managed to leave Brazil at this time. Can you help?'

Silence

'I have your number. I will call you back.' She hung up.

Within minutes, a diplomatic official called from Caracas and demanded more information. Lucan gave him details of a recent unsolved murder in Rio, of which there were many. The official said he would look into it. An hour later, Lucan had heard nothing and his flight was now boarding, so he joined the departure gate queue. Then his phone rang; it was the Caracas official.

'Under the circumstances the commissioner has informed his Brazilian counterpart that Venezuela is refusing entry to flight one four zero, their diplomatic flight. The pilot will be contacted shortly. Thank you for letting us know, goodbye.'

Curled up under blankets Mike and Savannah slept soundly throughout the 2,800 kilometre flight to Manaus Airport. Their dramatic escape had led to a long and terrifying day, and Colin saw no reason to wake them while the Hawker sat on the tarmac waiting to be re-fuelled. No one was in a hurry to do anything at that time of the morning, but the fuel eventually arrived and the Hawker was soon underway heading north to Venezuela.

Fifteen minutes from Venezuelan airspace the pilot received an urgent official message.'Abort flight. Entry into Venezuela is denied.'

The co-pilot demanded urgent confirmation, which came seconds from the Venezuelan border. The pilot changed course for Manaus and requested permission to return. Denying entry to a diplomatic flight was a serious matter and Brazilian officials were soon involved. Angry exchanges would follow; nasty letters written, trade deals renegotiated, borders tightened, pipelines halted and diplomatic flights denied entry.

The Venezuelan Commissioner was very sorry and said there was nothing else he could do.

As the Hawker touched down at Manaus in the early morning sun the control tower ordered the pilot to park beside the hangers and wait for instructions. Colin contacted his commander, Major Bell, who said the situation remained a political stand off, but talks were underway and told him to await further orders.

In the comfort of safe hands Mike and Savannah continued to sleep soundly, oblivious to the gathering political storm.

Brazilian officials asked several neighbouring countries for assistance. Colombia said they would think about it. A few hours later, they reached a tenuous agreement, which included no calls and a media blackout. They would allow the Hawker to land at La Pedrera, a small landing strip at the southern corner of the Amazon jungle, surrounded by native villages with limited access to roads in or out. A private jet would then transfer the subjects to Villavicencio airport. From there, a government vehicle would take them to the U.S. Embassy in Bogota.

That was the best they could do.

* * * * *

10-45 a.m. Friday, October 9th

Lucan smiled when he saw the Hawker parked by the hangers as his flight landed at Manaus airport. Disembarking with a smug grin he went straight to the terminal offices. Luiz, the manager, a short, overweight balding man in a crumpled beige suit offered his hand. Lucan waved his police badge in his face.

'There is a problem with flight one four zero. I want to see the flight plan, give it to me,' Lucan snapped, aggressively.

Resenting Lucan's bad attitude Luiz made him wait half an hour before handing him details of the flights to La Pedrera and Villavicencio airport. Lucan snatched the flight details out of his hand, and marching outside he called Rylan Mitchell.

'The kids are at Manaus airport. Someone has arranged to get them to Bogota via Villavicencio,' Lucan explained. 'They are due to arrive at around seven p.m. I will be waiting for them.'

Mitchell began pacing his luxurious hotel suite. He was back in business, and this time there would be no mistakes. 'You've earned that ten grand, Lucan. I'll get to Bogota tonight and check into the Venus Plaza Hotel I'll call you from there.'

'Bring the money.'

Lucan boarded the one p.m. flight to Villavicencio, giving him plenty of time to rent a car before the kids arrived.

The Brazilians had no choice but to accept the Colombian deal, which meant a six-hour delay while they organized a plane and a driver. The Hawker finally took off at 3:05 p.m. and headed south west over the dense Amazon jungle. Due to freak weather conditions, it was two hours before it landed at La Pedrera's short runway and taxied to a halt fifty yards from a black Cessna Citation 550 parked on the cracked tarmac.

When Colin explained why they had landed in Colombia it was as if a dark cloud had passed over Mike and Savannah. Still emotionally fragile after their terrifying ordeal they just stared at him with silent resignation. They had thought their nightmare was over, that they were safe, but that was clearly not the case.

Colin went on. 'The Colombians agreed to help, but they are prohibiting any calls or a military presence. They have however, guaranteed your safety to

Bogota's U.S. Embassy, so you should be home in a day or two. Oh, and I have a gift for you.'

Colin went to his kit bag. He felt uneasy. The sinister political move by the Venezuelans meant that someone else knew about the flight to Caracas, which was serious cause for concern.

Comforted by the thought of a government guaranteeing their safety to Bogota Mike and Savannah gazed at the thick jungle alongside the runway. Susan handed them some fresh coffee.

Colin marched back down the aisle and handed them each a black plastic bracelet with a gold band through the center. 'Put these on and don't take them off until you get home.' he said. It was an order not a request.

'Not exactly a fashion statement,' Savannah remarked.

Mike grinned. 'She's just kidding.'

'I know, at least you still have your sense of humour,' he said, lightly, and nodded to his men. 'Right, it's time to leave.'

The soldiers fanned out around the black Cessna, weapons at the ready; it was a dangerous part of the world. Thanking Susan for her caring help Mike and Savannah followed Colin down the short flight of steps and immediately felt the heat and humidity of the Amazon jungle, which after the Hawker's air conditioning seemed almost unbearable.

Colin stopped at the Cessna's steps. Alberto, a commercial pilot who was off duty when the Colombian officials called upon his services, stood at the door, with a pretty flight attendant. Colin ordered his men to inspect the aircraft, and as they boarded he asked Alberto to clarify his orders.

'My orders are to fly the youngsters to Villavicencio airport, which should take less than two hours, and then escort them out to a government vehicle that will take them to Bogota; a journey no longer than an hour and a half,' Alberto explained.

As a sign of respect for their courage, Colin's men saluted as Mike and Savannah climbed up the steps into the black Cessna. Colin had also grown fond of them, but attachments were taboo in the intelligence business, so goodbye would be brief, although their safety would remain a cause of concern until they were safely home. Leaving Mike and Savannah buckled up at the rear of the cabin Colin marched to the exit, and said, 'Good luck you two, and try to stay out of trouble.'

Before either could respond, Colin stepped out of the aircraft and returned to the Hawker.

He joined his men in the cabin and one remarked, 'I guess that's the end of Colin, sir.' Jamie nodded, and snapping open a can of beer he looked thoughtfully out the window.

The Colombian deal was the best they could have hoped for, but Jamie was unhappy with the exchange there were too many unknowns. Alberto, the pilot, appeared to be fine, but who was driving the car to Bogota, and who found out about the flight to Caracas, did they know about the exchange at La Pedrera too? Laying his head back on the leather seat he breathed out heavily and stared at the overhead lighting. Everything was a risk in that part of the world, but he had done all that he could to ensure their safety. Even so, if anything happened to the youngsters on his watch he would find it hard to live with.

Jamie's jaws tightened as the black Cessna roared along the cracked runway and soared into the Colombian sky, with Mike and Savannah alone onboard.

TWENTY-THREE

The two-hour flight was uneventful and as the Cessna made its final descent to Villavicencio airport, Mike and Savannah gazed out the window at the vast tropical forests passing by beneath them and melting into the Andes Mountains.

After a bumpy landing the Cessna taxied to a halt near a red brick terminal. The flight attendant opened the door and smiled as Mike and Savannah disembarked. Leading them into the building Alberto handed a government letter to an official, who glanced at it and irritably waved them through to the terminal. There was a sizeable military presence in the small air terminal, which Mike and Savannah found unnerving. The air reeked of sweat and stale perfume. Weary travellers were standing in queues with a look of hopelessness. Others lay stretched out on plastic seats, while their kids ran amok in the airless building. Street urchins, some no more than eight years old, were hustling to carry baggage or sell a cheap watch.

Welcome to Colombia, said a colourful sign.

Charismatic in his light blue pilot's uniform Alberto led them out the sweaty terminal to more chaos outside. Taxis were scarce and passengers dragging suitcases and holding onto their kids scrambled for a dusty bus. The air was humid and sticky. Recent rainfall had left steam rising from the worn out asphalt. They walked passed the empty taxi rank to a waiting area, where a short, dark-haired man in a navy suit held up a board with the name *Alberto* scribbled in black felt tip. Alberto questioned the man who promptly produced a letter of authorisation to drive two young Americans to the U.S. Embassy, in Bogota. Handing him twenty dollars he turned to Mike and Savannah.

'Everything is fine. The driver will take care of you. Good luck to you both,' he said, and walked back to the terminal.

The black Mercedes sped away and as the tiny airport faded behind them, Mike and Savannah sat back and bathed in its air conditioning. Armed soldiers, stationed along the roadside, eyed them warily as they drove by. Unconcerned, the driver took the slip road onto highway 40 and headed north to Bogota.

Traffic was heavy. Dark mountainous clouds loomed ahead.

After travelling in silence for about forty minutes, the driver asked in Spanish if they knew anyone in Colombia.

'Hablas Ingles, por favor,' Savannah told the man.

'Okay yes, I speak English. A man driving a red Volkswagen Vento, he is following us. He is there since we left airport. I lose him in Bogota if you want.'

They spun around and there was the red Vento maintaining a predatory distance behind them. 'Lose him,' Mike said, irritably, and looked at Savannah. 'Who the hell is that? It can't be Rylan Mitchell. No-one knows we're here.'

'Well somebody obviously does,' she retorted, with nervous anger. 'I hope no one else is looking for us.'

'Please, do not worry,' the dark-haired driver said, looking in his rear-view mirror, 'In Bogota he will vanish, you will see.

Highway 40 took them high into the Andes Mountains; the backbone of Colombia, which stretches from Venezuela to Peru, and upon which stands the capital city of Bogota eight thousand six hundred and sixty feet above sea level, the driver explained.

As the traffic began to congest on the outskirts of Bogota the driver decided it was time to lose the Vento, and after speeding through a succession of alleyways and narrow one-way streets it disappeared. Pleased with himself, he returned to the main road and rejoined the traffic flowing towards the city.

A sea of flashing blue lights loomed up ahead; it was a police roadblock and traffic was stacked up along the highway.

The driver shook his head. 'I am sorry, this is a problem. I can go no further,' he said, shrugging his shoulders. 'We may be here long time. You want to wait, no?'

Savannah looked at the road ahead. They were almost in the city. 'How far is the American Embassy?'

'Maybe twenty minutes. Follow this road to city center. You will see sign on right. Embassy is down that street in square.'

Savannah looked at Mike. He nodded. 'We will walk.'

Wrinkling his face apologetically the driver pulled over at a park entrance and they jumped out. He nodded and drove away. The park looked idyllically tranquil; families were strolling hand-in-hand and dog owners lovingly walking their pets. Just inside the gates a group of teenagers were noisily chatting on scooters. Old women with glazed eyes and dressed in black sat alone on wooden benches near a leafy pond in the fading light.

Having spent twenty-four hours under the protection of Colin and his men, Mike and Savannah now found themselves alone and vulnerable in a reputedly dangerous city and an acute sense of foreboding prompted them to move on.

It was almost dark and right on cue the lights in the park and surrounding city came to life, punctuating the skyline with neon signs advertising hotels, banks and conglomerates. Then as if a curfew were in force, the old women stood up and hurried away, shawls pulled tightly over their heads. Dog owners leashed their reluctant pets and dragged them along the sidewalk. The noisy teenagers roared away in a large group of scooters.

The park was suddenly silent as a graveyard. A police siren wailed somewhere. People hurried by on the sidewalk, their feet crunching on fallen leaves in the looming darkness.

Savannah snuggled up to Mike. 'Where did everyone go?'

'Who knows, maybe it's bingo night. I'm more concerned about the guy in the red Vento. How did he know we were here?'

Savannah yawned. 'Someone must have told him.'

'Maybe, but if he's looking for us in the traffic he won't see us on the sidewalk, and the moment we set foot inside the U.S. Embassy we're safe. Come on, let's go.'

Savannah grabbed his arm. 'Wait a minute. Greta once had a problem at a U.S. Embassy. I think it was in Madrid. She said that it only opened from eight till noon and closed at weekends.'

Mike absorbed that. 'Mmm, even if that's true there's gotta be an emergency number we can call.'

'Yes, but if the embassy is closed until Monday they cannot help us tonight, so we need to find a hotel. Our first problem is American Express. They may have cancelled your card in case the kidnappers force you to use it.'

Mike shook his head. 'Damn, I never thought of that.'

'We can try buying some clothes, at least we will know. The second problem is that we are minors and have no passports, which means the big hotels may turn us away. All we can do then is lie and hope they take pity on us,' Savannah said, bleakly.

Mike smiled. 'With your face how can they not believe you?'

They hurried along the sidewalk under the shadowy rustling trees. A brisk walk took them to the heart of the city where its glittering stores bustled with last minute shoppers. They figured the U.S. Embassy was only minutes away now, but aware that someone might recognize them, which could lead to all sorts of problems, they entered the store separately and picked out a mini wardrobe. Much to their relief the sales assistant didn't give them a second glance as she wrapped their selection. Using his AmEx card Mike paid the bill; two hundred and forty-one dollars, which confirmed that American Express had not cancelled his card and they had access to money. Lots of it.

Empowered by their anonymity they walked along the busy sidewalk until a sign for the U.S. Embassy appeared on the other side of the road. Dizzy at the prospect of going home under the protection of the United States Embassy, they crossed over and hurried towards a leafy avenue lined with stately buildings.

'Holy shit!' Mike exclaimed, staring wide-eyed at the smoke-filled avenue crowded with people.

Savannah gasped. 'Oh no, there has been an accident!'

'No, that's a fire and it looks bad. Come on let's go,' he urged, quickening their pace towards the smoking orange glow.

Halfway down the avenue a large crowd had gathered around a sea of flashing blue lights. Cars stood abandoned in the road and on the pavement. Several fire engines were at the scene. Fire fighters were hosing the upper floors of a building. Ambulances were racing back and forth at the other end of the square, which police had cleared for emergency services.

Weaving their way through abandoned vehicles they joined the burgeoning crowd and looked up at the sign on the burning building; **United States Embassy.** Their hearts sank in disbelief. Several people were staggering around in a daze. Paramedics were treating those with minor injuries at the scene; others lay burnt and bleeding on stretchers, waiting for the next ambulance. One woman wandered around with a glazed look amid the broken glass and charred remnants falling from the upper floors.

The square was in chaos.

Thick black smoke and flaming ash saturated the air.

People inside were screaming for help.

Jostling their way through the crowd of onlookers they stood at the yellow police cordon and stared at the horrific scene; their hopes of going home any time soon fading to ashes before them.

Savannah hated fires. Even more so now.

Another ambulance arrived, its siren whaling down the street. A woman frantically screamed for her husband, who apparently was still inside the building. A female correspondent with a TV camera crew described the horrific scene. Fire fighters hosed a burning dog as it leapt from a second floor window into a thick blanket held by police officers.

An explosion shook the building.

The crowd backed up.

Two strong hands suddenly gripped the back of their necks, and a deep voice said, 'You have given me quite a chase.'

Mike and Savannah stiffened with dread.

Lucan's vice-like grip tightened. 'Now, we are going to walk away. Behave yourselves and no harm will come to you.'

'What do you want with us?' Mike said, resisting his grip.

'Don't play games with me boy! Walk! Nice and easy.'

Savannah was no toughie, but having spent three years in a boxing ring with Henry Max she had skills. Overcoming her fear with anger she spun around and hit Lucan square on the jaw with her right fist. Shocked, Lucan stumbled backwards, arms flaying. Mike stuck out his foot and knocked him hard to the ground.

Savannah yelled out in Spanish, 'Help! Help us, please! This man is a kidnapper! He is trying to kill us!'

Onlookers gathered round. A police officer pushed his way through them and saw Lucan scrambling to his feet, his shoulder holstered revolver clearly visible inside his jacket.

Mike grabbed Savannah's hand. 'We're leaving let's go!'

They scrambled under the police cordon and ran away. Lucan ducked under the tape after them. The police officer withdrew his revolver and yelled at him to stop, but when he started to run he fired in the air. The crowd backed away. Lucan stopped, raised his hands and faced the burly officer, who stepped forward, revolver in hand, and ordered him to lie face down. Lucan smiled, pointing to his jacket and reached inside for his police badge. The officer fired twice. Lucan fell hard to the ground, dropping his badge in a river of water running into a drain from the fire hoses. Women screamed as the crowd looked on in horror. The officer removed the revolver holstered under Lucan's arm. Searching his pockets he found a cell phone and six hundred Reais. The man carried no ID and the officer had no reason to doubt the young girl who had claimed he was a kidnapper. Another police officer joined him and called in the incident.

The first officer stood up and surveyed the surrounding chaos for any sign of the youngsters. He saw them only briefly, but it was long enough for him to sense the fear in their eyes. They were out there somewhere, but with so many fire fighters, police, paramedics, the walking wounded and onlookers in the area it was almost impossible to see anything. He shook his head and was about to turn away when a sudden breeze swept the swirling black smoke high into the air. Searching through the ash-filled haze he caught a glimpse of Mike and Savannah as they slipped beneath the yellow police cordon at the far end of the burning embassy and raced away in the misty darkness.

TWENTY-FOUR

Richard Kinnerman had never raised his voice in a courtroom, either for dramatic effect or to sway a judge and jury. Now he had a case that would never reach a courtroom and he wanted to yell at someone; a case subject solely to the perpetrators demands, and he didn't like that one bit because he now represented the most important client of his career; his son.

Although JB had lightened his workload there were still not enough hours in the day, and without Beth he'd struggle to cope. He was tired, tired of the uncertainty, tired of people telling him how sorry they were, and tired of waking up in the early hours hearing his daughter sobbing for her missing brother, when all he could do is wait for a phone call that may never come.

When Greta offered her support in what was undoubtedly the family's darkest hour, Richard realised Mike's adolescent crush for her was not without merit, and that beneath her movie star looks was a woman with real character. Apparently, she fought with Harry Schlecker over a million-dollar reward he posted on the internet for any information leading to Mike and Savannah's whereabouts. This also went against the wishes of FBI Director, Vernon Bentram, who said that it would give a green light to bounty hunters, gangsters and corrupt cops to hunt the kids down, and may even encourage another kidnapping by a terrorist group.

Harry remained unrepentant, which left Greta wondering how a man with such vision could be so blind.

PocketMoney.com's inexorable rise to success continued, but those working at the company building remained sombre amid growing concern for its young founder. When Mike Kinnerman's mysterious disappearance hit the news, millions of kids around the world felt the only way they could show their support was to buy more shares, which they did; billions of dollars worth and it was still pouring in daily.

Friday morning, students at New Mayford High and Hartvale School said a prayer for Mike and Savannah, who had now been missing for six days. Many were in tears.

At Tokyo's Narita airport jostling reporters subjected Katie Kinnerman to a barrage of wickedly inane questions.

'It's been rumoured that you know where your son is Mrs. Kinnerman, any truth in that?' one yelled.

'Sources say he's in Canada, is that right?' asked another.

'Are you on your way to meet him?' A female asked.

'He apparently disappeared just after you left New York. Care to comment on that?' yelled another.

'Is your son's disappearance connected to the breakdown of your marriage Mrs. Kinnerman?' Another asked.

Refusing to dignify their crass remarks with a response Katie tearfully boarded the long flight to New York.

Richard had taken Friday off to meet Katie at JFK airport. Beth had cleared his diary and diverted office calls to her desk. That morning, as he drove Julieanne to school Richard explained what he planned to do about finding her brother.

'You've probably noticed that I don't go anywhere without this shoulder bag, Jules. It contains my passport, clothes and a few necessities. News of Mike's whereabouts will eventually come from somewhere, and when that happens, which could be at any moment, your Mom and I are gonna get on a plane and go find him. In that event, Sally will look after you and drive you to and from school.'

'I understand, dad. I wanted to come with you to meet Mom today, but I can wait until you get home. If you get that call, just go. I'll be okay, I promise. Jenny's Mom will drive me home.'

'We love you, Jules, and no matter what we'll come through this together,' Richard said, pulling up at the school entrance.

Hugging her father, she whispered, 'Love you too, dad, bye.'

She climbed out of the car and gave him a look of affection needing no explanation. Richard's lips tightened; his daughter had grown up and he hadn't even noticed. That would change starting now. She had promised her support, which, with Katie's imminent return, signified a sense of unity in the family's hour of crisis. Warmed by her affection he drove home and made a few calls before heading to JFK airport.

It was raining heavily and due to an incident at JFK's short stay, police directed Richard to another parking lot. He grabbed his black bag and boarded a bus to the terminals. Gazing out the window he thought about Katie and their once perfect marriage that had descended to indifference, and harbouring a deep sense of remorse Richard wondered how he allowed that to happen.

Katie had gone to Tokyo in an effort to save their marriage, only to learn that Mike had been kidnapped, and having endured the heartbreaking news so far away, Richard had no doubt that she was close to despair. Hopefully, they would find strength in their family unity, but if Mike's life was taken it was unlikely Julieanne would recover, neither would his parents.

Richard stepped off the crowded bus and entered the terminal. The incoming board indicated Katie's flight was due to land in thirty-five minutes, which meant that she'd walk through arrivals in about an hour. He recalled their last visit to JFK when he, Julieanne and Mike watched Katie's plane take off for Tokyo.

How he wished he could turn back the clock.

He bought a newspaper, coffee and Danish and sat outside the café, watching hoards of travellers struggle by with overloaded trolleys and handfuls of weary kids, while the airport PA system announced arrivals and departures.

A flurry of calls came from the trustees who had just bought Stella Electronics and were excited about the deal. Richard was in no mood to talk business and explained that he was meeting Katie at JFK. He would call them tomorrow.

Moose crawled out of bed at three forty-five p.m. and sat in front of his laptop; the nasty virus had gone. Trawling through his emails he came to one entitled SAV. Having read the message, he stood up and stared at the screen. The email had arrived at two-twenty p.m. on Thursday. He printed off a copy, underlined two words; *kidnapped, escaped,* and reached for the phone.

Unable to concentrate with any degree of interest Richard folded the newspaper and stared at his cell phone willing Mike to call him, but it remained silent and he ridiculed himself for such wishful thinking. Sitting at an airport café table watching a sea of human traffic pass by was not exactly thought provoking, and after drumming his fingers on the table for half an hour he'd had enough. Shuffling his way through the crowded upper floor he took the elevator down to arrivals and leaned against a pay phone waiting for Katie to walk through the barrier. Then his cell phone rang. 'Richard Kinnerman.'

'Mr. Kinnerman, it's Moose. I got an email from Mike.'

Richard stood wide-eyed, his throat tightening. 'What? Christ where is he, what did he say? Talk to me, Moose.'

'I think Savannah sent it. SAV was in the subject slot. I've never met her but Mike never stopped talking about her and...'

'Get to point, Moose.'

'She said they were kidnapped but they've escaped. I feel bad about this, sir. The email came Thursday but I was sick.'

Richard began pacing back and forth, his mind way beyond overdrive. Several flights had recently arrived and a crowd had gathered at the gate. In the chaos, the noise level began to rise from a mass of screeching trolley wheels, ringing cell phones and people calling out to love ones struggling through the barrier. He looked at the outgoing flight board and scanned the destinations going all over the world.

'Where are they, Moose, did she give you any idea?'

'No, I think Savannah was interrupted before she could finish the message. Even so, every email has a transitory code, sir, it's a kind of signature, and it's different in every country. Anyway, I checked it out and managed to trace it back to Rio de Janeiro.'

Richard stopped pacing and breathed out. 'Brazil. They're in Brazil. Moose, you're a goddam genius! Can you find the source of that email? I'm at JFK and after what you've just told me, I'm gonna get on a plane in the next few hours.'

'I'll call you right back, sir.'

U.S. citizens required a visa to enter Brazil and Richard knew the only way he could get visas now was to call JB, who had his family details and knew the Brazilian Ambassador well.

Minutes later, JB called back and promised to have the visas at JFK airport within two hours. Richard thanked him and said he would call to confirm they had arrived.

A thousand questions ran through his mind: why Brazil, who kidnapped them? Was it Rylan Mitchell, organised criminals, or maybe terrorists? They had escaped, made one call and sent an email, but where were they now, how were they surviving, how were they travelling? If Mike had used his American Express card the FBI would know about it, but he never had, why? These were all questions for which Richard had no answers. The only thing in their favour was that Savannah spoke Portuguese, which meant they had no language barrier to deal with. Thankfully, they had escaped, but the thought of a bunch of kidnappers pursuing them across Brazil was too terrifying to imagine.

He looked at the long list of flights leaving JFK and paced the floor as though his feet were on fire.

He checked his watch: 17:15. Katie's flight had landed forty-five minutes ago and he expected her at any moment. His blood was up, way up. Check-in was two hours before flight time and to have any chance of getting seats to Rio that evening he needed to book the tickets right away, but Katie would never forgive him if he wasn't there to meet her. Rio is an all-year-round destination, and getting last minute seats on the next flight was a long shot at best. He again called JB and explained his dilemma. JB said that he would deal with it, and ten minutes later, he called back.

'The firm's travel agent got you and Katie on the 21:15 flight to Rio. Your tickets are at the United Airline desk. They know your visas are on their way to you. Call me when you get there. No, call me anytime. I want to help, Richard.'

'You have, JB, and thanks, I'll call you tomorrow.'

Katie strolled through the barrier, along with two hundred fellow weary passengers all looking for a board with their name on it. Her emerald eyes were red and tearful and strands of her auburn hair fell abandoned to the side of her face. Pushing her baggage trolley looking physically beaten, Katie scanned the arrivals hall for her husband. Richard jostled his way through the dwindling crowd and made eye contact. Sighing with relief, Katie hurried towards him, her eyes misty with anxious longing and threw her arms around his neck sobbing.

'Katie, we're going to Rio.'

TWENTY-FIVE

8-50 p.m. Friday, Bogota

With the chaotic smoky avenue behind them Mike and Savannah turned right and then right again, which brought them back to main-street. It was dark now and the city had noticeably changed. The stores had closed and thick security bars were visible on the doors and windows. Shadowy groups of men lingered on the sidewalk where families had earlier window-shopped.

A black van pulled up at the kerb and two men jumped out. Mike grabbed Savannah's hand and dragged her into a dimly lit side street. A red neon sign **Hotel and Bar** reluctantly glimmered halfway down. They ran to the door, pushed it open and entered a crowded smoky bar. A table of drunks directed lewd comments at Savannah as they jostled their way through to reception.

A tall unshaven man with coal black eyes stood behind the shabby desk. He lit a cigarette and stared at them. 'You want room?' he asked, tossing the match on the filthy wooden floor.

A bearded drunk staggered by holding up an obese women, wearing a stained red dress, theatrical make-up, torn stockings and high heels. She laughed raucously as the man grabbed her long, unkempt hair and dragged her up the stairs.

Savannah whispered, 'We cannot stay here.'

Mike looked at her. 'Why not?'

'Trust me,' she said, dragging him back to the door.

'But we have to sleep somewhere,' he protested

'Yes but the bigger hotels are much safer. I need a hot bath, a clean, soft bed and room service. You can afford it you are rich, remember?' Savannah persisted. Mike didn't argue.

Hurrying back to the main road they turned left and headed for downtown Bogota. Hidden faces stared at them in darkened doorways as their ghost-like reflections floated by on the tinted windowed restaurants and bars. Police sirens wailed somewhere, several dogs were fighting over scraps of food in a nearby alley, and a blanket of mist hovered eerily beneath the yellow glow of the street lights. A man hurried by and glanced at them.

Gripping one another's hand, they quickened their pace down the almost deserted street until a multi-road junction forced them to stop. They looked around in the misty light unsure which way to go, then a distant glittering hotel caught their attention.

'That will do, come on,' Savannah said, urging Mike along the dimly lit sidewalk. 'Remember, look confident.'

The Venus Plaza Hotel; a five-star towering building with a bubbling fountain, pristine gardens and a grand entrance stood welcoming in the hazy evening light.

They marched up the driveway and entered through its glass revolving doors. Ignoring questioning looks from the staff and curious guests they walked arm in arm across the marble floor to the reception desk. Smiling sweetly at the receptionist, Savannah said, 'A twin suite for the night please.'

The dark-haired woman leaned over the black marble desk and gave her a condescending look. 'Your passports please.

Unconvinced their kidnap story would secure a room and that it would lead to all sorts of questions, which may endanger their lives, Savannah decided to lie. She smiled angelically.

'We are Americans on vacation and thieves have stolen our luggage and passports. The U.S. Embassy has closed due to a fire, and so a replacement is not possible. We have bought new clothes and need a room for the night, perhaps two. Then we plan to go north to Cartegena. Will American Express do?'

The receptionist raised an eyebrow. One moment,' she said, taking Mike's AmEx card to a rear office. She quickly returned with the hotel manager, Emile

Arnaud, a dark-haired grey-suited Frenchman. He nodded, glancing at their modest appearance and studied the American Express card. Being an avid news follower he knew exactly who Mike Kinnerman was and would certainly not refuse to accommodate the world's youngest billionaire, whatever the controversy surrounding his disappearance.

'Welcome to our hotel,' Emile said, with a company smile.

'Thanks,' Mike replied. Savannah uncrossed her fingers.

Having signed the hotel register, the receptionist snapped her fingers at a bellboy and handed him the key card to suit 106.

Emile Arnaud folded his arms and smiled with complicity. 'Let me assure you that your personal security is of paramount importance to us, and will remain so,' he said, clearly enjoying the pretence charade of not knowing who they were.

Mike read the look in his eyes. 'Thanks, we appreciate it.'

'Have a pleasant stay,' Emile said, returning to his office.

At level one they followed the bellboy along a blue-carpeted corridor to 106; a twin-bedded suite with a thick, beige carpet, a plasma TV, a mosaic tiled bathroom, a cloakroom, lounge-diner, mini-bar and a balcony overlooking the city. Savannah secured the door, and turning off the lights they huddled together at the window gazing at the mist-shrouded city of Bogota.

They were safe, at least for tonight.

* * * * *

Mitchell and Netty arrived at El Dorado airport, Bogota at seven-thirty p.m. and took a taxi to the Venus Plaza Hotel, where a suite awaited them on the eighteenth floor. Once they had unpacked and settled in Mitchell called Lucan. The number rang several times before a voice answered.

'Bogota Police.'

'Sorry, wrong number,' Mitchell said, and disconnected. The police officer called back. 'Senor Mitchell, your number is listed on this phone. What do you know about this man?'

Mitchell had no choice but to tell him. 'I've known him for many years. His name is Lucan Bezerra. He's an undercover cop in Rio. Is there some kind of problem here?'

'Yes, your friend is in the morgue. The police shot him dead last night when he attempted to evade arrest outside the American Embassy. We believe this man was a child kidnapper. Where are you calling from?'

The last thing Mitchell needed was to get involved with the Bogota police. 'I'm in Rio. I called to ask when he'd be back.'

'You need concern yourself no more. Your corrupt police friend will not be coming back. Goodbye.'

Mitchell poured himself a whisky and paced the thick, carpeted floor. 'Lucan's dead. The damn cops shot him outside the U.S. Embassy,' he said, strolling to the spacious window.

'Be grateful they saved you ten grand. Why'd they shoot him anyway?' Netty asked, but couldn't care less. He hated cops.

'Why? Maybe he followed the kids to the Embassy, maybe they recognised him and told the police, maybe he panicked and they shot him. What am I a psychic? How the hell should I know?' Mitchell yelled, looking out at Bogota's city lights.

Netty snapped open another beer and took a slug. 'Lucan said the kids are here, so all we gotta do is find 'em, right?'

'Right, but this is Bogota, Netty, and the only person I trust here is Rizzio. Problem is, he's no longer my best friend because those damn kids set fire to his boat, which had seven hundred and fifty million dollars worth of his cocaine onboard.'

'For Christ sake, the kid's worth billions. Give him a piece of the action,' Netty growled. He was tired of Mitchell's whingeing. If they'd done things his way, the ransom money would be in the bank and the kids would be underground. He drank more beer.

Mitchell stared into space. Netty was right. He had no choice but to call Rizzio. He reluctantly dialled the number and prepared himself for the insults. 'Si, hello?'

'Rizzio, its Mitchell.'

'Well well, Senor Rylan Mitchell. You are my least favourite person right now, but you already know that. What do you want?'

'Look, Rizzio, about that shipment. A couple of kids set fire to the damn boat and it sank with the stuff onboard. I'll make it up to you I swear. I'm in

Bogota and I need your help to find a fourteen-year old boy and girl. They're hiding somewhere in the city. The boy is Mike Kinnerman, an American, and he's worth thirty billion dollars. I'll make up your loss and give you a piece of the action. Whadaya say?' Mitchell said, and held his breath.

Rizzio laughed. 'Thirty billion dollars! You always were too greedy my friend. One billion is enough. If these kids are in Bogota, I will find them.'

'So do we have a deal.?'

'Do not stay long in Bogota Senor Mitchell, you have many enemies. I will be in touch.'

Mitchell knew that he'd made a big mistake. Rizzio would no doubt find the kids and he hadn't agreed a deal, which left him vulnerable. Rizzio was a powerful Colombian drug lord, and not someone he would want as an enemy. Maybe he would see things differently if he got the seven hundred and fifty million dollars back. There was however, a down side; if Rizzio couldn't find the kids, for whatever reason, he would certainly find Mitchell, and at that point life could get shorter. Mitchell decided to give him a couple of days to call, and then he would disappear; Bogota was fast becoming a dangerous place. Having shaken Netty out of his alcoholic stupor, they took the elevator down to the mezzanine restaurant and ordered dinner.

* * * * *

The number you have dialled is currently not in use, please try later. Mike sullenly put down the phone and exhaled.

Savannah looked at him. 'What?'

'Mom and Dad's cell phones are not available.'

'They may be out of the zone, or on a plane. Try later. Have a hot shower you stink. I will call room service and order dinner,' Savannah said, bossily.

She was right. It was a five-star hotel. They were safe, had room service and a phone. Once he had contacted his father, they could stay there until he arrived to take them home. Was he really on a plane? Mike wondered, heading for the bathroom.

Savannah ordered shellfish, rice, two steaks, vegetables and a selection of pastries. Feeling secure in the relative safety of their luxurious suite, she yawned wearily and laid across her bed until Mike returned drying his hair with a towel. She ran a hot bath and soaked in vanilla foam for twenty minutes before emerging wrapped in one of the hotels matching bathrobes. She sat down at the dresser and began drying her long, dark hair, and noticing Mike watching her in the mirror, she smiled, coyly.

A sharp rap on the door startled them. 'Room service!'

Mike peeked through the security eye and opened the door. A young man in a red buttoned-down uniform wheeled in a trolley to the dining table. Mike thanked him, and securing the door he sat down as Savannah dished out the first course.

'These are delicious,' he said, scooping shellfish and rice into his mouth. Savannah nodded, munching happily.

She took two small bottles of red wine from the mini bar to accompany their steaks, after which they finished off the pastries and had coffee. Mike began sweating profusely and sat back in his chair looking pale and his breathing laboured.

'Are you alright?' Savannah asked. 'You look weird.'

'I feel weird, I'm burning up,' he groaned, and clutching his stomach he slid to the floor.

Savannah knelt beside him. 'Are you allergic to anything?'

'I must be,' he croaked, curling up in agony, his body rigid and shaking as though he were having a fit. She felt his pulse; his heart was racing and his eyes had a glazed look.

She called reception. 'This is suite 106. Mike is sick! It was something he ate. We need a doctor, hurry please!'

The receptionist summoned the hotel's doctor. Shortly after, a well-dressed woman entered their suite carrying a shoulder bag. When Savannah told her what they had eaten the doctor knew right away what had caused the reaction. She gave Mike a shot of something and explained what had happened to him.

'He is suffering from Scromboid Toxicity. This occurs when the shellfish putrefies and releases histamine, which sometimes causes allergy-like reactions: sweating, convulsions, vomiting, cramp and diarrhoea.....No longer listening, Savanna looked at Mike lying helpless on the bed with his head to one side and his breathing laboured. The doctor squeezed her hand. 'Don't worry, he will be fine after a good night's sleep. I will examine him in the morning,' the doctor said, zipping up her bag.

As the doctor strode off down the corridor, Savannah secured the door and sat on Mike's bed holding his lifeless hand. He was dreadfully pale and she blamed herself for ordering the shellfish, but why had it not affected her too, she wondered.

She heard a noise outside the door and stood up, fear tearing at her stomach. Tightening her bathrobe she unlocked the door, wrenched it open and found a bellboy standing outside. 'What are you doing here?' she snapped. 'What do you want?'

The boy nervously stepped back. 'I…I'm sorry Miss. I have the wrong room,' he said, slinking off down the corridor. Securing the door she kissed Mike and climbed into bed.

* * * * *

Mitchell and Netty had a table on the mezzanine balcony, which overlooked the hotel's lobby and reception area. They disliked one another and having little to say, sat in morbid silence amid the bustle of the crowded five-star restaurant. A waiter hurried to their table with two thick steaks and salad. Mitchell thanked him and sipped his expensive red wine. Netty ordered more beer and staggered off to the toilet.

There was some sort of panic going on below. A woman with a shoulder bag hurried through the glass revolving door and as she crossed the lobby, the receptionist called out to her.

'Suite 106, doctor. It's a boy, an American. The young girl thinks it may be a food allergy.' The doctor nodded and ran to catch the elevator as the doors were closing.

Mitchell grinned and sipped his wine.

TWENTY-SIX

Friday, October 9th

A courier delivered Richard and Katie's visas to the airline desk in time for boarding their flight to Rio de Janeiro, which took off as scheduled. Unfortunately, a technical problem forced the pilot to make an unscheduled stop at Miami airport. After sitting on the tarmac for almost two hours, an official led the passengers to a transit area inside the terminal and a scramble ensued for the bar. Richard ordered two cold beers and pretzels. Katie wearily looked out the huge window at their broken jet, which had several technicians standing beneath it scratching their heads.

The room was hot and sticky. Tired kids were screaming, the toilets were blocked and two hundred angry passengers were pacing up and down, all wishing they were somewhere else.

The place stank.

Harry's Mansion Friday, October 9th

Harry and Greta arrived home around midnight after attending a charity function in New York City. Greta checked the messages but found nothing urgent. There had also been no further contact from Brimson, but their incriminating email had left a dark cloud hanging over her relationship with Harry, who had noticed her guarded conversation. Dismissing his concern

Greta said that she was just deeply worried about Mike and Savannah. Harry let it go and they went to the library for coffee and brandy.

Harry leaned on the grand fireplace and stared at the flames. Greta sat in an armchair and warmed her brandy. The private line rang; Harry grabbed it. 'Yeah?' he said, irritably.

'Mr. Schlecker, Agent Grant, FBI. I have some news of your daughter, Savannah.'

Harry's back stiffened. 'What is it?'

'We've just had conformation that Mike Kinnerman used his American Express card tonight in Bogota.'

Harry paced the floor. 'Colombia? Are you sure it was him?'

'Positive, sir. Report says they were shopping in downtown Bogota, which kinda puts a hole in the kidnapping theory.'

'Theory? If you were doin your goddam job you'd know they were kidnapped, schmuck.'

'I resent that, sir. We're doing our best to find them.'

'Your best? Then how dyou think they got to South America with no passports, hitched a lift with Mary Poppins?'

'We're looking at every possibility, sir.'

'Look at the facts you might get somewhere. What else?'

'Kinnerman bought clothing items at a store called MEX. He had a young girl with him, whom we believe was your daughter, Savannah. Apparently, they went to the Bogota U.S. Embassy, but it was on fire due to an explosion. American Express said they'll let us know if he uses the card again.'

'And you think they're on vacation. Did anybody see them?'

'One of the local cops did, but there was a shooting and they ran away. When we get more news I'll let you know, sir.'

'You do that!' Harry yelled, and slammed the phone down. 'That was the FBI, Greta. Mike and Savannah are in Bogota. Don't ask me how, but they got away and they're on the run.'

Greta jumped out of the armchair. 'Oh my God! Call the U.S. Embassy in Bogota.'

'It's closed there's been some kind of explosion.'

'Explosion…at the U.S. Embassy? It sounds like a goddam war zone. Harry, do something.'

'Like what? Jump in the jet, do a quick search and rescue and bring 'em home? Or perhaps we should call superman?'

Greta deflected the sarcasm. 'What about asking your friends in Chicago?'

'I already did. They talked to their sources, had a few people sniff around in Rio but came up with zilch.

Greta sipped her brandy. 'So what do we do?'

'Nothing, what else can we do? They went to the embassy and found the place blown up and burning. Apparently, a local cop saw them, but there was a shooting and they ran away.'

Greta's eyes widened. 'A shooting?'

'Yeah, well, that's Bogota. They could send in the boy scouts and search the area, but it's not that simple. If they're running from kidnappers they don't wanna be found. I know Colombia, it's nothing but mountains and jungle, and there's no point in wading through swamps and anacondas on a maybe. Until we get past a few sketchy details we let the FBI do what they're paid to do. In the meantime, I'll call Richard and let him know.'

Greta paced the floor. 'Who do we know in Bogota?'

'A few politicians, but I guarantee this has nothing to do with anyone in Bogota.'

'Call them anyway.'

* * * * *

Miami Airport

Katie was asleep on Richard's shoulder when Harry called and at that hour he expected bad news. 'What's up, Harry?

'I know where your son is.'

Richard jumped off the barstool. Katie slumped to the bar.

'What! Where is he, is he okay?'

'That I don't know, but they're in Bogota. They went to the U.S. Embassy for help, but there'd been some kind of explosion and it was closed. A cop saw them before they ran away.'

'Bogota? How dyou know that?'

'The FBI just called. Mike used his AmEx card tonight at a clothes store. Savannah was with him.'

This was the news Richard had hoped for. 'Mike's telling us where they are. Tell American Express not to cancel the card, Harry. We can use it to trace their whereabouts.'

A waiter dropped a tray of glasses. A roomful of passengers glared at him in angry silence. Katie raised her head off the bar, opened her eyes and lay down again.

'American Express are not gonna cancel Mike's card. They'll monitor the account and let the FBI know as soon as he uses it again,' Harry explained. 'Anything else?'

'Katie's back from Tokyo and we're in Miami on our way to Rio, but it looks like we're going to Bogota. Look in on Julieanne for me will you. We don't want her feeling isolated.'

'Sure, I'll go see her tomorrow. Look, if you're gonna play Sherlock Holmes go to the MEX store in Bogotá, that's where Mike used his card. We'll talk later.' Harry disconnected.

Katie's tired eyes barely flickered when Richard told her the good news. After a twenty-hour flight from Tokyo to New York and another to Miami she was clearly exhausted. Harry's news had raised their optimism, but it also confirmed their worst fears, and in the starkness of that stinking room the thought of Mike and Savannah fighting for survival in the dark alleyways of a far away city was impossible to contemplate.

It was a waking nightmare

Changing flights for Bogota meant accessing the terminal, but as they were stuck in transit and Katie's baggage was still on the plane, they had no choice but to wait until the airline cancelled their flight, which seemed likely.

The room continued to descend into chaos. Two hundred irate passengers were demanding to know what was happening. *What kind of airline is this?* Somebody yelled. Two miserable hours later, officials wheeled in a trolley full of coffee and sandwiches to the center of the room, which now stank of stale sweat and a thick layer of smoke, thanks to defiant smokers.

It was four-thirty a.m. Saturday, October 10th

Columbus Day. How ironic, thought Richard.

The night shift manager, forty-something, grey hair, grey suit and grey face swaggered into the crowded room and attempted to calm the situation. Without one word of apology he said that the airline had now cancelled the Rio flight and allocated hotel rooms for all the passengers. A bus would take them to the hotel and return them tomorrow morning for the midday flight. The room erupted with an angry barrage of questions, but he ignored them and walked off without looking back.

Scuffles broke out. Someone called security. The bar closed.

Katie was asleep with her head on the bar when Richard's cell phone rang. 'Mr. Kinnerman, its Moose. I had a problem chasing down the information you wanted.'

'Moose, it's four-thirty a.m., shouldn't you be in bed? Never mind, what've you got?'

Hearing the name Moose prompted Katie to sit up and yawn.

'Mike's e-mail came from Extron Computers in Rio,' Moose explained. 'The store's based at a mall called the Old Municipal Center. Like I said, looks like Savannah got caught using one of their computers before she could finish the message.'

'Good job, Moose, but things are changing by the minute. I can't go into details now it's still a bit sketchy, and I don't want to risk compromising Mike and Savannah's safety.' Katie held out her hand. 'Hang on, Katie wants a word.'

'Moose, I want you to call Julieanne and tell her what you found, and send her a copy of Mike's email, it'll cheer her up. If Mike contacts you again, call us right away. You got that?'

'Yes ma-am. Bring Mike home, I miss him.'

A tall brunette in a red two-piece suit, white blouse and high heels marched into the room holding a clipboard; her name tag said Rose. Having trawled through her passenger list and found everyone accounted for, Rose led the bedraggled group to the baggage claim area. After the usual conveyor-belt scramble for belongings, a herd of rattling trolleys followed her to passport control and a long, short-tempered queue.

Richard and Katie took the elevator to the check-in floor and headed for the airline desk, which looked deserted until a blue uniformed woman stepped out of the rear office. 'Yes sir?'

'Hi, our flight from New York to Rio has been cancelled and we'd like a refund or two round tickets to Bogota,' Richard said, business-like.

With an all hours company smile, she said, 'I'm sorry, sir, but if you are not continuing your flight to Rio the New York office will deal with compensation for that flight. Here is the number. It is quite simple I assure you.'

Pocketing the number, Richard bought two club-class seats on a direct flight to El Dorado airport, Bogotá`, which would take six hours and forty minutes and was scheduled to leave at seven-thirty a.m.. The dollar was strong in Colombia and there was no visa requirement for U.S. citizens. With three hours to wait a nap was more than tempting, particularly for Katie, but rather than run the risk of missing their flight they took the elevator to the ground floor and walked out into the early morning air.

A group of taxi drivers were milling around waiting for the first wave of tourists to arrive. On the distant horizon an orange glow gave the promise of a sunny day as Richard and Katie strolled in silence outside the terminal building. They watched the bus drive their fellow passengers away to a hotel, and wished that they too could have had a few hours sleep, but the thought of arriving in Bogota, where Mike and Savannah were seen only hours ago, superseded any desire for slumber.

It would prove to be a long day.

* * * * *

Venus Plaza Hotel, Bogota, Saturday, October10th

Netty opened the suite door and nodded expectantly to the well-dressed man who followed him inside closing the door. Rylan Mitchell swaggered across the room with his hand out.

'Good to see you, Javier. You want coffee?'

Javier nodded. Mitchell handed him an expresso.

'So, you've had problems,' Javier said, sipping his coffee.

'Yeah, the damn kids set fire to the boat and got away. Lucan reckoned some sort of military group got them to Bogota. By the way, the Bogota cops shot Lucan dead last night.'

Javier calmly lit a cigar. 'The kids, are they in this hotel?'

'Yes, suite 106,' Mitchell replied, with a grin

Javier walked to the window. 'I have done what you asked. The helicopter is ready and the pilot can be trusted. We need to frighten the kids into leaving the hotel. I will do that.'

Mitchell poured some coffee. 'Then what?'

'Netty will follow the kids to the airport. They will try to fly north. There is nothing south of here, only the Amazon, Peru and Ecuador, and without passports they cannot cross borders.'

'Can they get an internal flight without passports?'

'No, only Colombians can do that. When the kids realise they cannot fly, they will return to Bogota and hide in another hotel, hoping the U.S. Embassy will open on Monday. We will know where they are. They will not resist; a small injection will see to that. The helicopter I have arranged will then take us to a small airfield near the Venezuelan border, where a car will be waiting. There I shall take my leave of you.'

'Piece a cake,' Netty said, popping a beer. It was nine a.m.

Ignoring him Mitchell handed Javier a shoulder bag. 'Here's the thirty-five grand it cost you to set it all up. As agreed, you'll get a share of the ransom when it's done.'

'Very well. The driver will get you and the kids across the border, where a waiting helicopter will fly you to a farm south of Puerto de La Guaira, a port north of Caracas. A van will then take you to a cargo boat named *Blue Sea Rose*. Stay in the van they will hoist it onboard. The captain has arranged all the necessary papers for departure to Cuba. There, a black SUV will be waiting for you to drive to a farmhouse, which I have arranged for you to rent. Here is the realtor's number. He is expecting your call.'

Mitchell nodded. 'Pretty impressive, Javier. Looks like we'll have those damn kids back in four or five hours.'

'Yes, all I have to do is make one or two phone calls.'

TWENTY-SEVEN

Mike awoke to find Savannah lying beside him two inches from his face. 'Hi,' he said, grinning.

Wrapping her arms around his neck she kissed him on the lips. 'I was very worried about you,' she said, kissing his nose. 'How do you feel?' she asked, kissing his chin.

Mike gazed at her in awe. It was early morning and she still looked perfect; her coral blue eyes sparkling, her face flawlessly beautiful, her long, dark hair wild and tangled, and her body that of a slender young girl. Her Rio tattoo a reminder of when they first met in the stables in what seemed a lifetime ago.

'I'm okay. Muscles feel a bit sore, that's all.'

'Good,' she said, kissing his lips again. 'I have something to tell you, and let me finish before you say anything.'

Mike laid back, hands behind his head. 'Okay, what's up?' Savannah smiled, coyly. 'I have noticed the way you look at me sometimes. Your eyes give your feelings away.'

Mike felt his cheeks burning. They were the same age and yet Savannah seemed so much worldlier than he was. Do girls grow up quicker than boys do? He wondered.

She squeezed his hand. 'Do not be embarrassed, Mike, it is quite natural. My feelings are the same as yours. We are young, together in a far away place and our hormones are in turmoil.'

Mike didn't know where to look. He wanted to crawl under the sheets. He knew the basics but…..

Savannah continued, 'I want to believe that we will come through this, but whatever happens sharing this journey with you has convinced me that I shall never want to be with anyone else. Does your heart not tell you that we have become inseparable?'

Mike's hormones were certainly in turmoil now. 'Yeah,' he whispered, and gently pulling her towards him he kissed her and the inviting wetness of her lips and sensual warmth of her breath on his face stirred his emotions beyond anything he had ever imagined. As their mouths parted, he said, 'Savannah we...

She placed her finger to his lips. 'Shsh, I will give my love to you, Mike, but not here, not now, and not just because we can. We are too young to share the gift of such a physical emotion. That magical moment is something we can look forward to. We will know when the time is right, okay?'

Unable to respond with anything intelligent Mike looked at her as if for the first time. Kissing him again she rolled off the bed and padded to the bathroom, hips swaying.

The phone rang. Their eyes locked with a questioning look. It rang again. Savannah ran to the bedside table and grabbed it.

'Hello?' No answer. 'Hello!' A hushed breath. 'Who is this?' she demanded, but the line remained silent, so she slammed the phone down. 'It was a man. I heard him breathing. The call did not come through reception, so it must have been internal.'

'Someone wants to know if this is our room.'

Savannah's eyes widened. 'They have found us.'

Mike jumped out of bed. 'And they're trying to scare us.'

'Scare us? I am terrified!'

Someone knocked on the door. They looked anxiously at one another. 'Room service!' A voice yelled.

Breathing a sigh of relief, Mike peeked through the security eye. 'Did you order breakfast?'

'Yes, cancel it we have to leave,' Savannah insisted

'He's here now and we still have to shower,' Mike argued, and held open the door as the waiter wheeled in the trolley and took out last night's debris, then he locked it. 'Tell reception we need the limo. Then take a shower while I make some calls.'

Savannah grabbed the phone. 'Where are we going?'

'The airport. I'll explain later.'

She dialled zero. 'Reception, good morning.'

'Morning, we would like to pay our bill, and then go to the airport. Perhaps in fifteen minutes.'

'I'll have it ready Miss Schlecker. The limousine is outside.'

'Quickly devouring some scrambled eggs and a sip of mango juice Savannah hurried to the bathroom. 'I will be five minutes!'

The phone rang again. Gritting his teeth, Mike picked it up and yelled, 'Who the hell is this?'

'Reception, sir, the doctor is on her way up.'

'Oh, okay, thanks,' he said, and pulled on a bathrobe.

Arriving minutes later, the doctor examined Mike thoroughly, and declaring him fit and well she grabbed her bag and walked to the door. 'Do not be put off by this episode it really *is* very rare,' she said on her way out. Mike thanked her and secured the door.

Hungry for home news he flicked through the TV channels to CNN and killed the sound. Ignoring his breakfast he reached for the phone and dialled his father's cell phone.

Wrapped in a blue bathrobe Savannah returned to find Mike sitting long-faced on the sofa. 'Did you talk to your father?'

'No, I didn't speak to anyone they were all on voicemail. Can you believe that? I can always get Mom and Dad, but not today. Oh, the doc came and checked me out, said I was okay.'

She kissed his head. 'I already knew that. Did you leave them a message? We may not get another chance for some time.'

'Yep, also for Sally Brooks, and Jules, but my sister probably went shopping with Sally and left her phone at home as usual.

'Anyone else?'

'No, all the numbers are on my lost cell phone. I tried my school, but no one's there at weekends; even Moose's phone is no longer in service, but he's always getting new free-bees.'

'Did you try his home number?'

'Yeah, it just kept ringing. Moose shuts off at weekends and helps his Mom out; she's a landscape gardener.'

'The world does not stop just because we are missing, Mike. People go shopping; buy phones, clothes, whatever, that is life.'

'Well life sucks sometimes. I'll go drown myself.'

Savannah dialled Harry's private office line and his message service kicked in, which she knew meant that he and Greta were in a meeting with their cell phones switched off; a protocol Harry insisted on. 'Harry, it's me, Savannah……..

Keeping the details to a minimum she described their brutal kidnapping and dramatic escape to Bogota, where they found the U.S. Embassy in flames and the police shot one of the kidnappers when he tried to grab them.

She went on, 'They followed us to Bogota. We are at the Venus Plaza Hotel, but we cannot stay here. When we are safely out of Bogota I will call again. Follow the American Express receipts, and tell Greta I miss her terribly. Bye, Harry.'

Hearing Nanny's voice on the answer phone brought tears to her eyes, but it was also a reminder that she and Jonathan went out on Saturdays. Briefly explaining what had happened to them she promised to call again soon and hung up, placing her head in her hands wishing she could call her mother and father.

As Mike returned drying his hair their faces appeared on the TV screen. It was the photograph taken by Richard that fateful Sunday morning. Mike clicked on the sound.

- This is CNN news. I'm Henry Bower. The disappearance of Mike Kinnerman, the teenage founder of PocketMoney.com, and 14-year-old Savannah Schlecker remains a mystery. The debate as to whether or not they were kidnapped continues, but as no ransom has been demanded and that Kinnerman, or someone like him, is using his credit card, there is growing concern that it may be something more sinister, that a kidnapping went wrong and they were murdered, or even randomly killed. Some tabloids have cynically suggested the wealthy youngsters may have run away together. Savannah is the beautiful daughter of Wall Street genius Harry Schlecker, who has offered one million dollars for any information leading to their whereabouts. More on that story later, now here's Richie Bailer with today's sport update -

'Ran away together? Are they stupid?' Mike fumed, killing the sound. 'The FBI must know that we were kidnapped.'

Savannah stood up and paced the floor. 'The FBI is the least of our problems. I am more concerned about Harry's million-dollar reward. Do you realise what that means?'

'It'll make us a prime target for every crooked cop, criminal and terrorist south of the equator,' Mike said, cynically.

'Yes, and we need help. Did you call the FBI?'

'The FBI? No.'

'Do it now, hurry we have to leave.'

'Okay,' but as he reached for the phone it rang.

Their eyes locked; was it Richard, Harry or Nanny calling back, or was it the anonymous caller. It rang again. Savannah grabbed the phone. 'Hello?' She could hear heavy breathing. 'Who is this? What do you want you pig!'

A man laughed chillingly and disconnected.

She slammed the phone down. 'It was him again, and he was laughing. They are here, Mike, somewhere in this hotel.'

Mike jumped to his feet. 'Get ready we're leaving. We'll buy a cell phone at the airport. I got an idea how to contact the FBI.'

Dressed like a million other kids on vacation; baseball caps, jeans, sneakers, sweatshirts and sunglasses they hoped to become invisible among the tourists at Eldorado Airport. As a long shot, Savannah hid their dirty clothes under a pile of towels at the back of the linen cupboard, knowing that if Richard and Katie *were* tracing their steps, finding them would be inspirational.

They took the elevator down to the ground floor and glancing around the lobby for watchful eyes they cautiously made their way to the desk. The receptionist handed Mike their hotel bill and without looking it he paid with his AmEx card.

Savannah tugged his arm urging him to leave.

'Well goodbye, and thanks for taking care of us.'

'Oh, before you go, Monsieur Arnaud asked me to give you this.' The receptionist handed him a business card.'

Mike took the card. On the back was a short handwritten note. *If I can ever be of help, call. Emile Arnaud.*

'Tell him thanks a lot. We gotta go now…bye.'

Savannah noticed a bellboy staring at her. It was the young man she had found loitering outside their room last night. Their eyes met and he quickly looked away. Thinking no more of it she and Mike crossed the lobby floor and exited through the glass revolving door. It was warm and sunny, but as they approached the limousine, Mike froze and Savannah shrieked with terror.

Twenty yards away, leaning against a black Mercedes with their arms folded, Rylan Mitchell, Javier and crew-cut Netty were staring at them with murderous eyes.

Gomez, the Colombian driver, six-four and built like a Sumo wrestler walked around to the limo's side door and placed his hands on his hips. 'Is there a problem?' he asked.

Mike turned his back to Mitchell and whispered, 'Those guys kidnapped us, but we escaped and they followed us here.'

Gomez faced the men. 'What are you doing here, what do you want with these kids?' he asked, with attitude.

Netty clenched his teeth and took a step towards Gomez, who braced himself for trouble. Mike and Savannah backed away preparing to bolt. Then Emile Arnaud strode out, accompanied by a burly security guard.

'What *is* this, what is going on out here?' Emile demanded, glaring at Netty, who backed off unclenching his fists.

Mitchell pushed back his Panama hat. 'May I remind you that we're guests in this hotel, so kindly moderate your tone,' he said, his manner that of a Machiavellian Mississippi gambler.

'And I am the manager. What is going on out here?'

'We're just chilling out,' Netty snarled, ready to explode.

Gomez pulled Emile to one side. 'The boy told me these men kidnapped them. I believe him.'

Emile nodded, and turned to Mitchell. 'Very well gentlemen, I am calling the police you can talk to them.'

'Aw come on you got it all wrong. We're just being friendly that's all. 'We don't even know these kids,' Mitchell protested.

'Liar, you kidnapped us, but we escaped and you followed us here!' Mike yelled, pulling Savannah out of harms way.

'Leave us alone you pig!' Savannah yelled.

'Get the youngsters into the limousine, Gomez, they will not be harmed,' Emile said, producing his cell phone.

Mitchell turned to Netty. 'Follow the limo. I'll check us into Hotel de la Opera. Call me when they get to the airport,' he said, and whispered to Javier, who nodded with complicity.

Gritting his teeth as if he were about to commit murder Netty climbed into the Mercedes driver's seat. Growling the engine he pointed a finger at Mike as if it were a revolver and screeched away, leaving a cloud of dust in his wake. Shaking his head in response to Netty's inane volatility Emile told the security guard to stay there until the youngsters had safely left in the limousine. Giving Mike and Savannah a reassuring smile Emile returned through the revolving glass doors to the lobby. Savannah gave Mitchell a parting shot with her middle finger as she snuggled up to Mike in the limo's rear seat. Javier chuckled and lit a cigar. Mitchell's eyes narrowed with promised revenge.

Folding his huge frame into the driver's seat Gomez clicked the shift into gear, and keeping an eye on the rear view mirror he sped away heading for Eldorado airport.

Mike and Savannah sighed with relief.

Neither looked back.

TWENTY-EIGHT

They were alone in a dangerous country, and with Mitchell and Netty determined to hunt them down, it was only a matter of time before their luck ran out. Under any other circumstance seeking help from the authorities would be their ticket home, but with a million-dollar reward on offer and corruption rife in Colombia, another kidnapping was more likely than a possibility, and going to the police downright suicidal. They decided to ask the airport authorities for help. Like all international airports El Dorado had access to enforcement agencies around the world, making it a much safer bet. One call from immigration to the FBI and they could be on a flight home in a few hours. Maybe.

Mike sat in thoughtful silence. Savannah gazed out the tinted side window; something about that bellboy worried her.

Gomez caught their faces in the rear view mirror. 'That gorilla driving the Mercedes, he is following us,' he said, calmly.

They turned around and there was Netty pursuing like an assassin - blonde crew cut, sunglasses and his huge hands on the steering wheel. In the distance, Eldorado airport shimmered in a haze of heat, and once they were inside the terminal, Netty would be nothing more than a bad dream.

Gomez cruised down the slip road and veered right towards the airport. Then out of nowhere, a black van screeched across the road and smashed into the side doors. The limo skidded out of control and crashed into a line of canopy trees.

Mike and Savannah tumbled to the floor. Gomez flew across the front seat, smashing his head on the window and lay bleeding over the passenger seat. Four balaclavered men with automatic weapons jumped out of the steel-plated van and wrenched open the limo's rear doors. Savannah screamed in terror as one of the men dragged her out to the van. Another opened the front door and shot Gomez several times in the head.

When Netty drove down the slip road and saw the carnage he braked, reaching for his revolver, but he was too late; one of the balaclavered men fired at him, shattering the Mercedes' front and side windows. Head down, he slammed his foot to the floor and sped away as more bullets ripped through the rear windows. Safely out of range, he pulled the windowless Mercedes to the roadside and reached for his cell phone.

Curled up below the rear seat Mike held his hands to his face in terror. One of the men reached in and tried to grab him, but he kicked out with both feet. The man hit him on the jaw with the butt of his weapon and dragged him out to the van. The others poured gasoline inside the limo, and then tossing in a lighted match they jumped back in the van. The limo exploded into a fireball, and as the van raced away the men held Mike and Savannah face down and injected them with some sort of drug.

Then everything went dark.

At a rendezvous east of Bogota, they hauled the unconscious youngsters out the van and bundled them into a helicopter, which took off heading North to the Andes Mountains.

Mitchell's jaw dropped when Netty told him that a group of terrorists had just kidnapped the kids, and he wondered if it was Rizzio's handy work. Either way, he wanted nothing to do with militants. He cursed Rizzio, the kids, Rio and his damn bad luck and told Netty to meet him at the airport, secretly wishing he'd gone to Mexico with Wilson.

The game was up. It was time to disappear.

* * * * *

The terrorist camp, Saturday, October 10th

They woke up on the wooden floor of a shabby brick room; their mouths parched and their heads throbbing. A log fire blazed in a charred brick fireplace and a naked light bulb hung above from a rotting ceiling. Opening his bloodshot eyes Mike felt his swollen jaw and looked in horror at the metal shackle around his ankle, which their murderous captors had chained to the floor. Savannah woke up and immediately vomited; her face ashen and her hands trembling. Mike held her in his arms.

The door flew open. Two balaclavered men stormed into the room. Mike and Savannah huddled together afraid of what they might do to them. A woman in a green sweater, black skirt, boots and a red beret limped across the room and placed a tray of food beside them. She was young, but looked older than her years. She grabbed Savannah's hair and pulled her head back. *'Pretty girl,'* she said, her smoky voice void of any emotion. Then she spat in Mike's face and limped outside. Leaving a bucket, toilet paper and two blankets the men followed her out and locked the door.

Savannah unrolled some toilet tissue and wiped the stinking vomit off her clothes. Mike cleaned the phlegm off his face, and for the first time since their frightening ordeal began he saw a look of hopelessness in Savannah's coral blue eyes. He searched for words to comfort her, but none came. They were in the hands of a paramilitary group.

It was terrifying.

The tray contained a jug of water, coffee, bananas and black bread, but fear had suppressed any thought of nourishment. They sat as close to the fire as the chains would allow and bathed in its glowing warmth. Mike gazed thoughtfully into the flames. The room temperature was close to freezing, and in Colombia that could only mean one thing; they were somewhere high in the Andes Mountains surrounded by dense jungle, and their chances of escape were zero. If so, they were captives in one of nature's formidable landscapes, and their uncertain fate lay in the hands of political guerrillas, who ransom lives merely to fund their cause.

The most frightening thing of all was how they had murdered Gomez in cold blood.

It was sickening.

* * * * *

Bogota, Saturday, October 10th

Richard and Katie landed at El Dorado airport just after two p.m. and as they followed the signs to passport control, both their cell phones indicated new voicemails. Joining the queue at the barrier they listened to Mike's emotional message.

He was in Bogotá, only minutes away.

Harry called and for once he had good news. 'Richard, we got a message from Savannah today. Apparently those scumbags followed them to Bogota and they've made a run for it.'

'Did she mention a name, who took them?'

'No, just a quick rundown. She was real upset, saw the cops shoot one of the kidnappers dead outside the embassy when he tried to grab 'em. Christ knows how she'll get over that.'

'I doubt she'll lose sleep over him. What else did she say?'

'That they're scared but somehow surviving. Can you believe that? When I heard her young voice, I cried like a goddam baby. They're in real trouble and I wanna do something, but I honestly don't know what. Kidnapping is a way of life down there.'

'Mike left us a message and we feel the same, damn helpless. At least we know where to start looking. Anything else?'

'Mike paid their hotel bill with his AmEx card this morning. I called the hotel but they'd left. Go find em, Richard. If you need me, I'm a few hours away. Tell Katie I'll keep an eye on Jules.'

Passport control waved them through with the usual stare and they hurried to the airport desk; Carla was on duty.

Big smile. 'Can I help you, sir?'

'Yes, I'd like you to call the Venus Plaza Hotel and ask for the manager. It's an emergency.' Richard said, knowing that it was a long shot, but he might know something.

Carla spoke to the receptionist and handed him the phone. A moment later, a voice answered. 'Emile Arnaud.'

'Hi, I'm Richard Kinnerman. My wife and I just arrived from New York. We're looking for our son, Mike. He was at....

'Mr. Kinnerman, your son and Miss Schlecker left for the airport this morning. When they checked into the hotel last night Miss Schlecker said they planned to go north to Cartegena.'

Richard's heart sank. 'Cartegena, did they say why?'

'No, and I didn't think to ask. The news report here only said they had run away together, but three men apparently followed them to this hotel and they were very frightened.'

'Okay, thanks. I'll try the airlines.' Richard handed Carla the phone. 'Look, we're managing an emergency here. We're trying to locate our missing son, Mike Kinnerman and his girlfriend, Savannah Schlecker. They may have flown to Cartegena earlier today. Do you have passenger lists for internal flights?'

'Yes we do.' Carla scrolled down the list on her screen and shook her head. 'There is no Kinnerman or Schlecker listed, but there are other ways they could have travelled.'

'You mean private hire?'

'Yes, by jet, helicopter, chauffeured car or bus.'

'Mmm, what time's the next flight to Cartegena?'

Carla exhaled and shook her head again. 'I am very sorry, sir, there is nothing available today. All the flights are full and we have a long standby list.'

Richard gripped the desk and studied the floor. Katie turned away in a disgruntled manner. 'Can we get a train or hire a car?' he asked, without looking up.

'There are very few trains in Colombia; people fly or go by bus. The bus journey takes eighteen hours, and some take longer due to stop and searches by the military.'

Katie's eyes widened. 'Searches by the military? It sounds like a goddam war zone. Are there no other options?'

'You can rent a car, but tourists are advised not to drive into the mountains. We have a serious problem here with FARC - the Revolutionary Armed Forces of Colombia. They stop buses and cars at gunpoint, hoping to kidnap a wealthy tourist. They call it "Miracle Fishing" and you would be a prime target.'

'We'll fly. When can we go?' Richard asked, irritably.

'15:30 tomorrow. I advise you to book now we are busy at this time of year. May I ask how old your son is, sir?'

'He's fourteen, they both are, why?'

'Do they have passports?'

'Yes, but not with them.'

Carla exhaled. 'I'm sorry, sir, but…

'Wait a minute, you don't understand,' Katie interjected. 'A week ago, they were kidnapped in the U.S. and taken to Rio, but they escaped and made it to Bogota. Last night they stayed at the Venus Plaza Hotel, and this morning they came to this airport. That's all we know. Now are you gonna help us or not?'

Carla deflected the attitude. 'I am very sorry. You must be going through a terrible ordeal. I really am trying to be helpful here. Your son did not fly to Cartegena, even privately, because only Colombians can fly internally without passports.'

Richard looked at Carla. 'Wait a minute. If they came direct from the hotel to the airport believing they could fly, there's a chance that Mike could still be here. Can you page him?'

Katie gripped his arm. 'It's worth a try, Richard, but don't mention his name. Use something that only Mike would know.'

'Carla, say this; Richard and Katie are looking for Jules and Piffin. Please come to the airport desk.'

Carla announced the message in English. An irritable queue had gathered behind them. 'There are people waiting, sir. Would you mind standing aside for a moment while I deal with them.'

After paging Mike a second and third time, Carla sighed and gave up. 'I am sorry, sir, they are obviously not here. I have made a note of their names. Where can I contact you if they show up?'

Richard rubbed his face. 'The Venus Plaza Hotel.'

'Fine, I pray that you soon find your son. Meanwhile, try to enjoy our beautiful city,' Carla said, with an airport smile.

After queuing in the chaos outside the terminal, they climbed into an ageing Honda and sat cramped together in the back seat while the driver cruised along as though he was on lunch break. Neither noticed the burnt out limousine on the other side of the highway. The humidity was close to unbearable and with no air conditioning all the windows were down. A rumble of thunder rolled across the blackened sky, leaving thick spots of rain over the filthy windscreen.

Unconcerned, the unshaven driver tapped his fingers to some Latin female singer on a tinny radio, while Katie nodded off with exhaustion from her epic journey.

Richard looked thoughtfully out the open window and tried to figure out why Mike and Savannah would go to Cartegena, if indeed that was their plan. Maybe they changed their minds, got a lift, caught a bus, or something unforeseen happened. He shook his head; no, the men who followed them to the hotel must have been the kidnappers, what other reason would they have to leave Bogota in such a hurry? But if they didn't fly anywhere, where the hell did they go?

The taxi pulled up outside the marble entrance of the Venus Plaza hotel. A police car, abandoned by its occupants, sat in the middle of the drive-through, its blue light still flashing. The taxi driver gave a toothless smile at the tip and remained seated while Richard hauled Katie's suitcase and his shoulder bag out of the trunk. Then he drove off.

A teenage bellboy grabbed the baggage and led them through the glass revolving door to reception. Katie leaned on the black marble desk, visualising Mike and Savannah standing there a few hours ago. Perhaps if she had caught an earlier flight to New York....she bit her lip and let the thought pass.

'I'm Richard Kinnerman. I'd like to speak to the manager.'

The receptionist picked up a phone and mumbled something in French. Emile Arnaud promptly appeared from a rear office, accompanied by three police officers, one in plain clothes who introduced himself as Aldo. 'Mr. Kinnerman. I am Emile Arnaud, the hotel manager. You called from the airport about your son.'

'Yes I did, and this is my wife, Katie.'

Aldo, mid forties, five ten, dark hair and wearing a visible shoulder holster inside his leather jacket exhaled and spoke in English. 'Mr. Kinnerman, I am afraid I have bad news. We found the limousine that took your son to the airport; it was lying at the roadside burnt to a cinder. We found the driver's remains inside. He had been shot four times.'

'Oh my God!' Katie yelled, with tearful anger. 'What kind of goddam people do that?'

Richard reached out to her, but she turned away. 'Shot?' he said, almost choking on the word.

'Yes, but there was no sign of your son and his companion in the wreckage, which means they are probably still alive,' Aldo said, trying to show a little compassion.

'Probably is not the word I was hoping for. So what's the bottom line, your gut feeling?' Richard asked, curtly.

'Escape is unlikely; I believe they were targeted for kidnap, which sadly has become an epidemic in Colombia. I am sorry.'

'Sorry? What the hell good will that do?' Katie snapped.

Richard placed his arm around her. 'Look, we're a couple of days past bedtime, and to be told that our son has been kidnapped again is not the best news we were hoping for. We're kinda edgy here, so cut us a little slack.'

'I understand Mr. Kinnerman. I wish I had better news to offer you.' Aldo said, checking his cell phone messages.

A couple with a young son and daughter wearing "England" sweatshirts checked in at the desk. Katie looked away.

Keen to vindicate his impartiality Emile Arnaud leaned over the reception desk and clasped his hands.

'Your son and his lovely companion were very young to be travelling alone, but it was late and they needed a room for the night. They were clearly distressed and had nowhere else to go, and to turn them away would have been irresponsible. I hope you understand,' Emile said, his forehead creased with concern.

Richard waved him away. 'I'm not blaming you, Emile.'

'Of course not, but we are all deeply shocked by what has happened to them.'

'Oh really, then how do you think we feel?' Katie said, with tearful indignation. 'I arrived in this country two hours ago, only to be told that my son was kidnapped this morning and how sorry everyone is. Where I come from kidnapping is a serious crime, but here it seems to be a way of life. Why in Gods name won't somebody do something?'

Overhearing Katie's anguish for her missing son, the English couple looked at her with concerned sympathy as they followed the bellboy to the elevator, clutching their children.

Aldo raised his hands in a calming gesture. 'Look, I know you are very upset Mrs. Kinnerman, but a burnt out car tells me nothing. Until I know which group took them and how they knew the kids were going to the airport I am in the dark.'

'Do you have any idea?' Richard asked him.

'Not yet, but I will,' Aldo said, and walked off clamping a cell phone to his ear.

Richard's phone rang; it was JB Walsome. 'Hi, Richard, I'm glad you got the visas okay. Hope you and Katie are holding up. Guess you're in Brazil by now, any further news?'

'Yes, we're in Bogota, JB. A terrorist group kidnapped Mike and Savannah this morning, and we're pretty shaky, worse.'

'Bogota? Oh Christ no. If I can…well, you know the rest.'

'I know, thanks, JB. I'll call you.' Richard hung up.

Emile handed Richard a sheet of headed paper. 'I thought you might like to see this. It is your son's hotel bill.'

Katie joined Richard and went through their list of items: dinner, red wine, bottled water, breakfast and international calls. 'And what's this, ninety-seven dollars for a doctor?' Katie asked, with concern, knowing Mike was rarely ill.

'Your son became ill after eating shellfish last night, but the doctor said he was fine this morning,' Emile explained, folding his arms. 'They are nice kids, I hope….

Emile's voice faded to a foggy mumble as Richard and Katie, numbed by the dreadful news, held one another. For them the hotel receipt was a cruel reminder they had missed Mike and Savannah by just a few hours; a few hours in which their plane had broken down and they had sat in a stinking room at Miami airport; a few hours in which they just might have prevented their violent kidnapping by a terrorist group.

Now, for the first time since this wretched nightmare began, they were beginning to wonder if they would ever see Mike and Savannah alive again.

TWENTY-NINE

News that terrorists had killed Gomez and kidnapped two guests quickly spread throughout the Venus Plaza hotel, leaving shocked staff fearing for their lives. In an effort to placate their concern Emile offered transport to and from work, and assured them the incident had nothing to do with the hotel. At reception, worried guests demanded to know how they would get to the airport, since the driver and limousine were no longer available.

Devastated by the latest kidnapping and exhausted from her epic journey around the globe, Katie sat on her suitcase with her head in her hands, staring vacantly at the marble floor.

Pocketing his cell phone Aldo rejoined Richard and Emile at the reception desk. 'We have just received an anonymous call. It came from a woman who claimed to be a friend of Gomez, and she sounded very upset. She said a bellboy is responsible for his murder and disconnected. We traced the call to a payphone. How many boys work here?' Aldo asked.

'Six, two are here this afternoon, two are on duty at seven, and two others start at five a.m.'

Aldo noticed one of the boys standing by the reception desk with his hands behind his back, and intuitively sensed that he was listening to every word. He shared his suspicion with Emile, who summoned him in front of the desk. The boy's eyes widened, and panicking he bolted for the glass revolving door, but was quickly apprehended by another officer and brought before Aldo.

'What do you know about this boy? Tell me or I'll beat it out of you. I know you boys speak English, so let's hear it.'

Visibly shaking the boy spoke up. 'A woman, she cover her face. She want to know where Mike Kinnerman is. She give me a phone number and offer two hundred dollars,' he said, looking nervously at Richard. 'I don't say no more.'

Aldo slapped the boys face. 'Tell me what happened!'

He nervously rubbed his glowing cheek. 'I…call number this morning. A man, he tell me to go to the old market with white cloth in my left hand. I go there and a bearded man, he drag me into dark alley. He has big knife. I am scared. I tell him Mike Kinnerman is at Venus Plaza; he wants to pay his bill and have limousine to the airport. The man give me two hundred dollars and say he kills me if I tell anyone.'

'So that's how they knew the youngsters were going to the airport. Now Gomez is dead and two kids are missing because of you. Have you seen this man before boy?' Aldo barked.

'No sir. I am sorry. I need money for my mama, she is sick.'

'I am not interested in your excuses, give me the number.'

The boy held out his left wrist, which had a faded number written on it. Aldo wrote it down and nodded to the other officer to take the boy away. Emile studied his shoes and shook his head. A group of nearby guests muttered and tutted; a five-star hotel, are we not safe anywhere these days?

Aldo went on. 'Well Mr. Kinnerman, the youngsters appear to have been kidnapped, so we must assume they are alive.'

'Kidnapped? On the way to the airport? What kind of goddam country is this?' Richard growled.

'A troubled country,' Aldo countered. 'I will do everything in my power to find them, but it will not be easy. These groups are heavily armed, organized and ruthless. If we do not play by their rules, they will kill your son and the girl. You must understand, for them it is only about money, life is meaningless.'

'For God's sake! When is this going to end, when my son is dead?' Katie yelled. The hotel lobby fell silent. She was sick of crying, of being afraid and having her family torn apart by those with no respect for life. She turned away and wiped her eyes, her mind burning with hatred for those who took her son.

'Is there anything else I can do?' Aldo asked.

'No. Thanks,' Richard said, emphatically. 'I'll talk to the U.S. Embassy when it opens. If I need your help I'll call.'

Aldo handed him his card. 'Don't do anything stupid Mr. Kinnerman. This is Colombia, not America. I will be in touch.'

Richard turned to Emile. 'We'd like to offer our condolences to the driver's family. The terrorists only murdered him because he was with our son. I am truly sorry.'

Emile nodded sombrely. 'I will inform his wife of your kind words, she is my wife's sister. Will there be anything else?'

'Yes, we'd like suite 106, I'm sure you understand why, and dinner in the restaurant around eight.'

Emile checked the computer. 'That is fine, will that be all?'

'Yes, thank you.'

Richard signed the register and handed their passports to the receptionist, who snapped her fingers at the bellboy and gave him the key card. Grabbing their bags, the young man led them to the elevator and pressed floor one. A breath later, the doors opened and they followed him along a carpeted corridor to 106. Placing the key card in the door he led them into the luxurious twin suite. Richard told him to leave their baggage by the beds, and then handed him a tip as he left closing the door.

Katie softly ran her hands over the twin beds that Mike and Savannah had slept in only hours ago, and cursed the cruel twist of fate that had brought them to Bogota too late to save them. If only I had….she stopped herself, recrimination was pointless.

Venting her anger she searched for anything they may have left behind, in the closets, the drawers, under the beds, even the mini bar, but found nothing. Finally, having dragged everything out of the bathroom linen cupboard and thrown it on the floor, she stepped back wide-eyed with her hands to her mouth.

Hidden deep in the cupboard were two pairs of dirty jeans, t-shirts, socks and pants. Hearing Katie scream, Richard ran into the bathroom and found her on her knees holding the dirty clothes against her tearful face. He helped Katie up and led her into the bedroom, then hurrying to the dining area he took a bottle of mineral water from the mini bar. Returning to the bedroom, he found clothes strewn across the floor and Katie curled up in bed clutching Mike and

Savannah's dirty clothes. Smiling with her last ounce of strength she closed her eyes and drifted away.

Gently removing the clothes from Katie's arms he kissed her on the cheek. Then silently sliding open the balcony window he stepped outside and took a breath. The air was humid, oppressive and black clouds loomed over the city. Leaning over the balcony rail he tried to unravel Mike and Savannah's travel plans.

A pigeon landed on the next balcony and surveyed the view below. Richard watched, amused by the creature, then as it flew away to the nearby park, a thought occurred to him; a detail that he had overlooked. Without passports Mike and Savannah could not fly commercially, so how did they travel 2,800 miles from Rio to Bogota in one day? If they had somehow managed to hire a plane American Express would know about it, but they hadn't, which left only one possibility; they had help, but who was it?

He doubted the U.S. Embassy would know, but maybe Harry could find out. He dialled his number and the sound of kids in the park brought a lump to his throat as it rang. 'Yeah?' 'Harry, I have bad news. Terrorists kidnapped Mike and Savannah today near Bogota airport, and murdered the hotel's limo driver.

A dreadful silence filled the line.

Richard listened as Harry relayed the terrible news to Greta, who began sobbing her heart out. Apparently, she was holding a blue seashell with Savannah's photo imprinted on it, which had just arrived from St Lucia.

'Christ, Richard, this is goin from bad to worse. Who the hell are these bozos, any idea?' Harry growled, burning with rage.

'No.'

'Can you imagine what those kids are going through? They must be terrified outa their goddam minds. Maybe I should hire a bunch of mercenaries to kill the goddam lot of them; life seems pretty cheap down there.'

'Stay calm, Harry.'

'Stay calm? I've talked to the FBI and the CIA. I've had arms twisted in Rio. I've yelled at powerful people all over South America. I've offered a million dollars for any knowledge of their whereabouts. Now, a paramilitary group has my daughter and you're telling me to STAY FRIGGIN CALM!'

More silence

Harry blew out some air. 'Dyou want some company? I can fly down today.'

'No, but thanks. We'll try to trace their movements and hope for a break. Who knows, maybe we'll get lucky. And you know what? It's comforting to know that you're there, Harry. You can keep an eye on Julieanne, and the company. And should we need money, information, documentation, or a jet, I can call you.'

'Okay, but if they're in the hands of a terrorist group, it's a different ballgame. They're fanatics, and without military help you could get yourself killed, so forget any ideas about doin some kinda rescue. That said; what dyou want me to do?'

'You're well connected, Harry, and perhaps you can tap into someone who might know how Mike and Savannah got out of Brazil. They left Rio and landed in Bogota the same day, which is impossible unless…'

'They flew.'

'Right, but they have no passports, so it was not a scheduled flight; someone with clearance, possibly government or military, got them to Bogota. If we can find out who they are, then maybe, for a price, they'll help us get them back. It's worth a shot.

'Gotcha, lemme call you back.'

Harry called Larry Harbourne, who responded with his usual affable greeting. 'Harry! It's great to hear your voice my friend. Any news of your daughter yet?'

'Yeah, and it's not good. A terrorists group kidnapped Mike and Savannah today, in Bogota, and I wanna know how they got out of Brazil. Ask your CIA pal, it's important.'

The story had yet to hit the news and Larry, deeply shocked, felt partially responsible. 'Christ, Harry, this is bad. I don't know what to say. Leave it with me; I'll do what I can.'

'Call me right back.'

Larry called Ben Brakker, who took the official line. 'I can't comment on how they got out of Brazil. Leave it there, Larry. We know about the latest terrorist kidnapping, that's all I'm prepared to say. However, something is about to go down that might solve the problem, but I can't promise anything. I guess you're talking to Harry Schlecker, if so, tell him the Kinnermans need to stay put in Bogota. We never had this conversation.'

Larry relayed Ben's conversation to Harry, and said he would not comment on how the kids left Brazil. He hated lying, even though it was true. Harry hung up and called Richard back.

'They CIA refused to comment on how they got out of Brazil, but they know about the terrorist kidnap. The good news is, something's about to go down and they're advising you to stay in Bogota. They would not elaborate. Gimme a call as soon as you know anything. By the way, Greta saw Jules this morning.'

'Good, how is she?'

'Apparently, Mike left her a message and she keeps playing it. I take it you haven't told her about the terrorist kidnap.'

'No, and it's not something I'm looking forward to. She's on the edge, Harry. Keep an eye on her. I'll call the U.S. Embassy on Monday and find out what they know. We'll talk later.'

Richard hung up and went off to take a shower. Apart from spare underwear and a clean shirt, all he had were the clothes he was wearing and they stank, so he needed to buy some daywear, who knows how long they'd be in Bogota.

As the hot water bubbled over his face he thought about what Harry's contact had said. Some sort of operation was about to go down, and if the CIA was involved, it was probably military. Was that a coded way of saying they had found the terrorists, or was it just wishful thinking? Either way, nothing was about happen that day, not unless Mike called. It was not scintillating news, but at least they were no longer isolated in a foreign country, wondering who to turn to, which in itself was a small comfort. With that in mind Richard saw no reason to wake Katie. She had travelled halfway around the world, only to face more bad news. He would let her sleep through until morning; she was exhausted.

Reception directed Richard to a nearby mall where he bought an assortment of clothes, a suitcase and a pair of gold earrings for Katie as small a token of reconciliation. He returned to their hotel suite and looked in on Katie, to make sure that she was sleeping soundly. She was. Quietly changing into clean clothes he tiptoed out and took the elevator to the mezzanine restaurant. A waiter ushered him to a balcony table and took his order for the chef's special and a bottle of Amarone wine.

Then with a heavy heart Richard called Julieanne. Two rings and her bubbly voice answered. 'Hi, Dad, love you miss you.'

'Me too, sweetheart, you okay?'

'Moose sent me a copy of Mike's email, and guess what? Mike left a message on my cell telling me not to worry, that he would be home soon. It's was so great to hear his voice. I can't stop playing it. It's like he's in the room, you know.'

Richard sank back in his chair. 'Jules, listen honey, I have some bad news. A terrorist group kidnapped Mike and Savannah this morning, in Bogota, and we're devastated, worse.'

The line fell silent. Richard wanted to reach out to her, to hold her in his arms, to tell her that his heart was breaking too, that he would bring Mike home no matter what, but he knew the gut-wrenching news had shattered her growing optimism, and that promises would be meaningless.

'Can I talk to Mom?' Julieanne asked, tearfully.

'Your Mom's asleep, sweetheart, she's exhausted.'

The line went dead.

U.S. Surveillance & Intelligence Operations

Classified Document

Washington DC 20606

October 9th Memo: code X51204

Attn: Major Bell. Special Forces Unit. Brazil

Subject: American Hostages

Country: Colombia

Issue: Hostage Rescue Mission

Dear Major Bell,

As you are aware, a week ago three American female tourists; the daughters of Senator Goldman, Judge Hinkle and Carl Weisman, Assistant Director of the CIA were brutally kidnapped by a terrorist group in Bogota; an incident many high-ranking officers at Langley and the Pentagon consider a threat to U.S. security. Following discussions at the White House our Colombian operatives approached all known local subversive political networks. They threw money around, cajoled informers, made threats and called in favours. Forty-eight hours later, we had the terrorist camp location; an isolated farmhouse three hundred miles north of Bogota in the Andes Mountains. We negotiated a deal with the Colombians and they have sanctioned a covert operation by U.S. Special Forces to rescue the hostages. Location details will come via the usual method. Any questions call me.

Sincerely

Rachel Steiner – Director of Operations

THIRTY

At two-thirty a.m. Sunday, October 11th, a cargo plane landed and taxied to the hangers at El Dorado airport, Bogota. Eight heavily armed soldiers in combat fatigues jumped out and boarded two helicopters, which took off and headed north. Two hours later, after refuelling at a secret base near the Venezuelan border, they flew north west and touched down at a clearing five miles south of a farmhouse high in the Andes Mountains. The soldiers jumped out and quickly melted into the jungle. The helicopters turned south and headed back to the border base. At six-forty, having reached the perimeter fence, the blackened faced unit made a silent sweep around the farmhouse, and then vanished in the undergrowth.

The terrorist camp, seven a.m.

Banging open the door two burly masked men entered the room, followed by the young woman limping across the wooden floor, her face frozen with bitterness. Unshackling Savannah's leg-iron she dragged her out to a doorless bathroom with a filthy sink and a stinking toilet, and gave her five minutes to clean herself up. After subjecting Mike to the same indifference one of the men handed them a tray of coffee and black bread and stormed out locking the door. Savouring the warm, sweet coffee Mike and Savannah sat shivering on the wooden floor of the bitterly cold windowless brick room. The once glowing fire had dwindled to smouldering ashes and there had been no attempt to revive it.

Huddling together to keep warm they spoke in whispers of their uncertain future, and many questions remained unanswered; what if they should need a doctor or a dentist: could they survive years of captivity, won't the terrorists murder them anyway, would the FBI search for two kids held by terrorists in the Andes Mountains? It seemed unlikely, which left only one conclusion; they were alone and no one was coming to the rescue.

Their fears came to life when another masked duo entered the room, one having to lower his head through the doorway. The other man, holding a camera, handed Savannah the October issue of Vogue Magazine, its cover featuring a boy and girl chained to the White House perimeter fence, wearing gruesome masquerade masks. The caption read; Tourists or Terrorists?

'Una copia de Inglés?' *An English copy*? Savannah asked.

'Yes, from New York. Sit together and hold the magazine in front of you. I need to see the date. No smiles,' he ordered.

He took a series of photographs and retrieved the magazine. The tall man threw down two sweaters and told them to put them on as he removed their leg-irons. Both welcomed the warmth of the thick wool on their chilled bodies. Then a boy aged around twelve entered the room carrying a rifle, and nodding to the men he walked out leaving the door open. The men hauled Mike and Savannah out and bundled them into the back of a military jeep. The waiting silent boy bound their wrists and ankles and placed a blanket over their legs. Savannah tried using sign language, but the boy looked puzzled and walked off, glancing back.

Freezing mist shrouded the surrounding dense woodland.

A tall, heavy-set man, in army fatigues and his face hidden beneath a black balaclava, approached the jeep and spoke with a gruff voice. 'I know you are afraid, but no harm will come to you unless you attempt to escape, understood?'

Mike and Savannah nodded. His tone was menacing, but his huge stature and staring masked eyes made him terrifying.

'You are going to our base camp,' the man explained. 'There, our comrades will ensure you have all your basic needs. Ransom negotiations will begin soon, but these things take time, so be prepared to remain with us for a year or two, perhaps longer. Do nothing stupid and you will survive.' He nodded to the unmasked driver. 'Take them,' he ordered, and marched off towards the farmhouse, where the young crippled woman, wearing a belt of bullets over her a combat jacket, a red beret and sunglasses, stood on the porch smoking a cigar with her arm around the mute boy.

Crunching the jeep into gear the driver headed down a narrow ice-filled potholed track. A thick blanket of mist hung over the dramatic cliffs and sloping fields, where sheep and goats silently grazed in an ever-whispering breeze. Far below, the tangled mass of a dense steamy jungle stretched as far as the eye could see. The mountain looked cold, wild and desolate.

Mike observed the dark-haired driver, who looked to be in his early twenties and wore jeans, muddy boots, a thick sweater and a combat jacket. He smoked small, black cigars and showed a keen affection for the AK47 assault rifle beside him on the front seat. How many people had he kidnapped and killed? Had he grown up at the camp with no education, was this the only way of life he knew? Mike mused, almost feeling sorry for him.

Savannah despised him.

The driver suddenly cursed and braked, bringing the jeep to a skidding halt a few yards from a tree blocking the track. Grabbing his AK 47 rifle he climbed out and as he attempted to move it, a ghostly-faced soldier jumped out of the dense foliage, snapped his neck and dragged him down in the undergrowth. Frozen with fear, Mike and Savannah sat wide-eyed wondering if they were about to die. Seconds later, another seven heavily armed soldiers, camouflaged with leaves and greasepaint, emerged out of the undergrowth and gathered around the jeep.

'You seem to make a habit of getting yourselves into trouble,' one man said. The other blackened faces chuckled but their eyes were everywhere.

Mike and Savannah looked at the man in astonishment and spoke in unison. 'Colin?'

When the U.S. surveillance satellite revealed two blips at the terrorist camp location, Jamie had no doubt they were Mike and Savannah's, and that they were in trouble. Nevertheless, he was relieved to know that they were alive and on his radar, but he had not expected to find them sitting in an open top jeep.

'Indeed, you know the boys of course,' he said, motioning a hand to his men who were clearly in a high state of readiness for combat but managed a toothy smile.

Mike breathed out. 'I can't tell you how glad I am to see you guys,' he said, the colour noticeably returning to his face.

'Me too, but I almost died of fright,' Savannah said, holding out her hands. 'Would one of you please cut off this tape?'

As the blood circulation returned to their hands and ankles, they jumped out of the jeep and stretched their legs. Jamie folded his arms and smiled with admiration for their tenacity.

'The U.S. Embassy gas explosion was unfortunate. It killed a number of staff and left you vulnerable, which gave the terrorists an opportunity to kidnap you,' Jamie said, turning to one of his men. 'Get some grease and hats on these two.'

'It happened so fast,' Mike garbled. 'They rammed the limo, shot the driver, shoved us in a van and gave us some sort of drug, then we woke up in a freezing room. It was horrific.'

'They chained us to the floor, Colin. Can you believe that?' Savannah said, revealing dark bruising around her ankle.

Jamie nodded. 'Kidnapping is a very nasty business. When I saw those two blips on my screen, I knew that you were here and very much alive. How many others are in the house?'

Mike shrugged. 'Not sure, they wore balaclavas. Maybe six or seven guys, a woman and a mute boy.'

Jamie suddenly paid urgent attention to his earpiece. 'Damn it they know we're here, how the hell did that happen?'

One of the soldiers approached the jeep. 'We got company, sir. A chopper with nine players heading this way; ETA fourteen minutes,' he reported, calmly.

'Right, scan the jeep,' Jamie ordered. 'Can you drive?'

'Sure,' Mike said, frowning. 'Are we going somewhere?'

One of the men rubbed greasepaint on their hands and faces and gave them each a tropical military hat.

'Can we stay with you, Colin, please,' Savannah pleaded.

'No, I can't risk it. Our mission is to retrieve three female hostages. You are a bonus. Fortunately you have escaped, but you cannot stay here this area is crawling with terrorists. We believe there are nine targets in the house, and with nine more and maybe others on the way, a gun battle is inevitable. If I leave you here and the operation goes wrong they will certainly kill you, and I am not going to let that happen,' Jamie said, emphatically.

A soldier handed him a small disk. 'A tracking device, sir, it was under the jeep,' he reported, and returned to keep watch.

Jamie stamped on it. 'Thank God we found it or they would have tracked you down,' he said, opening a map over the jeep's bonnet. 'Now, I want you to follow this track down the mountain to the main road here, then turn right and head for Cartegena.'

'Cartegena? On our own?' Savannah objected.

'Yes, I want you off this mountain out of harms way, and this is the safest option. When these terrorists realise that you have escaped, their comrades will try to hunt you down, but we intend to keep them busy, and by the time this operation is over I want you safely hidden on a boat, so please do as I ask. Cartegena is only 130 miles north west of here, and the road is reasonable,' Jamie explained, looking at his watch again.

'So what happens in Cartegena?' Mike asked, with growing trepidation. He could drive but... down a mountain, in a jungle?

'Mingle with the tourists and find the marina. Look for a boat named Maitre d`, it's owned by a fisherman named Juan, whom I trust. You will be quite safe at sea. Juan will take you to the U.S. Embassy in Panama and they will get you home.

'Why can't we drive to Panama?' Mike asked.

'There are no roads between Panama and Colombia due to civil unrest and cattle infection. The strip of land between the two countries is known as, "The Darien Gap" 160 kilometres of dense jungle, inhabited by dangerous guerrillas. Any more questions?'

'I guess not,' Mike said, reluctantly climbing into the jeep.

Jamie saw the apprehension in Savannah's eyes. 'I know you are afraid, but please do as I ask. Once you are on the boat your fears will pass,' he assured her. 'You will reach the highway in a couple of hours. From there, it's a reasonable drive to Cartegena.'

A helicopter chattered somewhere in the distance. 'Gotta go, sir,' a soldier said, with a heightened sense of urgency.

The men dragged the tree off the road and nodded at Jamie to join them; it was time to face the enemy.

Tucking her hair beneath the hat Savannah climbed into the jeep. 'You mentioned two blips, what did you mean?'

Colin lifted her left sleeve. 'Those,' he said, pointing to the black bracelet he gave her in Rio. 'They are tiny transmitters that will enable me to keep track of you, so keep them on. Here, take this you might need it,' he said, handing her a wad of pesos.

Gunfire suddenly cracked in the air and as white-hot bullets strafed the ground, the soldiers melted into the forest.

'Go! Don't stop for anything!' Jamie yelled, and vanished.

Mike slammed the jeep into gear and as he put his foot down a bullet smashed the left side mirror, spraying chards of glass into the air. 'Get down, Savannah!' he yelled, and sinking to the floor she saw a revolver under the front seat.

With the crack of automatic weapons and exploding grenades erupting behind them, Mike crashed through the gears and sped down the ice-holed track. Savannah lifted her head and looked back, wondering if they would ever see Colin and his men again.

Ears popping they bumped down the mountain into a thick, steamy jungle, where eerie beams of sunlight shone on marauding mosquitoes through the dense overhead trees. The foul stench of decay forced Savannah to cover her face. Macaws' squawked and unseen wildlife chattered overhead as they passed by waterfalls and stagnant pools, in which giant anacondas lay in wait for their next meal beneath the murky water.

They followed the downhill path for almost an hour, then a helicopter suddenly clattered overhead. Mike pulled up under the low hanging trees and turned off the engine. In the distance, miles of open countryside lay before them: they had reached the foot of the mountain. The helicopter landed on the roadside ahead. Hidden among the trees Mike and Savannah watched as two men studied the road for fresh muddy tire marks. Shaking their heads, they climbed back into the helicopter and began circling above.

After a hovering treetop search of the area, they swung north and headed up the mountain. Mike booted the engine and drove out into the warm sunshine. On a distant hillside a small village and cattle grazing confirmed their return to the civilized world.

Savannah sighed with relief. *Surely, the worst is over.*

With plenty of fuel and a deserted road ahead their optimism returned. Mike silently thanked his father for the driving lessons in the BMW; the jeep was a piece of cake by comparison.

As the mountains became a picture postcard in the rear view mirror, sweeping savanna grasslands carpeted both sides of the narrow country road. The acrid smell of agriculture lingered in the air as they sped through tiny villages, in which the only sign of life was that of grazing cattle. The road eventually widened and tiny villages began to appear more frequently. Groups of farmers gossiping at wooden fences, turned their heads as the muddy jeep roared by hugging the center of the road.

After driving for almost two hours with no sign of the main road, their concern for getting lost in the wilderness heightened to near panic. Then a loud explosion suddenly boomed in the air and almost jumping out of her seat Savannah pointed to a distant army-type truck heading towards them. Mike quickly pulled up beneath the trees and killed the engine. Shortly after, an open-top truck slowly thundered by loaded with armed guerrillas. Then another explosion shook the ground and a jeep chugged by with guerrillas tossing grenades and firing automatic weapons into the roadside foliage. Terrified, Mike and Savannah sank to the floor as a hail of bullets ripped through nearby trees. The jeep slowly drove on, its mercenary crew continuing to rake the roadside with automatic weapons and grenades. Then an eerie silence fell. The guerrillas appeared to have gone. Savannah told Mike to leave quickly while they had a chance, but intuition told him otherwise. He waited; ten, fifteen, twenty minutes, then the jeep pulled out of its hiding place some distance away and slowly drove on, the indiscriminate firing and explosions continuing.

Mike gave it another ten minutes before he backed out and put his foot to the floor. Savannah kept watch on the road behind them. A few miles further on, they finally reached the main road where a sign pointed to the right: Cartegena 140 kilometres. Mike nosed the jeep out and gunned the engine.

It was a winding single-lane road and for the first hour they encountered very little traffic, other than a few cars, a tractor and a muddy green bus at the roadside surrounded by soldiers. As the miles rolled by they glanced at one another, their eyes wide with anticipation. Earlier feelings of foreboding had given way to a renewed sense of well being and they were beginning to believe their journey home had finally begun.

They trailed behind a logging truck for several miles unable to pass until the road widened into a highway. Before long, they were in heavy traffic and the city of Cartegena lay before them. Savannah found a toilet roll behind her seat and used it to wipe the greasepaint off their hands and faces, which had made their age indeterminable. Clever Colin, she thought, smiling.

At a stop light a group of boys pulled up alongside them in a rusting convertible. Mike gave them a cursory glance. One boy yelled something in Spanish, and the others joined in. Savannah grabbed the revolver beneath her seat and pointed it at them. Mike froze. The gun had obviously belonged to the driver. She yelled something in Spanish and the boys sat facing the front like statues. On green, the boys turned right and sped away, giving a selection of crude signs with their fingers en route.

Mike breathed out. 'What did you say to them?'

'I told them to shut up or I would shoot them.'

'Are you kidding? What were they saying?

'You do not want to know.' She hid the gun under the seat.

'Do you know how to use a gun?'

'Yes, Harry ordered me to have shooting lessons once a week as part of my self-defence training.'

'Do you have a gun at home?'

'No, Angela, my ex military instructor, brings them.'

'You're amazing. Maybe that's why I'm crazy about you.'

Savannah leaned over and kissed him. 'I feel the same about you. And in case you are worried, I hate guns.'

While Mike focussed on his driving Savannah touched the black bracelet on her wrist, realizing how lucky they were that Colin and his men were at the farmhouse. Without that incredible piece of luck they would have suffered years of captivity at a filthy terrorist camp, and perhaps even been murdered.

It didn't bear thinking about.

THIRTY-ONE

Bogota, Sunday, October 11th

Sharing an overwhelming sense of relief to be back in Bogota the three rescued females, badly shaken and bruised but most of all grateful, climbed into a waiting ambulance and sat blank-faced alongside one of Jamie's men, who had a bullet wound below his left ribcage. Airport security opened the gate and the ambulance sped away to a hospital unit opposite the U.S. Embassy.

Jamie saluted his unit as they boarded a cargo plane bound for Rio, then he drove to the U.S. compound, which accommodated embassy staff, dignitaries and ranked officers, and debriefed via a secure line to Major Bell in Rio.

'The gun battle lasted about an hour, sir, by which time most of the terrorists were dead and the rest had scattered. We found the female hostages chained to the floor in a cellar. I recalled the Hueys, blew up the farmhouse, and then brought them back to Bogota'. Other than one casualty the mission went to plan.'

'Good job, Jamie, what about the two American kids?'

'We managed to free them before it kicked off, but I couldn't risk keeping them there, sir, our conflict level had risen to critical, and so I sent them to Cartegena, and they appear to have arrived safely. My contact agreed to take them to the U.S. Embassy in Panama. I will keep you posted on their progress.'

'Very well. Look, I'm off to Washington and doubt that I'll be back before you go on leave, so enjoy you've earned it.'

Looking forward to a ten-day furlough at home with his father, Larry, Jamie called to let him know of his arrival.

'Hi, Dad, it's your wayward son.'

'Jamie! It's good to hear your voice. How's South America, are you staying out of trouble?'

'We've managed to keep our noses clean, apart from a few minor skirmishes, and I'm enjoying the hedonistic culture. The Brazilians really are nice people.'

'You sound great. Did you get those kids out of Brazil?'

'How did you know about that? Oh, of course, Savannah is…

'Harry Schlecker's daughter, and whatever you're about to say the answer is yes.'

'So you're the ghost financier. I know you were indebted to Harry, but does he know? It must have set you back some.'

'No, and it was worth every penny, because I knew you were heading the operation.'

'You've been talking to your CIA pal Ben Brakker.'

'Don't hold it against him, Jamie, he's a trusted friend. So did you get 'em out?'

'Yes, although they got into trouble again unfortunately, but we managed to send them on their way, and with the right wind they should be home in a few days.'

'Great, I can't wait to see you, son. What's your ETA?'

'15-00 hours, Wednesday.'

'I'll put the beers on ice.

* * * * *

Venus Plaza Hotel, Bogota

It was Sunday and there was little to do except wish that time would pass more quickly, but of course it didn't, so they joined a group of tourists and strolled around the cathedral. Richard kept looking at his cell phone, hoping it would ring but it never did and by mid afternoon they'd had enough. Back at the hotel, still groggy after her 14-hour sleep, Katie took a nap. Richard buried his head in the New York Times while CNN gave an update on the latest news and sport. Then a breaking news story caught his attention so he cranked up the volume.

- Three American females, brutally kidnapped a week ago in Bogota, were dramatically rescued today at a remote farmhouse in the Colombian Andes Mountains. The distraught women; the daughters of Senator Goldman, Judge Hinkle and assistant CIA director Carl Weisman were safely returned this afternoon to the Bogota U.S. Embassy, where they released a moving statement of gratitude to those involved in their rescue, and said they hoped to return to their families tomorrow. Kidnapping in Colombia has risen to epidemic proportions in recent years, and the United States continues to work closely with the Colombian Government to help stem the growing menace. More details on that story later, now here's Gary Flick with the latest weather report -

Richard called the Bogota U.S. Embassy and a voice message clicked in; *The United States Embassy has closed due to a fire. Business hours are Monday through Friday, eight till noon. In an emergency call,...* he dialled the number and left a message.

'Hello, I'm Richard Kinnerman. Terrorists kidnapped my son and his girlfriend yesterday in Bogota, and I'd like to know what you're doing about it. I'm at the Venus Plaza Hotel, suite 106.'

An hour or so later, reception put a call through. 'It's the U.S. Embassy Mr. Kinnerman.' 'Okay, thanks. Hello?'

'Mr. Kinnerman, Jerry Harper, U.S. Embassy. Sorry to hear about your son, hope I can help. We close weekends, but due to repairs after a major fire we gotta be here. Now, there were six kidnappings yesterday. Can you give me a few more details?'

'My son Mike and Savannah Schlecker were kidnapped by terrorists yesterday near El Dorado airport, and I wanna know –

'Hold it, sir, we do have knowledge of this case, in fact...he reached for a folder...the youngsters were seen this morning.'

Richard jumped up. 'What? They were seen, where?'

'Did you see the news report of three U.S. females rescued today at a farmhouse in the Andes Mountains?'

'Yeah, but what does that have to do with it?'

'Your son and the girl were at that farmhouse, but they got caught up in gunfire and were sent away for their own safety.'

'What! They were there, who sent them away? I wanna speak to that person.'

'I'm sorry, sir, that's classified.'

'To hell with that! I need to know who that person was and where they went.'

'Okay look, I'll see what I can do. I'll call you back.'

* * * * *

Cartegena Sunday, October 11th

Cartegena is a century's old port and although some areas have been modernised remnants of its long history remain intact. The grand colonial buildings, fortified by ancient narrow streets lined with restaurants and stores around the old part of the city, and the Caribbean coastline with an array of glittering hotels remains a magnet for our visitors. The marina, enclosed by sweeping stone sea walls, is home to hundreds of large and small boats moored in rows as far as the eye can see. Fishing boats come and go as they have done for centuries, and cruise liners hugging the skyline lie anchored at the main port. *Cartegena Tourist Authority.*

Savannah put down the brochure, which four pretty reps were handing out to drivers stuck in traffic, and realizing their muddy jeep had become a source of curiosity, she pointed to a hotel with an underground car park and told Mike to pull up at the barrier. The machine punched out a ticket giving the time as 14-37 and the barrier sailed up. Mike drove down to the dimly lit basement and parked the jeep. He dropped the keys down a drain and they hurried to the elevator. Lowering their heads as the doors opened at the ground floor, they strolled arm in arm through the crowded lobby and stepped out on to the streets of Cartegena.

Breathing in the sun-kissed air they walked passed the tourist shops lining the road down to the blue Caribbean Sea. The breezy seafront bustled with street vendors, cafes' and hoards of tourists capturing the ancient harbour with their digital cameras.

Mingle with the tourists, Colin said.

Standing at the center of a square amid rows of flowerbeds and palm trees Savannah studied the city's information board map. Sensing someone was watching her, she glanced up and saw a tall man in beige slacks, a white shirt and straw hat leaning against a palm tree staring at them. Turning her back to him, she spoke to Mike. 'Can you see the man with the straw hat?'

'Yeah, and he's not sightseeing. Let's go.'

Savannah noticed a sign pointing to the marina, and melting in the crowd they headed in that direction. Entrenched in a sea of heads they walked along the seafront, and then crossing the road they vanished in a labyrinth of backstreets crawling with tourists. Two police officers strolled by nodding and smiling to the city visitors. Mike pulled Savannah into a store and waited until they had gone. Unnerved that someone had recognised them, they eased their way through the crowded alleyways and circled back to where they first saw the man, but he had gone. Convinced that he was searching for them and would no doubt return they linked arms and headed for the marina.

Hidden among a colourful parade of camera-clicking tourists they meandered along the towpath, studying the names of boats bobbing up and down in their moorings. Then a green fishing boat caught their attention; it was the Maitre d`; an ageing rust bucket destined to be their home for the next few days.

An unshaven weather-beaten man in an oil-stained t-shirt, shabby grey slacks and worn out deck shoes appeared on deck. He smiled, and doffed his once white Captains hat.

'She's nice eh?' the man said, flapping his arms in an effort to frighten the seagulls away, but refusing to be intimidated they just stared at him. 'What do you kids want? No free trips round the islands today, okay,' he said, waving his finger.

'A friend said you'd help us. Are you Juan?' Mike asked.

Wiping the back of his neck with an oily rag Juan walked to the side of the boat. 'What friend?'

Savannah ran her finger along the rim of the boat. 'A soldier, tall, blonde hair and has an English accent. His name is Colin,' she said, wiping her finger on a filthy rag.

'Colin? Ah, you mean English with no name. I know him, nice man,' Juan said, with the gravelly voice of a hangover.

She frowned. 'What do you mean, English with no name?'

'He has many. Don't ask. Where you wanna get to?'

'Colin said you'd take us to Panama, to the U.S. Embassy.' Mike said, preparing for bad news.

Juan laughed, throwing back his head. 'Ha, just like that, eh? Panama, the embassy. Got any money?'

Mike held up his American Express card and Juan's face lit up. 'Okay, okay, but first we talk business man to man. I am fair, you will see. Come,' he said, motioning them on deck

Climbing onboard they studied the ageing rusty framework, wondering if the Maitre d' was seaworthy. A string of old tyres ringed both sides of the boat and the deck looked as though it hadn't been scrubbed for years. The engine gurgled with a deep throaty rasp as though it was gasping for oil. A stinking pile of old fishing nets lay abandoned on the starboard deck, which was no doubt attracting the seagulls perched on the stern seemingly oblivious to humans. Concerned that the man with straw hat may stroll by and see them they stood out of sight behind the bridge. Juan joined them but made no comment.

'How long will it take to sail to Panama?' Savannah asked.

'With no sightseeing, two and a half days, if the sea is kind to us,' Juan said, wiping the peeling paintwork as though it would make a difference after a lifetime of neglect.'

'How much?' Mike asked, business like.

'To you, only two thousand dollars,' Juan said, as if burdened by doing them a huge favour and continued polishing.

Mike knew the game. 'Three hundred dollars.'

'Three hundred dollars? You insult me. You are a criminal, have you no shame?' Juan ranted, flaying his arms.

Savannah stood between them and folded her arms. 'What is it with boys? You are always trying to score points. Can we reach a deal here and move on.'

Juan slammed his Captains hat on the deck. 'Fifteen hundred, last offer.'

'Seven-fifty, take it or leave it,' Mike said, and faced the sea.

Savannah rolled her eyes.

Juan picked up his hat. 'You take the bread out of my mouth my friend,' he moaned, placing it on his head. 'Okay, I will take you, but only as favour to English with no name. Come, we go down to my galley, this way.'

Savannah playfully ruffled Mike's hair as they followed Juan below. Surprised by the galley's quirky cosiness they began to realize that Colin was right. Leaving Colombia hidden on a boat was not only comforting it was a smart move. Their sea voyage would finally sever Mitchell and Netty's stalking torment and prevent the terrorist group from hunting them down. A few days at sea and they would be in Panama, their last place of refuge before returning to the United States.

'Do you have a cell phone, Juan?' Savannah asked.

'No, I hate these things. I have radio onboard, but this stays off at sea. I like peace when we sail.'

'Can we call home on the radio?' Mike asked.

'No, and I want no one to know you are here.'

Savannah's eyes narrowed. 'You know who we are. You saw us approach the boat and came out to meet us.'

Juan shrugged his shoulders. 'I see your faces on TV, how could I not know you?' he admitted, opening his hands. 'Okay, English with no name call marina office and say you are coming. For him, I look after you, but still you must pay. Come, we go to marina office, you pay me there.'

Leading them up to the deck Juan turned off the engine and jumped onto the quayside. Keeping their eyes peeled for any sign of the man with the straw hat they followed him to the marina office, where a thin, ageing official with thick glasses sat behind a dishevelled desk. When he mentioned passports they prepared to bolt, but Juan calmly shook his head. Grinning knowingly, the official handed Mike a one-page charter contract and a cheap pen. Having signed the contract and paid Juan's fee, Mike folded his arms and smiled, knowing that American Express was about to find out they had just chartered a boat in Cartegena.

With safe passage procured to Panama, they hurried back to the Maitre d' eager to set sail. Business had been slow lately and Juan was more than happy to be earning extra dollars. An evening at the tavern would doubtless be a certainty when he returned.

As Juan hurried off to the marina store for supplies, Mike and Savannah watched for the man with the straw hat. If they were seen leaving by boat the terrorists would surely follow, and what would happen then did not bear thinking about. Hidden beneath the aft rail they observed the passing tourists faces.

Juan returned with bags of fresh supplies and stowed them below. Then having studied the sky, he stepped inside the bridge and started the diesel engine, which growled to life with plumes of black smoke billowing out the rusting funnel. Squealing with resentment the seagulls reluctantly abandoned their perch on the starboard bow. Juan ordered Mike to release the mooring ropes and having done so, he quickly jumped back onboard.

The Maitre d' slowly chugged away from its moorings and sailed out of the marina heading seaward in the warm afternoon sunshine. Mike and Savannah watched the bow crashing through the crystal blue water as Juan navigated his way around a group of outlying islands and set sail for Panama.

THIRTY-TWO

Venus Plaza Hotel, Bogota

It was four-twenty p.m. when Jerry Harper called back from the U.S. Embassy. 'Mr. Kinnerman, I'm sorry it's taken so long to get back to you, but it is Sunday and I had to track a few people down. Anyway, the person you need to talk to has agreed to a meeting. But I must advise you that anything said at the meeting is strictly classified, do you understand?'

'Yes, of course.'

'Okay, be at the Serifino café opposite the zoo at two p.m. tomorrow. The man knows what you look like. Order a drink and sit at one of the garden tables. He'll find you.'

'We'll be waiting,' Richard said, and hung up.

At one-forty five p.m. the next day, the taxi dropped them off outside the Serifino café; a busy bar-restaurant coated in flowers. Across the road families and tourists were queuing at the zoo. They bought two beers and sat down at a garden table shaded by a red parasol. It was just after two p.m., and as they searched for a face in the crowd, a tall, blonde man in jeans, a t-shirt, cowboy boots, a baseball cap and sunglasses strode towards them holding a laptop. Introducing himself, Jamie sat down and ordered a beer. Sensing Richard and Katie were desperate for news he explained the tense political flight out of Brazil and the deal made with the Colombians, and added, 'There is one other thing; as a security protocol Mike and Savannah know me as Colin.'

Richard nodded. 'Fair enough. We knew someone had gotten them out of Brazil. So it was you.'

'Yes, and they are now on their way to Panama.'

Katie gripped Richard's arm. 'How do you know that?'

'I gave them tracking devices in the form of bracelets, and earlier today I ran a check on our surveillance satellite. Look, allow me to show you.' Jamie opened his laptop and logged onto U.S. Intelligence via a black van full of sophisticated electronics parked nearby. Entering an encrypted code, which initiated a GPS grid, he tapped in the coordinates and the screen zoomed in on two pulsating dots.

'Believe it or not those two little dots are Mike and Savannah. They are on a boat named Maitre d', about a hundred and fifty miles west of Cartegena,' Jamie said, cheerfully.

'Oh my God,' Katie exclaimed, touching the screen with her fingertips. 'Is that really them? Can we call them? Oh God, this is unbelievable.'

Richard placed his arm around her. 'You must understand that seeing our son as a dot on a screen when he's been missing for a week is kinda mind blowing.'

Katie exhaled. 'I'm sorry, Jamie, this is so surreal.'

Jamie had hoped that it would be inspiring, but he was clearly mistaken. 'I'm sorry, perhaps that was a little tactless given the circumstances. However, you will be able to contact them at the marina office in Panama City. The Maitre d' has a ship-to-shore radio,' he explained, closing the laptop.

Richard nodded. 'Why'd they go to Panama?'

The waiter brought a cold beer to the table. Jamie paid him and he walked off, collecting dirty glasses on his way.

'My orders were to extricate three female hostages from the farmhouse, but when Mike and Savannah came towards us in the back of a jeep, driven by a terrorist taking them to another camp, we stopped the vehicle and took out the driver.'

Katie frowned. 'Did Mike and Savannah see that?'

'I'm afraid so, but they were brave, and relieved to see us.'

Richard exhaled. 'Then what happened?'

'There were nine terrorists at the farmhouse, and nine more heading towards us in a helicopter, others showed up on foot. The youngsters wanted to stay with me, but I couldn't risk it. We faced a gun battle against a large and determined force. If we had been overpowered, they would have been caught and killed.'

Katie shook her head. 'So you sent them away.'

A little boy ran up to reclaim his football, which had rolled underneath the table. Jamie picked it up, patted the boy's head and handed it to him. The boy smiled and ran off.

'I had no choice, they were in grave danger. Fortunately, the terrorists were not aware that Mike and Savannah had escaped, or they would have used their network of informers to hunt them down. We found a tracking device attached to the jeep.'

Richard breathed out heavily. 'Seems the more we know the worse it gets. That was a tough call, Jamie, but those dots on the screen tell us that you made the right decision.'

'Yes, but this is South America and nothing is guaranteed. Juan, owner of the Maitre d', is a man I trust, and he will take them to the U.S. Embassy in Panama City. As far as I know, no one else is aware that Mike and Savannah are on the boat. If they encounter any problems, Juan will deal with it. He knows his way around the Caribbean, and Panama.'

Misty-eyed with gratitude Katie smiled. 'Thanks, Jamie, for making that difficult decision, and for being so candid, it means a great deal to us. We haven't slept in a week.'

'Feels more like a month,' Richard said, and sipped his beer.

'I can only imagine what you are going through, but let me say this; those youngsters are resilient and courageous and I have no doubt that you will be reunited. When you get to Panama City, go to the marina and speak to Eduardo, the harbourmaster. He is a good man and will help if you have any problems.'

'In the blink of an eye I'd go tonight,' Richard said, wearily.

Jamie finished his beer. 'If that makes you feel better, then do so, but bear in mind the Maitre d' is not due to arrive in Panama until late Wednesday afternoon.'

Katie brushed away those strands of hair that fell to the side of her face, and said, 'You know what? I'd be happy to wait on a quayside if I know my son will be there in a couple of days.'

Jamie nodded. 'Yes, of course,' he said, standing up. 'Well I think we've covered everything. I hope you sleep better knowing they are safe and well. It has been a pleasure meeting you, Katie, Richard. Good luck.' They shook hands, and he strode off.

Warmed by a renewed sense of optimism Richard and Katie took a taxi back to the Venus Plaza hotel. In 48-hours they would be standing on the waters edge of Panama City's marina waiting for Mike and Savannah to arrive. Although there was no cause yet for celebration, meeting Jamie had lifted their spirits and for the first time in a week they were hungry.

The hotel receptionist called the airline and booked Richard and Katie on the first available flight to Panama City, which was scheduled to leave at 15:30 the next day, that being Tuesday. At seven-thirty, having freshened up for dinner, they strolled to the mezzanine restaurant fully intending to order the best wine and cuisine the Venus Plaza Hotel had to offer.

A chilled bottle of chardonnay, courtesy of Emile Arnaud, arrived at their table. Richard asked the waiter to thank him and ordered two five-course specials. Katie reached for her cell phone and called Julieanne; she picked up. 'Hi, sweetie, it's me.'

'Hi, Mom, you okay? Miss you love you.'

'Me too, now get ready to smile. Mike and Savannah have escaped and they're on a boat heading for Panama. They're due to dock on Wednesday and we're going there to meet them.'

'They got away, on a boat? Oh my God, this is fantastic news. Have you called them? Can I call Mike?'

'No, sweetie, they only have a ship-to-shore radio. We'll try calling them tomorrow from the marina office in Panama.'

'Don't let it go wrong again, Mom. I'm not sure I can handle it, and I don't mean to sound…

'I know, sweetie. You can tell Sally the good news, but no one else must know, okay. I'll call you later tonight. Your father sends his love. I kiss you my darling, love you, bye.'

When Richard informed Harry that Mike and Savannah were on a boat sailing to Panama he leapt out of his office chair. 'If they're on a goddam boat, hire a chopper or a cruiser and go get 'em,' Harry yelled.

Greta stood up and paced the office floor.

'I'll go down that road when I get there, Harry.' Richard said, calmly. 'If we can contact the Maitre d' at the marina office, I'll find out where they are and go get 'em. It's owned by guy named Juan, a pal of a guy in U.S. Special Forces, who gave Mike and Savannah tracking devices, but to track their location we would need to access U.S. Military Surveillance, and that's never gonna happen. I'll look at hiring a chopper, but whether a pilot will be prepared to do a search and rescue at sea is questionable.'

'Na, they won't go for that, especially at night,' Harry said. 'And forget Military Surveillance; they wouldn't let you near that stuff if you were the President's best friend.'

'I know, so the marina office is our best shot.'

'Well if this guy Juan is a pal of Special Forces their in safe hands. Problem is, the Caribbean covers a huge area, and without their exact location you'd never find them. The other thing is; if you can't find them no one else will.'

'That did occur to me. Anyway, we'll try contacting the boat. If that doesn't work, we'll just have to wait it out.'

'Well maybe that's what you should do,' Harry went on. 'A sea search might alert the scumbags they're running from, and that's the last they need right now.'

'I'll make that decision when we get to Panama.'

Harry breathed out heavily. 'Listen, I'm ready to get in the Gulfstream and fly down to Panama tonight, but I got a problem. My clients have summoned me to Chicago for two days. They've organized a hotel suite and a limo to pick me up at the airport. I agreed, so if I cancel I'm breaking my word, which means they'll get upset, and the last thing I need is those people as enemies,' Harry explained. 'That said, call me as soon as you make eye contact with Mike and Savannah, and I'll come pick 'em up. Even those schmucks would understand that.'

'Nothing is gonna happen until late Wednesday, Harry. Go to Chicago and I'll call you as soon as the Maitre d' docks,' Richard said, realizing Harry was in a tough spot with his dubious clients, but his love for Savannah was certainly not in doubt.

'Okay, but if you need me, for whatever reason, I'm on red alert six hours away. Keep that in mind,' Harry reiterated.

Katie waved her fingers at Richard to hand over the phone. 'Hang on, Harry, Katie wants a word.'

'Hi, Harry,'

Harry warmed to her voice. 'How you holding up, Katie?'

'Well not good, but that will change when I get to hold Mike and Savannah. Thanks for looking in on Jules. I guess you know how difficult this is for her, she idolises her brother.'

'Yeah I know. Don't worry, Sally Brooks is taking good care of her. What a sweetheart she is. We're all in this together, Katie, same hope, same pain. Just get our kids back on Wednesday, and then we can start living again.'

'We'll call as soon as we have them, Harry.'

'I'll be waiting. Greta sends her love. Take care of yourself, Katie.' Harry hung up.

Richard and Katie managed to finish all five courses and the bottle of Chardonnay before calling it a night, which promised be a restless one. Tomorrow afternoon, they would arrive in Panama City, hoping to put an end to their dreadful family nightmare. In the meantime, they would take comfort in knowing those two small dots were safely on their way.

THIRTY-THREE

By sunrise, Juan was at the helm sipping his third black coffee and holding a steady course. Mike and Savannah emerged sleepy-eyed around noon, and he wondered how kids slept so long. He gave them strong coffee, juice and warm bread rolls, after which they sunbathed and fell sleep again. Jamie had warned him that they were still emotionally fragile, and so he left them to enjoy the afternoon sunshine. On Tuesday though, Juan had other plans. After another midday breakfast, he ordered Mike to take the helm, and ignoring his protestations took a nap, leaving him gripping the wheel and nervously watching the compass.

On the forward deck, wearing skimpy shorts and a makeshift bikini top, Savannah laid out a towel and sat down, her long, dark hair flowing over her shoulders. Embracing the warm sun on her smooth olive skin, she leaned back on her hands and looked out at the Caribbean Sea, staring into the past.

The frightening events of the past week had awakened her consciousness, and she was ready to face her demons. She shook her head recalling the anger that forced her to take refuge in the stables to shut out the world. Yet Harry Schlecker had saved her from abject poverty on the streets of Rio and given her a fairy-tail existence, but her tormented mind convinced her that he had only done so to clear his conscience for her the death of her parents, and she had cruelly shunned him. The disturbing memory of her beloved mother and father screaming in agony as they burnt to death when she was nine years old, had left a deep emotional scar. Now, five years later, having experienced a close encounter with death herself, Savannah realized the lamenting force that had driven her away from the world was her own and that her life was now one of privilege. She wiped her moist eyes, suddenly aware that she was finally growing up. Harry Schlecker was now her father and he loved her. If by good fortune they manage to find their way home, she vowed to seek his forgiveness and shower him with the affection he craved from his adopted daughter.

Early that evening, as a glimmer of the Panamanian coastline appeared on the distant horizon, Mike asked Juan how he would get them to the U.S. Embassy.

'Embassy? Ha! You think I am crazy?' Juan said, giving the boat another notch of speed as he lit a small cigar.

Mike frowned. 'But you said –

'I know what I say, but this is not so simple.'

'What do you mean?'

'There is one million dollars reward to find you, and your faces are at every airport, marina and seaport. You ask me for a miracle, and that I cannot do.'

Savannah folded her arms. 'But Colin said you would take us to the Embassy in Panama City.'

Weaving an overhead ballet a colony of squawking seagulls landed on the stern as the Maitre d' rolled with the swell. A huge cruise liner, inexorably heading for the Panama Canal, blew its horn as it sailed by amid a flotilla of small boats.

'Hah yes, but to sail to Panama City we must go through the Panama Canal. If police stop us, or my boat breaks down in canal with you onboard, no passports, they take my licence and I am in jail, so forget this,' Juan said, dismissively.'

Savannah persisted. 'Is there another way?

'Sure, if we sail round South America; this is why they build Panama Canal. 'Okay, look, Mike, he is rich and famous, and you are beautiful daughter of billionaire. Panama is nice country, but like all in South America they have criminals; bad people who make living from drugs and kidnapping. Panama is small country, so if one person see you, everyone knows you are here. Then it is short time and they find you. For me, it is simple to moor Maitre d' on northern coast and drive you to Panama City, but if corrupt police stop me at roadblock, or bad criminals follow us, they take you and shoot me. So forget American Embassy, this is too risky. Trust me, I know.'

Mike breathed out. 'So that's it, we just give up?'

'No, no, you find passage on big freighter or plane with pilot going to Florida. Many people do this.'

Mike frowned 'Why can't you take us to Florida?'

Juan shook his head. 'For me this is not possible, but I have friend; he fly goods to Florida, the Caribbean, who knows.'

Savannah leaned into his face. 'Is he a smuggler?'

Juan shrugged. 'I no say. Wanna meet him?'

She glanced at Mike, who shook his head hopelessly. Relying on a criminal was risky at best. 'Is he trustworthy?' she asked.

Juan chuckled. 'Trustworthy? This man, he is career criminal police never catch. He is like ghost. But when you pay for flight to Florida he keep his word.'

Sharing a sense of trepidation Mike and Savannah looked out across the white-tipped sea at the distant glowing coastline. There was something comforting about the knock of the diesel engine and the ceaseless crashing of the swell as the Maitre d' chugged ever closer to the sandy shores of Panama. With no other choice and no one to trust but Juan, they agreed to meet the man, hoping he would not betray them and cash in on their misfortune.

Venus Plaza Hotel, Tuesday, October 13th

Richard and Katie had stared at the ceiling for most of the night waiting for dawn to break. Knowing their hopes could still go horribly wrong, a fear fuelled by trepidation in a foreign country, they had become bystanders in a life and death drama over which they had no control, and were praying this was the final act.

Over a late breakfast they called everyone at home, including Beth and JB Walsome, who were relieved to hear that the end was in sight. Then while Katie packed for their flight to Panama Richard went out on the balcony and leaned thoughtfully over the rail. How were Mike and Savannah coping at sea; were they safe, were they nearing Panama? He wondered. His ringing cell phone snapped him back to reality. The caller was Penny Bowman, a tough lawyer not usually prone to emotional outbursts, but on this occasion he sensed she was ready to explode.

'As you know, I had reservations about buying Stella Electronics, Richard, well guess what? I was right. On Friday, we bought the company for 42 dollars a share. Then on Monday, Stella unveiled a new system that they've secretly developed, and the shares are now worth 109 dollars and rising.'

'What?'

'I thought that would get your attention, it sure got mine. A dark cloud is now hanging over the business sector and no one is returning my calls. The corridors of Wall Street are rampant with wicked innuendos that PocketMoney. com's trustees are guilty of insider trading,' Penny said, boiling with fury.

'Insider trading?' Richard repeated, with disbelief

'Yes, and I'm worried, Richard, something smells bad here.'

'You're damn right it does.'

'I can't imagine what you're going through right now, but I had to make you aware of the facts. If I get my hands on the son-of-a-bitch responsible I'll probably go to jail. You find Mike and Savannah, I'll handle the war,' Penny said, and disconnected.

Richard lowered his head and suddenly had a bad feeling. He gazed at the street below, his legal mind in overdrive. If that was true, then PocketMoney. com was in serious trouble, and the legal implications meant that those involved in the company could go to jail, including himself and Katie. He looked up at the dark clouds ominously hanging over the city. 'If it's gonna get worse then throw it at me now; at least I'll know what I'm up against!' he yelled, banging his fist on the balcony railing.

More calls came from the trustees who said that mud slinging and fraud accusations were rife, and that the media was having a field day at their expense. Traders were baying for blood at the NY Stock Exchange and Wall Street, and Stella had become a metaphor for who's going down first. PocketMoney.com was in deep water and the great whites were circling.

Richard disconnected and stared at his cell phone.

Insider trading?

How the hell did that happen?

He exhaled and began thinking like a lawyer. Why had Stella not mentioned their new system until after the purchase? That in itself was a serious breach of conduct, which supported Penny's theory that someone had a dirty plan. He recalled once losing an insider trading case when his client lied about gaining advanced knowledge of a technological breakthrough, before buying shares in a major company, a deception that involves at least two people, which, in Richard's opinion, amounted to conspiracy.

He burned up with anger, but what could he do. He was in South America trying to find his missing son. 'To hell with it, let them have a field day with the story. It'll have to wait until I'm back in New York,' he mumbled, determined not to let anything distract him from bringing Mike and Savannah home, and if that meant his career and credibility were on the line, then so be it.

Katie dragged him away from the balcony. 'Come on, let's go for a walk and get some air, we still have an hour or so to kill,' she said, heading for the door.

It was warm and humid and the streets were humming with shoppers, tourists and traffic. As they strolled by the downtown shopping malls and cafés, Richard broke the news to Katie.

'I've just had a string of calls from the trustees. Wall Street traders and the NYSE have accused PocketMoney.com of insider trading in the Stella deal, and apparently they're up in arms.'

Katie stopped and glared at Richard. 'Insider trading? Are you serious? She said, with a look of disbelief.

'Yep, and it's gonna get worse, a lot worse.'

'I do not want to talk about this, Richard. The crowded streets of Bogotá are no place to rationalize unfolding events in New York, and speculation is fruitless,' Katie said, quickening their pace along the sidewalk. 'Let's get our son home before we start worrying about Wall Street.'

When Richard and Katie arrived at reception to pay their bill, Emile Arnaud tore it up and wished them a happy family reunion. Thanking him for his kindness they strolled out through the glass revolving doors and climbed in the hotel's new limousine. Julio, Gomez's replacement, stowed their baggage and sped them away into the heavy traffic heading for the airport. Richard and Katie gazed out of the tinted windows, both painfully aware that every aspect of their life was crumbling around them.

Parking at the terminal entrance, Julio jumped out and hauled their baggage onto a trolley. Richard handed him a nice tip and followed Katie through the automatic glass doors to the airport desk. Carla was on duty and smiled as they approached.

'Mr. and Mrs Kinnerman, I hope you enjoyed your brief stay in our beautiful city,' she said, cheerfully.

Katie touched her new gold earrings. 'Yes we did, but better still, we've found our son and his girlfriend, and we're on our way to meet them. I can't tell you how good that feels,' Katie said, linking arms with Richard.

'I can only imagine. Sadly, kidnappings happen every day in my country, and many never return.' Carla said, handing over their tickets for the Panama flight. 'Here, go get your son back.'

Richard wandered off in search of the latest New York Times. Katie found a table outside one of the few cafés and restaurants at the departure level and ordered a pot of coffee. Katie had never liked airports, and though she had travelled extensively, to her they were cold and impersonal, a place to squander time beneath the bright lights and endless treadmill of confusion. However, on this occasion she was more than happy to spend an hour or so at El Dorado airport, seduced by the thought that it brought her closer to Mike and Savannah, and would be the catalyst to close the distance between them.'

A waitress brought their coffee to the table. Katie thanked her and poured a cup for Richard, who had his head buried in the newspaper. The front page was devoted to the outrageous scandal of a Senator and his mistress, an industrial spy, which was of no interest to him that day. He carelessly flicked through each page, and finding nothing of interest, turned to the money page.

The headline took his breath away.

WALL STREET ERUPTS! POCKETMONEY.COM MAKES SUSPECT KILLING WITH STELLA ELECTRONICS!

Details of the Stella purchase followed, including the names of PocketMoney.com's board of trustees, which the reporter had cleverly intertwined with innuendos of insider trading.

Wall Street and NYSE demand full investigation.

An FBI investigation is now a certainty after traders made a formal complaint. Apparently, sensitive information, leaked by an unknown source prior to the purchase of Stella Electronics, gave PocketMoney.com advance knowledge, of what many experts say is a revolutionary system developed by the ailing company. Unsurprisingly, the scandal made buyers twitchy, and as a result, markets were down six hundred and twelve points at close of business. Further announcements are expected tomorrow

Richard shook his head with contempt. A female voice on the PA system announced boarding for the Panama City flight would commence in thirty minutes. He handed Katie the article, which she read with growing anger.

Richard's phone rang; it was Harry Schlecker, who seemed unperturbed by the latest Wall Street revelations. 'I guess you're on your way to Panama right now. I'm stuck here in Chicago, but I had to let you to know that you've missed one hell of a day at the office,' Harry said, apparently thriving on the controversy.

'Yeah, well, the Times report suggested it was a little more serious than that, Harry,' Richard said, curtly. 'Your concern is not exactly overwhelming. What are you up to?'

'What am I up to? I'm making money, that's what I do; remember? What's up, getting jittery because we beat those schmucks at Wall Street to the Holy Grail?'

'No, insider trading makes me jittery; it's a federal offence and men in dark suits start knocking on doors. What's going on?'

'I'll tell you what's goin on. You're in the big league pal and you can't handle it!' Harry yelled, and disconnected.

Richard ignored Harry's abrasiveness; he was just blowing smoke as usual. Katie overheard the call but said nothing. Harry was in emotional meltdown over Savannah. More bad news came from trustee Winston Bliss, who was clearly beginning to panic.

'I guess you've read the Times article, Richard, but it doesn't tell you that all hell has broken loose in New York's financial world, and that criminal proceedings are imminent. I guess Harry Schlecker went to Chicago so he can avoid the flak.'

'No, I've read the article, Winston. We're clean.'

'Hold on, Richard, there's more. The NY Stock Exchange has suspended PocketMoney.com and Stella Electronics from further trading pending an investigation. The FBI has sealed the offices and told us to stay away. They're conducting a thorough search of the premises tomorrow. I'm real sorry to be the bearer of this bad news, but someone had to let you know.'

Richard disconnected, and buried his head in his hands.

Katie frowned. 'Richard? What is it, what's happened?'

THIRTY-FOUR

Their Avianca flight landed at Panama City's Tocumen Airport at 17:35, and after a delay due to an incident at passport control, they hurried out of the terminal and found a yellow taxi.

'The Marina,' Richard ordered. The driver nodded and sped away into the city-bound traffic. The journey took half an hour. It seemed longer. Pulling up at the marina office, he hauled their baggage onto the sidewalk and put his hand out. Richard gave him twenty dollars, and he drove off in a cloud of dust.

Standing at the quayside overlooking the bay the cabin-style marina office, according to its notice board, was an information center for tourists, cargo boats and private mariners. Beneath the overhead fan and fluorescent lighting fading photographs of long forgotten steamboats, shipping charts and local maps were pinned to its walls. A brass plaque, embedded in the varnished reception desk, explained that it was a remnant of a notorious pirate ship, behind which a glass door led to another office at the rear, where someone was talking in Spanish on the phone.

Richard leaned on the desk and shook the small brass bell. A grey-haired broad-shouldered man with bushy eyebrows and a square chin appeared and introduced himself as Eduardo.

'I'm Richard Kinnerman, and this my wife, Katie. We've just arrived from Bogota and we're here to meet the Maitre d', which I believe is due to dock tomorrow afternoon.'

Eduardo nodded. 'Yes, Juan called. Is there a problem?'

'Ten days ago, our 14-year old son Mike and his girlfriend Savannah were kidnapped in the states and taken to Rio, but they managed to escape. Then terrorists took them in Bogota, but they escaped again. Now they're on their way here on the Maitre d'.'

Eduardo rounded his cheeks and blew out some air. 'Holy Mother, I know about these kids, but the news report said they were missing, nothing more. Please tell me what I can do to help you?' he said, with grave sincerity.

Katie spoke up. 'If it's alright with you, Eduardo, we'd like to wait here until they arrive. Meanwhile, could you try contacting the Maitre d`?' she asked, her eyes wide and anxious.

Eduardo motioned for them to follow him into the rear office. Sitting down at his desk he grabbed a microphone and appealed for Juan to respond. With heightening anticipation Richard and Katie began pacing the creaky wooden floor. On the wall, a large clock ticked loudly; minutes passed, and when no response came from the Maitre d' their hopes returned to anxiety. Eduardo explained that Juan switched off his radio at sea, but defensively insisted that he was an excellent sailor. His assurances however did little to allay their concern, in fact it made matters worse. Katie was now visualising Mike and Savannah alone in the water clinging to life jackets.

Were there sharks out there?

She paced the floor, biting her lip.

Richard decided he'd had enough. 'Okay, that's it. I'm gonna go find them. Where can I hire a helicopter?'

Eduardo shook his head. 'It will be dark by the time you find a pilot and they are reluctant to fly over the sea at night. Even if you went out in daylight, without knowing their exact location rescuing two kids from a small boat is highly improbable. If I thought your son and his companion were in real danger Mr. Kinnerman, my answer might be different, but they are not they are with a man I know and trust. I assure you the Maitre d` will arrive tomorrow, with the youngsters safely onboard.'

With no experience in such matters Richard bowed to greater knowledge, though his heart was telling him to search for Mike and Savannah, who were probably no more than and hour or two away by helicopter. Eduardo, of course, was right and common sense prevailed, although on this occasion he wished it hadn't.

'There is a hotel not far from here. I will take you there if you wish,' Eduardo said, tidying his cluttered desk.

Katie winced at the thought of yet another hotel but resigned herself to the inevitable. Eduardo led them out to his red station wagon and helped Richard stow their baggage in the trunk. Katie climbed onto the rear seat and looked out the window at a sleek yacht entering the marina. The car radio, tuned to some sort of police frequency, crackled to life in Spanish, prompting Eduardo to chuckle to himself as they bumped along Panama's potholed country roads in the early evening light. Richard and Katie sat in thoughtful silence, both hoping that some unknown malevolent force would not prevent tomorrow's safe arrival of the Maitre d'.

A sleepless night was a certainty.

A glimmering hotel appeared in the distance.

Eduardo dropped them off outside the Red Dahlia; an old colonial style hotel, situated at the edge of a small village in the middle of nowhere. Having checked in at the desk, the elderly pink-haired receptionist handed Katie a large crusty key for room eleven; a creaky twin on the first floor, with an ancient bathroom and French windows opening onto a balcony, giving them a nice view of the surrounding arid countryside. The air conditioning resembled an old airplane propeller, which spun precariously above in the cracked ceiling, but as choices were limited there was no point in complaining.

Katie called Julieanne, who sounded nervous, edgy.

'Hi, Mom, guess what? A man and a woman from the District Attorneys office came to the house today with a search warrant. They took our computers and all the paperwork they could find. The woman asked where you were, and when I said you'd gone to South America, she huffed, gave me her card and left.'

'Don't worry, sweetie, your father will deal with that when we get home. Go to school, and don't talk to reporters.'

'I don't care about reporters, or the District Attorney. I want my brother back. He's been gone for ten days now and it feels like a lifetime. I miss you terribly, but please don't come home without him. Sally sends her love, me too, bye Mom.'

With the sun fading to a purple haze on the distant horizon Richard and Katie strolled to the village in search of something to eat. Much to their surprise they found a traditional Panamanian restaurant, with ageing candlelit tables and a creaky wooden floor covered in sawdust. Four people were just leaving. They ordered the day's special; sancocho de gallina; *chicken stew,* and a chilled bottle of local white wine. Katie yawned and rubbed her dark-circled emerald eyes. Emotionally and physically drained after her epic journey and ongoing family heartbreak, Richard knew that she was short-tempered and prone to tearful outbursts, but under the circumstances who could blame her.

As they sat in their own silence, hoping those two little dots were sailing safely towards them, Richard's cell phone rang; it was trustee, Malcolm Connors with more bad news.

'Richard, I spoke earlier with Rachel Summers at the Stock Exchange, and she said the FBI has subpoenaed every business transaction undertaken by PocketMoney.com.'

'That's normal practice in these cases, Malcolm. I understand your knee jerk reaction, but don't forget that we're all innocent here. The transaction with Stella was done in good faith.'

Overhearing the conversation Katie shook her head irritably.

'That's as may be, Richard, but it doesn't alter the fact that we look guilty as hell when we're totally innocent. The FBI took everything, including computers, and we've been ordered to stay away. They've also suspended PocketMoney. com's website until further notice. This heavy-handedness is unprecedented and very frightening. I know this is a difficult time for you, but we need your help. They're determined to put someone in jail.'

Katie's phone rang; it was Simon Wyler; her Tokyo boss.

'Hi, Katie, I just called to see if you're okay, but given the circumstances I suspect that's a stupid question.'

'I'm pretty wrecked, and so is Richard but we're coping.'

'If there's anything I can do let me know. I'd like to help.'

'Thanks, I appreciate that. We just got into Panama and I'm holding my breath because there's a good chance that this could be all over tomorrow. When I have my son back I'll call and let you know, and I will no doubt be tearful. I'm grateful for your concern, Simon, I really am. We'll talk soon.'

'You won't go to jail, Malcolm, I'll see to that,' Richard said, reassuringly, 'Hopefully, I will be home in a couple of days and we can look at this problem together.' It was not what Malcolm wanted to hear, but Richard was in Panama what could he do.

Malcolm didn't pursue it any further. 'Sorry I can't be more positive, Richard. We're all praying that Mike and Savannah…. well, I'll call with any further news.'

As Richard disconnected, his phone rang again. It was Greta, and she sounded uncharacteristically edgy. 'Greta, what's up?'

'Richard, I know what you and Katie are going through and I have no intention of adding to your problems, just hear me out. I've discovered a startling piece of information, and I'm not sure what to do about it. It's in relation to the purchase of Stella Electronics, which I'm now convinced is part of a conspiracy to destroy PocketMoney.com, and I thought you should know.'

Richard stared into space. 'I appreciate you telling me that, Greta, but I need you to elaborate. What is it?'

'I can't, Richard, that's all I'm prepared to say right now. You'll figure it out. Give my love to Katie.' Greta hung up.

Richard had considered the possibility of a conspiracy but dismissed it on the grounds of improbability. Greta now claimed to have discovered evidence to the contrary, and her refusal to give details worried him. He relayed Greta's call to Katie, who seemed unsurprised and sat in thoughtful silence. A conspiracy usually meant that someone on the inside was involved, and if Greta was right, that someone worked at PocketMoney.com.

The waiter, who looked about eighty give or take, shuffled to their table with two specials and shuffled back out to the kitchen. Richard chuckled; grandpa was obviously holding the fort but the place was in safe hands, even though they were a bit shaky. As they ate the delicious meal in silence, Katie uncrossed her knees and leaned forward. 'Let's suppose for a minute that Harry wanted PocketMoney. com. What would he do? He would destroy it, and then buy it, isn't that what Harry does? Remember that story about rigged phone-ins at NYTV, and the newspaper's refusal to reveal the source. Six months later, NYTV shares fell off the cliff. Enter Harry Schlecker, who bought 35 percent. That is Harry's M.O., he cuts the legs off a company before buying it,' she said, pushing away her empty plate.

Richard dealt with facts not speculation. 'Why would Harry Schlecker risk being involved in fraud, Katie? He's a goddam billionaire. It doesn't make any sense. In reality, it could be any number of people with some sort of a grudge, but without any evidence it's nothing more than finger-pointing and gut feelings. The Stella problem will undoubtedly get worse, and those critical of PocketMoney.com will fan the growing flame of discontent at Wall Street to their advantage.'

Grandpa shuffled to their table, and handing Richard the bill he made his way back to the kitchen.

Katie nodded. 'I agree, but the bubble is bound to burst, and with no other suspects to muddy the water, the FBI will have no choice but to charge all those at PocketMoney.com with fraud.'

Richard rubbed his eyes. 'Yep, and the damage to careers, including ours, will be life changing. Come on, let's go.'

Katie paid the bill and left a tip for grandpa, who responded with a crinkly smile. Stepping out into the village darkness they strolled towards their hotel along the deserted street, in which the only sign of life was that of a dog barking and several windows glimmering behind tightly drawn curtains.

Back in their stuffy room, Katie turned on the fan and opened the balcony windows. Outside, the crickets and bullfrogs were in full chorus, along with other nocturnal creatures all seemingly talking to one another. Low in a starlit sky a full moon they could almost reach out and touch shone like a celestial beacon through the open windows into their darkened room.

Richard and Katie's silhouettes embraced for a long time, and finding comfort in one another's arms neither wanted to let go. Their lives, family and careers were on hold and everything they held dear was now in jeopardy.

CHAPTER

THIRTY-FIVE

Tuesday, October 13th

At seven a.m., Harry was sipping coffee aboard his Gulfstream jet en route to Chicago, where he had a meeting with union bosses keen to invest money from the pension funds. Although it was quite legitimate the FBI believed that organized crime families controlled the unions and its vast finances, which involved money laundering from drug dealing and other illicit businesses. When Harry got a call from Don Silvio Belachi, he cancelled everything and flew to Chicago, no questions asked. A suite awaited him at the Intercontinental Hotel on North Michigan Avenue.

Meanwhile, dressed in a sweat suit and her hair in a ponytail Greta entered Harry's huge office. The phones, already ringing, diverted to a message service, which she monitored. The split-level room radiated with success, but other than Harry's walnut desk, grandiose in the light of the French windows, Greta found it impersonal. She disliked the beige floral carpet, peach oriental rugs and drapes, crystal chandeliers, black glass conference table, black marble drinks bar and black and gold sofas; it resembled a 1950's movie set, in her opinion. But that was Harry, black and white no grey areas. Orchids and various plants breathed life into the room, and subtly lit priceless paintings by Picasso, Van Gogh, Turner and Monet incongruously hung on the oak-panelled walls, alongside portraits of Savannah, Greta, the U.S. President and photographs of Harry posing among politicians, movie stars and golf pro's. Screens showing the world's financial markets were visible everywhere in the room. Greta's glass and chrome desk faced Harry's, which he had insisted on to maintain eye contact and secretly admire her long legs. This was Harry's domain; a decadent shrine reminding him daily that he was once a penniless orphan who became a billionaire.

Greta believed there were lines that Harry would never cross, even though he had been involved in several shady deals; one of which was Rylan Mitchell's property scam some years ago, to which she had turned a blind eye. Mitchell had used an offshore company to purchase land cheaply from suffering farmers unable to survive the downturn. Some he sold to property developers and retained a share; others went to suspect military-security firms via a Pentagon source, who organized the land purchases in return for a sunset bank account. Harry invested the profits wisely and the Pentagon source became an offshore millionaire. Everyone was happy with the arrangement and swore to keep it a graveyard secret; that is, until Rylan Mitchell went to jail for fraud, thanks to Harry's evidence, and they were no longer pals. Greta recalled Mitchell calling Harry from jail and yelling at him to return his lockbox key, in which sat ten million dollars; Harry hung up.

Greta had monitored the FBI's closure of PocketMoney.com, and read every allegation of insider trading made by Wall Street. With hindsight, she regretted not having confronted Harry with Brimson's incriminating email. Had she done so, perhaps he and his conspirators would now be facing justice.

She read the email again and felt sick to her stomach.

> Harry, $75,000 is in the account. Thanks. As agreed, the fax alert will arrive at 2:20 p.m. next Thursday, and will recommend PocketMoney.com buy Stella Electronics on Friday prior to the last bell. I will also attach a copy of the sensitive details you provided. Matchmaker

Greta couldn't figure out why Harry hadn't deleted the email when it was so incriminating. Had something distracted him, she wondered. Whatever the reason; she was now between a rock and a hard place, and though it was a tough call, having discovered a document that clearly proved Harry was conspiring to destroy PocketMoney.com, her conscience would not allow her to remain behind a cloak of impartiality. Conflict of loyalty is never easy, but with such compelling evidence Greta had no choice but to commit an act of betrayal; one that Harry would never forgive.

She took a breath. It was time to discard her emotions and be decisive. First, as a little insurance against retribution, she copied Mitchell's shady land deals file and some of Harry's questionable business transactions. Then she called Robert Stone, whom she had dated at university, and who now owned a news agency.

'Are you sure about this, Greta? You got a front-page story here and it's worth a lot of bucks. You're also gonna make some powerful enemies, one in particular,' Robert cautioned.

'I'm not looking for money, or revenge, Robert, and this is not a decision I have taken lightly. I am simply trying to prevent a conspiracy against someone I really care about.'

'Okay, you'll remain an anonymous source. Email the disk to me, and promise you'll leave right away.'

'I'll call you from Burlington. And thanks, Robert.'

She clicked send, and then quickly deleted the electronic trail. It was two-thirty p.m. Her sweat suit was soaked, her hands were shaking and the phones were ringing. She checked the messages, but there was nothing urgent. She ran her hands over her face and breathed out heavily. Guilt-ridden and haunted with regret that her relationship with Harry had ended in betrayal, she looked at her beautiful portrait on the wall, wondering what his reaction would be to the note now lying on his desk.

She took one last look at the room in which they had worked together for five years, and recalled the dramas, disappointments, arguments and celebrations, of which there were many. Then her private line rang. She ran to her desk and looked at the screen; it was Harry. Closing her eyes, she took a breath and picked it up.

'Hi, Harry, homesick already?' she said, brightly as though it was just another day at the office.

'No, my business here's almost done. I was gonna fly home and take you to dinner tonight. It's our anniversary.'

'We have an anniversary?'

'We've been together five years today. I was planning a nice dinner for two at the Waldorf, but these schmucks in Chicago insist on showing me the town. They get insulted if you say no. Believe me I'd rather be with you at the Waldorf tonight.'

'Thanks for the thought, Harry, when are you back?'

'I got lunch with the Don tomorrow, so I'll be back around six. Have some bubbly tonight. I will too, bye.' Harry hung up.

Greta sat at her desk. Five years to the day Harry had said, and she had to admit that throughout those years he'd been more than generous. Now she was leaving like a thief in the night, and it bothered her, but she could not allow Harry to destroy Mike Kinnerman's dream, especially when he was fighting for his life somewhere in South America unable to defend himself. She had made the right decision, of that she was certain and it was time to leave, to be somewhere else, anywhere, it didn't matter. Harry would never find her. She would start a new life, in another city, another state, or perhaps even return to Europe.

Hurrying to her apartment she dragged two suitcases out of the box room and started packing. Then she called the airline and booked a seat on the 17:30 flight to Burlington. Ten minutes later, Charlie brought her blue Mercedes around to the side door and stowed her baggage in the trunk. With heavy snow forecast in Burlington Greta had put on a dark suede coat, a Russian fur hat, a red sweater, jeans, boots and gloves.

Outside, whipped up by the icy wind, the autumn leaves flew around like locusts in frenzied circles. Tightening the suede coat around her Greta climbed into her Mercedes and drove away, glancing at the lake as she followed the stony road to the iron gates, which opened as her car approached. Pulling up outside the gates, she took one last look at Harry's distant glowing mansion, and then tearfully headed for the freeway.

Greta owned a five-bedroom house overlooking a lake near Milton, Vermont, and having not been there for six months, she was looking forward to its comfortable seclusion.

Entering the terminal seemed to confirm a chapter in her life had ended, and waves of regret swept through her mind. Greta hated endings; they left craters of sadness that evoke feelings of vulnerability and solitude, and at that moment the airport seemed the loneliest place in the world. Collecting her ticket at the desk, she hurried to the gate determined not shed any more tears. *This is what I have to do,* she said to herself. Although the words gave her no comfort, they were a stark reminder of why she was at LaGuardia airport, all alone, without a career and soon to be despised by one of the wealthiest men in America.

As the aircraft thundered along the runway and soared into the darkening wintry sky, Greta gazed ruefully out the window at the shimmering city of New York slowly fading behind her.

Harry would never forgive her.

The Red Dahlia Hotel, Wednesday, October 14th

Richard called his office. 'Hi, Beth, it's me. Looks like we'll have Mike and Savannah back in a few hours, all being well.

Beth choked up. 'Oh thank God. How's Katie holding up?'

'Wrecked, but she's coping. What about the ranch?'

'Hectic. I paid your credit cards and dealt with the mail. JB's a tad upset about the insider trading problem and media flak.'

'Me too, we'll get to that. Call you later.' Richard hung up.

Katie called Julieanne, whom she knew was desperate to hear good news. 'Hi, sweetie, we're almost there. Mike and Savannah are due to arrive soon and we're waiting to meet them.'

'Oh Mom, get me on a plane. I wanna be there.'

'Let's wait until they're safe, Jules. We have no control over this it's a real cliff hanger. Just be patient, okay?'

Julieanne slammed down the phone.

Katie knew that Julieanne's outbursts were nothing more than teenage angst, but since Mike's disappearance they had become more intense, causing severe asthma attacks. Her devotion for her missing brother was understandable, but Katie was worried about her state of mind, and thanked God that Sally Brooks was caring for her in their absence. She pocketed her phone, hoping those problems would be gone in a few hours.

Richard called Eduardo several times that morning, but there was still no contact with the Maitre d'. At two-thirty, unable to stand the waiting any longer, Katie summoned a taxi and arriving at the marina office twenty minutes later, they scrambled out and hurried inside, hoping for some good news, but there was none. Disappointed, Katie leaned on the desk, her frustration visible and her optimism beginning to fade. Eduardo continually tried to contact Juan, but without success, and Richard reproached himself for not hiring a helicopter. Had he done so, they probably would have rescued Mike and Savannah and be heading home by now. Instead, they were anxiously pacing the marina office floor with no contact or sign of the Maitre d.'

THIRTY-SIX

On Wednesday afternoon, having navigated his way through the San Blas Islands, an archipelago comprising 378 tiny islands off the northern coast of Panama, Juan steered the Maitre d' into the mouth of a wide estuary and headed for a small fishing village east of Portobelo, to which he regularly brought tourists.

Juan had sailed around Panama's beautiful coastline for most of his life and it still took his breath away. Now, almost legendary in those waters, patrolling police boats gave him nothing more than a friendly wave. That day however, proved to be different. A police launch raced up alongside and ordered him to stop. Mike and Savannah scampered below and hid under the table, holding their breath as two armed officers jumped onboard. One officer went to the stern and looked around before joining his partner.

Rubbing his three-day stubble, Juan stepped out of the bridge and handed the burly officers two cold cans of beer. 'What's up?' he asked, nonchalantly in Spanish.

'We are looking for two American kids,' officer two said, showing Juan a photograph of Mike and Savannah. 'They were last seen at Cartegena's marina on Sunday. Have you seen them?'

Listening below, Savannah translated. 'Someone saw us at the Cartegena marina, probably the man with the straw hat.'

Mike nodded, placing a finger to his lips.

Juan shook his head. 'No, I see only local kids wanting free trips. Business for me is slow, so I am visiting my cousin.'

They popped open the beers and took a long slug. Wiping his mouth officer one strolled to the galley steps and started making his way down, when he noticed Savannah's towel on the forward deck. Climbing back up he crossed the deck and picked it up. 'Is this yours?' he asked, glaring at Juan.

'Of course, it was out to dry. It must have fallen to the deck,' Juan lied, and took it from him.

'If you see those kids, call us. And tell your cousin that car he sold me is shit,' officer two said, tossing the can over the side.

'I will tell him!' Juan yelled, as they jumped back onboard the police launch, and giving Juan a sullen look they roared away, leaving the Maitre d' rocking in its wake.

Juan opened the throttle. 'You kids can come out now!' he yelled, as the Maitre d' bounced across the bay.

Joining him at the helm, Savannah said, 'A man with a straw hat followed us in Cartegena. He probably saw us at the marina, but not which boat we boarded, and told the police.'

'Which means that he was an informer and the cops are after the reward, right?' Mike added.

Juan nodded. 'For sure, but these police do not return. I know them they go to tavern now,' he said, waving to an old man at the helm of a passing boat as he steered the Maitre d' into a small harbour and gently docked at the quayside. 'In this village I have friend; he will borrow me his truck. Then I ask pilot for taking you to Florida,' Juan said, and jumping to the quayside he tied the mooring ropes. 'Stay below till when I am back, okay?'

Juan strolled off towards the ancient village houses, where the only sign of the 21st century were satellite dishes on the terracotta roofs. Below in the galley, Mike and Savannah reflected on their sea voyage, which had given them a safe haven, albeit short lived. Suddenly, footsteps clomped along the deck and a man yelled, 'Juan!' They sank beneath the table and held their breath. 'Juan! Are you there?' he yelled again and plodded down the galley steps stopping half way. Muttering under his breath he made his way back up to the deck and clambered onto the quayside. They peeked through the porthole and saw an old man with a sailor's hat hobbling on a walking stick towards the village. Breathing a sigh of relief they sat at the table, comforted by the fact that only Juan knew their whereabouts. Nevertheless, they were still a long way from home, and relying on a dubious pilot to fly them to Florida was risky, and things could go horribly wrong, of which they had first hand experience, especially if there were criminals involved. They would trust no one.

An hour later, a rusty pick-up truck pulled up and parked on the quayside. Slamming the door, Juan jumped onboard and went below to join his young passengers.

'We have very great news,' he said, lighting a small cigar. 'Santo, my friend, he fly you to Tampa, Florida for five thousand dollars cash. But this is nothing, you are rich, no?'

Mike breathed out irritably. 'But we don't have any cash.'

'Bah, you Americans, always worrying,' Juan said, flaying his arms. 'Leave this for me. My cousin help, you will see.'

Sticking to the back roads Juan drove south for about fifteen miles, and pulling into an auto dealership he parked the truck out back. Mike and Savannah jumped out and followed him through rows of used cars parked beneath lines of flags flapping in the breeze like carnival washing. Opening a glass door, he led them into a showroom, and as they strode across the shiny, black floor, a man approached with a big smile and his hand out. He looked to be in his early fifties and grossly overweight. His head was bald, but a thin curled moustache lined his upper lip. Wearing a beige suit with a rose in the lapel, a white collarless shirt and canvas shoes, he could be mistaken for a camel trader, in Cairo, in Savannah's opinion, who disliked him on sight.

His name was Alfredo.

'Mmm, five thousand dollars is a lot of money,' Alfredo said, acting badly. 'However, I might be able to arrange a transaction for six thousand. Would that be agreeable?'

Juan shook his head and sauntered to the tinted showroom window. His cousin had always been a heartless cheat, but taking advantage of two helpless youngsters was a new low, even for him. He felt ashamed and regretted having brought them there. Savannah glared at Alfredo behind the thick sunglasses she had borrowed from Juan, along with a baseball cap, under which she had tucked her long dark hair, in an attempt to look like a boy, but her beauty betrayed her.

Gaunt and tanned with dishevelled hair Mike could pass as a local. 'You're charging me twenty percent,' he protested.

Alfredo placed his stubby arm around Mike's shoulder. 'You are in no position to bargain my friend. Five thousand for you and one thousand for me is fair. I have expenses.'

Mike produced his AmEx card and paid six thousand dollars for some sort of Toyota saloon, which Alfredo would buy back for five thousand dollars a few weeks later.

Alfredo would fill in the dates.

They followed him to a ram-shackled office at the rear of the showroom. A large TV screen showing CNN news dominated the left wall. Opening a drawer of his paper-strewn desk, he took out five thousand dollars and held it up. Savannah snatched it out of his hand, and grabbing Mike's arm they headed for the door, until they heard their names mentioned on CNN.

They spun around and faced the screen.

- This is Graham Docherty at the CNN news desk. Mike Kinnerman, the young whiz kid, as he is known, is still missing with Savannah Schlecker. The FBI has remained sceptical about their kidnapping, and with no demand for ransom, many believe that Kinnerman and Miss Schlecker ran away together. However, in what you might call "an ironic twist of fate" a terrorist group kidnapped the youngsters Saturday morning, after murdering their driver near El Dorado airport, Bogota, Colombia. Incredibly, according to local sources, they managed to escape and are now on the run. My God, this story is unbelievable, and it gets worse. Kinnerman, founder of the giant company PocketMoney.com, which the FBI has suspended following allegations of insider trading in the purchase of Stella Electronics, is also a suspect in the ongoing investigation of fraud. I guess it's fair to say that he's in deep trouble. -

Mike and Savannah's smiling faces appeared on the screen.

-Harry Schlecker, who helped found the company, is furious. Here he is giving an interview in Chicago earlier today. -

'Whoever dreamed up that story is full of crap, so lemme put the record straight; Mike Kinnerman did not run away with my daughter, they were kidnapped, and God help them.'

'What about PocketMoney.com, Harry? The company's in real trouble, according to the reports published today.'

'Maybe you should ask the person who wrote that report. Those kids are dodging bullets in South America, and you wanna know who's screwing the company? Lemme tell you somethin; if the agencies don't get off their asses and find 'em, there won't be a company, and if that happens, a generation of kids are gonna get mad, and I'm gonna start a war. Is that clear enough for you?' Harry growled, his face taught with anger.

- That was Harry Schlecker in Chicago. Now it looks like trouble is brewing over Senator Belmont's campaign to….

A warm feeling swept over Savannah when she saw Harry, particularly as he was defending Mike. She gripped his arm.

Realizing that it was Mike's face on the screen Alfredo killed the sound and sheepishly approached him. 'I owe you an apology. When Juan said two kids needed money I had no idea that it was you, Mike. PocketMoney.com was a brilliant concept.'

Showing no interest in Alfredo's compliments Mike grabbed Savannah's hand. 'Come on let's go,' he said, mortified that the FBI had suspended PocketMoney.com and that it was now under investigation for insider trading. How did that happen?

To avoid police roadblocks, Juan weaved through the narrow back roads heading south east. Annoyed by Alfredo's trickery he stared tight-lipped at the road ahead in silence. Savannah assured him that he was not to blame, but he sullenly ignored her.

Mike found the allegations of fraud difficult to comprehend. The trustees were impeccable and could only acquire companies with unified agreement. PocketMoney.com would have bought Stella Electronics in accordance with the rules and favourable terms to both companies. Harry Schlecker had no doubt brokered the deal, and all parties must have signed an agreement before the shares changed hands.

How could that lead to insider trading?

On a narrow road running parallel above the highway, Juan pulled up and pointed to a sea of flashing blue lights below. 'See, this is police roadblock. If we drive this highway, they stop my truck and you disappear.'

'That guy who saw us in Cartegena must have friends here,' Mike said, watching the blue lights fade behind them.

Juan nodded gravely. 'If these police know you are here, so do many criminals, trust me.'

'How do you know they are looking for us?' Savannah asked.

Juan huffed. 'You want to find out?'

There was no response. Switching off the truck's lights Juan cautiously drove through the dark country roads. He was nervous, and had every reason to be.

Richard anxiously paced the marina office. Katie stared out the window at every passing boat, but there was no Maitre d'.

Somewhere north of Chilibre, a small airport with a high-wire perimeter fence appeared out of nowhere. Driving through the open barrier Juan followed the road to a white building with a sign above the entrance *Aeropuerto Officianado* and parked the truck outside. Mike and Savannah jumped out and followed him through reception to a dimly lit corridor, which led to an office, where a man sat in a leather chair smoking a cigar with his feet on the desk. His name was Santo; a slim, tanned Colombian in his early thirties with black combed-back hair, who looked as if he'd stepped right out of the Godfather movie.

Removing his feet from the desk Santo motioned for them to sit, and said. 'These are the rules. I don't want to know who you are, why you are hiding, or where you are going. You are paying me to fly you to Tampa, nothing more. Agreed?'

Savannah stiffened; she had a bad feeling about him.

'Agreed,' Mike said, and handed him the $5,000.

Santo blew a pale of smoke into the overhead fan. 'Okay, we leave at ten. Wait outside,' he ordered, and handed Juan $500.

Mike wrote his home number on a slip of paper. 'Santo, can I call my Dad and let him know that we're going to Tampa?'

'No calls, no names, you were never here,' Santo said, curtly.

Savannah strolled outside, and leaning against the building she looked out at the misty darkness around the deserted airfield. Then a silver aircraft on the runway fired her curiosity.

Juan joined her and lit a cigar. 'This is Douglas DC3, some say best cargo plane they make. I think they build first one 1950. You fly to Florida with this plane,' he explained.

Savannah said nothing. Mike came out and stood beside her. Juan strolled off onto the grass and looked out at the dark airfield, his conscience bothering him. He could have told them that Santo was a drug courier for the cartels, and that they would have to jump out the plane in parachutes. But had he not brought them to Panama, saved them from corrupt police, found a pilot? He had kept his word, his honour. It was time to leave.

They accompanied Juan back to the truck and as he opened the door, Savannah threw her arms around his neck. 'Thank you for our sea voyage, Juan, we will never forget you.'

Mike handed him the slip of paper. 'That's my home number. Buy a cell phone and call me,' he said, shaking Juan's hand.

Forcing a weak smile Juan climbed into the truck and started the engine. Watching them wave in his rear view mirror, he drove away with a lump in his throat and a troubled conscience.

Juan decided to take the highway. If the police stopped him at a roadblock he would lie; he had been to Panama City on urgent business, but as he approached the slip road a sign forced him to stop. "Closed for repairs" Cursing, he crossed over the bridge and headed south to Panama City, hoping to turn around at the next junction. The highway looked ominously empty. He drove faster. Then his stomach turned when the flashing blue lights of a police car raced up alongside and forced him to pull over. Juan remained seated, his back stiffening as two armed officers strode towards him. He knew them and smiled. Wrenching open the door, officer one dragged him out to the ground.

'Hey, hey, hey, what's going on?' Juan protested.

Officer two kicked him in the ribs. 'Where are the American kids?' he demanded, menacingly.

Juan groaned rubbing his side. 'What American kids?'

Officer one grabbed him by the throat. 'Tell me where those damn kids are, or I will leave you on the roadside with a hole in your forehead.'

Juan knew that these men were corrupt and dangerous, and if he didn't keep a cool head they wouldn't hesitate to kill him. 'I don't know where any kids are, I swear. I borrowed the truck to visit my cousin, Alfredo. Why would I lie? My life is in Panama.'

'Get up,' officer one barked, producing a photograph of Mike and Savannah. 'Take a look at this.'

Juan struggled to his feet and leaned against the truck. He took the photograph and studied it. 'Yes, I have seen them on TV news,' he said, rubbing his ribs.

'They were last seen in Cartegena, and we've been told they got a boat to Panama. You sailed from Cartegena, no?'

'Yes, to Portobelo. The coastline police searched my boat; they are also looking for these kids, but I have not seen them.'

Officer two. 'Many people in Panama are looking for them. We want to find them first.' He took a step closer. 'We spoke to your cousin, Alfredo. He said you came to borrow five-thousand dollars. What was that for?'

'To repair my boat, but that shit refused, so I have to ask the Panama City Mariners Bank for loan and pay interest.'

The officers looked sceptically at one another. Officer two turned to Juan. If we find out you have lied to us, Juan....

'You know me. I sail twice a week to Panama. I am not lying, I swear,' Juan said, offering the flat of his hands.

The officers jumped back in their patrol car and sped away. Juan brushed the dust off his clothes, and feeling a sharp pain in his ribcage he climbed back in the truck and continued along the highway. Having told them he was going to Panama City Juan had no choice but to go there and park overnight at the marina. He noticed the highway was suddenly busy. The police must have opened the roadblock, and he wondered if it had anything to do with him. Keeping eye on the mirror he put his foot to the floor.

Mike and Savannah strolled onto the runway and stood under the DC3 cargo plane. Circles of oil had dripped onto the tarmac from the engines, and loose rusty rivets held a patchwork of metal to the ageing bodywork. It was like the Maitre d' with wings, in their opinion, but as they were a little short on options, dwelling on the downside only made matters worse, so they returned to the main building and sat outside waiting to board.

Santo's private line rang. 'Yes?'

'Is everything arranged for tonight?'

'Yes. Is the new passport okay?

'Couldn't be better, the name George Mason is perfect; it's nobody. Any problem with the merchandise?'

'No, it's in a sealed metal container. Four cases arrived from Colombia this morning, no questions asked,' Santo reported.

'It's a well-oiled machine. What about the airport?'

'Security is taken care of. It's a cargo airport about twenty-five miles south of Tampa. A truck will collect the container from there at eleven tomorrow morning, as you requested.'

'Very well, anything else?'

'Yes, I have two paying passengers.'

'What! Are you crazy?'

'Don't worry; it's just two American kids.'

'American?'

'Yes, they were desperate to get to Florida, so I took their money. I don't know who they are, and I don't care. I will drop them in a field long before we get to Tampa.'

'Is that a dark-haired boy about fourteen, and has a pretty girl with him about the same age?

'Yes, why?'

'Listen up; I've been summoned to a meeting at the Panama City Hotel. Big guns from all over South America will be there, including Rizzio, who wants to patch things up.'

'Good, I am sure you will sleep better, knowing the contract on your life has been cancelled,' Santo remarked.

'Whatever. Anyway, as a gesture of good faith to Rizzio and his bozo friends, I agreed to organize delivery of their cocaine shipment to Tampa. I hate goddam drugs. I usually get guys who know what they're doin to deal with that stuff, but they didn't exactly give me a choice.'

'You're lucky; Rizzio rarely gives anyone a second chance.'

'Yeah, well, the upside is, when it's done and dusted we'll all be pals again. And you know what? It couldn't have worked out better, because in light of what you've just told me, and don't get busy with questions, we're gonna make a little detour to Santiago, Cuba, so change the flight plan, and don't leave without me.'

'There is a storm brewing further north so I will be taking off at ten sharp.'

'I'm looking forward to it.'

THIRTY-SEVEN

Juan pulled up alongside the marina office and sighed with relief as the engine stopped. It was just after nine. He climbed out and slammed the door, fully intending to head for the nearest tavern. A few beers and his conscience and bruised ribs would no longer bother him. Tomorrow at first light, he planned to drive back to the village and return his friend's truck, then hopefully pick up a few tourists and set sail for Cartegena. He could hardly wait.

Hearing a screech of tires and a slamming door, Katie hurried outside and looked inquisitively at the pick-up truck. Stopping to light a cigar, Juan made eye contact with her.

'Can I help you?' he asked.

Katie took a step forward. 'I'm looking for Juan, owner of the Maitre d.' she said, as Richard came out to join her.

'I am Juan, what do you want?'

'My son, where is he you son-of-a-bitch?' Katie snapped.

'Whoa whoa, wait a minute,' Juan said, raising his palms a little shocked.

'No you wait a minute!' Richard yelled, pointing a finger at him. 'Where's the Maitre d'? There were two kids onboard, and you're gonna tell me where they are right now!'

Two couples strolled by laughing and chatting in the yellow glow of the quayside streetlamp and glanced at the heated scene. A sleek yacht, ablaze with lights, silently sailed by behind them in the mist blanketing the marina's watery darkness.

Juan's eyes danced nervously from Richard to Katie. 'You are Mike Kinnerman's parents, no?'

'Yes. Where are they?' Katie demanded.

'I sail them from Cartegena to small village near Portobelo on Panama northern coast. Then I am taking them to American Embassy, Panama City, but my friend call marina office before we sail, he is soldier…'

'You mean, Jamie?' Richard asked.

'You know him?'

'We've met. What'd he say?'

'A police informer, he see the kids look at boats in Cartegena marina. Now police search all boats, and many bad people in Panama look for them: kidnappers and criminals. Corrupt highway police, they stop me and kick my ribs. They think I bring these kids here. I lie pretty good.'

Richard breathed out. 'Christ, this gets worse by the goddam minute. So where the hell are they now?'

'Jamie say to get them out from Panama if trouble come. So I call my friend, Santo, he has plane. They pay him five thousand dollars for flight to Tampa, Florida.'

'Florida? Oh my God, tell me this is not happening!' Katie yelled, with both anger and frustration.

Richards back stiffened. 'Tampa? You mean the airport?'

Juan shuffled uncomfortably. 'No…not airport.'

Katie glared at him ready to explode. 'Then where the hell are they going?'

'They drop to field…in parachute.'

Katie's eyes widened with horror. 'Parachute!'

Richard stood in Juan's face. 'What kind of people are you? They're just kids, for Christ sake! When did they leave?' he snarled, clearly on the verge of losing it.

'Santo, he like to leave at ten, but this depends on cargo and destination,' Juan explained, his face pale and anxious.

Richard checked his watch; 9:13 p.m. 'You mean they're still here, in Panama, at an airport?' he said, with menacing optimism.

Unsure what Richard might do next Juan backed up. 'Yes, I think so. Why you blame me for this when I….

Katie ran forward and slapped Juan's face. 'Tell me where my son is goddam you!' she yelled, and slapped him again.

Juan stepped back, rubbing his cheek, his eyes moving swiftly from Katie to Richard. 'You do not understand. I do this to help them, I swear.'

Richard grabbed Juan's shirt with both hands and lifted him off the ground. 'Help them? Help them! Knowing they'd have to jump out of a plane in a goddam parachute?'

Katie tugged his arm. 'Richard, we don't have time for this.'

'How far is the airport, what's it called, and where is it?' Tell me damn you!' Richard yelled, his face contorted with rage.

Unable to move, Juan held back his head and his captain's hat fell to the ground. 'Chilibre airport, I think is forty kilometres north east from here. I show you if you want...

Eduardo stepped out the office door. 'What is going on?'

'Eduardo, tell him I am honourable, a good man!' he yelled.

Eduardo, a retired police officer with a distinguished career and a string of medals for bravery, ordered Richard to let Juan go. Now somewhere in his fifties he had settled for a quiet life as harbourmaster of the marina, watching the boats come and go.

Tonight he sensed fate would call upon his police skills.

Richard released Juan and turned to face Eduardo. 'Mike and Savannah are at Chilibre airport, with a guy named Santo, a pilot. Apparently, he's flying them to Florida at ten o'clock, and if we don't leave now they'll be gone, maybe forever.'

Juan picked up his hat. 'You are angry, this I understand, but corrupt police would have these children now if I do not take them to Chilibre.'

Eduardo shook his head. 'Maybe so, but all you have done is save them from one evil and given them to another. If you had kept your radio on, as you are supposed to do, we could have met you at Portobelo, but you did not do that did you Juan. No, you placed those kid's lives in the hands of a ruthless criminal to earn extra money, and that my friend is unforgivable.'

Katie stamped her foot. 'For God's sake let's do something!'

Eduardo turned to Richard. 'I know Chilibre airport, and this criminal Santo. Allow me to offer my services; I think you are going to need them.' Richard nodded gratefully. 'Very well, you and your wife get in the back of the station wagon. Juan, you get in front, and let us pray that we are not too late.

* * * * *

Panama City Hotel, Wednesday, October 14th

Six CIA operatives gathered for a final briefing at an apartment in a suburb of Panama City; two of whom were attractive females specially trained for covert operations. The so-called "Drug lords" had chosen the Panama City Hotel as neutral ground to discuss their ongoing wars, unaware that the CIA had installed powerful listening devices and micro video cameras linked to a roomful of hi-tec equipment on the third floor. These notoriously violent men were undoubtedly the most dangerous criminals in South America, and covert observation was an effective way of gathering hard evidence to bring them to justice.

That evening would prove to be invaluable.

At nine p.m., wearing an assortment of hats, silk shirts and black baggy slacks, eight men swaggered into the hotel lobby, each with two armed bodyguards and an excessive amount of jewellery and scars. Laughing and cursing crudely they entered the conference room, followed by their heavily armed entourage. The two CIA females gave them a welcoming smile and began opening bottles of red wine. Nervously eyeing one another, the sixteen bodyguards lined up along the wall as their feared bosses embraced one another before sitting down at a long table.

Amid the crude Spanish chatter echoing in the domed ceiling, the females calmly handed out glasses of wine to the bosses.

Two men entered the hotel lobby; one had a gambler Panama hat, the other a long scar across his face. They pushed open the conference room and went inside.

Rizzio stood up and folded his arms, as Rylan Mitchell entered the room and nodded to the staring faces around the table before sitting down. Netty stood at the wall with the other bodyguards, who glared at him menacingly. One of the females, serving drinks and bread rolls, stood next to Mitchell and poured him a glass of wine. He glanced up and her eyes danced with provocation. As she turned to walk away Mitchell's hat tumbled to the floor. Apologising profusely she bent down to pick it up, and in doing so planted a tiny device inside the headband before returning it to the table. Mitchell waved her away, and bowing like a peasant she hurried off to the kitchen. Netty was too busy admiring her legs to notice her slight of hand and the bodyguards were too busy watching each other to notice anything.

'Señor Mitchell, you will apologise to my friends for losing our shipment and our schooner,' Rizzio ordered.

The bosses glared at Mitchell as he stood up, and he was sure they would have shot him had Rizzio not come to his defence. 'I apologise,' he said, lowering his head as a mark of respect.

A chilling silence fell as Rizzio walked around the table and kissed Mitchell on both cheeks. The men applauded, giving a sign of their forgiveness, but there would be no second chances.

Rizzio returned to his seat. 'Señor Mitchell, we want you to find new ways of getting our cocaine into the United States and Canada. Last month, their enforcement agencies confiscated eight of our shipments. This has cost us a billion dollars.'

'I'll look into it,' Mitchell lied. He would do nothing.

After conferring with the bosses, Rizzio turned to Mitchell. 'It is agreed; deliver our cocaine shipment to Tampa and you will regain our trust. I will contact you in one month. You may go.'

Mitchell nodded and left the room. Netty followed him out. He was playing a dangerous game, which he knew could be fatal, but once Rizzio's cocaine landed safely in Tampa, he'd be off the hook and have the kids hidden in Cuba. His Italian contact would negotiate the ransom and arrange for the kids to be found as soon as the money arrived in his secret account. Then having moved it around the world until it was untraceable, he'd go lie on a beach.

After that, to hell with them.

* * * * *

Chilibre Airport 9:47 p.m.

The Douglas engines sprang to life with a roar. Buckled up at the rear of the hold Mike and Savannah sat staring at the parachutes on the floor. Then a helicopter floated in and landed alongside the runway. Mike pressed his face against the window, and when he saw Mitchell and Netty jump out and Santo hurrying out to meet them, his blood turned cold. Someone had betrayed them. He alerted Savannah and they both stiffened with dread as Mitchell and Netty entered the hold, grinning.

'Well well, you kids have been a pain in the ass,' Mitchell said, pushing back his Panama hat. 'You cost me a lot of money and I intend to get it back, so here's the deal. You're gonna sweat in the dark, stinking room of a Cuban farmhouse until the ransom is paid. And if that don't happen, I'll give you to Netty.'

Netty leaned down to Mike's face. 'If you give me any more grief, I'm gonna be your worst nightmare sonny' he growled, chillingly, then turning to Savannah he spoke as though she were a doll and touched her hair. 'Hi, sweetheart, you look in better shape than your boyfriend here.' Savannah spat in his face and kicked his crotch. 'Ah, you little bitch....' Netty raised his fist.

Mike shielded her with his body. 'Leave her alone!'

'Stop it, Netty!' Mitchell yelled.

Wiping his face, Netty glared at Savannah, as she snuggled up to Mike. Mitchell took a call from the helicopter pilot who was keen to take off. 'Wait until the plane's in the air in case we have any problems,' he ordered, and disconnected.

As they headed for the cockpit, Santo stopped beside a metal container. 'Rizzio's shipment is in here,' he said, patting it gently. 'I'm glad you're pals again. He's a dangerous man.'

Mitchell said nothing and walked on.

Haunted by dreadful imaginings of their uncertain future Mike and Savannah sat huddled together, wondering who had betrayed them. Mitchell's furtive appearance had dealt a final blow to any hope of finding their way home, and after crossing a continent determined to escape his stalking menace, it seemed ironic that fate had brought them full circle. Now, numbed by a desolate sense of hopelessness, they were preparing for the inevitable, and having abandoned any hope of rescue or means of escape, were steeling themselves for months of solitude and possibly death on the Caribbean island of Cuba.

Chilibre airport's perimeter fence appeared on the left side of the road. Eduardo tightened his grip on the wheel and pushed his foot to the floor. The road would take them around the airfield to the entrance gate, but he had another plan and told Richard and Katie to brace themselves.

Gazing out of the hold window Mike whispered sorry to his beloved sister, knowing that her heart would be breaking. His future had promised great things, which he had hoped to share with Savannah. Now, engulfed in an air of palpable resignation, they sat holding one another's hand, their future doubtful.

Then a moving flash of lights in the distant darkness jolted him back to reality. Wiping the glass, he looked again and sat bolt upright. A station wagon had just crashed through the perimeter fence. He pressed his face hard up against the window, his mind racing with possibility, and nudging Savannah he pointed to the distant moving headlights.

Leaning over him to the window, she saw the oncoming headlights, and whispered, 'Mike, I think your father is here.'

Bouncing over mounds of earth and concealed debris the red station wagon streaked across the airfield. Eduardo could clearly see the pilot and two others in the cockpit, and with the propellers spinning he knew they were preparing for take-off. He bumped the station wagon onto the runway and skidded to a halt. Two old aircraft tyres lay abandoned in the nearby grass. He told Richard and Juan to roll them on to the runway. Then opening the rear door, he dragged out two large plastic bottles of gasoline. Richard helped him splash the fuel over the tyres and runway, then setting it ablaze they quickly jumped back in the station wagon. Eduardo slammed his foot to the floor and as they raced along the runway towards the spinning propellers, Katie gripped Richard's arm and stared wide-eyed at the looming aircraft.

Santo froze when he saw the runway in flames and headlights speeding towards him, and pointing through the cockpit window he yelled over the engine noise. 'Look, we have company!'

'Who the hell is that?' Mitchell yelled.

'Who knows, but it looks like trouble. I'm taking off. Secure the hold door, Netty, quickly!'

The DC3 could take off on grass or concrete, but with unseen debris littering the airfield, Santo had no choice but to use the burning runway, which he knew was risky. If the flames licked the passing wheels during take-off the plane could explode into a fireball in seconds. It would be close.

Having locked the hold door, Netty grinned at Mike. 'You're gonna love Cuba,' he said, and laughed his way to the cockpit.

The engines suddenly roared and the aircraft began to shake. Mike jumped out of his seat and frantically searched the hold for another exit. Surely, there must be another way out.

Fully powered for take-off the ageing DC3 shuddered under the stress of the engines' forward thrust. Then the emergency exit door light began flashing above the control panel. Santo tapped it with his fingers but it made no difference. 'That's another thing I'll have to fix on this old crate,' he mumbled

Mitchell stared at the burning runway, his eyes narrowing.

The helicopter pilot decided it was time to leave and with a surge of power he took off into the night.

Mitchell cursed him and yelled at Santo, 'For Christ sake take off before it's too late! They'll be a goddam contract on my life if we don't get Rizzio's shipment to Florida.'

Santo pulled back the throttle and the engines responded with roar of power. Shuddering and rattling the DC3 quickly gathered speed along the cracked runway. Wiping his sweating hands on his jacket Mitchell gritted his teeth as the flaming tyres and burning runway came hurtling towards them.

Gripping the wheel Eduardo stared deer like at the aircraft's' beaming lights racing towards him, and as they loomed closer he knew the pilot was determined to take off or be damned. Banging his fist on the steering wheel he pulled off the runway onto the grass and brought the station wagon to skidding halt.

Richard and Katie scrambled out as the DC3 roared towards them, lights blazing and its wheels tearing at the runway. Eduardo raised his hands in a futile effort to deter the pilot from taking off and as it thundered by, Richard and Katie caught a glimpse of Mike Savannah clawing at a window screaming for help. They frantically waved and called to them, and in that fleeting moment Katie saw Mike yelling "Mom!" as the aircraft took to the air, its undercarriage folding beneath it. Then they were gone. Katie fell to her knees sobbing. Richard knelt beside her and together they watched the DC3's tail lights fade into the night.

An empty silence fell, bringing with it an overwhelming sense of finality. In the harrowing darkness a breeze swept across the runway and rustled through the surrounding trees. The stench of aviation fuel lingered in the air like a bad memory.

Mike and Savannah had gone, perhaps never to return.

Time had stopped for Richard and Katie Kinnerman.

Eduardo reached for his cell phone and called Jose` Martinez; manager of Panama City Airport. He told him exactly what had happened, and added, 'I think they are heading north west.'

'They will have a big problem. There is a bad storm further north,' Jose` reported. 'We will track the DC3 and alert all local airports that two kidnapped kids are onboard. When we have any further news I'll let you know.' Jose` hung up.

Pocketing his phone Eduardo approached Richard and Katie, who were on their knees seeking comfort in one another's arms. He solemnly expressed regret for his inability to stop the DC3, and promised to do everything in his power to find it. When neither responded he walked to the deserted runway and looked up at the endless night sky.

The youngsters had gone. Words were meaningless.

Still on her knees and inconsolable Katie leaned forward and wept in her hands. Emotionally and physically drained and no longer empowered by her seemingly limitless optimism, all hope had gone with the fading plane's tail-lights. Richard helped her up and held her in his arms; she was broken, in despair.

They both were.

Juan sheepishly joined them. 'I am sorry. I try to help them. I am honourable man,' he said, clearly distraught. 'Santo, he will keep his word to drop them in Tampa, you will see.'

Eduardo shook his head. 'No, there were other men on that plane and they refused to stop when they saw us. Those poor youngsters are now in the hands of kidnappers. I hope you are proud of yourself, Juan,' he said, harshly.

Juan lowered his head and sullenly walked back to the station wagon, wondering who else was aboard the DC3.

Eduardo sensed, understandably, that Richard and Katie were on the very edge of despair, but experience told him to keep them involved, no matter how painful, or they may lose their resolve.

'Come,' Eduardo said, beckoning a hand, 'there is no point in staying here any longer. Let us go back to the marina office.'

Without responding Richard and Katie climbed in the station wagon's rear seat and shut the door. Eduardo slammed the shift into drive and screeched away to the exit. No one looked back. Following the highway to downtown Panama City, he pulled up outside his old police station and ordered Juan inside. 'Tell them everything you know, do you understand? Everything.'

Juan nodded, and shuffled up the steps to the entrance.

Back at the marina office Eduardo called the coastguard and Tampa police. Katie sat down and stared at the floor; her eyes glazed with hopelessness and her mind haunted by the memory of Mike and Savannah clawing at the window screaming for help as the DC3 thundered by on that God-forsaken runway.

Richard gazed out the window, wondering what he would say to Julieanne. He rubbed his hand over his face and tried to think positively. He doubted the plane would go to Tampa now, if so, it would need permission to land elsewhere, which would give the authorities time to alert local police and implement a rescue plan. Surely pilots can't island hop without a flight plan can they?

But this is South America, he recalled Jamie saying. He paced the floor desperate to do something, anything.

After speaking at length to the aviation authorities, Eduardo reported his findings to Richard and Katie. 'All Central American airports have been alerted to track the DC3,' he said, his voice charged with optimism. 'I am confident the aircraft will be found, but there is nothing more we can do until morning, so allow me to drive you to your hotel.'

Wincing at the thought of returning to their dreary hotel room, Katie stood up and walked to the office window. Richard leaned against the wall, his mind somewhere over the Caribbean.

They were obviously still in shock and Eduardo felt reluctant to leave them alone in such an emotional state, particularly as they were in a foreign country. 'I have a better idea; come with me to the marina members club. A stiff drink and a light supper would do you both good,' he urged, persuasively.

They indulged Eduardo's kindness, but neither were the least bit hungry, and after several brandies and little conversation Eduardo drove them back to the Red Dahlia hotel. With barely a thread of hope to cling to they went up to their dark, stuffy room and sat on the beds staring at the floor, not knowing what to say to one another, both certain they would never feel more desolate than at that moment.

Early next morning, looking pale and drawn after a sleepless night of anguish, Richard and Katie returned to the marina office praying for good news, but they were to be disappointed. Eduardo handed them each a strong coffee and proceeded to explain.

'The DC3 did not go to Florida. The authorities tracked it heading north to Nicaragua, and then it vanished off their radar. Santo is a good pilot and knows the Caribbean, but this is still hurricane season, and further north there was a bad storm last night, which could explain their sudden disappearance.'

Katie sullenly shook her head. Storm was bad enough, why did he have to mention hurricane?

Richard decided to call the Panama U.S. Embassy, and after explaining to a female official what had happened, she transferred him to Sheila Macavy, the emergency duty officer.

'We are all very sorry this has happened Mr. Kinnerman. I assure you we'll do everything in our power to find the missing youngsters. Kidnappings are always a priority here, but gathering information takes time and I would advise you, as painful as it is, to go home and wait for a breakthrough. The U.S. has people on the ground in every Central American country, and we'll use that network to find out what happened to this aircraft.'

Sheila took down all their contact details. Richard thanked her and put down the phone. There was nothing else he could do.

Katie dreaded breaking the bad news to Julieanne, but she could not allow her to find out by watching CNN. She pressed her daughter's cell phone number and tried to sound positive.

'Hi, sweetie, you okay?'

'Hi, Mom, why didn't you call me last night, where's Mike?'

'Darling, they didn't know we were here and we couldn't contact them. They bought passage on a plane to Tampa.'

'What! You mean they're on their way to the U.S.?'

'By the time we found the airport, their plane was taking off. I saw them at the window. They were taken, Jules, by whom we don't know. The authorities are tracking the airplane, and police are on red alert to rescue them as soon as it's located.'

Julieanne did not respond. There were no tears, just silence, and then the slamming down of the phone. Katie called back and spoke to Sally Brooks, who was staying at the house, and told her the dreadful news. It took Sally a moment to compose herself.

'Oh my God, Katie, this is so awful. Now I understand why Julieanne ran screaming up to her room in a flood of tears. Just do what you have to do. I'll take care of her.'

'Thank you Sally. I'll call tomorrow,' Katie said, feeling an overwhelming sense of emptiness as she disconnected.

Lost in a thickening fog of despair Katie stood at the marina office window, watching the sailboats silently pass by. She could no longer fight the growing sense of hopelessness, and for the first time since their terrible nightmare began, doubted she would ever see her son alive again.

THIRTY-EIGHT

Thursday, October 15th

WALL STREET KING HARRY SCHLECKER
LINKED TO SCANDAL WITH PENTAGON.

The headline hit the news coast-to-coast, along with details of Rylan Mitchell's fraudulent dealings with the Pentagon. Greta had anxiously waited for the story to break and for the phone to ring. The note on Harry's desk informed him of her betrayal and the end of their relationship.

I leaked the story, Harry. I had to. There is no easy way to say this, I truly am sorry. Goodbye. Greta.

Homeward bound from Chicago in his Gulf Stream jet Harry watched the article unfold on CNN. He didn't give a damn about the accusations, but he *was* concerned about who stabbed him in the back. He offered newspaper editors fifty-thousand dollars for the name of the source, but there were no takers.

When Harry arrived home in his helicopter at six-thirty Henry was out jogging and the mansion seemed strangely quiet. Finding his office door locked, he marched up the marble staircase and knocked on Greta's apartment door. There was no response. He paced back and forth along the airy landing. This was Greta's sanctuary; the one place that she could walk around naked, yell or do whatever she wanted. He knocked again, and with no answer forthcoming he cautiously opened the door and went inside. The apartment was empty; Greta had gone, but where, and why? He hurried down to his office, unlocked the door and clicked on the lights. Greta's intoxicating perfume lingered in the air. He took a breath and looked around. 'What's happening, what the hell *is* this? He yelled, reaching for the phone.

Then he saw the note.

Harry had never been the emotional type, but with Greta it was different. Betrayal by the woman he loved was a stab in the back and he was bleeding with disappointment, as if she'd ripped his heart out. His haggard face, distorted with rage, stared at him in a sixty-thousand dollar mirror on the opposite wall. Lashing out, he threw a crystal glass ashtray at his reflection and watched it shatter like his dreams of happy ever after.

Having spent most of his early life in institutions, Harry was hardened to disappointment, but when Richard informed him that Mike and Savannah were once again at the mercy of kidnappers, this time in Panama, he broke down.

Greta's goodbye note was the final straw.

Harry was used to adversity, but not this pain, this heartbreak. He had been away for two days and lost everything that he loved. His beautiful daughter had disappeared in a cargo plane, which aviation authorities believed had crashed in the sea, and Greta, the woman with whom he hoped to spend the rest of his life, had left him and he had no idea why. Now, for the first time in his life, Harry felt alone and his magnificent mansion, filled with the trappings of enormous wealth, suddenly seemed worthless.

* * * * *

Burlington Vermont

Thursday morning, Greta sat in front of a blazing fire revelling in its warmth. Her five-bedroom house, which she had painstakingly redesigned, was now a spacious luxury home, with dark wooded framework, glowing fireplaces, red brick walls, leather sofas and antique tables dotted around a thick, green-carpet, with matching velvet drapes falling to the floor in the bay windows overlooking the lake. If her dreams never materialized, she planned to live there and perhaps write a book or two.

She spent the afternoon walking around the lake deliberating over her uncertain future. The cold October air and magnificent scenery created an ideal sense of isolation in which to find solace. Only the sound of her boots crunching in the newly fallen snow disturbed the silence of her frosty winter land. Then as daylight began to fade, casting long shadows from the surrounding ageing conifers, she trekked back to the warm glow of her house and the life she had left behind suddenly seemed far away.

Showered and wearing a sweater and jeans she uncorked a bottle of French white burgundy to accompany her slowly cooked chicken chasseur, and an old movie. The phone rang; she looked at the screen. It was Harry Schlecker. Allowing it to ring several times she prepared herself for a confrontation. She saw no point in mentioning the incriminating email yet. Harry would have to explain that at the appropriate time. Instead, she decided to steer the conversation in another direction, one that would undoubtedly infuriate him. She picked up the phone. 'Hi, Harry.'

Melting to the sound of Greta's voice Harry took a breath and calmly said 'I'm disappointed in you.'

'I know you are, but it was time to put my cards on the table.'

Sitting behind his huge walnut desk Harry stared at Greta's note, trying to figure out why she had betrayed him. 'What the hell are you talking about?'

Greta sipped her chilled burgundy. 'Do you really want me to spell it out?'

Harry stood up. 'Yeah, go ahead spell it out.'

'You gave me the job of a lifetime, Harry, and for that I'm grateful. But there is one thing; I've known how you felt about me since day one, and though I care about you deeply I have often wondered about the sincerity of your motive.'

Now pacing the room Harry pulled off his tie and unbuttoned his shirt. 'It was strictly-business,' he said, clenching his fist.

'Really? Then tell me why you destroyed David's New York antique business and forced him to return to London with his tail between his legs? You remember David, my fiancé.'

Silence

Harry stopped pacing. 'I had nothing to do with that he made some bad investments.'

Greta began pacing her kitchen. 'Bullshit! You had his name removed from the society list, his club memberships cancelled and paid the press to give him a roasting until he quit. I'm not a fool, Harry, so don't treat me like one. I deserve better than that.'

More silence.

Somewhat shocked by Greta's angry rebuke Harry glanced at her exquisite portrait on the wall above her desk. 'No, Greta, you're not a fool.' Long pause. 'Yeah okay it's true, I'm sorry. So is that why you betrayed me, revenge?'

'I'll let you figure it out.'

'What else could it be?'

'Think about it.'

'Think about what? You're the best, Greta, that's why you worked for me. I'm also crazy about you, but you know that.'

'Yes I do, and I never, ever wanted to hurt you.'

Harry knew this was no good. He needed to be face to face with Greta to find out why she had left him, but now was not the time. She sounded upset, angry, and he had no idea why. He calmed down. 'Are you in Vermont? I just wanna know.'

'Yes.'

Harry screwed Greta's note into a ball and threw it in the wastebasket. 'We need to talk, Greta. Come back to New York whenever you're ready. I'm not goin anywhere.'

* * * * *

Panama City.

Richard and Katie spent a further ten days talking to the U.S. Embassy, local police and aviation authorities. They also made a plea on Panama's TV news channel "Telemetro" to anyone who knew of Mike and Savannah's whereabouts, but their efforts were in vain. Eduardo remained sympathetic and called the authorities daily for any news of the missing youngsters, but to no avail.

Monday, October 26th Richard and Katie reluctantly returned to New York and spent the whole journey staring blankly out the window. Both felt a cold sense of finality as their Delta flight landed on La Guardia airport's icy runway. Once stoic in her belief that Mike and Savannah would somehow return, Katie was now convinced they were dead; killed in plane crash somewhere in the Caribbean. She sat in morbid silence, steeling herself for a heartbreaking reunion with her distraught daughter, for whom they were both deeply concerned.

Mike and Savannah's "adventure" as some had named it, was still headline news, and when Richard and Katie walked through arrivals a mob of reporters, intent on hearing the details, gathered round them in a news-hungry frenzy. Halting the baggage trolley, Richard asked them to stop yelling, and then gave an impromptu press conference to a bunch of hand-held recorders.

One smart-mouthed female reporter asked, 'How do you feel about going to jail for insider trading Mr. Kinnerman?'

Richard and Katie headed for the exit.

Two unsmiling FBI agents jumped out of an illegally parked black SUV and produced their badges. 'Please come with us Mr. and Mrs. Kinnerman,' one said, opening the side door.

Richard was in no mood to argue and placing their baggage behind the seat he sat beside Katie. The van sped away through the city and pulled up in a reserved bay at 26 Federal Plaza; FBI Headquarters. Ordering Richard and Katie out they escorted them into the building and up to a room on the third floor, where two criminal investigation agents sullenly sat behind a desk. The first offered sympathy for their missing son, and then read them their Miranda rights. The second warned that they were answerable for the crime of insider trading in the purchase of Stella Electronics. Questioning followed, and after an hour-long short-tempered interrogation, Richard and Katie took the Fifth Amendment. Yelling, desk banging and threats followed, then snapping shut their folders the agents furiously marched out the room.

New York's District Attorney, Jim Lawrence strode into the room with a thick folder. Grinning he shook Richard's hand, and said, 'I'm real sorry to see my old friend and one of New York's finest lawyers in trouble with the law, Richard.'

Richard had barely known him at university, but he sensed a little gloating. 'Who says I'm in trouble?'

Katie was furious. 'A smug sorry, is that all you can say? The FBI has accused us of insider trading, which is nothing short of libellous. Got any evidence to prove these allegations?'

Jim smiled. 'Well now, we found a two-page fax hidden in Richard's desk drawer at the PocketMoney.com building, which arrived the day before the company bought Stella Electronics. Attached were details of Stella's ground-breaking system, which was not due to be unveiled until the following Monday morning, thus motivating PocketMoney.com to buy the company, knowing the share value would increase greatly.'

'I don't know anything about a fax and vehemently deny any involvement in insider trading. Will that do?' Richard growled.

Katie huffed derisively. 'Have you considered the possibility that someone could have planted a fax in Richard's desk?'

Jim shrugged dispassionately. 'I'll tell you what I do know; indictments will be served on all those involved in the scandal, and I will personally see to it that every one of them stands before a grand jury. Sorry pal, I'll be in touch.' He opened the door.

'I want a copy of the fax and a list of everything else you've taken from the building,' Richard demanded.

Jim Lawrence strode down the corridor and waving his finger without looking back, he yelled, 'All in good time, pal.'

An FBI agent drove them to JFK's perimeter parking lot and left them standing in the icy rain clutching their suitcases. Katie paid the bill at the office, while Richard brought his BMW to the barrier. Tossing the baggage into the back they climbed in and headed for the freeway in the freezing rain.

An hour later, as they drove through New Mayford and turned into Beechwood Avenue, Katie said, 'Let's talk about this fax problem tomorrow, Richard. Right now, Julieanne needs us.'

Richard nodded and pulled up in the driveway. Katie jumped out and hurried to the front door while he brought in the baggage. Piffin greeted them with his usual doting affection, but there was no way of telling him why they were so unresponsive. Leaving the baggage cluttering the hallway, they ran upstairs and found Julieanne lying in her bed staring at the wall, clutching a broken doll. The curtains were drawn and Sally Brooks, sadness written all over her face, sat holding her hand.

David Morton, the family doctor, whom Sally had summoned days earlier, arrived at the house and examined Julieanne once again. Having administered to her needs since she was born, David knew that in spite of her asthmatic problem she was a healthy kid at a delicate age. He went on to explain her condition.

'Julieanne is suffering from emotional trauma, which occurs when the mind is confronted with something it cannot face and shuts down. She is refusing to accept that her brother may never return. God forbid that happens, but if it does, given time she may come to terms with it, but don't expect a miracle.'

Katie gently held her daughter and sobbed.

Julieanne's boyfriend Jake had been in Philadelphia for two weeks and called at the house to see her. Richard explained that she was unwell and could not receive visitors right now. 'We'll call when she's feeling better, Jake. Okay?'

Nodding morbidly he sauntered off down the pathway.

With Savannah missing and Greta having walked out of his life, Harry cancelled his monthly business ball, the Christmas Eve party, the New Years Eve ball and every other event, except the Christmas day party for the local orphanage. He told his staff that things would return to normal when Savannah came home, but they were not convinced. Harry was no longer taking calls. All the curtains were drawn and the mansion was in darkness. Alone in the library, he morbidly sat in front of the fireplace, his eyes lost in the blazing flames and refused to speak to anyone, except Henry, who was always close by whenever Harry was troubled.

Horrified by Mike's latest kidnapping and saddened by news of Julieanne's withdrawal Ms. Wilmont called Katie to express her sorrow. JB Walsome and Beth, both deeply concerned, told Richard not to worry about the office; it would be there whenever he was ready to return. Sheriff Carver had to take a deep breath when he saw how feeble and sickly Julieanne had become. It was heartbreaking. Moose called, hoping for any news of Mike, but Katie had none to give him. Sally Brooks continued to be a family blessing. Linda Greenberg remained resolute that Mike and Savannah would return safe and well, and promised to call Katie every day until that happened. Regular phone calls came from the trustees, but conversations were stiff, mainly because no one knew quite what to say, other than how sorry they were.

Meanwhile, furious NYSE officials and Wall Street traders demanded that New York's District Attorney serve grand jury indictments to all those involved in the fraudulent purchase of Stella Electronics.

Someone had to go to jail.

Jim Lawrence was working on it.

Still isolated in Burlington Greta emailed Harry, expressing her sorrow over Mike and Savannah's disappearance in Panama, and urged him not to give up. Harry did not respond. Greta then called Katie to offer her support, and asked if she could come to Beechwood Avenue for a week or so. Katie relished the thought of intelligent female company, and when Richard welcomed the idea she invited Greta to come stay at the house.

The Kinnerman house, once the hub of activity in Beechwood Avenue, now looked as though it was in mourning. The curtains remained drawn and a dark gloominess shrouded its now famous red brick walls. The autumn leaves, swirling around the lifeless garden in the blustery October wind, seemed to make it even bleaker. Neighbours offering their support left hastily written notes in their mailbox, and messages of hope continued to arrive in abundance from Mike and Julieanne's school friends.

It was cold and raining heavily.

The reporters had gone.

The avenue looked deserted.

Late one night, when the house was dark and silent, Richard and Katie entered Julieanne's bedroom and sat beside her in the light of the bedside lamp glowing softly on her tormented face. Piffin had lain at her feet with his head on his paws everyday since her withdrawal as though he could sense she was sick and troubled. Gently holding her lifeless hands they watched her sleeping and silently prayed for her to come back to them. The evil that had taken their son had now infected their daughter and there seemed no end in sight to their family misery.

THIRTY-NINE

Monday, October 26th

After a ten-day furlough with his father, Jamie received orders to report to Major Bell in Bogota. Juan had called to inform him of Mike and Savannah's Panama abduction, which had yet to hit the news, and he felt responsible, angry, they trusted him. Marching into the major's office at 14:30 he saluted stiffly.

'Good to see you, Jamie, have a seat. Now unfortunately we have a problem; the kids you sent to Panama are missing.'

Jamie sat facing the major's desk. 'They were taken, sir.'

'Yes, so it would seem, but there are other factors involved. The NSA is concerned about a growing wave of anger, not only in the U.S., but also around the world. Apparently, millions of youngsters are convinced young Kinnermans' disappearance and PockMoney.com's closure is a part of a government conspiracy, and accusations of a cover up are now flooding the internet and news channels. As a result, market prices and the U.S. dollar have fallen sharply, and Langley has ordered us to find them, quickly.

'Mike Kinnerman is an icon to a generation of kids. They believe in him, sir. I will need a partner.'

'Very well, just keep me informed. I'll be in Brazil.'

Jamie chose Judy Cassano, a tough veteran, aged 27, five ten, with brown eyes and short auburn hair who spoke fluent Spanish. Jamie's security status rose to level three, giving him access to sensitive documents, satellites and unlimited travel.

Jamie searched the satellite surveillance system for Mike and Savannah's two blips, but found no sign of them. In addition, according to CIA reports, a female operative had placed a small tracking device in Rylan Mitchell's hat at the Panama City Hotel, but that was not showing either, which seemed ominous and he could only assume they had either discarded the homing devices, someone discovered them, or they were all dead.

The next morning, Judy spoke with the Panamanian Aviation Authorities who just quoted their report; the DC3 vanished off the coast of Honduras. Then she called the Honduran Authorities and asked the duty officer what he saw that night.

'We followed the DC3 heading north east towards Jamaica,' he reported. 'Then it disappeared off the radar, probably due to the bad storm. However, it could not have flown any further than Cuba because the fuel tanks would have been empty by then and it was running on vapour. That is all we have, I am sorry.'

Judy reported her findings to Jamie, but he was suspicious, and said so. 'The DC3 either slipped through the net or it crashed in the Caribbean. If the plane did go down, Mike and Savannah would not have survived and we could be chasing ghosts, but something tells me that's exactly what they'd like us to believe.'

Judy nodded. 'I agree.'

Three weeks later, having talked to Venus Plaza hotel's staff, detective Aldo, Juan, whom police released without charge, staff at Chilibre airport, Eduardo, Panama's Shipping Office and those who tracked the DC3, they returned to Bogota with no new leads.

Jamie paced his apartment. 'That damn DC3 pilot wanted us to believe that he crashed in the sea, but he landed alright, about here,' he said, circling Cuba's southern coast. 'Get us on a flight to Santiago, Judy. I'll get our visas from Major Bell.'

Arriving in Santiago late the next morning, they took a taxi to the Melina Beach Hotel and checked into two rooms. There were a number of intelligence agents in Cuba, one of whom Jamie had toured with in Iraq. His current name was Graham Manion; ghost owner of a tourism business in Havana. He touched base with Graham and arranged a three-thirty rendezvous at Plaza de Armas in Old Havana. Their flight from Santiago to Havana would take an hour and thirty-five minutes, Judy confirmed.

For Jamie, Havana was a captivating city vibrant with music, exotic food, sunshine and a constant hint of danger. Ageing signs of Fidel Castro's rebellion against Batista's government forces, which gave birth to antihero Che Guevara in 1958, were still visible on the baroque buildings. As Havana is the most popular destination in the Caribbean Jose` Marti` airport was predictably buzzing with tourists arriving and departing. A glamorous tour guide, leading a flock of new arrivals, wiggled her way out of the crowded terminal, clutching a clipboard.

Jamie smiled; those were the days, he thought to himself as he and Judy jumped into one of many taxis eager for fares.

Graham Manion arrived at exactly three-thirty and after an old pals greeting, he led Jamie and Judy to a bar-restaurant, with red-clothed tables and matching parasols outside in the square.

'We need to find the DC3 and its occupants, probably two men,' Jamie explained. 'They are unlikely to have checked into a hotel, with two kidnapped kids in tow. If they made it to Cuba, and I am convinced they did, my guess is they rented a house somewhere. I want you to check all properties rented in the last four weeks, and find out anything you can about the DC3. It landed somewhere in Cuba, of that I am certain.'

'I'll look into it, Jamie, but things don't happen overnight in sunny Cuba, time runs on a different clock down here, pal. Don't worry, if those guys came here I'll find them.'

After two hours of exotic food, war stories and cold beer, Jamie and Judy caught the 19:30 flight back to Santiago. They sniffed around for four days, hoping for a lead, but when neither information nor intuition led them anywhere, they joined the tourists at the hotel's pool and waited for Graham Manion's call.

The call came late the following day. 'Okay, get this, Jamie; the day after the DC3 went missing, a realtor rented a farmhouse about ten miles from Bayamo to an American for three months.' Graham confirmed. 'The guy was tall, had a big gut and wore a beige suit and Panama hat. His name was George Mason.'

Jamie smiled. 'That's our boy. What's the address?'

The next day, Tuesday, November 24th, driving a rented black Hyundai TQ van they headed for Bayamo, a small town sixty miles north of Santiago. Graham's map took them through the deserted Cuban countryside to a remote farmhouse nestled on a hillside overlooking a valley of golden cornfields.

They pulled up a short distance from the farmhouse, and there appeared to be no sign of life, other than a dusty, black SUV parked at the rear. Jamie hid the van among a cluster of trees and decided to wait until sunset before entering the house.

As dusk fell, they rounded the property and cautiously entered through the unlocked rear door. Rotting food, covered in a mass of flies, sat abandoned on the kitchen table. Empty beer cans and shattered glass lay strewn across the wooden floor. The sun had almost disappeared, leaving the ground smouldering with mist and an eerie light casting shadows through the broken blinds of the stinking room. Finding no sign of life in the hallway and two rooms at the rear, they warily entered a large living room. Both gasped and took a step back as the pungent smell of death forced them to cover their nose and mouths.

Covered in dried blood Rylan Mitchell and Rick Netty sat slumped in armchairs with their heads back and mouths open. Both had multiple gunshot wounds and had been dead for some time. A homing device and Mitchell's hat lay crushed at their feet. They searched the bedrooms for anything belonging to the kids, and then beneath one of the single mattresses Judy found a gold crucifix, which Jamie was certain belonged to Savannah.

'The kids *were* here, which means that they are alive,' Jamie said. 'But someone else arrived, and it was no stranger because there's no sign of forced entry or a struggle. Whoever committed these murders took Mike and Savannah with them, but to where?'

* * * * *

The Kinnerman House

After their traumatic events in Panama, finding Julieanne in such a dreadful state had devastated Richard and Katie, and they began to wonder if things could possibly get any worse.

'Why is this happening to our family, Richard? Our kids have never hurt anyone, why them, why?' Katie said, hopelessly.

Since returning home Richard had slept very little and Katie had woken up screaming in the early hours, unable to escape the recurring nightmare of standing on that runway as the plane thundered by, with Mike and Savannah clawing at the window.

Sally Brooks could find no words to ease their pain.

As the autumn days turned colder, Richard and Katie came to accept there was little they could do but pray, and though they would never give up, the flame of hope that had driven them to believe their son would return had begun to flicker and dim. In happier times they would be looking forward to Thanksgiving now, but with Mike and Savannah lost and Julieanne emotionally disturbed, there seemed little to celebrate.

One day at a time was the best they could hope for.

When Greta arrived at Beechwood Avenue's famous house, her effervescent smile brought a sparkle to an otherwise gloomy atmosphere and a warm welcome awaited her.

'Your room is ready, Greta, make yourself at home,' Katie said, with surprising alacrity, 'I hope you like blue.'

'It's my favourite colour,' Greta yelled, dragging her suitcase up the stairs, followed by Richard carrying another.

Greta was clearly one of those rare creatures who could light up a room by simply walking into it. She was a butterfly, but also a good listener, which prompted Richard and Katie to talk about their heartbreaking journey to South America. Observing their pale, drawn faces and the despair in their eyes, Greta had no doubt that with the added pain of Julieanne's comatose state they were almost at the end of their tether. Adding to their misery were the anticipated indictments for insider trading.

When Greta saw Julieanne lying in bed, her eyes swollen and her hands clenched into fists, she was visibly shaken. She had seen this once before when her best friend's mother died in a car wreck, and refusing to accept her death she withdrew into a dark shell. Greta sat with her lifeless friend for two long weeks before having to leave to begin her studies at Harvard. This time, she would stay until Julieanne recovered, however long it took.

Greta soon made her presence felt, much to Sally Brook's relief, who nevertheless sat with Julieanne daily. Every morning at seven, fresh coffee, juice, eggs and toast awaited Richard and Katie, served with her Hollywood smile.

Richard drove to his office each day looking drawn and his shoulders sagging. Katie dotingly nursed Julieanne, but in need of a distraction, she asked Andrew Stell for a little work to occupy her mind for a few hours, while Greta put on wildlife movies for her daughter. Andrew didn't hesitate. Time passed, and with no further news of Mike and Savannah and Julieanne still silent, Katie was at her wits end as to what else she could do.

The following Friday, Andrew Stell asked Katie to have lunch and spend the afternoon at the office. Katie was reluctant to leave Julieanne, but Greta said that it would do her good and persuaded her to wear something glamorous. Riddled with guilt she drove to Manhattan, calling Greta several times en-route.

Since arriving at the house Greta had sat with Julieanne and stroked her hands, brushed her hair, talked to her and put on her favourite movies, but there had been no response. That afternoon, for no apparent reason, Julieanne unclenched her fist and gripped Greta's hand. Piffin sat up on the bed. Gently stroking her face Greta told her to come home, that she was very beautiful, that her mother and father loved and missed her very much.

At first, there was little response, just the turning of her head and a slight groan. Then her whole body stiffened, and opening her eyes she stared at the ceiling. Greta talked to her, kissed her, caressed her face and held her hands. Then, as if prompted by an unseen force, Julienne sat bolt upright gasping for breath and vomited. Taking her in her arms, she whispered, 'Julieanne, it's Greta, can you hear my voice?'

'Greta?' Julieanne croaked, and gave a deep rasping cough.

'Yes, sweetie, I'm here to look after you until you're better.'

Julieanne coughed and rubbed her matted eyes. Greta laid her on the pillow. Piffin raised his paw and moaned. 'Am I sick? I feel sick,' she said, her voice hoarse and her lips cracked.

Greta kissed her pale cheek. 'Yes, you've been asleep for a little while, but you'll be just fine now darling.'

'Where's Mom and Dad?'

Piffin's tail wagged as though he knew she had returned.

'They'll be home soon darling, and you can't imagine how happy they'll be to see you.'

'What happened, Greta? I feel weird.'

Greta knew that she had to choose her words carefully. There could be no mention of Mike, not yet anyway.

'You've been somewhere dark, haven't you?'

'Yes, I was trapped. It was dark and cold and I couldn't get out,' she said, and vomited again. Greta grabbed a box of tissues and wiped Julieanne's face. 'Sorry, Greta, I can't seem to…

Greta held her. 'Don't worry, sweetie, I'll change your bed in a minute. Can I get you something; water, tea, hot soup maybe?'

'I need to go to the bathroom.'

Greta helped Julieanne out of bed and propped her up. She was frail and had difficulty standing. Piffin followed her to the bathroom and lay down as she reached for the toothpaste. Greta ran a bath and laid out clean towels, and then changed her bed.

Just after five p.m., Katie parked her Lexus and went inside the house. When she entered the living room and saw Julieanne lying on the sofa wrapped in a blanket sipping a bowl of soup, she shrieked with joy and fell to her knees beside her. Greta had to bite her lip to suppress her emotion. Julieanne sobbed for the first time since Mike's disappearance, and the pain in her young voice soared through the house as the torment buried deep inside her flooded onto her mother's shoulder.

Katie thanked God for the miracle that Doctor Morton said may never come, and for Greta's caring perseverance, but most of all for Richard, whom she had loved since the moment they first met. She had counted on his strength throughout their ongoing family nightmare and he had not disappointed her. Lately though, he seemed to have aged, and for the first time looked burdened, almost defeated. His once sparkling brown eyes now appeared lifeless, but now, perhaps…..

Leaving his BMW at the front door, Richard went inside the hallway and hung up his thick, blue overcoat. Looking weary and dark-eyed he strolled into the living room and seeing Julieanne, he froze, dropping his briefcase.

Julieanne smiled. 'Hi, Dad, do I get a kiss?'

Richard dropped to his knees and held her in his arms, his shoulders no longer sagging under the weight of despair and his heart beating with renewed hope. 'Sure you do, sweetheart.'

'Thanksgiving arrived early this year,' Katie said, and wiping away a tear she called Sally to tell her the good news.

Squealing with delight Sally swept into the living room and wrapped her arms around Julieanne. Shortly after, Sheriff Carver and Jake arrived, bringing a warm smile to her young pallid face.

Sunday morning, the doorbell rang, and opening the door Katie found Harry Schlecker standing outside in his golfing attire and a blue baseball cap with his initials on the peek. Charlie backed the limousine into the driveway. Giving Katie a peck on the cheek, Harry said, 'How's my Julieanne?'

'Come and see for yourself,' Katie said, walking off towards the kitchen.

'Good to see you, too,' Harry muttered.

Harry had to take a breath when he saw Julieanne's fragile state, but said nothing as he sat down and handed her a small gift-wrapped box. Opening it, she found a solid gold bracelet with an inscription inside, *for my darling Julieanne, love Harry.*

Placing her cracked lips on his cheek, she whispered, 'Thank you, Harry, this is beautiful. I will treasure it always.'

For the first time in many weeks a warm sense of joy filled the Kinnerman house. The subject of Mike and Savannah's well-being however, remained closed. There had been no further news since their abduction in Panama, and no one wanted to mention it, especially in front of Julieanne. Harry, affable as usual, made no mention of the heartbreak that he felt for his missing daughter, or Greta's betrayal, even though she sat next to him. Richard sensed a serious rift between them, and wondered if it had something to do with Greta's conspiracy discovery, but said nothing.

Curled up in her mother's arms Julieanne remained the focus of attention throughout lunch. Then Harry said he had a meeting to attend in New York City and needed to go home and change. He kissed Julieanne goodbye and as he stood up to leave, she said, 'I'm so sorry about Savannah, Harry.'

An uncomfortable silence filled the room.

Harry leaned down to her, and said, 'I told her to stay away from boys. She's in deep shit when I get her home.'

Julieanne smiled. Katie fought back a tear. Harry nodded to Richard, and ignoring Greta he strode out closing the front door.

Late afternoon on Monday, November 30th, Katie and Greta were busy preparing dinner in the kitchen when the house phone rang; Richard took the call.

'Richard Kinnerman.'

'Mr. Kinnerman, it's Sheila Macavy. I'm now working at the U.S. Embassy in Bogota. I have some news for you.'

Expecting to hear the worst, Richards' back stiffened and his knuckles whitened. 'What is it?'

'About a week ago, a Mr. Rylan Mitchell and Mr. Rick Netty were found murdered at a remote farmhouse, in Cuba. Both had multiple gunshot wounds, and our people believe that it was a revenge killing. A gold crucifix, identified as belonging to Miss Savannah Schlecker, was found in one of the bedrooms.'

Richard took a breath. 'What are you implying; that it's over, that they're dead?' he said, bitterly.

Greta raised her hands to her mouth. Katie stood wide-eyed with a look of horror. Julieanne had gone upstairs to change for dinner. Sally Brooks was running her a bath.

'Not at all sir, on the contrary, if they were going to kill the youngsters it would have happened at that farmhouse, but they did not, which means they are being held captive and are very much alive. Whoever murdered Mr. Mitchell and Mr. Netty took your son and Miss Schlecker, which, according to our people, narrows things down considerably.'

Richard nodded positively to Katie. 'That is good news, and I appreciate you letting me know, Sheila. By the way, did they find the missing airplane?'

'No, sir, but Mitchell and Netty were found in Cuba, which means the airplane did not crash in the sea. Hang on to your faith Mr. Kinnerman, we'll find those kids. I'll be in touch.'

When Richard reported the hope-filled news to Katie, she walked to the kitchen window and looked out towards the distant river, wondering if she dared wish for another miracle.

FORTY

Julieanne soon regained her strength, thanks to Doctor Morton who said that physically she had recovered, but accepting the loss of her brother would take time, and suggested that being at school with her friends might be the tonic you won't find at a drug store. Julieanne begged her mother to let her go, and after speaking with the principal, Ms. Wilmont, who promised to keep a close eye on her, Katie drove her to high school the next morning.

Parked at the entrance, she said, 'Have you got your inhaler?'

'Mom, you've already asked me three times.'

'Oh did I? Are you feeling okay? Did you bring your...

'Mom, I know you're worried about me after what happened, but I'll be fine, I promise, okay?'

Reluctantly kissing her daughter goodbye she watched her run excitedly up the steps to the school's entrance, where a group of friends quickly gathered round and made a huge fuss of her.

Katie smiled; Julieanne was going to be okay.

* * * * *

The scandal relating to Harry's illicit dealings with the Pentagon had all but faded away, until Rylan Mitchell's killing hit the news. The malicious headline **"MURDER AND CONSPIRACY"** linked to a subtext of innuendos that a revenge killing by Harry Schlecker may not be far from the truth made Harry furious, especially since the FBI now believed Mitchell was a prime suspect in Mike and Savannah's brutal kidnapping and possible murder.

Harry threatened to sue the tabloids and terrestrial stations for ten million dollars unless they made a public retraction. Lawyers gravely huddled around long tables, and after studying the text concluded that Harry would win a libel case. As a result, the late editions printed an apology, and major TV networks, which had embraced the story, reluctantly apologized. Greta chuckled when she heard the primetime apology. Having been around the block a few times, Harry loved to bring the media down a notch or two, particularly when he couldn't lose. Predictably, the press had the last word by publishing everything they had on the insider trading allegations made against those involved in the purchase of Stella Electronics. It was not pleasant reading but Harry didn't think it was worth getting into another row over it.

When a pal at the district attorney's office informed Richard that the insider-trading indictments were imminent, he arranged an urgent meeting with the trustees, to discuss the charges made against them by the FBI. When they agreed that there had been no impropriety in the Stella acquisition, Richard, not wishing to involve his own firm, asked Michael Brimmer, one of New York City's finest litigators to look at the case.

Brimmer's first call was to the FBI, to whom he made it clear that he wanted to see the fax they claim to have found, and any other evidence pertaining to the allegations, including statements given by defendants and witnesses, the paperwork taken from the PocketMoney.com building, and bank statements and credit card receipts. He also called Harry Schlecker, for whom he had once litigated in a courtroom brawl against a multi national, and asked him for a notarised statement of his involvement in the purchase of Stella. He then summoned the Kinnermans and the trustees to his office at eleven the following morning.

Greeting them at the 19th floor of the towering Manhattan building Brimmer's PA, Avril Loman smiled businesslike and ushered the group into a wood-panelled office overlooking the city, in which Michael Brimmer sat behind a large desk, glasses perched on his nose studying a thick legal document.

Avril nodded, and left the room.

'Good morning,' Brimmer said, getting to his feet. 'Richard, Katie, my dear friends. I am praying for the safe return of Mike, and of course, Savannah.

I cannot begin to imagine how you are coping and sincerely hope that I can assist you in your grief.'

Thanking Michael for his kind words Richard, Katie and the trustees followed him to a conference room and gathered around an oval mahogany table.

Brimmer held up a sheet of paper. 'This fax the FBI claim to have found in Richard's desk came from Brimson International at Wall Street, and it undoubtedly informed the trustees of Stella's intention to announce their new system the following Monday. It also recommended that PocketMoney.com buy the company prior to the closing bell that Friday. The sender could not be identified.

Brimmer handed out copies of the fax.

Richard quickly read it. 'So it *was* a goddam conspiracy,' he said, confirming Katie's and the trustee's suspicions.

Brimmer removed his glasses. 'I'm afraid so, the whole thing was a set-up pure and simple.'

'You're damn right it was, and we know who's responsible,' Penny Bowman said, slamming her pen on the table.

Richard exhaled. 'Penny, you're a damn good lawyer, but that kind of talk will only lead to a libel suit.'

Jenny Grant agreed, and poured a liberal dose of sanity on the growing vigilantism. 'Look, we may think that Harry Schlecker is involved, but there's not one shred of evidence linking him to any of this, and acting like a lynch mob will get us nowhere, so let's be sensible here,' Jenny said, business like.

Malcolm Connors nodded. 'Jenny's right, until we know for sure who's behind this I don't think we should say anything, it'll just make us look desperate.'

'We are desperate, that's why we're here,' Penny countered, and in case you've forgotten, Malcolm, insider trading is a federal offence, and if we don't start defending ourselves we'll all go to jail. Still wanna keep quiet?'

Malcolm huffed and shook his head hopelessly.

Brimmer went on, 'Whoever planted the fax knew that when Stella's revolutionary system was unveiled the following Monday morning, Wall Street traders would erupt with accusations of insider trading by PocketMoney.com. In short, it was an insidious plot to discredit every one of you.'

Winston Bliss spoke up. 'If the fax came to Richard's office Thursday afternoon, why didn't anyone pick it up?'

Brimmer removed his glasses. 'No one picked it up because it was hidden in the bottom draw of Richard's desk. Someone is trying to destroy PocketMoney. com, and this is a very nasty way of going about it. As Penny said, insider trading is a federal offence, resulting in a long jail sentence and the destruction of careers. If the FBI can substantiate their case, none of you will ever work in the financial world again.'

Silence fell in the room.

Avril Loman sensed the underlying tension as she brought in a large tray of coffee and biscuits. Brimmer thanked her as she left closing the door. Katie poured the coffee and handed the cups around the gloomy table.

Richard never speculated he wanted details, which prompted him to recall Harry Schlecker standing at the boardroom door at around 2:15 p.m. on the day they discussed buying Stella, and his exact words as he left the room, *I have something to attend to, I'll be back in fifteen minutes. I know you'll do the right thing.*

Katie asked the question on everyone's lips. 'Can you really find out who's responsible for this, Michael?'

'Yes, but it will take time. There were no fingerprints on the fax, and the lack of hard evidence will make progress difficult. However, I have strenuously denied that you had any knowledge of this fax, and were therefore not privy to details of the new system prior to its unveiling the following Monday morning.'

'But if we're completely innocent, how could they possibly prove otherwise? Katie persisted.

'These cases are difficult because the perpetrator can erase evidence long before it becomes public knowledge. Those guilty of this fraud will be caught, but time and circumstantial evidence is against us. The district attorney and the FBI are determined to subpoena all those involved in this scandal to appear before a grand jury, but I intend to uncover the real culprit before then, which of course, will exonerate you all.'

They left Brimmer's office, believing PocketMoney.com and their reputations were in safe hands, but as the crowded elevator sailed to the ground floor, Richard's thoughtful silence led Katie to believe that all was not as it seemed.

* * * * *

Santiago, Cuba, Tuesday, December 1ˢᵗ

Graham Manion spent three days tapping his sources for clues to the DC3's whereabouts, but no one was talking, which he found suspicious, and said so. Meanwhile, Jamie and Judy decided to do another search of the farmhouse where Mitchell and Netty were murdered, but they were out of luck; a forensic team had sealed up the building as a crime scene. Judy suggested that it might be worth asking the neighbours if they had seen or heard anything. Jamie agreed, and a picturesque farm a crows-mile north of the sealed farmhouse seemed like a good place to start.

Judy rapped the metal door knocker and a small, wrinkled old woman in a long, black dress, a purple blouse and her grey hair tied in a bun opened the creaking door, and seemed distressed to have visitors. Softly in Spanish, Judy explained who they were.

Giving her a cautious look the old woman said her name was Silvana Souza de Belara, and explaining that her husband was out she led them into a small wooden-floored parlour, in which a patchwork of fading photographs, probably as old as the house, were pinned to the cracked walls. Sinking into a creaky armchair in front of the charred fireplace she folded her arms. Judy sat in a chair opposite her and leaned forward resting on her knees.

Jamie looked through window across the valley and could see the farmhouse where the murder took place.

Judy asked Silvana, who spoke only Spanish, if she had heard anything strange recently, but neglected to mention the grizzly murders, fearing that it would be too upsetting for her. She was old and frail, and very frightened.

'Yes, my husband Ernesto and I heard gunshots. Not bangs, it was tat-tat-tat, like one of those machine guns they used in the revolution,' she said, with a far away look. 'It is so quiet here you can hear a mouse scratching itself in the valley, let alone a gun going off. I think it was late afternoon, perhaps three or four weeks ago. I was frightened and told Ernesto to draw the curtains. We are simple farmers, quiet people, you know.'

'Yes, I know,' Judy said, gently patting Silvana's hand. 'Did you see anything at all; a car perhaps?'

'No, but one of our young workers did. He said it was a black Mercedes. He is a car fanatic and dreams of owning one like that one day. Nice boy.'

Judy smiled. 'Is he here, can we talk to him?'

Somewhere in her eighties Silvana stood up and walked to the back door. 'Come, he is outside. His name is Angel.'

They followed her out to the barn, where someone was busy repairing an old tractor. She called to him and a dark-haired boy of around fifteen came running out. Silvana gripped his hand and explained why Judy wished to speak to him.

Angel's eyes lit up. 'It was a Mercedes, a black GL Class off-roader. There are not many cars like this one in Cuba. They are fantastic, but very much money.'

'Did you see anyone?' Judy asked.

Jamie was standing a few feet away with his arms folded.

Angel looked down and put both hands in the pockets of his oil-stained overalls. 'Will there be trouble?' he asked.

Judy pulled him to one side and spoke softly. 'No, Angel, there will be no trouble for you. Two men were murdered in that farmhouse four weeks ago, and we just want to know if you heard or saw anything.'

'I heard gunshots, it was an automatic weapon. I saw four men go inside the house, but I was over there in that cornfield and could not see their faces. They were only in there four or five minutes. After the gunshots, they backed the Mercedes up to the front door for a moment, and then left. When they had gone, I crept inside the house and saw the dead bodies, it was horrible.'

Judy gripped his oily hands. 'Thank you, Angel, you are very brave. There is no need to tell Silvana or Ernesto what you saw. Those men will not be coming back, okay?'

Angel nodded and strolled back to the barn. Judy thanked Silvana, and assured her that there would be no more gunshots. Standing in the doorway, Silvana waved goodbye, her long black dress swaying in the breeze as they sped away across the valley.

'Your handling of Silvana was brilliant, Judy, and thanks to you we've made a break though. Well done,' Jamie said.

Jamie asked Graham Manion to find a car rental that had a black Mercedes GLR. Ten minutes later, he was back. 'Ocean Car Rentals, Beach Road, Santiago have one, but you won't find much; rental car firms are government owned and their vehicles are professionally cleaned. Good luck, pal.' Graham hung up.

Jamie wanted to see that car, cleaned or not. They took a taxi along the breezy seafront and soon pulled up outside *Ocean Car Rentals,* a medium size business lot with an assortment of cars. Jamie paid the driver, who nodded and sped away.

Entering the company lot they strolled around the rental cars. Jamie scanned the grounds for security cameras, which may have captured the murderer's face, but there didn't appear to be any. A woman hurried out of the office and approached them.

'You want to rent a car?' she asked, in English.

'Yes, the black Mercedes GL,' Jamie said, pointing to the car inside the showroom. 'When was it last used?'

The woman frowned. 'Why do you ask?'

'I believe the person who last rented it may have murdered two men at a farmhouse north of here, and we would very much like to know who that person was.'

'Who are you?' she asked, her eyes narrowing. Jamie gave her his ID, and having studied it, she looked into his icy blue eyes. 'It must be serious if U.S. Intelligence is involved. They are not exactly popular in Cuba. I am Rafaela Ramos. Come, we'll go to the office,' she said, and continued talking as they crossed the lot. 'The GL was last used some weeks ago. It was returned with an electrical fault and has yet to be cleaned, I'm sorry.'

Rafaela was in her mid thirties, slender, five seven with dark hair, soft brown eyes and had a twelve-year old son, Anier. Her husband had died two years ago in a Venezuelan oilrig accident, she explained to Judy as they neared the office.

'Do you mind if I take a look at the car? 'Jamie asked.

'No, help yourself.' Rafaela replied, opening the door of her portacabin, which had florescent lighting and one large window. On her desk at the window was a photo of her son, a telephone, a cell phone, a large notepad, a small radio, and a coffee percolator. A leather shoulder bag hung over the back of her chair. On the far wall, a shelf of blue folders stood in a neat line above a table with a photocopier and printer. A huge poster of the latest BMW SUV and a board with car keys hanging on brass hooks all but covered the rear wall space.

'Please, come in,' Rafaela said, grabbing the Mercedes keys and handing them to Jamie, who nodded and went outside. Then reaching for a folder on the shelf she sat down at her desk. Judy pulled up another chair and gave her a brief account of Mike and Savannah's brutal kidnappings and Mitchell and Netty's grisly murders. Horrified, Rafaela gently ran her fingers over her young son's smiling photo. 'Evil has no conscience. I will do what I can to help you,' she said, spreading the booking forms across her desk. 'Ah, here we are. Elian Lopez Garcia, a Cuban, rented the Mercedes for two days on Thursday, November 5th. He paid with a credit card and returned it Friday, November 6th. Here is his address and telephone number.'

Judy called Graham Manion and gave him Garcia's details. Graham chuckled, and said he'd call right back. Jamie returned to the office and handed Rafaela the car keys.

'I want to hire the Mercedes GL for two or three days, just as it is. Is that alright?'

Needing no explanation, Rafaela nodded.

Graham called back. 'Elian Garcia does not exist, Judy. The guy was a total fake,' he said, as if it was no surprise. 'There's no such address, his cell phone was prepaid, and the credit card was cloned. If you get anything else, call me.' He disconnected.

The hirer's criminal anonymity only re-enforced Jamie and Judy's belief that one of the murderers had rented the Mercedes GL, and the fact that he used a false name indicated that he was not Cuban. Even so, they were a step closer to finding the killers, thanks to Rafaela, whom they were certain would never reveal their reasons for renting the Mercedes for two days. She had gone out of her way to be helpful in an unfavourable political climate, but had dismissed their gratitude as they sped away with gloved hands in the black SUV to a CIA forensic facility.

The next day, a forensic team painstakingly searched the Mercedes for fingerprints, DNA, hair, bloodstains, anything that might link it to the suspects. Jamie and Judy had taken samples of hair, the carpet, the sofa and bedding from the farmhouse and needed a match to confirm their intuitive evidence. Twenty-four hours later, forensics discovered a positive match, which proved beyond doubt the assassins had used the car. They also found one strand of long, dark hair beneath the rear seat, which intrigued Jamie, and he wondered if it might be Savannah's. He shared his thoughts with Judy, who immediately called Harry Schlecker and explained that she worked for U.S. Intelligence.

'The investigation into Mike and Savannah's whereabouts is ongoing Mr. Schlecker, and we need Savannah's DNA. I assure you there is nothing ominous about the request. Look for some strands of hair on her hairbrush or bedding, it's very important.'

Minutes later, Harry was back. 'I got a few strands of her hair, but better yet, my doctor took a sample of her blood when she arrived in the U.S. and he'll supply some for a DNA test.'

'Excellent, address it to Judy Cassano at Guantanamo Bay U.S. military facility. Someone will collect it from you within the hour by helicopter. His code will be "Serum"

'Serum. Okay, just find her, Judy.' Harry hung up.

Early next morning, Harry's package arrived at Guantanamo Bay. Two hours later, Judy signed for it and drove to the forensic lab. The match proved to be conclusive; it was Savannah's hair all right, and as a long shot she had stuck it beneath the seat.

Clever girl, thought Jamie. Judy smiled with admiration; she was fast becoming a fan of this young lady.

Convinced they were now on the right track Jamie called Major Bell and debriefed. 'The DNA found in the car matches the DNA in the farmhouse, sir; it's the killer's. I'm afraid we've had no luck with the DC3; no one seems to know anything about it. However, if Mitchell and Netty made it to Cuba, then it didn't crash in the Caribbean and the killers may have used it to escape with the youngsters, but to where I don't know.'

'Someone in Cuba knows where they went, Jamie, just keep digging,' Major Bell ordered. 'Our friends at Langley are getting anxious. They want the youngsters found, and quickly.'

'I'll do my best, sir.'

They spent the next five days checking every possible source that might give a clue as to how the assassins escaped from Cuba, with two kidnapped kids, including commercial and private jets and every type of boat that sailed around the time of the murders. Unfortunately, corrupt officials and those too afraid to speak up conspired against them in a wall of silence. Nevertheless, Jamie and Judy were certain that Rylan Mitchell knew his killers and that they had followed him to Cuba.

It smelled of drugs and revenge.

Using his laptop Jamie replayed the CIA recording of the drug cartels meeting at the Panama City Hotel, which Mitchell and Netty had attended. For Major Bell's reference, Judy narrated the Spanish dialogue in English, which Jamie recorded.

Judy described the scene. 'They're furious with Mitchell for losing seven hundred and fifty million dollars worth of cocaine hidden aboard their schooner, which caught fire and sank in Rio's marina, and the bosses have voted to have him killed.'

Jamie nodded. 'Well there's a motive for Mitchell's murder. Mike and Savannah set fire to that schooner when they escaped, which may have provoked the bosses to seek revenge by killing Mitchell and taking the youngsters.'

'Wait, Mitchell's just arrived and Rizzio has ordered him to apologize to the bosses. He does so, and they agree give him one more chance, but they're not happy. The bosses want Mitchell to find new ways of getting their cocaine into the U.S. and Canada, and to regain their faith, they have given him a cocaine shipment to deliver in Tampa, and hey...

'Let me guess, that shipment was hidden inside a container on the missing DC3,' Jamie said, stopping the recorder. Then his cell phone rang; it was Manion. 'I hope this is good news, Graham, we could do with some.'

'Well you're gonna love this, pal. I've just had a call from one of my informers about the missing DC3.'

'Hang on; I want Judy to hear this.' Jamie put his phone on audio. 'Go ahead.'

'The plane landed at a small airfield about twenty miles west of Santiago. It was dark, stormy and almost deserted. Santo, the pilot, had pals there. My source, who was one of them, said two men and two kids left after a train-load of cash changed hands.'

Jamie and Judy glanced at one another. 'You mean they just walked out the airport?' Jamie asked.

'Not exactly, apparently a black SUV and a van pulled up alongside the airplane. George Mason, better known as Rylan Mitchell, handed out wads of cash, then he and his sidekick Netty got in the SUV while couple of guys bundled the kids into the van. No questions asked they drove off in tandem, simple as that.'

'What happened to the DC3?' Jamie asked.

'My informer helped refuel the DC3 and he overheard Santo telling Mitchell not to worry about the merchandise arriving in Tampa, he'd take care of it. Apparently, Mitchell was worried about a cocaine shipment belonging to a Colombian cartel boss named Rizzio. However, good ole' Santo never went to Tampa. He flew south to sunny El Salvador and vanished, presumably a wealthy man. I guess that's about does it on the DC3. You owe me one, pal. Hope you find those kids breathing. If you need any more help, call me.' Graham disconnected.

Jamie closed his laptop. It had suddenly all become clear; the grisly murders, the cocaine, and the revenge. 'We're on the right track, Judy, but we're in the wrong country.

Judy nodded. 'I agree. I think Rizzio murdered Mitchell and Netty because he believed they had stolen the Tampa cocaine shipment, which meant that he lost face with the bosses, so as an investment he took the kids with him, probably in a private jet.'

Jamie leaned back in his chair. 'Which means?'

'Mike and Savannah are in Colombia.'

FORTY-ONE

Monday, December 14th

Greta had brought some much-needed sunshine to the Kinnerman house, but with Christmas approaching and Mike's 15th birthday due in February, a cloud of anticipated grief hung in the air. Mike and Savannah's ever-smiling photograph, taken by Richard that fateful Sunday, appeared regularly on the news channels and it was heartbreaking. Nevertheless, as difficult as it was life had to go on. Julieanne's return to high school had lifted her spirits and rekindled the sparkle in her emotionally burdened eyes. She still sobbed every night for her brother, clinging to the hope that he was alive, but like her parents, had accepted there was nothing she could do other than pray for his safe return.

Katie's ex boss Andrew Stell, with whom she had recently lunched, advised her to think carefully about her career before the doors of opportunity closed. Having had no time to think about her future, Katie decided to take Piffin for a walk that afternoon, to consider her options. Meanwhile, Richard had gone to meet with JB Walsome and the partners, who were concerned about his involvement in the insider trading scandal.

As the elevator doors opened at JB's floor, Richard wondered if the partners were planning his exit. He had always believed that it was every man for himself at the firm, but as he entered the oak-panelled boardroom, his misguided scepticism faded to relief when he realized they were genuinely rallying round.

Richard explained the Stella deal and the anonymous fax to the partners, and said that it was part of a conspiracy to destroy PocketMoney.com. When no one disagreed, JB offered the firm's resources for his defence. Richard thanked him for his generous offer and said that he had given the case to Michael Brimmer. JB smiled, understanding his reasons for doing so, but insisted he shed more of his workload until the insider trading and family crisis was over. Richard didn't argue, and thanking JB and the partners for their support he went to his office.

He told Beth to retain his four major clients and hand the rest to the partners. Then he left to pick up Katie and arrange delivery of a new car before collecting Julieanne at school.

Nodding to the security guard at the ground floor, he walked out through the glass doors, and stopping in the crowded square, he breathed out, thankful his career was still in tact.

Wearing winter boots and a warm coat and hat Katie walked to the river with Piffin at her heels and stood beside Mike's favourite willow tree. Having spent many joyful summer days on that riverbank with her children, Katie could not imagine how terrifying Mike and Savannah's kidnapping must have been that fateful Sunday morning. Unable to accept that they may be dead she wrapped her arms around herself and tearfully cursed the evil men who had taken them. She would never give up, and having just relived those fond family memories, only reinforced Katie's determination to forget about her career and devote every waking moment to her daughter's future.

She angrily threw a stone into the river, knowing that until Mike and Savannah's safe return the pain would never go away. Finding small comfort in the fact that the kidnappers were dead she called to Piffin and headed home, eager to prepare dinner for her broken family; a chore that she would revel in.

Back at the house, she called Simon Wyler and thanked him for his support at a time of crisis. 'It meant a lot to me, Simon, and it pains me to say that I won't be returning to Tokyo.'

'I'm not surprised, Katie. We'll keep praying for your family reunion, and I'm here if you need a friend, good luck.'

Lately in the silent darkness of the early hours, Richard had chosen to find solace in his den. Heartbroken and his mind foggy with recrimination he listened to Mike's voicemail message from Bogota over, and over again, finding it hard to accept that he may never return. For company, he had a bottle of fine brandy, which only distorted his misguided sense of failure.

His immersion into solitary grief had not gone unnoticed.

That evening, the door opened and Katie walked in wearing a long, silky nightdress, and sat beside him, strands of hair falling to the side of her face and her emerald eyes pleading for her life back, for some kind of sanity. Touching his lips with her soft fingers she rested her head on his shoulder, her gold earrings flickering in the light a reminder of when they held one another in that far away hotel.

Gazing into his mournful brown eyes, she whispered, 'I don't want to be alone tonight, Richard.'

Washington DC, Thursday, December 17*th*

At 6:30 a.m. Geoff Wickerby, Head of U.S. National Security Agency (NSA) arrived at FBI headquarters, Pennsylvania Avenue and took the elevator to FBI Director Vernon Bentram's office. After the weak smiles and limp handshakes, Bentram filled two polystyrene cups with strong coffee from his thermos flask and handed one to Wickerby. 'So what's the urgency?' he asked, sipping the home blend he held in both hands.

This PocketMoney.com scandal is becoming a national sore, Vernon, and a lot of people are starting to get twitchy, including the President.'

Vernon gulped his coffee. 'Twitchy, why?'

'Because it's global, and the fact that it was designed just for kids has led some smart asses at the White House to believe that it might have political implications.'

'Political? It's just a company, for Christ sake,' Vernon said, tossing his empty cup in the wastebasket.

'No, Vernon. Mike Kinnerman is an icon to millions of kids. When he went missing and the FBI closed his company, the kids got mad and demanded to know what happened. Now they're on the rampage yelling, "America is corrupt" and some folks on Capital Hill are beginning to get a tad nervous.'

Vernon rubbed his face. 'They'd get jumpy if the grass didn't grow quick enough.'

Wickerby threw up his arms. 'Yeah, okay, but what if they're right? The President's charm is already down twenty points.'

'Kinnerman and the girl were kidnapped. The CIA found 'em and lost 'em. Latest report says they're probably dead, killed by a drug cartel,' Vernon stated. 'As for the company, it was closed because of fraud, and those damn kids know that.'

'Wrong, they're convinced that it's a government conspiracy, engineered by shady people at the Pentagon, and if we don't put out the fire this could turn into a political nightmare.'

Vernon disliked politicians but somehow managed to conceal his irritation. 'According to our friends at the CIA, Mitchell and Netty were responsible for the kidnapping, and they're dead. As for who's screwing the company, we have a list of suspects but no conclusive evidence at this time.'

'What if you're wrong, what if this is connected to a political agenda? Intel sources tell us there's a growing wave of anger out there, not just in the U.S., but also globally. Can you imagine what would happen if millions of kids start taking to the streets around the world because they believe the U.S. Government and Wall Street ripped them off?' Geoff said, dramatically.

Vernon had a stack of reports on his desk about people who hated the government. It was only seven a.m. and he was already tired. 'What do you want me to do?' he asked, wearily.

'Talk to the President; tell him this is serious, that it could end up biting him in the ass. Make him listen.'

'I spoke to him about this a week ago and he almost threw me out of the Oval Office for disturbing his golf practice,' Vernon said, glibly. 'I'll talk to the Attorney General.'

'Okay fine. Tell him we need indictments served on all those involved with the Stella deal, and make it public. At least it'll make us look as though we're doing something, and who knows, we might even flush out the real culprit.'

Vernon rubbed his eyes. 'I'll see what I can do.'

* * * * *

Greta had gone out to dinner with an old friend that evening and wouldn't be home until late. Katie had cooked pot roast, a family favourite, and as they gathered around the dining table, Julieanne announced she would not be going to school for a while.

Raising an eyebrow, Katie passed her the vegetables. 'Why not, sweetie?'

'The kids are boycotting school, they're going on strike.'

Richard put down his knife and fork. 'On strike? What the hell…are you kidding?'

'No, Dad, I'm serious. The FBI closed PocketMoney.com and they're demanding to know what happened to the money they've invested. They believe that the government targeted the company because it's gotten too powerful, and that it'll use that power to politically manipulate future generations. They're also convinced that Mike was disappeared by some shady organization at the Pentagon, which has a mandate to destroy potential enemies of the state. In short, they think it's a government conspiracy.'

Katie dropped her knife and fork. 'Conspiracy? How about UFO's or rendition? Or why not simply tell them the truth; Mike was kidnapped by criminals.'

'Because I think they are right but for the wrong reasons,' Julieanne stated. She was like her brother; articulate and spoke with a spirited passion about anything she believed in. 'There *is* a conspiracy. Someone *is* trying to destroy PocketMoney.com and the kids are not prepared to stand by and let it happen, so they're going on strike until it's resolved. If my brother was here he would agree,' Julieanne said, her throat tightening.

Katie and Richard glanced at one another but said nothing.

Richard leaned back in his chair. 'You know what? I'm all for standing up for what you believe in, and I think you have a point. But I'm not sure boycotting school is the right way to go about it. Are we just talking about the U.S.?'

No, kids all over the world have been communicating on the internet, and they've persuaded corporate and local companies to sponsor posters, banners, sweatshirts and baseball hats. They've also organized demonstrations outside major banks, and massive gatherings in cities and town squares, even in poorer countries. They can't sweep this under the carpet, Dad.'

'Not if it's worldwide. That's pretty serious.'

Dinner continued in silence, which Katie attributed to her culinary expertise. Then she and Richard brought up the subject of Christmas, which this year would be a tough one, and asked Julieanne if she'd like to go away, maybe to Florida.'

'No, Mike and I swore that we'd always spend Christmas at home with our parents, and that's what I intend to do,' Julieanne said, and kissing them goodnight she went up to her room.

FORTY-TWO

A global strike by millions of angry kids soon got everyone's attention. Their demonstrations became so widespread they were unstoppable, and with schools and colleges empty delinquency increased worldwide. Senators called an emergency meeting to discuss the crisis. The U.S. President had already spoken to many heads of state, in an effort to calm things down.

As usual, America was to blame.

Cell networks and the internet reached an unprecedented user level and the media were having a field day with the rebellion. As millions of young protestors gathered outside banks and stock exchanges, TV camera crews scrambled to capture them burning U.S. flags and holding up huge placards displaying their anger; **U.S. CONSPIRACY! WALL STREET IS CORRUPT!**

Facing international outrage, the Federal Government pledged to resolve the scandal, and those in the corridors of power were bracing themselves for an unprecedented political backlash.

State Governors ordered late night emergency meetings with education authorities and social services in order to minimise civil disruption. To prevent looting and vandalism the National Guard began patrolling schools and colleges around the clock. Thousands of businesses supplying daily goods to schools sat on mountains of perishable stock, causing financial ruin for many. With no kids to collect, thousands of school busses stood empty in depots around the country. Parents, keen to show their support and to protect their kids, joined the huge protests. Police chiefs cancelled all leave and ordered a large community presence, to assuage angry groups of youngsters roaming the streets.

A curfew was under consideration. The Dow Jones plunged overnight, wiping billions off the stock market.

The world was suddenly in chaos.

Monday, December 21st the United States Attorney General subpoenaed PocketMoney.com's five trustees, Richard and Katie Kinnerman, Greta Hortchfelt, Stella Electronics CEO Harvey Maybank and Harry Schlecker to attend a ten a.m. meeting on Thursday, December 24th at the FBI building in New York City. Michael Brimmer would also be present as legal council.

Greta had no choice but to attend the meeting, which the FBI had obviously arranged to bring the insider trading scandal to a head. Knowing that she would have to reveal Harry Schlecker as a conspirator and there would be no going back from betrayal; it was time to move on. Richard and Katie pleaded with her to stay, at least to celebrate the New Year, but she remained adamant and thanked them for their valued friendship. An hour later, Greta was on her way to New York's Downtown Marriott Hotel.

* * * * *

FBI Headquarters, New York City, December 24th

- This is CNN news-desk. The insider trading scandal, linked to the giant company PocketMoney.com, looks set to continue as kids around the globe refuse to go to school until their company is back in business. Here's a report from Paris, Europe. -

- As you can see, what is happening here is unprecedented. There must be fifty thousand kids standing in this Parisian square yelling for justice, and there's very little the authorities can do about it. No laws have been broken, and with parents backing the action they can't arrest them. I have never seen anything like it. Fast food chains, hotels and locals are supporting the youngsters who have gathered arm-in-arm outside financial institutions and refused to move. Any use of force against these kids would surely cause an international outcry, which could lead to ostracism of governments and send the dollar and euro into a nosedive. This has become a global problem, and until those responsible for the financial scandal, which has brought disrepute to Wall Street, and insider-trading accusations to PocketMoney. com, go to jail it will no doubt continue. Marty Holdmen, CNN News, Paris, Europe –

Vernon Bentram turned off his wide-screen TV, leaned on his cluttered desk and ran his fingers through his greying hair. 'What a nightmare,' he muttered to himself.

Doris Brook, his soon to retire personal assistant, knocked and entered the room. 'Attorney General Boyd and Mr. Wickerby have arrived, sir.'

'Thanks, Doris, show them in,' Bentram said, quickly hiding sensitive files inside his desk draw and locking it. He distrusted the other agencies, especially when they came to his office.

The attorney general and Geoff Wickerby sombrely entered the room. 'Have a seat, coffee?' Bentram asked, reaching for his thermos flasks. He didn't trust the city water.

'Yes, as it comes,' the Attorney General replied, and tossing his leather briefcase onto Bentram's desk he removed his thick navy blue overcoat.

'Black, four sugars for me, Vernon,' Wickerby said, taking off his hat, coat and scarf.

Bentram handed them plastic cups of coffee and nodded to the milk and sugar. 'Our friends will be here in a few minutes,' he said, lowering himself into an ageing chair behind his desk.

Parking himself at the edge of the desk the Attorney General sipped his coffee, and said, 'The President wants closure on this scandal today, Vernon, any problem with that?'

'I'll let you know when the meeting's over,' Bentram replied, and handed them each a thick, blue FBI folder.

'What about the two kidnapped youngsters, any further news, Vernon?' Wickerby asked.

'We think a Colombian cartel boss named Rizzio kidnapped them after killing Mitchell and Netty, but with the world's media covering the kids rebellion and the U.S. Governmental dragon beginning to breathe fire, my guess is he dumped them.'

'I really hope you're wrong about that,' the Attorney General commented, but having read reports from several Colombian CIA assets, he had a feeling that Vernon may be right.

'We'll keep looking,' Bentram added, tossing his empty cup in the wastebasket. 'They'll turn up somewhere, hopefully alive, but the odds are slim at best.'

Doris knocked and entered. 'Sir, the guests have arrived.'

'We'll go to the conference room. Follow me gentlemen.'

Just before ten, Richard and Katie entered the FBI building and after a rigorous search for weapons and devices, a burly agent told them to take the elevator to the top floor. They were met by smiling Doris, who ushered them to a reception area, where Greta, the trustees, Michael Brimmer and Stella's CEO Harvey Maybank sat quietly reading out of date magazines as though they were at the dentist.

After exchanging sombre greetings, Doris led the group to a conference room, in which a dusty glass chandelier hung above an imitation mahogany table standing on a cheap blue carpet. To the far left, a portrait of the President dominated the wall between U.S. flags. To the right, a gilt-framed black and white photograph of J. Edgar Hoover kept a watchful eye over the proceedings. A large window in the outer wall gave a splendid view of the falling snow and grimy skyscrapers across the street, opposite which a one-way tinted glass window concealed two FBI agents behind a hidden recording desk.

Director Bentram, Geoff Wickerby and the Attorney General stood up as the anxious group entered the room. After the formal introductions, Bentram asked everyone to take a seat and opened his thick FBI folder. Doris went off to organize powdered coffee and biscuits, but immediately returned with Armani-suited Harry Schlecker, who nodded nonchalantly and took a seat at the head of the table. Greta shuffled uncomfortably in her chair. Richard, Katie and the trustees gave him a collective nod.

Attorney General Boyd, a tall, thin man with an abundance of silver hair wore a black suit, a white shirt and a black ribbon tie. His commanding stature, dark piercing eyes and long fingered hands gave the distinct impression that he was a direct descendant of Abraham Lincoln. Looking gravely around the table he spoke with a deep authoritative voice.

'Good morning. I ordered this meeting at the request of the President, who is determined to put an end to this insider trading scandal, which is now affecting the global activities of American companies, and as a result, the dollar is becoming a dirty word. If we allow this to continue, America could take a financial fall, which will reflect around the globe, putting millions of people out of work, and could take years to recover. To resolve this problem we needed you all present at this meeting.'

Glancing at the sullen questioning looks around the table the Attorney General opened his FBI folder and continued.

'I must advise you that anything you say will be recorded for legal and reference purposes. Be in no doubt that the President wants this fiasco to end today. He is furious that these fraudulent activities have brought disrepute to the financial institutions of the United States, and has ordered me to ensure an example is made of all those responsible. White House Chief-of-Staff, Avery Carlton has arranged for the President to make a statement on national television this evening, in an effort to bring closure to this disgraceful episode. Before we continue, is there anything you wish to add Mr. Wickerby?'

Wickerby looked up from his thick, blue FBI folder. 'Feel free to ask questions during this meeting, but you are never to speak of it outside this room.'

Greta glanced at Harry and folded her arms. The trustees eyed one another, clearly uncomfortable. Doris entered and brought a tray of coffee and biscuits to the table. 'Let me know if you need anything else, sir,' she said, leaving the room.

Jenny Grant stood up. 'Attorney General Boyd, why are we here? Are we being blamed for this? If so, I am deeply offended and demand an explanation.'

'No one is guilty of anything unless proven otherwise, Jenny. As a trustee, you are hands on at the company, and it is therefore logical that we ask you questions.'

'But this is hardly a fishing trip, is it, sir? There's no one else here, which clearly means that we're the prime suspects, and that pisses me off,' Jenny snapped, and sat down heavily.

'I'm with her,' Penny Bowman added. 'And don't sit there with that smug look, Harry, you've got a lot to answer for, so say something for Christ sake.'

Harry's back stiffened but he chose to ignore Penny's vitriolic outburst. Katie poured coffee for herself and Richard.

Stern-faced the Attorney General leaned forward and clasped his hands. 'I'm sorry you feel that way, Jenny, but I am afraid you have little choice. This problem will not go away until we get to the bottom of it, so please, I urge you, do not make this any more difficult than it already is.'

Folding her arms defiantly Jenny sat back in her chair. Penny Bowman slammed her pen down on the table. Katie, speaking to no one in particular, said, 'Hey, let's not forget that we're all innocent here. We have nothing to fear by answering questions.'

No one responded. Backs remained stiff. The air simmered.

'Well let's start with the basics then shall we,' Richard said, as though he were in a courtroom interrogating a witness on the stand. 'Why didn't Stella announce their new system prior to selling the company? They never mentioned it in their portfolio, and it's for that very reason we're sitting here today.'

'I can answer that,' Harvey Maybank said, getting to his feet. He was fifty-something, grey hair and wore a dark suit, a white shirt, a red tie and a hearing aid in his left ear.

'Go ahead Mr. Maybank, enlighten us,' the Attorney General said, curtly, turning forward several pages of his blue folder.

'Thank you. Some months ago, someone circulated a wicked rumour that Stella was about to lose its government contracts, and as a result its share value dropped thirty-six percent. Stella was indebted to the bank and they refused to lend us any more money. Unfortunately, our agreement with them stated that if we sold the company the bank would not only redeem the loan, they would take a chunk of the profits, which would be less than attractive to potential buyers. Therefore, we had no choice but to ask them to renegotiate or file for bankruptcy under Chapter 11. The bank accepted a fifty-one percent cash deal, which we raised by selling several stock holdings and assets. Twelve months prior to that, to protect our future interests, we set up a new company, in Panama and acquired a research facility. Our U.S. science team resigned and joined our Panama crew, to continue developing our satellite communications system, which proved to be groundbreaking. On October 1st, having found a friendly bank, we transferred all our remaining assets back to the U.S. and re-floated the company. PocketMoney.com bought us on Friday, October 9th. On Monday October 12th, to regain our stock market credibility, we unveiled our new advanced system. By four p.m., Stella's share price had quadrupled and PocketMoney.com had made a profit on their investment. I have nothing further to say.' Maybank sat down.

Harry Schlecker shook his head and smiled derisively amid a growing sense of disbelief around the room.

Incensed by their irresponsibility, Richard said, 'That's all very cosy Mr. Maybank, but Stella's purchase agreement didn't mention any of those details. It might just be legal, but it's damn underhanded, and I suspect the bank weren't too happy either.'

Penny Bowman banged the table. 'You're damn right! We paid six point eight billion dollars for Stella Mr. Maybank, and now you have nothing to say? You're a disgrace and a charlatan and I promise to haul your ass into a federal court to answer for this despicable fraud!' she bawled, and taking off her red glasses, she sat back and glared at him as if he were a serial killer.

Maybank sank further into his seat and studied his fingernails. Jenny Grant offered Penny some strong coffee, but she shook her head; she needed a cigarette.

Elder trustee Malcolm Connors spoke up. 'We came here in good faith, but I fear this meeting is becoming a witch hunt.'

'Damn right it is!' Mike Coswell yelled. 'We know nothing about any of this. What the hell is goin on?'

Penny Bowman slapped the table. 'I'll tell you what's going on. Someone in this room is guilty. Aren't they…HARRY?'

Director Bentram raised his hand. 'Whoa, come on, Penny. I know you're angry, but let things take their course.'

Greta could no longer remain exiled between truth and loyalty she had wrestled with her conscience long enough. She had given Harry the opportunity to admit his involvement in the conspiracy, but he had not done so and it was time to speak out. Greta stood up, and said, 'Attorney General, I have irrefutable evidence that will exonerate the trustees and the Kinnermans of any involvement in this scandal.'

All eyes turned to Greta in silent shock. Harry leaned forward and shook his head with angry disappointment.

'Why did you not come forward sooner Miss Hortchfelt?' the Attorney General asked, sharply.

'I was torn between loyalties, sir. This has been a difficult decision for me to make.'

'Everything is difficult today Miss Hortchfelt. Proceed.'

Harry looked at the woman who was about to betray him, the only woman he had ever loved. If she crossed that line he would lose her, probably forever. He could not allow that happen. 'Stop, Greta, you don't know what you're doing,' he growled.

Hearing the coarseness of Harry's voice, Greta flinched with surprise and took a breath. Surely she couldn't be wrong she had a copy of the email. Harry was just playing poker as usual. For a split second though, she hesitated in a fog of emotional turmoil, doubting her judgement, questioning her motive.

Harry glared at her. 'Greta, you're making a big mistake.'

'Be quiet Mr. Schlecker, let us hear what Miss Hortchfelt has to say,' Wickerby ordered.

'What's up, Harry, truth touch a nerve, or just getting twitchy cause you've been found out?' Penny Bowman sniped.

Tension bubbled in the air and as the thickening snowflakes patted the window in the blustery north wind, for Greta, the world seemed as cold and grey inside as it was out.

This was the last page of the chapter in her life with Harry. The agony of indecision was over and it was time for the final betrayal, but as she reached into her Italian shoulder bag, Director Bentram leaned forward, and said, 'Miss Hortchfelt, I advise you not to say anything at this time.'

The Attorney General frowned, but said nothing.

Greta looked inquisitively at Director Bentram, but his dark eyes gave nothing away. She glanced at Harry, but he continued to brood and stare at the table. 'Sir, I can prove that Harry Schlecker conspired with others to destroy PocketMoney.com. I have here a copy of an email sent from Brimson International to his laptop Sunday, 4th October, six days before PocketMoney.com bought Stella, which I believe you will find self explanatory.'

Greta's surprising statement, for which she had forfeited her career to defend Mike Kinnerman and those in the room, sent shock waves around the table. Greta had informed Richard weeks ago that she had discovered evidence of a conspiracy to destroy PocketMoney.com, but had not disclosed her findings until now, which she had clearly done at great personal cost, and he could only admire her selflessness. The trustees however, were less than happy that Greta had chosen not to mention this sooner, but understood her reasons for not doing so.

All eyes now focussed on Harry Schlecker, who continued to stare at the table, his eyes blazing with disappointment. The air, thick with anger and betrayal, silently simmered as a buzz of intrigue sailed around the table like a Mexican wave.

Greta handed the Attorney General the copied email and sat back in her chair. She sensed Harry's eyes staring at her, shouting at her, screaming at her, and was desperate to leave. There would be no going back, not from this, but she had no second thoughts, no pangs of guilt and no regrets; her conscience was clear.

Smouldering anticipation circled the conference room as the Attorney General studied the contents of the email. Then placing it in front of him he leaned forward on his elbows, his piercing eyes staring directly at the head of the table.

'Well, Mr. Schlecker?'

FORTY-THREE

Harry Schlecker stood up and spoke with a measure of calmness not befitting a guilty man. 'I'm disappointed by the accusations made against me,' he said, 'but I'll try to put the record straight.'

Silence

'Early September, one of my contacts informed me that Stella Electronics was in trouble, and suggested I look at their books. They had a cash flow problem, but the banks were no longer interested, in fact, they'd called in the loans and the company was drowning. Just for the record, Stella never mentioned the Panama research center, or their new satellite communications system, to me, or in their portfolio. Anyway, after several meetings with the board of directors, I convinced them that PocketMoney.com was in a position to offer a financial package. I knew there'd be other offers, but they agreed, at least in principle, to go with us. All I had to do was convince the trustees that it was a good deal, but that turned into a one-day war.'

Penny Bowman huffed and shook her head derisively.

Harry ignored her. 'About four years ago, I gave evidence against Rylan Mitchell that sent him to jail for fraud, and he'd been plotting revenge ever since. Stop me if I'm going too fast for you boys in the control room,' Harry said, waving at the tinted glass window. 'Then on Sunday, October 4th, six days before we bought Stella, a suspect email arrived on my laptop at two a.m., and I knew right away it was a set-up.'

Greta sat forward and placed her head in her hands.

'So I hired Brian Chancey, the best private investigator in New York State, and Chancey's first port of call was Brimson International, Wall Street. Using gut instinct and a little payola he found the phoney email hidden among an automated mail-shot that Brimson send out weekly as a marketing probe. How it got there nobody knew, but Chancey kept on sniffing. He scanned the security videos and found a section showing a gentleman by the name of Ramon Salero, Brimson's marketing director, talking to none other than Rylan Mitchell in a basement stairwell at three- twenty p.m., Thursday, October 8th, the day before we bought Stella. I had no idea that Mitchell was out of jail, but Chancey knew, and he knew that meeting was no coincidence.'

The room fell silent with expectant curiosity. J. Edgar Hoover looked down solicitously from his gilded frame, while director Bentram, unmoved by the tension, sat poker-faced.

Michael Brimmer spoke up. 'It all sounds very convincing, Harry, but how could they have known that PocketMoney.com had offered to buy Stella when it was privileged information.'

Winston Bliss jumped in, 'Yeah, and this guy Ramon Salero, what the hell's he got to do with anything?'

'I'm coming to that,' Harry growled, irritably. 'Now what I'm about to tell you involves trustee Mike Coswell, and he knows nothing about this.'

Coswell opened his hands and shrugged his shoulders. 'Beats me,' he said.

Harry went on. 'Mike and June Coswell divorced eight years ago, which ended in a custody battle for their daughter, Mary. June was an alcoholic and, I'm sorry, Mike, also a drug addict, so when she lost custody of Mary, she'd lost everything, and was, understandably, a very bitter woman. However, some years later, having straightened herself out, June remarried and got a job at immigration. She was doing fine, but she never forgave her ex husband. And here's the twist; June is now Mrs. June Salero, wife of Ramon Salero, our little friend at Brimson International.'

'Oh my God, this is unbelievable.' Katie said, sinking back in her chair.

'I knew she'd gotten married but…' Coswell shook his head and stared at the table considering the implications.

'Wait, it gets better,' Harry continued, 'Rylan Mitchell was a member of "The Domingo Club" a gentlemans' drinking joint two blocks from Wall Street, and having just got out of jail, he was keen to renew friendships and call in favours. That's where he met Jonathan Shelleck, an ex employee of Stella, in

Panama, who was fired because of his drug habit. Stella sent Shelleck back to New York, unaware that he had copied the plans of their new system, and that those plans were now up for sale.

The trustees shook their heads in disbelief. Harry glanced at Greta, but she remained focussed on her red polished fingernails.

Richard said, 'Impressive stuff, Harry, but gathering that kind of detailed evidence means crossing lines. So how'd you do it?'

'Chancey can be very persuasive.'

'Wipe that!' Bentram yelled to the agents in the control room. 'Watch what you're saying, Harry.'

'Okay. In jail Mitchell's bible was the Wall Street Journal, which told him that Stella was in trouble, but it didn't say who'd offered to buy it. When Shelleck revealed that PocketMoney.com had made a serious offer, Mitchell paid him fifty thousand dollars for Stella's stolen plans. We know that because Chancey accessed Shelleck's bank account. He also took a peek at Ramon Salero's account and found a seventy-five thousand dollar transfer from a Cayman Island bank sent the day before we bought Stella. The exact amount the email said I'd paid for services rendered.'

'Hold on, Harry' Jenny said. 'Salero sent *you* the fake email, and then a fax to Richard with a copy of the stolen plans, right?'

'You *are* paying attention. Now, so that you understand the gravity of this email, I'm gonna read it to you.' Harry reached into his pocket and pulled out a folded sheet of paper.

Greta wanted to bolt for the door.

And I quote: Harry, $75,000 is in the account. Thanks. As

agreed, the fax alert will arrive at 2:20 p.m. next Thursday,

and will recommend PocketMoney.com buy Stella Electronics

on Friday prior to the last bell. I will also attach a copy of the sensitive details you provided. Matchmaker.

Harry held it up for all to see. 'This was sent to me five days before the seventy-five grand arrived in Salero's bank account, which proves the money did not come from me. Pass this around, Katie. And gimme some more coffee.'

Greta sat staring at the table, her eyes glistening with regret. Richard and Brimmer shared a look of satisfactory surprise. Katie handed Harry a cup of coffee. Penny Bowman abandoned her pen and sat back smiling. The Attorney General said nothing.

Harry continued. 'The Cayman bank refused to divulge the source of the seventy-five grand sent to Salero's bank account, so I asked a couple of pals in Chicago to pay them a visit.'

'Strike that!' Bentram said. 'You can't say that, Harry.'

'Okay, the seventy-five grand in Salero's account came from Goldsand Real Estate, which belonged to Coastline Ventures, which belonged to Green Valley Homes. All three companies, using different banks, belonged to a holding company in Canada; the Minton Mining Corporation, which is owned by…'

'Rylan Mitchell,' Penny Bowman interposed.

'Bingo, Rylan Mitchell,' Harry said, glancing round the table.

Richard and Katie squeezed hands. The trustees were ready to go out and celebrate. Greta forced a smile.

Harry loosened his tie. 'Mitchell wanted to put me in jail, so he asked Ramon Salero, who owed him money, to send the email and plant the fax in Richard's desk. Now to tie all this together, we go back to when he was in jail. Mitchell hooked up with a Mr Netty, a nice character, who saw Mike Kinnerman on TV and decided to kidnap him. How dare a 14-year old boy have billions of dollars in the bank when Netty was broke? Pathetic isn't it.'

'Harry, how could you possibly know what Mr. Netty was thinking?' Brimmer asked.

'One of the kidnappers, a Mr. Colin Wilson, cashed in and fled to Mexico. A few weeks later, police arrested him for a drug-related murder. Fearing for his life, Wilson contacted the U.S. Embassy in Mexico City and offered information on a recent U.S. kidnapping. The FBI decided to pay Wilson a visit and invited Chancey to come along. Offered extradition to the U.S., Wilson gave them every detail of Mike and Savannah's kidnapping; how and why and who planned it, that's how I know. Apparently, Mr. Wilson was murdered in his cell ten days ago, by unknowns.'

Brimmer removed his glasses. 'This is a remarkable piece of investigation, Harry.'

'It's unbelievable,' Malcolm Connors concurred.

Harry nodded. 'Yeah, anyway, Mitchell agreed to finance the kidnapping, which he thought, quite rightly, would bring billions of dollars in ransom. Not only did Mitchell set me up for an insider trading scam, he would have also walked away with a fortune in ransom money, so for him it was a double whammy. He may have gotten away with it too if I hadn't hired Brian Chancey. Let's be honest, you all thought this was my doing. So I hope this get-together has restored a little faith in my integrity,' Harry said, looking directly at Greta, and sat down.

Katie sank back in her chair. 'Harry, this is wonderful news, but why on earth didn't you tell us sooner? We've been going through hell believing you were responsible.'

'I couldn't, Chancey's report didn't arrive until last night and I sent it straight to Director Bentram.'

Geoff Wickerby, short, grey hair, mid forties said, 'Great job, Harry, but there's one detail you forgot to mention. Who put the goddam fax in Richard Kinnerman's desk?'

'Trina Cano, a cook, maid and cleaner for the trustees. Trina works solely on the executive floor and loves her job, but she's an illegal. That's where June Coswell, now Mrs. Salero, came in. As an immigration officer, June could go anywhere, so when her husband needed someone to plant a fax at PocketMoney. com she paid us a visit and checked out our staff list. The next night, she followed Trina home and threatened to have her deported if she didn't play ball. Poor kid was terrified; she's only twenty-two. June told Trina exactly when the fax would arrive and forced her to place it in Richard's desk draw. Chancey found Trina's rubber gloves and had them analysed. Inside of course, were traces of her DNA and perfume, which were also found on the fax, making the evidence conclusive,' Harry explained.

Director Bentram added, 'No charges will be brought against Trina Cano. She wants to keep her job and become a U.S. citizen, so I've arranged for her to get a green card.'

Coswell breathed out heavily. 'I can't believe June would do anything like this. This Salero guy must have forced her into it.'

The scale of the conspiracy astounded Richard. 'This is so goddam devious it's almost unbelievable,' he said, dramatically.

Doris knocked and entered. 'Agent Benaro asked me to give you this, sir. Says its urgent,' she said, handing Bentram a blue FBI folder. He opened the file and quickly read it.

Winston Bliss, who had said very little, spoke up. 'Harry, I can't believe that you let us go through weeks of uncertainty and finger-pointing when you suspected Mitchell all along.'

'Suspecting someone can be dangerous, as you all know. The real culprits were a mystery to me until I got Chancey's report.'

Bentram closed the folder. 'As Harry said, I got his report last night. Since then, our agents have been knocking on doors, and their report, which I've just received, corroborates every detail of Chancey's findings,' he confirmed.

A collective sigh of relief came from around the table. Greta feigned a look of relief and glanced at the exit.

Wickerby closed his FBI folder. 'One hell of a job, Harry.'

Bentram went on, 'Ramon and June Salero and Mr. Shelleck are in custody and have been charged with conspiracy to defraud, theft, criminal solicitation and attempting to pervert the course of justice. The kidnappers, Mitchell, Netty and Wilson are all dead. There were others, but they vanished. Finally, on a personal note, I pray the missing youngsters turn up safe and well.'

The Attorney General clasped his hands. 'I am sure that is something we are all praying for,' he said, sombrely. 'I would like to thank Mr. Schlecker for his tenacity in bringing this conspiracy to a close. As for PocketMoney.com, I believe those entrusted with its future will ensure that it continues to flourish as a beacon of inspiration for youngsters around the world.'

Wickerby pursed his lips and nodded in agreement.

Bentram sat back. 'Well I guess that about wraps it up.'

Jenny Grant jumped to her feet. 'Wraps it up? Are you saying that we were ordered here today and put through this charade when you already knew who the culprits were?'

'Stop the tape,' Bentram ordered.

'On the contrary,' the Attorney General replied. 'Until a few moments ago, all we knew was that Mitchell had kidnapped the youngsters. However, and Mr. Schlecker knows nothing about this, Chancey is ex CIA and considered it his duty to inform me of his findings, so he also sent me a copy of his report last night, which as you know, was uncorroborated until now. So the answer to your question is no, we had no idea who the culprits were, and without Chancey's report uncovering this insidious plot may well have proved impossible, which would have been disastrous considering what is happening around the globe.'

'I'm not sure that makes me feel any better, sir, but thanks for your candour,' Jenny said, dispassionately, and sat down.

The Attorney General went on, 'There is something else you should be aware of. The President wanted this inquiry televised globally from the Caucus Room at the Russell Senate Building, with the Senate Committee questioning you before an audience of hand picked press and democrat sympathizers. He was convinced that if the outcome were just another headline it would look like a political whitewash. However, after receiving Brian Chancey's astounding report, I managed to persuade the President that we could resolve the matter in the privacy of this conference room. The alternative would have been very humiliating.'

Jenny huffed and folded her arms. Winston Bliss shook his head disparagingly. Penny Bowman shuddered at the thought of answering to one Senator let alone a Committee.

Having visited the Caucus Room as a law student, Richard knew the history of its dramatic inquiries, such as *The Titanic disaster, Pearl Harbour and Watergate,* and had no reason to believe that a Senate Committee PocketMoney. com enquiry would have been any different. The outcome may have been the same, but their reputations would have been headline fodder, and he was grateful not to have suffered that indignity.

Saddened that his vengeful ex wife had ended up in jail, Mike Coswell felt sure that her estranged daughter Mary would want to visit her mother and try to build a relationship. He hoped so. Greta, already frozen with humiliation, thanked God that she had not made a fool of herself on global television, and was now considering ways to leave the room unnoticed.

Harry continued to stare at the table.

Closing his FBI folder the Attorney General went on, 'In short, Mr. Schlecker's investigation and this informal meeting have resolved the problem with minimum discomfort to you all. This evening, the President will denounce the conspirators on national television. He will also speak directly to those angry millions of youngsters around the globe, and personally exonerate all those at PocketMoney. com from any wrongdoing. Your presence here has helped to make that happen. My thanks to you all, and have a very happy Christmas. This meeting is now closed.'

FORTY-FOUR

The false insider trading accusations had been a living nightmare, especially for Richard and Katie, who had their own nightmare to cope with, and as they filed out to reception the air hummed with whispered relief. Amid the hubbub, Harvey Maybank called for everyone's attention, and the room descended into angry silence. Sheepishly apologising for Stella's underhandedness he rambled on about being honourable, which gained him nothing but a wall of unforgiving stares. Sensing the hostility, he grabbed his coat and hurried out the door, brushing past Linda Greenberg, who, having heard the outcome of the meeting from Harry Schlecker, strode in, wrapped in a camel coat, and marched over to Katie.

'Shouldn't you be happy? You look as though you're going to jail,' Linda snapped. 'If you don't smile, I'm gonna get mad.'

Katie grinned. 'Better? We were all suspects, Linda, and we damn well resented that, it was humiliating. Thankfully, we were exonerated, but they're a little short on apologies.'

'It's called due process. You'll get over it, gimme a hug.'

A palpable sense of relief filled the reception area, even Doris was smiling, but when Harry strolled in with a smug grin no one quite knew what to say or where to look.

Linda Greenberg, not exactly known for mincing her words, interrupted the uncomfortable silence. 'What the hell is this, a wake? You should all be celebrating, for Christ sake. Harry, do something. I can't stand this guilt bullshit.'

Harry offered the flat of his hands. 'Look, I don't blame you for thinking it was me I looked guilty as hell, but I was supposed to it was planned that way. It's behind us now and we all smell of roses, so let's move on we got a company to run.'

Immersed in feelings of regret Greta stood at the window watching the snowflakes pat the tinted glass. New York suddenly seemed a cold and lonely city and she was desperate to get away, perhaps to her house in Burlington, to consider her future.

To show that he bore no resentment Harry shook hands with each of the trustees, and Richard and Katie, to whom he made it clear their friendship was never in doubt, but despite the growing celebratory mood, inside Harry was bleeding for Greta.

Brimmer joined Richard and Katie. 'My dear friends, I have to leave, but my thoughts will remain with you this Christmas.'

Richard shook his hand. 'Thanks, Michael, we'll talk in the New Year.' Brimmer nodded, kissed Katie and strode out.

Harry, clearly agitated, still had the rift with Greta to resolve, which hung in the air like a storm waiting to break, and for those about to leave the outcome was too intriguing to miss.

Linda pulled Greta aside. 'What's going on, what happened? I feel knives in the air.'

Harry glanced at Greta as she grabbed her coat and explained her untenable position to Linda, who would have none of it.

'Okay, you were wrong. Say you're sorry and get it over with. If you don't, you'll regret it for the rest of your life, and you won't be the exceptional woman that I think you are.'

Those present feigned a disinterest, including Harry, who had his arm around Katie's waist, which she suspected was only to conceal his desperation. Then as Greta tearfully headed for the door, Harry broke away and called out to her.

'Greta, don't go. We need to talk,' he said, almost pleading.

All eyes focussed on Harry and Greta. Doris stopped typing.

Without turning around, Greta paused at the door and shook her head as though she had nothing left to say.

Harry desperately wanted to reach out to her. 'Greta, I had no idea why you were mad at me until today. Whether you were right or wrong doesn't matter. What you did took a lot of guts and I'm proud of you, honestly.'

Greta turned her head and looked at Harry, her beautiful face glistening with tears of remorse and uncertainty.

The room descended into an expectant silence.

Doris, an avid reader of romantic novels, watched misty-eyed as the drama unfolded.

Greta stepped forward, and hesitating briefly, folded her arms around Harry's neck. Clenching his jaw in an attempt to suppress a flood of emotion welling up inside, Harry sighed, revelling in the warmth and sincerity of Greta's embrace. Closing his eyes, he visualised her crumpled note in the basket beneath his desk, and recalled the desolate feeling when he had read the word *goodbye*. Having waited five years for this moment, he wrapped his arms around Greta and bathed in the silky warmth of her tears as she whispered, 'I'm so sorry, Harry, please forgive me.'

Oblivious to the surrounding smiling faces Harry and Greta remained locked in one another's arms. Doris sniffled, wiped her nose and continued typing. Prompted by their romantic reunion Richard and Katie glanced at one another.

It was time to leave.

Wrapped in thick overcoats Richard, Katie and Linda headed for the elevator, followed by the trustees who, for the first time in many weeks, could look forward to a favourable headline, which would put an end to the miserable saga and enable them to return to business in the New Year.

Having had to cope with Mike's kidnap, Julieanne's illness and the insider trading scandal, Katie had given no thought to seasonal shopping. Today was Christmas Eve and she would not allow the evil that had taken her son prevent her from revelling in the magic of buying presents for her daughter.

Amid the sound of cheery carol singers warming the snowy sidewalk, Linda, Richard and Katie exchanged seasonal greetings with the trustees, who promised to light candles for Mike and Savannah as they departed to join their loved ones.

Linda linked arms with Katie and said, 'Before we part for the holidays, I wanted you to know that Mike's dream of a global TV network for kids is now a reality, and it's scheduled to go on air late February. Mike will love it, I promise.'

Katie smiled, recalling Mike wanting his own company when he was twelve; a boyhood dream destined to change the world.

'You really are amazing, Linda,' she said, giving her a hug.

'Hell of a job, Linda,' Richard said, unsurprised. 'I guess with so much going on we haven't given it much thought lately.'

'I know, and now I'd like you to do something for me,' Linda said, and opening her leather shoulder bag she handed Katie two gift-wrapped boxes. 'Put these under your Christmas tree; they're for Mike and Savannah.' Then hugging them both she hurried away in a sea of Christmas shoppers.

Placing the gifts in her bag Katie reached for her cell phone and called Julieanne, who was at a friend's house. 'Hi, sweetie, it's me. You'll be happy to know that your father and I are not going to jail. The FBI caught the bad guys and put them away.'

'Thank God. I always knew that you were innocent. We have to celebrate. What time will you be home, Mom?'

'Well as we're here in New York your father and I are going shopping. We'll be home around five-thirty, is that okay?'

'Yes, but drive carefully it's snowing here in New Mayford. See you later, bye Mom.' As soon as Julieanne disconnected, she called Jake and some of her friends and asked them to help her put up the Christmas decorations.

By the time Richard and Katie arrived home a thick blanket of snow had covered the house and streams of fairy lights glowed in the windows and doorway. Happily surprised, they carried the gift-wrapped boxes into the hallway and stamped the snow off their feet. Wagging his tail Piffin followed them to the kitchen, where Julieanne stood smiling with her arms folded. Giving them a warm hug, she whispered, 'I'm glad you're not in handcuffs.'

Dinner was in the oven and a bottle of champagne sat in ice on the kitchen table. In a corner of the spacious living room the Christmas tree sparkled with joy, which Julieanne and her friends had adorned with festive decorations; a scene made complete with a glowing fire and a candlelit dining table.

'Do you like it?' Julieanne asked, bubbling with excitement.

Katie smiled. 'It's just perfect, sweetie, gimme another hug.'

At six p.m., sitting behind his oval office desk, the President appeared on television. 'Good evening my fellow Americans,' he began, his voice sombre. 'I'm sure that most of you are aware of the international insider trading scandal that has rocked the very foundations of America's financial institutions, a crime for which we have been blamed. This dreadful episode, which involved the kidnapping and probable murder of two innocent youngsters, has now been resolved, thanks to many dedicated people, and those responsible for this disgraceful affair are now either deceased or in jail. Because of the sheer scale of this crime, and to dismiss any criticism of the judicial outcome, an evidential report and the perpetrators photographs will appear on the FBI website for all to see. The evidence contained in that report clearly vindicates all those at PocketMoney.com of any involvement. Furthermore, this administration hopes that the company will continue to flourish on behalf of its young investors around the world, whom I now urge to return to school and continue their education. Your voices have been heard,' the President said, earnestly, 'we will not allow this to happen again. This Christmas, I hope that we can all...

As the President wished the nation a happy Christmas, ABC News called wanting an interview. Richard reluctantly agreed. Shortly after, jubilant calls came from JB Walsome, Beth, Sheriff Carver, Jake and friends near and far, including Sally Brooks.

'Katie, I was so relieved when I heard the President's speech. Now I'm praying for the best Christmas present of all; Mike and Savannah's safe return. I'm visiting my kids in Santa Barbara, but I'll be home New Year's Eve, you can count on it. Give Julieanne a kiss for me. I'll be thinking of you Christmas Day.'

'Thanks, Sally, we miss you too, Merry Christmas.'

As it was their family tradition, Richard, Katie and Julieanne walked to the town square and joined a candlelit carol service, led by the local choir. The snow had stopped, leaving the night air still and crisp. The joyful event concluded with a prayer for Mike and Savannah, and after sincere good wishes from the townsfolk they trekked home to enjoy their daughter's cooking.

At 8:30 p.m., a helicopter landed at the corner of Beechwood Avenue. Shortly after, the doorbell rang. It was Diane Sawyer, a much-loved ABC presenter, and a camera crew. Diane began by interviewing Richard, Katie and Julieanne sitting by the fire in front of the Christmas tree. Responding to her warm sincerity, they described their heartbreaking South American journey and played Mike's emotional voicemail from Bogota, which moved Diane, a veteran war reporter to tears. She asked if they would like to give Mike and Savannah a message, just in case they were out there somewhere watching Christmas Day.

Katie: 'Darling Mike, darling Savannah, wherever you are I have you in my heart. We will never let go, I promise.'

Julieanne: 'If someone out there knows where my brother is, call the number on the screen. Please. I miss you, Mike.'

Richard's eyes narrowed as he looked into the camera; 'I'm talking to the person who has Mike and Savannah. I'm asking you, no begging you not to hurt them. They are just two innocent kids. Let them go. Please. I'll find them.'

Richard placed his arms around Katie and Julieanne as the camera panned away and zoomed in on Mike and Savannah's smiling photograph on the wall above the flickering fireplace. Katie sniffled, and offering to make some coffee she dragged her daughter out to the kitchen.

Diane and her crew went up the stairs to Mike's bedroom and filmed his toy collection, model aircraft, school clothes, football heroes, pop star posters, and finally his empty bed. Then reading aloud to the camera Diane quoted some of the Christmas cards sent to Mike and Savannah from all over the world, of which Julieanne had pinned up as many as possible in the living room and boxed the rest away.

As the crew packed their equipment, Diane said, 'How will you cope without Mike this Christmas?' Richard and Katie put their arms around Julieanne. Diane tightened her lips and nodded. 'We're all rooting for you at ABC, and if I can help in any way give me a call,' Diane said, and then giving them all a warm hug, she followed the camera crew out to the waiting helicopter.

That night Richard and Katie sat with Julieanne until she fell asleep, both aware that Christmas would be heartbreaking this year, especially for their daughter who needed the warmth and security of family love around her. Mike had been missing now for almost three months, and though they would never give up hope, it seemed unlikely that he would ever return.

Just after midnight, Harry called, and he sounded emotional. Katie prepared herself for bad news, but she was wrong.

'Katie, you're gonna think this is weird, but hear me out. We got a bus load of orphans coming to my place for their Christmas party tomorrow. It's something we do every year, but I've asked Henry and the staff to take care of it. What I'm coming to is this; Greta and I would like to spend Christmas with you, Richard and Julieanne. We're all floating in a black hole over our missing kids, and I thought we might find some comfort in spending the holiday together. It's gonna be a tough one. I nearly cancelled it this year, but I couldn't do it, that'd be like giving up.'

Katie smiled. 'Hang on, Harry.' She ran Harry's request by Richard and Julieanne, who both agreed that it was a wonderful idea. 'We'd love you to spend Christmas with us, Harry, but there is one thing I have to ask, and I don't wish to sound indelicate or presumptuous; should I prepare a room for you, and Greta?'

'Yeah, I'll explain when I see you.'

'What time can we expect you?'

'My pilot will drop us off around eleven.'

'Okay, we'll see you then.'

FORTY-FIVE

Thursday, December 24th Bogota

When Sheila Macavy called from the U.S. Embassy on Christmas Eve, Jamie knew it was no social call. 'A woman named Mariana Valero de Vasquez just called. Says she knows where the missing kids are. Wants to meet ASAP. Sounds genuine.'

'This could be the break we've hoped for, Sheila. Arrange a five p.m. meeting at Bogota National Park's main entrance. And get her cell number.' Jamie hung up and called Judy.

With the festive holiday only hours away most people were last minute shopping and the park was predictably quiet. Jamie and Judy found a bench with view of the entrance and waited. It was after five. A dozen cars came and went and it began to look as though Mariana wouldn't show, then a blue Mercedes stopped just inside the entrance. Cautiously surveying the area the female driver inched forward and pulled up in the parking lot.

Jamie called the cell number Sheila Macavy had given him. A voice answered expectantly. 'Hello, this is Mariana,'

'Are you driving a blue Mercedes?' he asked.

'Yes,' she replied, looking around for the caller.

'Good, I can see you. Get out of the car and walk left towards the lake for about seventy yards.'

Following Jamie's instructions Mariana found them waiting on a wooden park bench beside the lake. They stood up as she approached. 'I am Mariana,' she said, offering her hand.

'Good to meet you. I'm Jamie, and this is my partner, Judy. Let's have a drink at the restaurant. It's quiet this evening, so we can sit outside and talk in private.'

'That will be fine,' Mariana agreed, her left hand clutching the strap of a leather shoulder bag.

Dressed in a beige skirt, matching shoes, a pale pink blouse, gold earrings and sunglasses Mariana epitomised the meaning of elegance, in Jamie's opinion. Somewhere in her forties, she was tall, slender and attractive, with long auburn hair, tanned skin and a generous smile.

A waiter hurried over as they sat down at a corner table. Judy ordered a beer and two glasses of merlot. Mariana seemed a little apprehensive, which Jamie suspected had something to do with what she was about to tell them. Producing their credentials, they made her feel at ease and got down to the business. 'So tell us how you know where the youngsters are, Mariana,' Jamie said.

The waiter brought their drinks to the table. Judy thanked him, and as he walked away, Mariana removed her sunglasses.

'My dear husband, Sebastian was an architect, a fine one,' she said, with a soft velvety voice, her English endeared by a rich Spanish accent.

'Was?' Judy asked.

'Yes, Sebastian is no longer with us, but I will get to that. He designed and built a palatial house in the Andes Mountains near the city of Medellin, for a man known only as Rizzio. His real name is Rizzio Antonio Perez.'

Jamie and Judy glanced at one another. 'Yes, we are aware of him,' Jamie stated. 'Five nine, stocky, has a short neck, black pony-tailed hair, a thick moustache, badly pockmarked face and always wears black. A dangerous man by all accounts.'

Mariana sat back in her chair and lit a menthol cigarette. 'He is a monster,' she said, blowing smoke into the evening air.

Judy twirled her Chilean merlot. 'So what's the connection?' she asked, intrigued by her coolness.

Mariana's brown eyes narrowed. 'He has the two American youngsters you are looking for. He also cold-bloodedly murdered my husband, Sebastian.'

Judy sat back and exhaled. Jamie nodded sombrely, and no longer having any doubts about Mariana's credibility he leaned forward making closer eye contact. 'You obviously know this man Rizzio, so why did he murder your husband?'

A young couple sat down at a table a short distance away.

Mariana gazed across the lake, and shaking her head in silent thought she returned to Jamie. 'When Sebastian completed the house Rizzio threw a party, and we of course, were invited. I was very proud of my husband; the house was beautiful. Later, in his usual drunken state, Rizzio told Sebastian of his plan to build an underground cocaine distribution laboratory, and asked him to design and build it, money no object. Sebastian wanted nothing to do with it and flatly refused, which apparently lit the fuse for an argument, and that is when Rizzio shot him.'

Judy leaned forward. 'You saw him kill Sebastian?'

'No, I was with an acquaintance outside on the patio. Rizzio came running out, waving his arms, and said that one of his crazy bodyguards had killed my husband. He led me into the kitchen and forced the guard, who was kneeling with his hands on his head, to confess. Then Rizzio shot him, right there in front of me. I knew he was lying, but what could I do?' Mariana said, turning towards the lake to wipe away a tear.

Jamie and Judy quietly absorbed Mariana's horrific story. The sun had all but disappeared and a warm breeze sailed across the grassland, picking up swirls of dust from the distant parking lot in its wake. Lines of coloured lights suddenly lit up around the bar-restaurant, prompting a colony of bats to flick by overhead as the crickets began their nightly chorus.

Judy cracked the silence. 'I'm sorry about your husband, Mariana. People like Rizzio have no respect for life, which is why we need to talk about the missing youngsters?'

'Yes, of course. They are at Rizzio's house.'

'You saw them?' Jamie asked, his ice-blue eyes hardening.

'Yes, I was there two days ago. Rizzio called and asked me to attend his birthday party. I agreed, but only because I planned to kill him. He sent his limousine, and when I arrived the house was full of corrupt police, politicians and bankers. I hated them all. Rizzio was charming, but only superficially, so for the sake of my plan I went along with it. He had redecorated the entire house and insisted on giving me a tour. Then he led me outside to the rear garden, which backs up onto a mountain, and pointed to a newly built small house at the far end of the lawn. He bragged about using it as a private bordello. Then his cell phone rang and he ran inside yelling that he would be back in a moment. Intrigued by the small house, I went inside and walked around, but it was quite basic. Upstairs there were four bedrooms, and as I gave each one a cursory look, I saw the two children. They were sound asleep, filthy and chained to a mattress on the floor of a dingy room at the far end of the hallway. The room stank of human excretion. The barbarity of it horrified me and I felt dreadfully ashamed for leaving them there, but I was helpless. I wanted to be sick. I ran down the stairs and went outside for some air. When I rejoined the party Rizzio and his friends were high on cocaine and he had completely forgotten about me. I was upset and no longer had the courage to use the pistol in my bag, and so I asked the chauffeur to drive me home.'

Judy said. 'If you had shot Rizzio you wouldn't be here now, so forget any feelings of guilt. Because of you we have a chance to save those kids and deliver devil's justice to Rizzio.'

Mariana stubbed out her cigarette. 'I pray to God that is true.'

'Do you still have the plans of Rizzio's house?' Jamie asked.

Mariana withdrew a drawing from her bag and rolled it out across the table. 'I am also an architect and have added several details that you will need to know; the power supply, security cameras, the most accessible way down the mountain at the rear of the house, and the bedroom where the children are. There are six vicious dogs roaming the grounds, which remain chained up whenever Rizzio throws a party, but if they are released you will have to kill them. Finally, Rizzio has twelve armed bodyguards, whom he lovingly calls "The Apostles"

Jamie did a quick study of the drawing and rolled it up. 'This information will give us the edge we need to end Rizzio's reign of terror,' Jamie said, aching to get him in his sights.

Judy added, 'Your motive for coming forward is clearly two-fold, Mariana, and we are grateful that you did. Is there anything we can do for you?'

Mariana crossed her long legs and sipped her wine. 'Yes, slay Rizzio and you will cut the head off the dragon.'

'Anything else?' Jamie asked.

'No, if my husband's death is avenged, I want nothing more. I am a wealthy woman.'

'Very well, we have your cell number. I advise you to stay in Bogota until this is over,' Jamie said, waving to the waiter who hurried to the table and cleared the empty glasses. Jamie gave the young man a handful of pesos and he strode back inside

With the bag strapped over her shoulder Mariana stood up and strolled alongside Jamie and Judy to the parking lot, which was dark now and almost empty. Brushing strands of her long auburn hair away from her face she opened the Mercedes door and tossed her bag on the passenger seat.

'I will pray for the children,' she said, sliding onto the front seat closing the door. "Good luck" she mouthed, and then sped away to the park entrance, glancing at the rear view mirror.

Judy drove them to her apartment and while she freshened up, Jamie called Major Bell and reported Mariana's eyewitness account of Mike and Savannah's captivity at Rizzio's house near the city of Medellin. With a heightening sense of urgency he requested permission to mount a rescue operation, for which he would need eight men, himself, Judy and two helicopters. Aware that time was against them Major Bell reminded Jamie that a U.S. military operation would need the Colombian's approval, and promised to deal with it immediately at the highest level. He had to admit however, that getting hold of anyone with the right level of authority late on Christmas Eve would take a miracle.

The Major was right; those in power were unavailable and not to be disturbed, especially regarding an American problem, so he went the long way round. Early Christmas morning, he called the home of Colonel J. Williams, a legendary marine who now had an office at the Pentagon, and explained the situation. The Colonel told the Major to send him an encrypted report and promised to do what he could. Having read the report, he sent it to White House Chief-of-Staff, Avery Carlton, and then called him. Avery said the President was unavailable, and unless war was declared he could do nothing until the morning.

At nine a.m. December 26th, Avery called the President, who in the early hours had returned after meeting with the Saudis, to spend the remainder of the seasonal holiday with his family at Camp David. When the President read Major Bell's report, he ordered Avery to call the Colombian President and patch him through on connection. It was three-thirty p.m. before the two presidents greeted one another. They spoke candidly about the planned rescue assault, which the Colombian President agreed to without hesitation, but stipulated that he would need twelve hours to notify his military commanders. The President understood the delay and thanked him for his co-operation. Then he reconnected with Avery Carlton who was at his desk awaiting orders.

'Avery, the rescue mission has been authorised for tomorrow. Keep me informed,' the President said, sternly.

'Yes Mr. President.' Avery hung up and called Colonel. J. Williams, who immediately informed Major Bell that the mission had been authorised to take place Sunday, December 27th, by the Presidents of the United States and Colombia.

* * * * *

On Christmas morning, Harry's Bell 430 helicopter landed on the open ground behind the Kinnerman house, which the overnight snow had transformed into a winter wonderland glistening in the lukewarm sunshine. Leaving a fresh trail of footprints to the rear door as the helicopter took off and headed home, Harry and Greta entered the kitchen laden with gifts, overnight bags, wine and champagne and stamped the snow off their feet. Piffin, wearing a red ribbon around his neck, wagged his tail and barked excitedly. Harry and Greta made a fuss of him.

After the hugs and seasonal greetings, Katie took their coats and hung them up in the hallway. Richard carried the overnight bags up to their room. Julieanne was still upstairs getting ready.

Harry placed the champagne in the fridge and closed the door as Richard and Katie returned to the kitchen. 'I can't tell you how good it feels to be here with you today,' Harry said.

Greta wanted Julieanne to have all the attention, so she had put on a plain green sweater, a beige skirt and tied her hair in a ponytail. Linking arms with Harry, she said, 'There's nowhere else we'd rather be today, Katie, this is just perfect.'

'Well that goes both ways, Greta,' Katie replied, noticing a large diamond ring on her left hand. 'There is one thing though, and Richard and I talked about this last night.'

'Feeling guilty about enjoying ourselves?' Harry asked.

'Something like that,' Richard said, pouring more coffee.

'Richard, I've been there. Whenever I laugh at a joke, enjoy a meal, good wine, or whatever I've thought, how can I do this when Savannah is out there suffering. But if we do that it means we've all been kidnapped, because like you and Katie there's not a day goes by that I don't think about Mike and Savannah. And you know what? I don't believe our kids would want us sitting in a dark room staring at the walls with the drapes drawn. That's why we wanted to be here today, to find some sort of emotional refuge in our friendship with you and Julieanne. If we find a little Christmas spirit along the way, then so be it.'

Katie grinned. 'Coffee, Harry?'

Harry had hit it right on the head, and from that moment on emotions were no longer subject to scrutiny. Katie handed Harry and Greta mugs of coffee, and as they warmed themselves by the fire, the sound of feet tramped down the stairs. Julieanne gushed into the living room, wearing a red sweater, a black skirt and shoes, and Harry's gold bracelet on her right wrist.

'Merry Christmas!' she said, brightly, affectionately passing around a kiss.

Greta gave her a hug. 'You look beautiful, sweetie.'

'Thanks, Greta, I have two great role models,' she whispered.

Harry refused to let her out of his arms until Katie handed her daughter some coffee. Richard's phone rang; it was JB Walsome.

With carols softly playing around the house and the aroma of a traditional lunch in the air, Katie, the image of her daughter, looked thoughtfully at her family and guests and suddenly felt warmed by their presence. Harry was right; what better time could there be to share the bond of friendship uniting them in grief for their missing children.

On the stroke of two, Katie and Greta served Christmas lunch and ordered everyone to sit down at the candlelit dining room table, which Katie had prepared for seven. They joined hands and said a prayer for Mike and Savannah, throughout which no one was able to mask their tears, especially Julieanne.

Two spaces, with neatly laid cutlery remained empty.

After a splendid two-hour lunch, enhanced by companionship and vintage wine, Richard and Katie knelt beside the Christmas tree and glanced at one another, remembering that a year ago they were doing exactly the same thing, only Mike was there excitedly waiting for his present; a new laptop.

Richard took a gift from under the glowing tree. 'This one is for someone called Julieanne, from Harry and Greta.'

Katie grinned and handed Richard another gift; a tradition the family enjoyed, especially their kids. Harry had predictably bought expensive gifts, especially for Julieanne, but that was who he was, and Greta had no doubt encouraged him, Katie thought, revelling in the warm feeling of togetherness.

Ten gifts for Mike and Savannah remained under the tree.

Greta, a carbon fanatic, gathered up the torn wrapping paper and placed it in a neat pile for recycling. Piffin playfully picked it up and spread it around the room again, much to her annoyance. Harry, who was on the phone to Nanny Coombes in St Lucia, seemed to think it was hilarious.

As Julieanne sat happily fiddling with her new I-Pad, Richard handed her a small gift-wrapped box, and quickly ripping it open she found a set of keys. Puzzled, she looked at her mother, who responded with a surreptitious smile, and said, 'Why don't you look in the driveway.'

Julieanne grinned and raced to the front door. Parked in the driveway was a bright red Volkswagen Beetle convertible, with a white ribbon around it. Squealing with delight she hurried out to inspect her new wheels. Harry, Greta and her smiling parents joined her as she excitedly sank into the driver's seat and started the engine. Richard leaned inside the door. 'We got your learners permit, but you can't drive in New York just yet,' he explained, but she was too absorbed in gadgets to hear him.

Like her brother Julieanne was already a proficient driver, thanks to her mother, and would certainly have no problem with her new Beetle. She adjusted the seat, checked out the gears, CD player, Satnav and revved the engine. 'Oh I love it, I love it, thanks Mom, thanks Dad,' she said, her face a picture of delight.

A small distraction from her ongoing grief was the best that Richard and Katie could hope for right now, but the Beetle would also give Julieanne the independence she needed and enable her to drive to high school, which she would no doubt do with a smile on her face in the New Year.

Katie coaxed Julieanne out of the car and grabbed her hand. 'We'll go for a long drive when the snow clears, sweetie. Right now I'm freezing, let's go in the house.'

Richard garaged the Beetle and followed them inside.

Julieanne and her father cleared the remnants of lunch from the dining table, while Greta attempted to recapture the wrapping paper from Piffin. Katie, happily redundant, cornered Harry in the kitchen and linked arms.

'You look suspiciously happy, Harry, what are you up to?'

'It's a big surprise, Katie,' Harry said, and filling five glasses with champagne, he called everyone into the kitchen and handed them out. Smiling ridiculously, he placed his arm around Greta's slender waist, and said, 'I proposed to Greta last night and she said yes. I can't begin to tell you how happy I feel right now. My pal at Continental has arranged for us to join a world cruise in South Africa, and we're getting married in Mauritius.'

The news came as no surprise to anyone, least of all Katie, who wondered why Harry had waited so long. Julieanne, keen to show her approval, gave them both a warm hug. 'I always knew you two belonged together,' she said, delighted.

'It took you long enough, Greta,' Katie said, mischievously.

'I know, but it's a big leap and we'd never fully connected. Now we have, and it's wonderful,' Greta said, deliciously smug.

'A world cruise? That's not a honeymoon that's retirement,' Richard said, chuckling. 'Here's to you both. Good luck.'

They all raised their glasses. Julieanne disliked champagne, so she took a sip and gave the rest to Piffin.

Still grinning boyishly Harry pulled out a large Havana cigar. Julieanne frowned and shook her head. Harry rolled his eyes and tapped his forehead; how could he forget that she was asthmatic. He kissed her on the cheek and put it away.

'It's a three month cruise, but I can still keep an eye on the business,' Harry explained. 'We got a VIP suite, which has all kinds of gadgets, and a private deck with a pool. If a miracle happens and we get news of Mike and Savannah's whereabouts, we'll jump ship and fly straight home in the Gulfstream. Christ, wouldn't that be some wedding present.'

Harry went out to the rear garden for a cigar. Standing alone in the fading winter light he looked out across the ghostly white landscape. Savannah was out there somewhere; was she trying to call, trying to find her way home? 'I don't know where you are princess,' he whispered, 'I just want you to come back to me.'

Richard reminded everyone that the ABC interview was on at five p.m., but there was no interest, so Julieanne put on her new wildlife movie. Katie prepared a buffet for dinner, with which she allowed her daughter two small glasses of wine. Later, Richard dug out the family albums and together they journeyed through the past. Julieanne cringed at her younger self and ran her fingers over Mike's photographs, while her misty-eyed parents relived happier times. Lost in one another's arms, Harry and Greta danced around the house to romantic Italian songs.

Just after midnight, Julieanne kissed everyone goodnight and went up to bed looking tired but happy. Harry and Greta stayed for coffee and brandy before also retiring for the night. Left alone in the kitchen, Richard and Katie held one another.

'We did okay, Richard,' Katie whispered.

He pulled her closer. 'Yeah….we did okay.'

They spent the next morning taking calls from friends near and far who had watched their moving interview on ABC's Christmas Show. Harry and Greta couldn't help but admire their strength and family unity in the wake of their adversity. At noon, Sheriff Carver and Jake arrived with gifts for Mike and Julieanne. Both stayed for lunch much to everyone's delight.

At three p.m., Harry's pilot arrived to take them home. They had yet to pack for their long voyage, which began with a flight to Cape Town, South Africa. After an emotional farewell, Harry and Greta boarded their helicopter and frantically waved goodbye as it clattered away in the grey wintry sky.

Christmas had been an unexpectedly joyful event for Richard and Katie, bringing with it a warm sense of family unity and a deepening of their friendship with Harry and Greta.

In the early hours, Julieanne lay on her pillow in the light of the bedside lamp and smiled, visualizing her brother's face when he saw her red Beetle convertible. Closing her eyes, she made a silent wish and turned out the light.

Lying in one another's arms Richard and Katie succumbed to an explosion of emotion they had denied one another for so long.

* * * * *

Bogota, Colombia. Sunday, December 27th

The delay to the rescue mission had annoyed Jamie, but he knew that delicate politics were involved. He ordered his unit to report for briefing at 16:00 hours in the hanger at El Dorado airport, where two army helicopters were fuelled and ready to go. He had considered calling Richard and Katie to let them know that Mike was alive, but decided against it. So many things could go wrong, and to give false hope to a family after suffering months of torment would be irresponsible. He would make that call when the youngsters were safely back in Bogota.

Judy and the men were checking their equipment when Jamie strode into the hanger, and as he marched towards them with a look of purpose in his blue eyes, they stiffly saluted. Jamie had hand picked each of his men, and as a unit they had shared many high-risk covert operations, which had led to a unique bond borne out of mutual respect. Nothing would ever change that.

Jamie rolled out Mariana's drawing of Rizzio's house across the wooden table and walked his unit through the assault plan. Judy handed him a mug of strong coffee.

'The Andes Mountains separate at the heart of Colombia and continue north in a V-shape. To keep the noise to a minimum, we'll fly in low between these two ranges and land on a small plateau half way up the west range. The terrain is harsh but the mountain is a reasonable climb. From there, it should take us no longer than twenty-five minutes to reach the summit.'

Judy and the men listened carefully as Jamie explained every detail of their forthcoming operation. Their lives depended on one another and precision timing was critical.

'Communicate with me at all times. I will advise when Judy and I have Mike and Savannah. At that point, assemble outside the rear wall and we'll pass them over. One more thing; there are six vicious dogs on the premises. If they are unleashed when it kicks off you will have to shoot them. Here's a photograph of Rizzio. If you spot him, kill him. Any questions?'

'Yes, sir, when do we leave?' One of the men asked, sparking off a round of laughter.

At 17:00 hours, in combat fatigues and their faces blackened, Jamie's small but deadly force loaded their considerable arsenal into the helicopters and climbed onboard. Minutes later, with the sprawling city of Bogota slowly fading behind them, they headed north over the dense jungle towards a sea of dark, stormy clouds swirling above the formidable Andes Mountains.

The Colombian sunset in December was around 6 p.m., Judy confirmed, and although political wranglings had delayed their mission for two days, which could mean life or death for Mike and Savannah, Jamie decided to wait until late afternoon before setting off. His primary concern was for the safety of his unit, and to give them maximum advantage the assault would need to take place under the cover of darkness.

As the distant mountains loomed closer, Jamie gazed out the window at the tiny villages and misty patchwork of fields passing by below in the fading December light. He knew from experience that every mission had its problems, but his men were highly trained soldiers, and unless something went drastically wrong he was confident the rescue assault on Rizzio's palatial house would be successful, as long as Mike and Savannah were still alive.

He just hoped they were not too late.

FORTY-SIX

The Andes Mountains, near Medellin, Colombia

It was pitch dark when they landed at a small plateau half way up the western section of the Andes Mountains. The area was barren and the rocky terrain easily navigable. The Special Forces Unit jumped out and gathered their equipment. Jamie gave an all clear to the pilots and the helicopters quickly sank down the cliff face, heading south to a designated waiting area.

A light wind drifted over the mountains, and with no moon and their faces blackened they were invisible. Jamie was right; the ascent was not too difficult and they reached the summit in less than thirty minutes. Using a night-vision monocular Jamie zoomed in on Rizzio's house, and as expected saw no activity, knowing the patio and swimming pools were on the other side. In the silent darkness they followed a steep, rocky trail down to the high perimeter wall at the rear of the house. A band was playing somewhere in the grounds. The men crouched down and checked their weapons, communications and explosives.

It was time.

The deadly unit separated and silently rounded the wall of the palatial building, which overlooked a wide valley dotted with a scattering of distant lights from tiny mountain villages. This was Rizzio's domain; the most feared man in South America, whose disregard for life and vengeance for betrayal was legendary. Little did he know his reign of terror was about to end, thought Jamie.

On the garden patio, a seven-piece band was playing to about thirty guests, who had clearly abandoned their inhibitions. Some were splashing about in the heart-shaped swimming pools; others were dancing, laughing and drinking in small groups.

Heavily armed guerrilla-type guards patrolled the grounds.

The unit moved into position; one, a sniper invisible in a tree set his scope to take out the cameras and bodyguards. The other seven men silently dropped over the ten-foot wall in the darkness behind the shrubbery. Unseen in the shadows Jamie and Judy slid down the wall into the rear garden and crawled along a narrow pathway towards the garden house Marianna had described.

The minimal lighting at the rear of the building enabled them to move swiftly and remain virtually invisible.

The small house looked dark and lifeless as they reached the front door, and Jamie wondered if they were too late. He turned the handle and slowly pushed it open. Judy stood opposite him, Glock revolver in hand. They cautiously went inside and searched the ground floor. The band was playing so loud no one could hear them moving stealthily from room to room. With the ground level secured, Jamie crept up the bare wooden stairs. Judy watched his back. Reaching the landing, they crouched down. Judy nodded, and pushed open the first bedroom door on the left. Jamie rolled inside onto one knee and turned 180 degrees, both hands on his Glock revolver. The room was empty and in total darkness, as were the second and third. The fourth was the room in which Mariana said that she saw Mike and Savannah.

As Judy pushed open the last bedroom door, gunfire suddenly cracked outside. The band stopped playing. Screaming party goers scrambled for safety. Dogs barked. Men started yelling. Jamie suspected a bodyguard saw one of his men and kicked off a gun battle, leaving a blanket of smoke and spent cordite hovering in the night air, but he knew they could handle it.

Remaining calm and focussed Jamie and Judy crept inside the room. There were no lights, no carpet and it stank of excrement. Adjusting to the darkness they surveyed the area. It was empty, other than a filthy double mattress on the floor, upon which lay Mike and Savanna seemingly oblivious to what was happening around them. They knelt down and gently tapped their faces, but there was no response. Both appeared to be comatose, and with their shackled ankles chained to the floor and filthy t-shirts and underpants covered in excretion they looked horrendous.

A light came on beneath a door at the far side of the room, followed by the scraping of a chair on a tiled floor. Jamie knelt by the door. Judy crouched opposite him as he cracked it open. A guard, revolver in hand, stood at the window attempting to see what was happening outside. Hearing the door creak as it opened, he spun around, Judy fired twice and he fell heavily to the floor. Jamie searched him, and finding a bunch of keys he quickly unshackled Mike and Savannah. Judy knelt down and examined them; their eyes were dilated, their pulses erratic and their arms and legs covered in sores and needle marks. They were clearly in a drug-induced coma and in urgent need of medical attention.

In the mayhem outside Jamie's men continued their mission.

Seven bodyguards were dead; four of whom lay stretched out on the lawn. The other three had fallen into the swimming pools, turning the water a light shade of purple.

Rizzio had so far remained elusive.

Like ghosts appearing out of thick smoke blanketing the air the blackened faced unit entered the house to plant incendiary devices. Several guests cowered behind sofas and tables; others ran up to the bedrooms in an effort to escape the invaders.

The determined force swept through the building room-by-room and ordered everyone out immediately. Hidden beneath the kitchen table, a lone bodyguard began spraying the hallway with his AK 47 assault rifle. A spontaneous response from the unit proved fatal. The guard reeled backwards onto the floor in a pool of blood. He looked no more than sixteen-years old.

Four guards remained unaccounted for, and there was still no sign of Rizzio. The unit continued their unrelenting search of the sprawling house; no one would escape their ruthless pursuit.

Then the dogs were let loose. Shots rang out. Two fell dead.

With Mike and Savannah wrapped in filthy sheets over their shoulders, Jamie and Judy made their way down the wooden staircase to the front door. Nudging it open, they warily stepped outside. The acrid smell of spent bullets and death hovered in the cool mountain air. The gunfire had stopped and an eerie silence had fallen around the building. Jamie spoke to his mini-com. 'Targets secured. We are leaving the small house. Move out.'

Hidden in the shadows Jamie and Judy crept low along the wall, then somewhere in the darkness they heard the dogs growl and froze. Turning to face them, they reached for their revolvers. Four huge Dobermans, bearing their teeth, raced across the lawn towards them. Both fired rapidly. Three dogs whimpered and fell to the ground. The other, just a few yards away, leapt at Jamie, its eyes wide and its jaws rabid. Judy fired one head shot and the dog fell at his feet. Stepping over the monstrous animal they hurried to the designated retrieval spot at the wall.

A lone bodyguard crept around to the back of the house and crouched in the darkness next to the trashcans. Reaching for his shoulder holster he withdrew a revolver.

Jamie passed the comatose youngsters up the wall to his men, who handed them down to those on the other side. Then as he lifted Judy up in his cupped hands, the crack of gunfire rang out. Judy recoiled, squealing in agony. The men quickly dragged her over the wall and passed her down. Jamie spun around and fired rapidly at the bodyguard until he fell lifeless to the ground. Then springing up a rope on the wall, he jumped down the other side and knelt beside Judy, whose upper thigh was bleeding heavily from a gaping bullet wound. Using his belt as a tourniquet, Jamie tightened it around the top of her leg and hoisted her up.

Two of the men volunteered to carry Mike and Savannah and hoisted them onto their shoulders. Jamie wrapped his arm around Judy, who was limping badly, and led his men up the mountain to the summit. There, they stopped for a breather while Jamie called the pilots and ordered the retrieval of his unit. Far behind them down the unforgiving mountain Rizzio's house suddenly exploded, lighting up the night sky with an orange mushroom visible for miles, bringing smiles to Jamie's men.

Jamie scanned the scene with his night-vision monocular. Those whom Rizzio had tormented would surely be smiling now, he thought. Then he saw the tail lights of a black sedan speeding away across the distant valley, leaving a cloud of dust in its wake, and instinctively knew that it was Rizzio. He had eluded them.

With Judy on his arm and Mike and Savannah in safe hands Jamie led their downward mountain trek to the plateau. Then a distant noise set off alarm bells, and it was closing. Fast. The unit crouched down low. Then all hell broke loose when an old army Huey came clattering over the summit towards them, spotlights blazing. At the open side door, three men were firing automatic weapons at anything that moved. The Huey swooped hard right and came around again, spraying the ground with a train of white-hot bullets. Jamie's men quickly dispersed in the shrubbery, with Mike and Savannah over their shoulders. Judy hit the ground next to Jamie. Both reloaded their revolvers.

Jamie ordered his men to fire at the engine while he and Judy took out the spotlights. Bullets showered both ways until a plume of black smoke poured out of the Hueys spluttering engine. The pilot attempted to regain control but it spiralled down the cliff face like a stone and exploded. A cloud of black smoke sailed up from the glowing wreckage far below. No one shed a tear.

Their ride home was waiting when they reached the plateau, and with no time to lose Jamie and two of his men hauled Judy, Mike and Savannah into one Huey and jumped onboard. The rest quickly scrambled into the other and the pilots took off heading for Bogota. Judy poured some water on Mike and Savannah's lips but there was no response. They were pale, lifeless.

They landed in Bogota at 3:17 a.m., and paramedics quickly hauled Judy, Mike and Savannah into two ambulances and sped away to the U.S. hospital opposite the embassy. Waiting at the emergence entrance, three nurses prepped to deal with one adult gunshot wound and two youngsters in a critical state, possibly suffering convulsions, opened the rear doors and retrieved the gurneys. One nurse rushed Judy straight to the operating theatre. The other two wheeled their young patients along a corridor to an emergency room. Lifting them onto rubber mattresses they cut off the stinking sheets, t-shirts and pants and threw them in the incinerator bin. Then having clinically bathed and dressed them in hospital gowns, a doctor arrived to examine them.

Drowsy and cold from loss of blood Judy stared at the ceiling as the surgeon irrigated the open bullet wound, which had passed through her thigh. After stitching the gaping puncture, he gave her a sedative and said she'd be fine in a few weeks.

Jamie thanked his team, including Judy before she passed out, for a job well done, and promised them a few beers the following night. Then he called and woke Major Bell, who had ordered him to do so as soon as he returned to debrief.

'Good job, Jamie, They'll be many happy faces at the White House and elsewhere tomorrow I'm sure. Have you called the youngster's parents yet?'

'I'm about to do that, sir, but I need to shower first.'

'Fine, then get some rest and we'll talk later.'

Using the hospital's pristine facilities Jamie took a hot shower and scrubbed off the stench of secretion, stale sweat and cordite. Wearing clean jeans and a sweatshirt he found a corridor bench and sat waiting for news of Mike and Savannah's state of health. A pretty nurse came by and handed him a sandwich and a mug of coffee. He nodded and smiled wearily.

It was four-twenty a.m. Time to call Richard Kinnerman.

Richard's cell phone rang several times before he rolled out of Katie's arms. 'Hello…Mike, is that you?' he croaked.

'Mr. Kinnerman, it's Jamie, we met in Bogota.'

Richard rubbed his eyes. 'Yeah, I remember. Don't you guys ever sleep? What is it, what's up?

'We found Mike and Savannah.'

Katie opened her eyes. Richard sat bolt upright. 'What! You found them? Are they alive, are they all right?' He took a breath. His heart was pounding. If Mike and Savannah were dead…he closed his eyes dreading the answer.

'Yes, they are alive,' Jamie said, not wishing to go into detail. 'Safely tucked up at a U.S. hospital in Bogota, and they are both going to be fine. The doctor is with them right now.'

'Oh my God,' Katie said, placing her hands to her mouth.

Richard rubbed his face. 'Christ, this is unbelievable news. Tell me, how badly are they hurt?'

Katie pulled him down to the pillow and shared the phone.

'They're in a bad way Mr. Kinnerman. They've been given a large quantity of drugs.'

Katie grabbed the phone and sat up. 'Drugs! My God, how bad is it, Jamie? We need to know what to expect.'

'Well it's not good I'm afraid. Right now, they are in a comatose state, but the doctor said, with the right treatment, they should fully recover. Look, perhaps it would be best if you wait a few days before…'

'To hell with that, we're coming to Bogota right now,' Katie snapped.

Jamie smiled. 'I know you are. Go to the U.S. Embassy and they'll direct you to the hospital. Have a safe trip.'

Overwhelmed by the news Richard and Katie looked at one another in disbelief. Katie screamed with joy and leapt out of bed. She had never felt so awake in her whole life.

'I'll shower and pack a suitcase. You book the airline tickets, Richard,' Katie said, hurrying to the bathroom, and stopping at the door, she looked up and whispered, *thank you.*

It was the second miracle Katie had not dared to hope for.

Richard managed to buy three seats on a ten a.m. direct flight to Bogota, which meant that they had three hours to drive to JFK, collect their tickets and go through the security check. He went into Julieanne's bedroom and gently woke her.

'Jules, we have wonderful news.'

'What, what is it?' she asked, rubbing her sleepy eyes.

'They found Mike and Savannah.'

Julieanne looked at her father; her eyes wide with hope but her mind still clouded with disappointment. 'They're alive?'

'They are at a U.S. hospital in Bogota, and they're gonna be just fine. Your Mom and I are going there right now, and we want you to come with us. I got your ticket.'

With tearful eyes, Julieanne said, 'No, Dad, don't ask me to go. Something always goes wrong....I can't take that anymore, I just can't. I know you won't understand, but that's how I feel.'

Richard cupped his hands around her tormented face. 'Sure I do sweetheart, but they are safe now and nothing will go wrong. We'll only be gone a few days and...'

'You said that before, Dad, and I want it to be true more than anything in the world, but I won't believe it until my brother walks through the front door.'

'I understand sweetheart, but he will, I promise. Look, we have to go now. We'll call you as soon as we get there, okay?' 'Yes, all right,' she said meekly, her eyes suddenly distant, and turning on her side she stared at the wall.

Richard kissed her on the cheek and hurried off to shower. Katie called Sally Brooks. It was 7:50 a.m. in Santa Barbara.

'Hi, Katie, did you have a nice Christmas?'

'Christmas just arrived. They found Mike and Savannah.'

'What! Oh my God! Are they alright, where are they?'

At a U.S. hospital in Bogota, and we're leaving right away to bring them home. We'll be gone for a few days and…

'Do whatever you have to, Katie. I'll get the next plane home. Tell Julieanne that I'll be there tonight and I'll cook her favourite dinner. Oh my God, this is wonderful news.'

'Thanks Sally, I really don't know how we could have coped without you.

'It's called devotion, Katie. Your kids mean the world to me, and I can only imagine how you and Richard must feel right now. Sounds like you're gonna have one hell of a trip.'

'It'll be the best ever. I'll call you tonight, Sally, bye.'

Katie replaced the receiver and smiled. This time they would not come home alone, of that she was certain.

FORTY-SEVEN

Due to a forty-minute delay at JFK their United flight landed at El Dorado airport, Bogota at 15:35, and following a long, irritable queue through passport control they entered the busy terminal, both sharing a sense of deja vous. Carla, seemingly a permanent fixture at the airport desk, smiled as they approached and couldn't help but notice a spring in their step.

'Mr. and Mrs. Kinnerman, I didn't expect to see you again so soon. Are you still looking for your son and his girlfriend?'

'Not any more, they've been rescued,' Katie said, brightly.

'And we're here to take them home,' Richard added, wishing he could have said that months ago. 'Do me a favour, Carla. Call the U.S. Embassy. I need to speak with them urgently.'

Carla dialled the number. 'I can only imagine how you must feel,' she said, handing Richard the phone.

'The embassy was closed. A message told him to press seven if it was urgent. A woman answered, 'U.S. Embassy.'

'Hi, my name is Richard Kinnerman and I'd like to speak to Sheila Macavy about our son. Is she there?'

'One moment, sir.' The line went silent, and then clicked.

'Mr. Kinnerman, we have wonderful news,' Sheila bubbled.

'Yeah, I know. Jamie called this morning. We just arrived in Bogota and we're gonna check in at the Venus Plaza Hotel.'

'Oh, then come straight to the embassy. We close at noon, so you'll have to ring the bell. We'll expect you.'

An air-conditioned yellow taxi drove them downtown and parked outside the Venus Plaza Hotel's entrance. A keen bellboy grabbed their baggage out of the trunk and led them though the familiar revolving glass doors to reception, where Emile Arnaud was saying farewell to three ageing guests. He turned, and with a look of surprise welcomed them back to the hotel.

Richard explained that Mike and Savannah had been rescued and they were there to take them home. Emile clasped his hands and exhaled. 'Well, this is wonderful news. Allow me to offer you suite 21, courtesy of the hotel management.'

Katie accepted his offer, which prompted Richard to smile as he signed the register. Katie was her astute self again it seemed.

'We're going straight to the U.S. Embassy, and we'd like our baggage taken to the room,' Richard said, eager to leave.

Emile handed their key card to the bellboy and leaned on the desk, 'Our limousine is at your disposal Mr. and Mrs. Kinnerman. It sounds as though this visit will be a joyful one.'

Katie thanked Emile, and linking arms with her husband they headed for the revolving glass door. Everything seemed different this time, she thought; the hotel, the sunny weather and the city were beautiful, even the taxi ride was enjoyable. Their last visit, clouded with fear and uncertainty, was prohibitive of any sense of well-being and had left them dispirited. Thankfully, the anguish was almost over and hopefully life would return to a semblance of normality. Mike and Savannah were now in safe hands just a few minutes away and every step suddenly seemed effortless.

The limousine sped away and after a brief encounter with city traffic, Richard rang the bell outside the U.S. Embassy. A marine opened the door and told them to take a seat. Shortly after, the sound of quickening heels clacked along the corridor as a tall, dark-haired woman approached with a smile and her hand out.

'Mr. and Mrs. Kinnerman, Sheila Macavy. I'm delighted to meet you. This is a good day for us all. Please come with me,' she said, striding towards the exit.

They followed Sheila across the road to a building, with a blue and gold sign above the entrance, **United States Hospital Unit.** Pushing open the glass doors she led them to a circular reception desk, where two female assistants in crisp white uniforms were busy tapping computers and answering ringing telephones. One looked up as Sheila approached.

'Carol, this is Mr. and Mrs. Kinnerman. They are here to see their son Mike, and Savannah Schlecker. Sign them in and I'll take them along,' Sheila said, matron-like.

Carol told Richard and Katie to sign the visitor's book and handed them each a security badge to wear whilst in the building. Clipping them on they followed Sheila along a highly polished corridor. Nurses were busily going in and out of rooms and the unmistakable aroma of disinfectant lingered in the air. The place looked immaculate. 'This is an ultra-modern hospital unit and has all the latest technology,' Sheila explained. 'And here we are.'

They stopped outside room 24. Richard and Katie stared at the door hardly daring to breath.

Sheila squeezed Katie's hand. 'The doctor will be here shortly Mrs. Kinnerman. Try not to worry, they're in good hands,' she said, and briskly walked off down the corridor.

Minutes later, Jamie strode towards them with his hand out and Mariana at his side. 'It's good to see you again Mr and Mrs Kinnerman,' he said, as they shook hands. 'This time we really do have reason to celebrate, don't you agree?'

Richard exhaled. 'Yeah, although to be honest it hasn't quite sunk in yet. We're still a little shell shocked,' he said, wondering what to expect on the other side of that door.

Katie folded her arms and paced back and forth. 'It feels as though we're hanging on a cliff by our fingernails.'

'That will pass in good time Mrs. Kinnerman,' Jamie assured her. 'I'd like you to meet Mariana Valero de Vasquez. Without her help we may never have found Mike and Savannah.'

Mariana stepped forward and offered her long-fingered hand. Jamie had advised her not to mention the bomb planted in her house last night, which had left her homeless.

'I'm Katie, Mike's mother, and this is my husband, Richard. I can't thank you enough, Mariana, and I do so with all my heart,' she said, taking her hand in both of hers.

'Thank you, but I could not let that evil man do those terrible things to them,' she said, clearly still haunted by what she saw.

'They are in there I can feel them,' Katie said, staring at the door. She was just a heartbeat away from rushing in and taking them in her arms. Richard placed a comforting arm around her.

'Yes, but they are in a bad way and have been sedated.' Jamie explained, aware of their anguish. 'You can see them, but I must warn you to prepare yourselves. Come, follow me.'

Richard and Katie's stomachs turned with both excitement and dread as Jamie pushed open the door. They stepped inside the pristine room and breathed in the antiseptic air. The blinds were closed and the overhead lighting dimmed. Mike and Savannah were sound asleep, their beds three feet apart. Both wore oxygen masks and had intravenous needles inserted into their arms. An assortment of high-tec equipment monitoring their life signs bleeped softly in the corner of the room.

'Oh my God!' Katie gasped, raising her hands to her mouth.

Visibly shaken, she leaned against the wall and looked at their faces in disbelief. Dreadfully emaciated with swollen eyes and skin a sickly shade of yellow they were hardly recognizable. Richard, also deeply shocked, sat on the edge of the bed and held his son's lifeless hand. Mariana turned away. Jamie held her.

Katie knelt between the beds and caressed their hands, kissed their stricken faces and stroked Savannahs long, dark dishevelled hair. Choking back her emotions, she turned to Richard with tears flooding down her cheeks. 'What in Gods name have they done to them, Richard, they are barely alive.'

The door opened and Dr Lugo entered in a white coat. 'Mr. and Mrs. Kinnerman, would you step outside for a moment,' he said, holding open the door. He was a tall, dark-haired Colombian in his late forties and had a reassuring tone to his voice.

Horrified by their sickening appearance Katie tearfully looked over her shoulder at Mike and Savannah's deathly faces as they followed the doctor out to the corridor.

'Let me explain what has happened to them so that you will understand what we are doing to make them well again,' Dr Lugo said, compassionately. 'I have given them an intravenous injection of dextrose, which is sugar and water to speed up the flushing out of narcotics in their bodies, and also rebalance the fluids and minerals in their system.'

'I can't tell you how upsetting this is doc. These kids have never taken drugs, and we need to know what to expect,' Richard said, determined to have some sort of understanding of what they were up against. 'We'll also need a report from you to give to our physician, in case he needs to continue the treatment.'

'Of course,' Dr Lugo said, and continued, 'Blood and urine samples show that a large amount of cocaine and heroin entered their systems while they were in captivity, and it will take time to flush it out. These powerful drugs are extremely addictive and can induce vomiting, convulsions, respiratory and heart failure. In some cases, the blood pressure can go so high it causes bleeding in the brain and can cut off the blood supply, resulting in brain damage or death. We are inducing sleep for at least seventy-two hours while their bodies discharge these drugs, by which time the immediate danger should be over. Unfortunately, throughout their recovery they will suffer painful withdrawal symptoms, such as convulsions, nausea, kicking out, shaking and vomiting.'

A nurse brushed passed them and entered room 24.

Mortified by the horrendous details Katie shook her head in disbelief. 'My God, how could anyone give heroin and cocaine to children? It's sickening,' she said, finding it difficult to come to terms with the fact that her son was in a drug-induced coma. 'These kids have never been involved in that world,' she went on, her face torn with anguish, knowing an evil presence now lurked in the veins of two innocent children. 'It's just unbelievable.'

'It might help if I explain doctor,' Mariana said. He nodded sombrely. 'Rizzio, the man who held these children, is the most powerful drug lord in South America. He has many heroin and cocaine factories. He kidnaps children, some only eight years old, and forces them to work for him by making them addicts. Rizzio treated your son and the young girl like animals. He chained them to the floor, forced heroin and cocaine into them, fed them little and left them covered in excretion for days at a time, simply to show his criminal friends that he had two famous Americans at his mercy. Eventually, he would have put them to work or given them to a terrorist group to bargain for ransom. He is an animal, and I wish he were dead.'

Satisfied with her half-hourly check, the nurse stepped out of room 24, closed the door and walked off down the corridor.

Katie was utterly horrified. Mariana's report of drug-induced children chained to the floor covered in their own excretion was, at the very least, disturbing, particularly as it was in relation to her son, and she was on the verge of screaming.

'I think we've heard enough stories for now,' Richard said, placing his arm around Katie's waist.

Jamie nodded. 'I agree. Come on, Mariana, I'll escort you to your hotel. See you here tomorrow Mr. and Mrs. Kinnerman.'

Marianna smiled weakly to Katie as she left with Jamie.

Dr Lugo assured them Mike and Savannah would be awake in four days, and may possibly be lucid enough to speak to them. He glanced at his watch and intimated that it was time to leave, but the torment on Richard and Katie's faces persuaded him to allow them to sit with the youngsters for a while. Richard thanked him and as he strode along the corridor, they returned to Mike and Savannah's bedside and watched them silently sleeping. Unable to imagine what terror the two young souls had endured, Richard and Katie wondered if they would ever fully recover.

Hours later, two nurses arrived and asked them to leave. It was time for the youngster's medication and a clinical bath one explained. Reluctantly stepping out into the corridor, Katie stared at the door. Richard pulled her away and headed for the exit.

Richard had decided not to call Harry and Greta until Mike and Savannah were awake, which would undoubtedly be the best wedding present that they could hope for. Right now, they were deliriously happy somewhere on the Indian Ocean, so why, for the sake of a few more days, dampen their joy with uncertainty when things could only get better.

Katie called Julieanne. 'Hi, sweetie, we're in Bogota.'

'Hi, Mom, are Mike and Savannah really there?'

'Yes, your father and I sat with them for a few hours.

'Oh my God, I can't believe it. Did you speak to Mike, is he hurt, is he sick? Talk to me, Mom.'

'No, we can't talk to them yet the doctor has sedated them. They looked exhausted, but he said they'll be fine in three or four days.' Katie avoided mentioning the horrific details; that would be far too upsetting for Julieanne.

'I can't imagine how you and Dad must feel. I wish I'd gone with you now. I didn't mean to be so…you know.'

'Forget it, sweetie, we understand, and when Mike is safely back home all those troubling doubts will disappear.'

'I know that, and don't worry, Mom, I'm okay, really. Sally's here now and she's staying with me. Kiss Mike for me, please.'

'I will. We're at the Venus Plaza hotel, Bogota. I'll call you and Sally in the morning, okay? Night my darling, we love you.'

The next morning, Richard and Katie returned to the hospital and as expected Mike and Savannah were still sleeping soundly. Kneeling between their beds they whispered words of comfort and caressed their hands until the duty nurse arrived and asked them to wait outside as the doctor was due any moment.

Alone in the corridor they sat staring at the walls. Nurses and staff hurried by, their shoes squeaking along the polished floor. There was little to do but wait, which only heightened their sense of helplessness. Richard alerted Katie to the fact that Mike and Savannah may suffer psychological damage, and if that were the case they would have to deal with it. Katie did not respond.

Jamie arrived with his arm around Judy who was hobbling on crutches. Both looked red-eyed after a celebratory evening with their comrades. As they sat quietly chatting about Judy's gunshot wound, Dr Lugo hurried down the corridor; his eyes burdened with the problems of others and entered room 24.

Katie stood up and paced back and forth outside the room, the strain of uncertainty evident on her face.

Richard exhaled and turned to Jamie. 'How the hell did Mike and Savannah become so emaciated and frail?'

'People can survive great hardship, but it does depend on the circumstance. By the time we rescued Mike and Savannah they had spent fifty-nine days chained to the floor in a drug-induced stupor on a filthy mattress. Throughout that time, Rizzio not only forced heroin and cocaine into their bodies, he also deprived them of any form of exercise or nourishment, which caused a dramatic loss of weight and muscle depletion,' Jamie explained.

Katie exhaled. 'I could kill that guy for what he's done.'

'In your place, I'd feel the same,' Judy said, 'and I know they look in horrendous shape right now, but they're young and will soon recover their strength with nutritious food and exercise.'

Richard said nothing. Katie burned with hatred.

The door to room 24 swung open and looking grim-faced Dr Lugo stepped out into the corridor. 'It will be at least forty-eight hours before I can allow them to face a family reunion, and even then it may be too soon. I am sorry. You can sit with them for a while if you wish,' he said, and marched off down the corridor.

Jamie and Judy said they had to leave and would to return in the morning. Continuing their bedside vigil Richard and Katie observed Mike and Savannah's sleep-filled eyes and motionless bodies, with only a pulsating machine to remind them that they were alive. Trapped alone in a dark, frightening place they were neither alive nor dead and had yet to return. Katie kept glancing at the breathing machine, terrified that it would suddenly stop.

At seven p.m., the duty nurses politely asked them to leave, which they found increasingly difficult. After the exhilaration of knowing that Mike and Savannah were safely in Bogota, finding them in a drug-induced coma had horrified Richard and Katie. It was if they were not there at all; that they were still somewhere far away fighting the evil presence lurking in their veins, and with their arms and legs covered in needle marks and sores, their skin sallow and breathing labored they seemed barely alive.

Julieanne would never have coped with this, thought Katie.

It was horrendous. Barbaric.

The next two days were spent much the same; sitting in the dimmed hospital room, hoping for the slightest sign of recovery from the young souls, but they remained lifeless.

That evening, they strolled to the old part of the city and sat outside a café` in the square, where they had coffee and croissants many blurred weeks ago. Katie remembered that it had rained that day. She was exhausted from her trip and they were both on the edge of despair. It was a stark reminder of how bleak it all seemed then and how much had changed in their lives since.

An hour or so later, as they strolled arm in arm back to the hotel in the hazy Colombian evening air, Katie wondered how they had found the resolve to come through it all. There had been times, especially on that God-forsaken runway in Panama, when their future as a family seemed destined for a lifetime of misery, a nightmare from which there seemed no escape.

Yet somehow, in the depths of hopelessness, she and Richard had rekindled their affection, Julieanne had fully recovered from her traumatic withdrawal, the insider-trading conspiracy had been resolved and, best of all, Mike and Savannah were now safe in a U.S. hospital, and in the caring hands of Dr Lugo they would soon be well enough to return home.

Arriving at their glittering hotel's entrance, Katie pushed her way through the glass revolving doors, and feeling the warmth of Richard's hand in her own she smiled, realising they had much to be thankful for.

FORTY-EIGHT

The following morning, having bought Mike and Savannah some warm clothes for their journey home, they returned to the hospital corridor bench and found Jamie and Judy awaiting their arrival. At eleven a.m., Dr Lugo hurried down the corridor, his white coat flapping behind him, and entered room 24. Katie anxiously paced back and forth, wondering what was happening behind that door. Nurses hurried by. A long hour passed. Then Dr Lugo stepped out into the corridor, and this time he was smiling.

'Come back at four,' he said, almost triumphantly. 'They are groggy but conscious, and will hopefully be responsive by then.'

Katie gripped her husband's arm. 'Four hours and we'll have them back,' she whispered, as the doctor marched away.

Richard exhaled. 'Feels like the jury's still out.'

Jamie insisted on buying lunch and led them to a small family restaurant tucked away in one of Bogota's backstreets. Antonio, a portly man with glowing cheeks and an operatic voice, greeted Jamie like an old friend, and ushering them to a circular table he hurried off to the kitchen. After a frenzy of activity, four specials arrived with warm bread and a decanter of wine. As they dined amid the hum of Spanish chatter, Jamie and Judy spoke of their admiration for Mike and Savannah's courage. Richard agreed. Katie kept glancing at her watch. Then Antonio approached their table and introduced his wife Maria, his son Miguel and daughter Juliana, who served them coffee and pastries.

Their innocent faces, glowing with the warmth of family life, stirred Katie's longing to reunite her own family. A long awaited pleasure in which she and

Richard would immerse themselves throughout the coming weeks of their recovery. She checked her watch, it was three-thirty p.m. 'Surely they must be awake by now, Richard, the doctor said -

'Easy, Katie, we're almost there,' he said, reassuringly.

Judy squeezed her hand. 'It'll be fine, Katie, I promise.'

At four p.m., breathless with expectation, Richard and Katie hurried along the hospital corridor to room 24. To allow their family reunion some privacy, Jamie and Judy sat in the corridor. Barely able to contain her excitement Katie turned to Richard, her eyes wide with anticipation. Giving her a comforting smile he opened the door. Katie hesitantly stepped inside and gasped, raising her hands to her mouth. Mike and Savannah were sitting upright holding hands - their faces pale and gaunt and their eyes swollen. Mike attempted to speak but only managing a croak he reached out to them. Savannah's face wrinkled with emotion.

Richard and Katie sank to their knees between the beds, and with an overwhelming sense of relief embraced them as though they would never let go; their long awaited tears of joy flowing onto one another's cheeks. Still numb from the remnants of drugs left in their veins Mike and Savannah melted in the warmth and safety of their doting affection. No longer would they suffer the terrifying nightmare that had tormented them for so long.

It was finally over.

'I can't tell you how relieved we are to see you. We've been out of our minds with worry,' Katie said, sniffling tearfully. 'I'm sure you feel lousy, but you look wonderful to me.' Savannah burst into tears. 'It's alright, sweetie, cry as much as you want to. It's over now and we're taking you home.'

'I thought we were going to die,' she said, whimpering.

Katie wrapped her arms around Savannah as though she were her own daughter. Mike hugged his father and warmed to the safety of his arms about him.

'We were somewhere dark, Dad. It was like we were falling. I could see Savannah, but she let go of my hand and -

Richard cupped his hands around his son's face. 'It's all right, Mike, it's over and you're safe now.'

The talking and hugging continued, but no mention was made of their kidnappings or near-death experiences they had suffered at the hands of

Mitchell, Netty and Rizzio, and Richard and Katie did not intend to broach the subject. Details of their painful ordeal would unfold when they were safely home and the nightmares had stopped, of which there would no doubt be many. Right now, Mike and Savannah needed the warmth and security of a family environment if they were ever going to put this dreadful episode behind them. Katie reached for her phone and called Julieanne, who had yet to overcome her cynicism.

'Hi, Mom, something is wrong isn't it, what's happened?'

'Hold on, sweetie, someone wants to talk to you,' Katie said, handing Mike her phone.

'Jules, it's me,' Mike croaked. The line went silent. He could hear her sobbing. Knowing that his disappearance had broken her heart he made light of it. 'Hey, it's okay, we're coming home. I got all my teeth, no broken bones and we're in a U.S. hospital. Mom and Dad are here and we're gonna be fine.'

Julieanne fought to regain her composure. 'Oh Mike, I never thought I'd see you again,' she said, sniffling.

'It came pretty close. Feels like I've been in a war zone.'

'You sound terrible. Is Savannah alright?'

'We look like shit but we're okay. Have you missed me?'

'Are you kidding? Just get home will you.'

'The doc says it'll be a few days before we can travel we're pretty exhausted. Tell Moose I'm coming home will you.'

'I'll tell everyone "My Brother's Coming Home!" she yelled. Julieanne was with a group of girls at a friend's house and they gathered round her. 'It's Mike, he's coming home!' she yelled. The girls screamed and whooped. 'That's your fan club, Mike. I can't wait to see you.'

'Me too,' he said, and kept chatting until Katie motioned for her phone. 'Hang on, Mom wants you. We'll talk later, okay.'

Katie took the phone. 'Feeling better, sweetie?'

Julieanne giggled, joyfully tearful. 'It's like the world just started turning again. Pretty special day, huh, Mom?'

'The best, and they're gonna be fine with a little TLC. I'll call you tonight before you go to bed, and don't be late home.'

'I won't, Mike's calling. Love you, Mom, and Dad, bye.'

Katie knew that hearing her brother's voice was the only tonic Julieanne needed. Her demons would bother her no longer.

Richard called Harry Schlecker's cell phone; Greta answered the call. 'Hi, Richard, what a nice surprise. Harry's in bed right now. The ocean is a little rough today and he swears the captain's doing it on purpose. Are you okay?'

'Better than that, we found Mike and Savannah.'

Greta almost dropped the phone. 'What! Oh my God, are they alright? What happened, where are you?'

'Bogota, they're in a U.S. hospital. Special Forces rescued them several days ago. They've just woken up.'

'Stay with me, I'll wake Harry.' Richard listened as Greta padded through their VIP suite to the bedroom. 'Harry, wake up! Mike and Savannah have been rescued. They're in Bogota. Here, talk to Richard.' Greta handed him the phone, her hands shaking.

Harry rolled over in the king size bed and sat up looking very pale. 'Christ Richard, this is unbelievable. I never thought…are they okay? Talk to me,' he said, climbing out of bed. He clicked the phone to audio. Greta handed him an aspirin in water.

Richard leaned over and handed Savannah the phone. 'Dad, it's me, Savannah.'

Greta turned away and sobbed.

Harry stood perfectly still, his eyes misty and his throat taut at the sound of her young voice. She had never called him Dad and he was almost lost for words. 'Savannah, I can't tell you what I'm feeling right now. Just hearing your voice is tearing me up.'

'I want you to know that I am alright, and that I love you.' Harry completely lost his composure and ran his hand over his face. 'I'm…. oh Christ, I got tears running down my face. Pretty stupid, huh?

'No, it means that you love me,' Savannah said, revelling in the warmth of finally committing herself to her adopted father.

'I honestly thought…..' Harry stopped and took a breath, 'Did they hurt you? Are you okay?'

'Yes they did. We are in a U.S. hospital and I would rather not talk about it right now.'

Richard and Katie could only admire Savannah's fortitude after all she had been through, but there was something else; she seemed different somehow, older, in control, more complete.

'What hospital? Gimme the doctor,' Harry barked.

Savannah coughed. 'He is not here right now. The kidnappers injected us with heroin and cocaine while we were asleep, and he is treating us for drug overdose. We look terrible.'

Silence.

Greta's mouth dropped. She looked wide-eyed at Harry.

'Heroin? Cocaine? Jesus Christ!' Harry hated drugs he knew what it could do to people. If Savannah had been subjected to the evil of heroin she could suffer for weeks, maybe months. 'Who the hell did this to you?' He was pacing the cabin now.

'A Colombian man, his name is Rizzio.'

'Sonofabitch, I'll have him killed. We're coming to get you. Gimme the address of the hospital.'

'There is no need to worry. Richard and Katie are taking us home as soon as we are well enough to travel. The doctor said it would take a few more days.'

Harry breathed out heavily. 'Okay, at least I know you're in safe hands. Just as well, it would take us a few days to get there. Listen princess, there is something I gotta tell you, and I hope you're not gonna get all upset.'

Savannah frowned. 'What is it, not Sugar Bay?'

'No. Greta and I are getting married. We're on a cruise ship sailing to Mauritius. Are you surprised, angry, what?'

Savannah smiled, feeling her lips crack open. 'Angry? No, I am happy for you. I always knew you would. Is Greta there?'

'I'm here, sweetie. I've missed you... her voice tailed off.

'I missed you, too. I am really happy that you and Harry are getting married, but I might have a problem calling you Mom, Greta, you are my best friend.'

Greta sniffled. 'I'll be your Mom and your best friend, and I'll always be Greta. I can't wait to see you, sweetie. Are you okay? You sound so tired and frail.'

'Yes, we are both exhausted, but the doctor has told us to stay awake until bedtime. Tell Henry I am coming home will you. Is Sugar Bay all right?'

'Sure, he's pining for you, so is Henry, and when hears the good news he'll seriously party. Hang on, Harry wants a word before you go. I'll call you later when you're rested and had some decent food. I love you, sweetie. Always. Bye my darling.'

Savannah hung on while Harry checked when they were due to dock in Mauritius. Greta called Captain Marsh and explained the happy situation. Greta nodded positively to Harry, indicating the Gulfstream would be ready to leave in the morning.

Harry was back. 'Okay, princess here's the plan. We're gonna jump ship in Mauritius and fly back to New York. Meanwhile, I'm sending the Gulfstream to Bogota and it'll wait there until you're ready to go home. We'll be at JFK when you arrive. Call us anytime if you wanna talk, you got that?'

Savannah smiled. 'Yes, all right.'

'I'm so happy right now I'm gonna let you in on a secret, a little surprise that I was saving until you were older.'

'What is it?'

'The house in St Lucia is yours princess. I put it in your name for your 21st birthday. I know how much you love it, so when you come of age you can live there, have vacations, whatever.'

'The house in St Lucia is mine, my house?'

'Yep, every brick, the gardens and the pool you love.'

'Oh, I will never sleep now. Thank you, thank you, Dad.'

'We can't wait to see you, and when I tell Nanny, Jonathan and Jeremy the good news they'll wanna see you, too. So take it easy and get some nourishment. We'll call you later, Greta has the hospital number. Now lemme have a quick word with Mike.'

'All right, bye.' Having shown affection to her adopted father after five years of angry indifference, Savannah suddenly felt a warm sense of contentment as she handed Mike the phone.

A nurse arrived to check their temperatures, blood pressure and pulse, and ordered them to drink some water.

'Hi, Harry,' Mike croaked.

'Christ, you sound as though you've swallowed razorblades. How're you holding up, kid?'

'I've felt better,' Mike said, finding it hard to speak. He was sweating and shivering at the same time and his head ached.'

'It's just great to hear your voice, Mike. Take it easy you're in safe hands. We'll meet you at JFK in a few days, okay?'

Mike suddenly started coughing. Richard took the phone and explained to Harry that he had a raging thirst and told him to call back later. Satisfied with her half-hourly check the nurse puffed up their pillows. Katie opened the door and invited Jamie and Judy to come in and they strode in through the doorway.

'I believe you've met Jamie,' Katie said, beaming.

Savannah grinned, and winced as her lips cracked open again. 'Jamie? I knew Colin was a phoney CIA name,' she said, trying not to smile but failing.

'Oh dear, now I will have to kill you,' Jamie said, drolly.

The emotionally charged room lit up with laughter, including the nurse as she left closing the door. Richard was just relieved that Mike and Savannah did not appear psychologically damaged, though he knew it was still early days. Katie, still revelling in the joy of their reunion, looked thoughtfully at the roomful of happy faces and felt a warm sense of family unity, on which, until a few days ago, she had almost given up hope.

There was something else; Mike and Savannah were acting like a couple. Their eyes spoke to one another and their hands remained locked. Richard and Katie had both noticed it. Mike seemed older. Perhaps it was his emaciated state, but there was definitely something different about them both.

Standing at the end of the bed, Jamie said, 'Savannah, this is Judy. She was one of the team that brought you home. You of course, wouldn't remember because you were asleep at the time. She's a big fan and wanted to meet you.'

Savannah's eyes misted with admiration as Judy sat beside her with her leg outstretched. 'Hey, no more tears, okay? You're the bravest kids I've ever met,' Judy said, glancing at Savannah's hands, which had begun to shake uncontrollably. She looked up at Jamie. 'I think we need the doc.'

Savannah's eyes suddenly rolled and her body stiffened, then she began shaking and kicking out. Her skin, though sallow and cold, was sweating profusely. Mike tried to call out to her. Judy gripped her wrists. Katie wrapped her arms around her. Richard held on to Mike as he reached for her. Jamie ran out of the room and returned with doctor Lugo, who took one look at Savannah and ordered everyone to leave immediately. 'Come back in the morning,' he said, as two nurses rushed into the room.

Richard and Katie went outside and stared at the door, both suddenly aware of the agony Mike and Savannah were suffering. Jamie reiterated that it was a necessary part of their recovery, but neither responded; they just held one another, sickened, horrified.

Their recurring attacks went on for two days. Several became so severe Dr Lugo contemplated using Methadone; a synthetic narcotic used to suppress withdrawal symptoms for 24 hours, but decided against it, believing the worst was over.

Richard called Harry and described the agony that Mike and Savannah were going through, but he was not surprised.

'I know what heroin does, Richard. A pal of mine got hooked on that stuff and wasted away. The guy had a nice family and a great future. He was thirty-one when he died. It was awful.'

'That's not gonna happen to our kids, Harry. If we have stay with them every minute of every day until they get rid of this goddam curse, then so be it,' Richard said, burning with anger.

'Let's get 'em home first, then maybe we'll all go to St Lucia while they recover. I can't wait to see you, pal.' Harry hung up.

When Richard told Beth, JB Walsome, Linda Greenberg, the trustees and Sheriff Carver the good news there was jubilation, but when Katie explained the grim details to Sally Brooks she was devastated. 'I'm a director of three charities, Katie, and I've seen those horrendous withdrawals. It'll be tough, but they *will* come through it, and I can't wait to give Mike a hug. I just pray that it's soon. I'm here if you need me…Sally hung up in tears.

The next day, Dr Lugo led Richard and Katie to his office for a chat. 'The youngsters are over the worst and recovering nicely. We will monitor them overnight, but in my opinion they will be well enough to fly home tomorrow afternoon,' he explained, and handed Richard a medical report. 'Give this to your doctor.'

Richard nodded. 'Thanks doc, for making them well again.'

'And for letting us sit with them, it meant a great deal to us doctor,' Katie added, with heartfelt sincerity.

Dr Lugo smiled a little embarrassed by their gratitude. 'Very well, tomorrow then,' he said, and walked out humming.

After their long flight from Mauritius to JFK, Harry and Greta sank in the limo's rear seat and by the time they hit the freeway, Greta was asleep on his shoulder. Harry's phone rang; it was Richard calling to let him know that Mike and Savannah were well enough to fly home tomorrow afternoon. Harry immediately called Captain Marsh and told him to prepare the Gulfstream for a flight to JFK tomorrow at three p.m. Then he called Dr Lugo at the hospital and explained that he wanted a physician monitoring Mike and Savannah throughout their homeward flight to JFK. He offered $5000, an overnight stay at a five-star hotel and a first class return flight to Bogota. Dr Lugo agreed to arrange it.

Having observed Mike and Savannah closely for several days, Richard and Katie were convinced their ordeal had connected them in a way that no one else would understand, and that their affection for one another had gone way beyond the boundaries of teenage infatuation. Their extraordinary experience had clearly elevated their innocent relationship to a level of inseparability, and ironically, the one thing that may inadvertently upset their unique bond was the journey home to JFK airport, where saying goodbye, albeit temporarily, could prove heartbreaking.

FORTY-NINE

Richard and Katie leapt out of bed at dawn and by seven-thirty, having showered and packed, they were having breakfast on the balcony. The early morning air was still cool but it was gloriously sunny; a good omen on such a special day, thought Katie. They were however, concerned about Mike and Savannah's emotional state, and though she and Richard kept hugging one another, both agreed the tears had to stop, beginning with the flight home.

With growing excitement they took the elevator down to the lobby and headed for the desk. The receptionist smiled as they approached and snapped her fingers at a bellboy, who stepped forward and hauled their baggage out to the limousine. She then informed Emile Arnaud that they were now at reception and he promptly appeared from his office smiling

'Mr. and Mrs Kinnerman, I am sure this visit has been joyful. How are your son and lovely Miss Schlecker?'

'Getting better every day, Emile,' Richard said, cheerfully.

'We're taking them home today,' Katie added, beaming.

'Wonderful, everyone here is delighted. Please visit us again soon,' Emile said, offering his hand. 'Au revoir, bon voyage.'

Hurrying across the lobby floor they exited through the glass revolving door to the waiting limousine. When they arrived at the hospital a huge crowd had gathered outside the entrance. Julio jumped out and retrieved their baggage. Richard handed him a nice tip and followed Katie through the glass doors.

That morning, a White House press release gave out sketchy details of Mike and Savannah's dramatic rescue, which quickly went viral, delighting millions of kids around the globe. Editors warned reporters that the youngsters were extremely ill and not to be pursued, but they were ignored; it was a front-page story.

Jamie had ensured details of their hospital presence and flight home remained secret, with the exception of immigration at El Dorado airport. Unfortunately, earlier that morning someone had posted their whereabouts on Facebook, and as a result, mountains of get-well cards and flowers arrived at the hospital unit, along with hoards of kids and reporters already gathering outside. Richard and Katie wheeled Mike and Savannah out to a black six-seater SUV belonging to the U.S. Embassy. Sheila Macavy, Dr Lugo and many hospital staff came out to the entrance to wave goodbye. Behind a makeshift police cordon excited youngsters and well-wishers yelled to them from across the street, and a wall of reporters and camera crews clambered to take their pictures as Jamie and Judy helped them into the vehicle's rear seats. Richard stowed their baggage and joined Katie in the center row.

Judy clicked the Yukon XL into drive and as they pulled out of the hospital entrance, a mass of voices started yelling amid a sea of waving hands. Hoards of idolizing kids raced along the sidewalk, hoping to get a glimpse of Mike Kinnerman through the tinted windows, and then they were gone.

Jamie and Judy had never seen anything like it.

The hospital staff, deeply moved, returned to their duties.

Mike and Savannah sat with their hands locked as the black SUV hummed along the highway. Then as Judy turned onto the slip road heading for El Dorado Airport, they tightened their grip, recalling the men in black balaclavas and the terrifying violence of their kidnapping. The grassy verge and trees, now a blackened space where their limo had burnt to a cinder with Emilio inside, was a stark reminder of how lucky they were to be alive. Katie followed their staring eyes through the window to the burnt out area. Then it dawned on her that their terrorists kidnapping had taken place near Eldorado airport, and she suddenly realized that this was where it had happened. Sickened by the evil barbarity of it she shuddered as the charred remains, a landmark of extreme violence, faded to a bad memory behind them.

Pulling up at the airside gate, Judy lowered the window and handed the security guard her ID. He nodded, and raising the barrier waved her through to the airfield. Savannah felt a warm tingle of relief when she saw Harry's Gulfstream jet gleaming beside the open hanger, the hanger in which they had boarded the silver Hawker and flown to a tiny airport in the Amazon Jungle, with Jamie and his men, in what seemed like a lifetime ago.

Jamie and Judy did a security check; Rizzio was still on the loose and they were taking no chances, even though the aircraft belonged to Harry Schlecker. Harry was taking no chances either; he had told Captain Marsh to turn off the cabin radio and TV monitors. He knew the last thing Mike and Savannah needed was an inflated news report reminding them of their worst nightmare.

Jamie hauled their baggage onboard while Richard and Katie escorted Mike and Savannah up the aircraft's short flight of steps. Shocked by Savannah's sickly, gaunt appearance Captain Marsh, co-pilot Alan Cobb and flight attendant Angelina Rosa gave her gentle hug as she and Mike boarded. Showing no interest in the gold-trimmed interior and hand-made leather seats they shuffled through the thick, blue-carpeted eighteen-seat cabin and curled up together beneath a blanket on a leather sofa. Richard and Katie couldn't help but admire the luxurious fifty-nine million dollar aircraft; it was breathtaking.

A short, dark-haired man carrying a shoulder bag entered the cabin and before he could take another step, Judy dragged him to the floor and ripped away his bag.

He protested vehemently. 'Stop, I am a doctor!' he yelled utterly terrified. 'Dr Bartolo Perez. Here are my papers.'

Jamie called Dr Lugo, who confirmed that he had arranged for Dr Perez to monitor the youngsters throughout the flight at Mr. Schlecker's request. Captain Marsh apologised to Jamie. He assumed Harry had told him there would be a doctor onboard. Jamie let it go, and helping Dr Perez to his feet he explained the reason for security. Forcing a smile, the doctor brushed the fluff off his clothes and proceeded to examine his patients.

Satisfied that Mike and Savannah's condition was stable, he gave them each a mild sedative, and said they must drink water to prevent dehydration. Overhearing his comments Angelina strode to the galley and returned with two chilled bottles of mineral water, which Katie offered to administer, as she and Richard were to remain at their side throughout the flight.

Dr Perez explained that because they were in a pressurised cabin he would continually monitor the youngsters. Richard had given no thought to the effects of cabin pressure, and praised Harry for having the foresight to hire a physician. Although Mike and Savannah's horrendous withdrawal attacks had become less frequent, they were, nevertheless, unpredictable, and under those circumstances having a doctor onboard throughout the flight was more than comforting.

Katie chuckled. Harry never ceased to surprise her.

Angelina handed Dr Perez a mug of coffee. He nodded and looked at his watch. A hotel suite awaited him in New York and tomorrow he would return "first class" to Bogota. He reached for his cell phone and called his wife, Maria. She was worried about him he had never travelled anywhere without her.

When Jamie and Judy sat beside them, Mike and Savannah knew that it was time to say goodbye and they would probably never meet again. Still weak and emotionally fragile, Savannah began to sniffle. Gently placing his arm around her, Jamie gave Mike strict orders to take good care of her. Mike gave a solemn promise to do so; it was a promise he would never break.

Still feeling emotional, Richard said, 'Words somehow seem inadequate to thank you for risking your lives to bring Mike and Savannah back to us. We will always be indebted to you, Jamie, and to you Judy, and of course, your heroic men.'

Katie added, 'Because of you, Mike and Savannah have a future and we have our family back. God bless you.'

Jamie nodded. 'Your gratitude will mean a lot to my men. Our missions rarely have a happy-ending. Thank you, and have a safe journey home,' he said, as they shook their hands.

Judy kissed Mike and Savannah. 'Good luck,' she whispered.

Without looking back Jamie and Judy exited down the short flight of steps, and as they strolled to the terminal, Jamie said, 'It's difficult not to get attached sometimes.'

Judy wiped her eyes and did not respond.

The Gulfstream's engines suddenly roared to life, signifying their journey home was about to begin, and an air of excitement filled the cabin. It was just after four p.m..

Richard and Katie smiled at one another.

Words were not necessary.

New York was only six hours away, but Katie was taking no chances with the air-con or anything else. Mike and Savannah were frail and susceptible to all sorts of bugs, in her opinion. So having conspired with Angelina she ushered them into Harry's small stateroom and tucked them in bed with hot chocolate. By the time the Gulfstream left the runway they were sound asleep.

Part way into the flight, Mike curled up into a ball and began yelling, clenching his fists and kicking out. Richard, Katie and Dr Perez held him down as he fought the agony until sleep finally returned. Thankfully, the episode lasted only five or six minutes, but it had left him shaking and soaked with sweat.

The incident had woken Savannah and she began sweating and moaning, clearly in pain. Katie gave her a few sips of water, and then gently rocked her in her arms until she fell asleep.

Mercifully, the remainder of the flight was uneventful and at ten-forty p.m. on January 5th - ninety-four days after their first kidnapping that fateful Sunday - the Gulfstream landed at John F. Kennedy Airport. Angelina handed Mike and Savannah mugs of hot tea as the aircraft taxied to a dimly lit hanger, where Harry, Greta and two FBI agents sat waiting inside the warm limousine.

Harry knew the last thing Mike and Savannah would want to travel home in was a helicopter.

Clearly relieved to have landed Dr Perez examined his young patients, to ensure they had not suffered any adverse effects from the pressurized journey. They had not, and reaching into his bag he handed Katie a small bottle of mild sedatives.

'Give the youngsters one of these when you get home. They will help them to sleep soundly,' he said. 'Your doctor will need to monitor their progress for several weeks, or maybe months, it depends how quickly they recover. Also, in my opinion, they will need trauma counselling,' Dr Perez added, rather sombrely.

Glancing at one another Richard and Katie thanked Dr Perez, who nodded modestly and gathered up his belongings. A limo awaited him outside the terminal. He was already homesick.

Looking sleepy-eyed and a little confused Mike and Savannah stepped out of the stateroom and stood shivering in the aisle with their arms wrapped around one another.

Katie grinned. 'No, it's not a dream my darlings. We're in New York. You're home. Now give me a hug.'

As Mike and Savannah had no passports, Richard was gearing himself up for a war with immigration, but Jamie assured him Major Bell had notified U.S. authorities of their arrival, to ensure entry without documents would not be a problem.

The door opened and rush of freezing air entered the cabin as the steps whirred to the ground. Chauffeur Charlie came onboard and hauled the baggage out to the limo. The flight crew gathered at the exit and wished Mike and Savannah a speedy recovery. Both smiled weakly as Richard and Katie helped them down the short flight of steps into the dimly lit hangar.

Richard had warned Harry and Greta that Savannah looked dreadfully emaciated and frail, but their reaction as Katie helped her down the steps was one of horror. Harry had to take a breath; she was barely recognisable. Masking her emotions, Greta ran to Savannah and wrapped her arms around her. Both burst into tears. Harry Schlecker held them and wept unashamedly. For the first time in his life he had a family, which, until Richard's call to the cruise liner telling him that Savannah was alive and safe in a U.S. hospital, he thought he had lost forever.

FBI agents Hadley and Brooks climbed out of the limousine and introduced themselves. Richard's back stiffened.

Harry tried to put his mind at rest. 'Don't worry, they just wanna confirm they really are Mike and Savannah, that's all.'

'Of course, we may have rescued the wrong kids.'

Harry chuckled. 'Yeah, well, FBI Director Vernon Bentram said he'd like to meet them when they're feeling up to it.'

'Along with a camera crew no doubt,' Richard said, bitterly.

'I take it the FBI is not on your list of favourite people.'

Richard said nothing.

Once they were convinced Mike and Savannah's identity was indeed genuine, Hadley and Brooks confirmed their findings to Director Bentram, and then sped away in a black van. Dr Perez said his goodbyes and headed for the terminal.

They agreed to celebrate their homecoming at the Kinnerman house when Savannah felt well enough. She and Mike had a stack of gifts waiting for them under the Christmas tree, which they would no doubt enjoy opening together. Then in a rare display of affection Harry hugged Richard and Katie for bringing Savannah safely home, and said that he would call in the morning. Wrapped in one another's arms in the dimly lit hanger, Mike and Savannah whispered goodbye and reluctantly parted.

Richard and Katie quickly linked arms with Mike and headed for the terminal, their suitcases rumbling behind them. Savannah kept nervously looking back as Harry and Greta escorted her to the limousine. Reaching the open rear door, she broke away and screamed for Mike, who instinctively hurried to her as if they were still on the run and held her in his arms.

Unsurprised, Richard and Katie returned to the limo. Harry stepped forward to retrieve Savannah, but Greta grabbed his arm.

'No don't, Harry, look at them; they're inseparable.'

It was a very delicate moment and no one quite knew how to respond. Their son and daughter were clinging to one another; anguish written all over the faces. Greta sensed they were hurting. Richard had expected this. Katie wanted to reach out to them; they looked lost, frail and vulnerable, but as they walked arm-in- arm towards her she knew the answer was forthcoming.

A jumbo jet thundered by overhead.

'I know you're worried, but there's nothing wrong,' Mike said huskily. 'It's just that...we've been through so much together and never spent a moment apart, so it's kinda hard letting go.'

Richard and Katie understood where this was coming from, but Harry and Greta had no idea of the depth of their relationship.

'So you're pretty stuck on one another, is that it?' Harry said.

Savannah smiled, a little embarrassed. 'Yes.'

Richard said, 'Tell you what I think. You were pretty-much smitten before any of this happened, and so it's not surprising that you've become even closer. Now you're going home in separate cars and you're confused, and I don't blame you. But you're not well and we're concerned, so these are the options: we can check into a hotel, find a restaurant, go to the mansion, or just go home. Whatever you two decide is fine with me. But you know what? After a good night's sleep in your own beds, I think you'll see things differently, and don't forget that we're all gonna meet up tomorrow, if you're feeling up to it. After that, you can see each other whenever you want to. So what's it gonna be?'

Mike and Savannah nodded to one another. 'Go home.'

Harry reacted spontaneously. 'Okay, get everyone get in the limo, Richard, we'll drop you at the parking lot,' he said, nodding at Charlie to open the rear door.

Mike and Savannah sat in silence.

When the limousine pulled up at the parking lot gates, Mike and Savannah embraced and kissed as though they were lovers, and Richard wondered if they had ever crossed the line. Harry tightened his lips and stared out of the window. Katie and Greta intuitively knew they were innocents. Aware of the stiff silence Mike reluctantly let Savannah go and whispered goodbye.

Charlie retrieved the baggage from the trunk, and once Mike and Katie were safely out of the car, Richard gave Harry the nod and the limousine sped away. Savannah tearfully waved to Mike at the rear window, her dishevelled hair and gaunt face a haunting reminder of all they had been through together. Mike stood there until the tail lights faded into the night.

Then she was gone.

Savannah gazed out the tinted window into the darkness; her mind filled with dreams of the future and her beautiful house in St Lucia. She glanced at Harry and Greta, who were looking at her with great concern and affection, and relished the thought of growing up in their loving care; she would want for nothing. The anger and bitter resentment, which had tormented her for so long, she had left behind in sorrowful tears on the gave of her mother and father.

She would never forget them.

Soon she would see the iron gates, the lake and the glow of the mansion; a home that she had bitterly rejected and would now embrace with all her heart. She would attend the parties, play the piano for her father and dance with New York's rich and famous. But her heart would always belong to Mike Kinnerman, the boy to whom she had promised her love.

* * * * *

As the BMW sped along the freeway towards the distant glow of New Mayford, Mike sat in the back staring out the window into the passing flickering darkness. He wondered if Savannah was thinking about him, about their future together. That final kiss and her forlorn look as the limo drove away suggested she was, and that they had much to look forward to.

The glow of a passing headlight danced over his face and he blinked returning to the moment as though it were an awakening. Whether it was the headlight or the fact that he was nearing home he wasn't sure, but it suddenly dawned on him that no one had mentioned PocketMoney.com, which seemed ominous. His mind rolled back to Alfredo's car showroom in Panama, where he and Savannah had watched CNN's report of insider trading and the FBI's closure of PocketMoney.com. The devastating news had left him wondering how it could possibly have happened. Did someone go to jail? Was the company in administration? He was almost too afraid to ask, but there was no point in evading the issue he would find out one way or another. He took a breath and spoke to his father, secretly dreading his response.

'Dad, why is no one talking about PocketMoney.com? If it's because you're afraid I'll get upset, you don't have to worry. We saw a CNN news report in Panama saying the FBI had closed the company because of insider trading.'

Katie glanced at Richard and shook her head, reminding him that they agreed not to talk about it yet. Richard looked at Mike in the rear-view mirror. 'I planned to talk to you about that when you are feeling better, Mike, and I'm not gonna get into it now, but I'll say this; PocketMoney.com is still in business and it's thriving. I'll fill in the details when you're up to it.'

Mike exhaled. 'Thank God. When I saw that story on CNN I couldn't believe it, and neither could Savannah. I thought I'd lost everything, my future, my career and the company.'

Katie turned around and faced Mike. 'There's something else that you might like to know. We met up with Linda Greenberg on Christmas Eve and she told us that the global network for kids is going on air in February, and that you'll love it.'

'Are you serious?'

'That's what she said. Nice 15th birthday present, huh?'

'It sure is,' Mike said, laying his head back smiling. He had been right about Linda Greenberg; she was a dynamo. He made a mental note to call her in the coming days. Right now, he was tired and weak, and most of all grateful to be alive. He saw his reflection in the darkened window and barely recognised himself.

Richard took the slip road to New Mayford.

It was almost one a.m.

Mike felt his stomach flutter with anticipation as they passed the Beechwood Avenue sign and pulled in the driveway of their beautiful home. Grabbing the baggage out of the trunk, Richard followed Katie and Mike up the snowy path to the front door.

Mike ran his eyes over the house he thought he would never see again - the red brickwork, the bay windows, the veranda bamboo table where he and Savannah had sat together that fateful Sunday morning, and the snow-covered lawns and flowerbeds Piffin loved to trample.

It was in that memory, Mike recalled, that he found strength and comfort when he and Savannah found themselves chained to the floor of a rundown farmhouse in the Andes Mountains and the young crippled woman had spat in his face.

Katie turned the key in the lock.

He ran his fingers over the door frame admiring his paintwork, a chore that took a weekend to perfect last spring.

Katie opened the front door.

Mike followed his mother into the hallway and absorbed the smells and fond memories of the home in which he had spent his childhood. Then bounding into the hallway with his tail wagging Piffin jumped up and licked his face, almost knocking him over. Mike knelt down and made a huge fuss of him; he was part of the family and he loved him. Then with Piffin close at his heels he followed his mother and father into the kitchen and bathed in its warmth and familiarity.

He wondered if Savannah was home yet.

Katie found a note from Sally Brooks, which she had left on the breakfast bar. *Richard, Katie and darling Mike, when you get home wake me, please! Love Sally.* Sally's simple message had confirmed the end of a dark chapter in their lives, and the words had such a profound effect on Katie she began to cry.

'Mom, are you okay?' Mike asked.

Katie held Mike in her arms. 'Just tears of happiness my darling. I missed you so much I thought my heart would break.'

'Savannah and I felt the same. That was the hardest part of all.' Mike said, revelling in the warmth Katie's embrace.

'I got a lump in my throat just seeing you standing there, son,' Richard said, unable to conceal his emotion.

Mike hugged his beloved parents. 'I talked to Savannah about you. She's really taken to you and wanted to know everything. Things looked pretty bleak and we weren't sure if we'd…

Katie placed her finger on Mike's lips. 'I know, and neither were we, but you're home now and that's all that matters.'

The sound of hurried feet suddenly thundered down the stairs as Julieanne frantically screamed, 'Mike! Mike! Is that you?'

Katie smiled, gripping Richard's arm. Mike braced himself.

Pausing at the open doorway, Julieanne looked wide-eyed with horror at Mike's frail, sickly appearance, and with tears running down her cheeks she ran across the room, wrapped her arms around her beloved brother, and whispered, 'You've got one hell of a lot of homework to catch up on….'

Then the phone rang; It was Savannah…..

9 781967 820467